PRAISE FOR *WHITE OUT*

"Readers will cheer the dogged Kylie on . . . Girard tells a story."

—*Publishers Weekly*

"[*White Out* is] full of just the right number of misdirections and surprises. The characters, especially Lily, are appealingly vulnerable."

—*Kirkus Reviews*

"*White Out* is a superb thriller—intense, intricate, and so intriguing. Detective Kylie Milliard is a badass, and Girard is one heck of a storyteller. The start of a fabulous new series."

—J. T. Ellison, *New York Times* bestselling author of *Good Girls Lie*

"Girard excels at creating kick-ass heroines in high-stakes, high-tension thrillers. Lily Baker and Detective Kylie Milliard ensure *White Out* is the start to another white-knuckle series."

—Robert Dugoni, #1 Amazon and international bestselling author of the Tracy Crosswhite series

"I loved *White Out* from page one until the jaw-dropping conclusion. I do this for a living, and Danielle Girard spun me in so many circles I was dizzy when it was over. The pacing is pitch perfect, the plot taut as a high wire, and the characters will stick with you long after you've read the shocking finale. I can't wait to read Danielle's next adventure in the sleepy little town of Hagen, North Dakota, which calls to mind Benjamin Franklin's famous quote: 'Three may keep a secret, if two of them are dead.'"

—D. J. Palmer, *USA Today* bestselling author of *Saving Meghan*

"Tantalizingly and seductively chilling. The story lines twist and turn and combine, revealing loss, fear, and love in a rivetingly compelling—and constantly surprising—tale of lives forgotten and lives found. Danielle Girard delves revealingly into deep emotions and hidden motivations in this original and supremely satisfying thriller."

—Hank Phillippi Ryan, national bestselling author of *The Murder List*

FAR GONE

ALSO BY DANIELLE GIRARD

BADLANDS SERIES

White Out

DR. SCHWARTZMAN SERIES

Exhume

Excise

Expose

Expire

ROOKIE CLUB SERIES

Dead Center

One Clean Shot

Dark Passage

Grave Danger

Everything to Lose

OTHER WORKS

Savage Art

Ruthless Game

Chasing Darkness

Cold Silence

FAR GONE

DANIELLE GIRARD

This is a work of fiction. Names, characters, organizations, places, events, and incidents are either products of the author's imagination or are used fictitiously. Any resemblance to actual persons, living or dead, or actual events is purely coincidental.

Published by Thomas & Mercer, Seattle

www.apub.com

ISBN-13: 9781542018258
ISBN-10: 1542018250

Cover design by Shasti O'Leary Soudant

Printed in the United States of America

For Rebecca Scherer,
for the years of generous cheerleading,
sharp editorial guidance, and friendship.

CHAPTER 1

Hannah

The pills Hannah Visser had taken were hitting her bloodstream, softening her vision and rendering her limbs tingly and loose, when she reached the Garzas' door, late to babysit their infant daughter. She paused on the walkway to respond to her brother's third text, then shut off her phone to end the conversation. He was out of town with their mother tonight, which meant no one would be home. Bonus. Her knuckles had barely grazed the front door when it swung open, revealing Nadine Garza in a bright-yellow blouse with white cheetah print and the kind of black jeans that were actually leggings. Jeggings. An old-person thing, but in Nadine's defense, she *did* just have a baby.

"Hannah. So good to see you," Nadine said and looked as though she might hug Hannah. Instead, the woman stepped aside and waved her into the house. "Come in, come in."

"Sorry I'm late," Hannah said.

"No worries. I appreciate you getting yourself out here. Ben will take you home."

"Sure," Hannah said, wishing once again that she could fast-forward the twenty-one months until her sixteenth birthday so she could drive herself. Those after-babysitting car rides from dads were usually weird, but Ben was better than most. He talked to her about the world. About leaving Hagen and coming back. He treated her like an adult, like she mattered. He might be the only one. Her older brother and her parents treated her like a kindergartner. *Where are you? When will you be home?*

"We're almost ready," Nadine said. "You hungry?"

The drugs were a warm buzz. She couldn't imagine feeling hungry ever again. Every inch of her was full and calm. The embarrassed rush she normally felt when forced to make eye contact with adults was absent. She could speak clearly, be confident. It was the most perfect sensation in the world. "I'm fine," Hannah said honestly.

"Well, you can help yourself. There's a bottle ready for Tiffany and two more in the fridge. Plus there's always formula in the container beside the coffee maker."

This wasn't the first time Hannah had babysat Tiffany, but it was the first time she had watched the baby at night. The other times had been a few hours during the day so Nadine could go to a meeting or do a few hours of work. Nadine was an accountant at Chase Visser Interiors, Hannah's much-older brother's business.

"Nadine always thinks Tiffany is going to eat like a linebacker when she's not around," Ben Garza said, coming down the hallway from the bedroom in a white button-down shirt. Where Nadine was broad shouldered and stocky, Ben was narrow and lean. It wasn't hard to imagine Nadine could take him in a fight, not that Hannah had ever seen the Garzas fight. Unlike her own parents, who were at each other's throats constantly.

"It's true," Nadine said, laughing with her husband.

With Ben and Nadine making final preparations, Hannah made her way to Tiffany, who lay sleeping quietly. The Garzas had put a wicker bassinet in one corner of the great room, which, Nadine had explained, was the only location in the space where the baby wouldn't feel a breeze every time the front door opened or closed. Tucked out of view of the front door and along the wall between the coat closet and the entrance to the bathroom, the spot was its own little weather system.

Hannah dropped her backpack and lined up several pairs of boots that were spilling out from the closet. Living in North Dakota meant owning a lot of coats and boots. Her own mother had a system for boots that limited each member of the family to one pair at the front of the house. Everything else was relegated to the mudroom. Her mother had a lot of rules.

Hands freed, Hannah stood over the bassinet, where Tiffany was bending and straightening her legs like they were attached with springs. Tiffany wore a gummy smile as Hannah leaned over to kiss her. The motion made her momentarily dizzy, the strength of the drugs showing itself. Adam had warned her that two pills would leave her on her ass—of course, he'd warned her after she'd taken them. She only hoped the Garzas would leave already. If Nadine realized Hannah was high, then it would be no time before her whole family knew.

Holding the bassinet to steady herself, Hannah leaned down and kissed the baby on one rosy cheek. "Hi, sweet Tiffany."

Hannah was about to lift the baby when the front door opened and closed with a whine of hinges and a thwack as it struck the casing. Had they been expecting someone else? Just what she needed—one more witness to how high she was.

"Neither of you move." The man's voice was commanding.

The words startled Hannah into looking up. But the front door wasn't visible from where she stood. A joke? But Nadine's face had gone white, her palms midair and body frozen. Instinct drove Hannah backward, first behind the closet door, then farther into the dark hollow of coats.

A boot sounded on the linoleum entryway, directly opposite the closet wall. The single step propelled Ben into action. He dropped Nadine's coat and stuck out his palms as though to halt an oncoming truck. "What the—"

"Hands up." The man's voice again.

Both Ben and Nadine raised their hands into the air while Hannah took another step backward, rolling her ankle on one of the boots on the floor. A cry corked in her throat as she caught herself against the closet wall, fighting to be silent. Her heart beat hard and heavy under her ribs. By shifting left and right, Hannah could see the Garzas through the opening on the hinge side of the closet door.

"What the hell are you doing?" Ben asked. "No!"

Hannah cowered as Ben cried out. When she looked up, he staggered and dropped to his knees, then fell like a stone. Was he shot? She hadn't heard gunfire.

Nadine shrieked, lunging toward him.

But the man barked something unintelligible, and Nadine froze. Hands in the air, she shook her head. "What are you doing? Why are you—"

Nadine was still speaking when a gun fired, an explosion of sound.

Hannah jolted, stunned at the volume of the noise. The echo of the bullet ricocheted in the quiet house. In her bassinet, Tiffany's legs kicked, but she made no noise. How was that possible? *Stay quiet, sweet girl.* When nothing happened, Hannah thought it had been a warning shot. Ben lay on the floor, but he had been there already. His eyes were open and moving. He was alive.

Nadine had shifted sideways, a little stumble, but she was still standing. Her mouth was moving, but there were no words. And then Hannah saw it—the red blossoming like a flower across the bright-yellow blouse. The realization was slow to sink through the drugs. Blood. Nadine's blood was soaking her blouse. That man had shot Nadine.

A silent scream coursed its way from her toes as Hannah pressed into the body of coats, fighting to hold it in. This was a nightmare. A side effect of the drugs. She would wake up and never take another pill, as long as she lived. She just needed to wake up. Squeezing her eyes closed, she dug her fingernails into the heels of her hands, fighting panic. When Hannah opened her eyes, the red flower on Nadine's blouse had grown. Nadine's eyes were wide, her mouth like one of Hannah's father's trout—open, closed, open, closed, in a silent struggle.

The tiny closet space grew smaller. Hannah's pulse drilled into the wall behind her head as she witnessed Nadine topple face-first onto the carpet.

This is real. This is real. Hannah tried to stop fighting what she saw. This wasn't a hallucination. She blinked. Did it twice more. A man had shot Nadine.

Minutes earlier, Nadine had been so alive.

And now she was probably dead.

The house was quiet, the thrumming of her own pulse the only sound. Her feet tingled where they were falling asleep from her awkward crouch. She tried to wiggle her toes, to keep her eyes open. How badly she wanted to close them.

A shadow crossed into the hallway, then vanished. The shooter had gone to the bedroom. Hannah reached out to pull the closet door toward her but stopped. If the shooter saw the motion of the door, if he noticed a change in its position . . . no. She crossed her arms over her stomach, pressing against the desire to throw up.

Ben groaned from the floor, and suddenly, as though he'd only just gotten control of his voice, he shouted his wife's name, a cry of grief that Hannah felt in her knees.

The light shifted again, the shooter returning. Hannah didn't dare look.

Ben's sobs filled the empty space.

"Shut up," the man warned, and there was the sound of swallowed hiccups and heavy, stilted breaths from Ben.

The next thing Hannah heard was a low grunt of exertion. She thought of her father, the sound he'd made struggling to unearth the ugly juniper bush from the front yard last summer. Hannah edged forward to peer through the crack in the hinges. She saw the man's back, light-brown hair cut short. A tan jacket, Carhartt, she thought. The same kind every man in Hagen owned, including her brother and her father. Ben was seated in a chair. His hands were bound behind him with a piece of red-and-blue striped fabric. The triangular cut at the bottom told her it was a man's necktie.

Ben slumped forward, chest heaving.

Hannah leaned back, pressing her hand to her mouth as tears streamed down her face. Was this man going to torture Ben? Was she going to be here for hours? She couldn't hide that long. She'd give herself away; then she'd be dead. Like Nadine.

The man spoke softly, his words too quiet to distinguish. Speaking to Ben. Something about his tone was familiar. When she inched forward again, she watched the shooter tie Ben's legs to the chair with two more neckties. He'd taken off his coat, and the muscles in his shoulders and back were visible through his navy T-shirt as he maneuvered the ties around Ben's legs. But why? Why was he doing this?

Ben struggled against the restraints, twisting left and right. A long strip of duct tape crossed his mouth. The man pressed a hand on Ben's shoulder and spoke softly to him.

Ben reared up, standing and bringing the chair with him. But the man shoved him down. The chair tipped and Ben fell over, landing on his shoulder.

The man cursed and hoisted the chair upright again.

Then the gun was pressed to Ben's head.

He froze.

She heard the man say the word *baby*.

Every cell in Hannah's body screamed, *No. No, please. Not Ben.* The baby needed her daddy. Every girl needed her daddy. She pressed her knuckles to her teeth, biting back her screams.

Ben shook his head. His chest lifted, his shoulders set in preparation to fight.

Please let him get away.

The gun exploded again. Hannah heard her breath in her throat, covered her mouth, choked and sobbed. Tiffany's bassinet trembled as the baby kicked, but still the baby was silent. When Hannah looked again, the left side of Ben's head was gone. A divot remained, filled with what reminded her of raw meat. Blood and bits of tissue were sprayed as far as the wall. Ben's brain.

She huddled into the closet, gagging as her mouth filled with vomit. She swallowed it down, acid burning her throat. She was alone. Ben and Nadine were dead. She was next. Unless she stayed silent, stayed hidden. She pressed herself harder against the closet wall as though it might open up and swallow her, make her disappear.

The shooter grunted, and there was a rasp of the duct tape being ripped from Ben's mouth. She leaned in to see. Ben's hands were loose at his sides, the neckties removed from his wrists and ankles. The shooter tipped the chair, and Ben dropped, lifeless, to the floor.

Bits of tissue and blood sprayed out around him as he fell, and Hannah clamped her mouth shut. Fought down the next wave of bile that flooded her throat.

She leaned back and closed her eyes. *Don't watch.* She heard more sounds, working sounds. A zipper and then the crinkle of a plastic bag. And then another gunshot that made her heart rocket to her throat. Her eyes shot open at the thought of Tiffany. But the bassinet was in her line of sight, and the man nowhere close.

The light seemed to wink at her; teasing or comforting, she couldn't tell. It all felt surreal. As she eyed the coats around her, she had the thought again that maybe all of this was an invention of her mind. The Garzas had put on their coats and gone on their date. She was alone in the house with Tiffany, the drugs playing tricks on her. Had her dealer given her a hallucinogenic as some kind of sick joke? Would Adam do that?

The thud of the killer's boots on the floor returned her to the cruel reality. Nadine and Ben were dead. It was true. Boots crossed the carpet with muffled thumps as the man made his way through the house. Several moments passed before the boots crossed a hard floor. The kitchen? She heard the screech of springs. A screen door. He was going out the back.

Don't move. Don't do anything. She'd be okay. He was leaving.

It would all be over.

As the screech of the springs crested to its highest note, Tiffany let out a piercing wail from her bassinet.

CHAPTER 2

Lily

Lily Baker was only a half hour into her shift in Hagen's emergency department when a man brought in his nineteen-year-old daughter with a fever and pain in her neck and back. "She's lethargic and won't eat. And she never gets sick," the girl's father said. "Ever."

The girl, Stephanie, wore a hoodie at least two sizes too large, the hood up and the sleeves pulled over her hands. Only the oval shape of her face was visible, skin pale, her eyes flat and dull. Lily flipped through the registration forms and checked for allergies, risk factors, current medications, anything to explain the symptoms. The patient was negative on all three. It was only October, early for flu, though it was not unheard of.

Lily took the girl's vitals and temperature. Her blood pressure and pulse were in the normal range, though a fever of 101 was a little concerning. Higher would certainly be cause for worry. Lower and probability was on some sort of virus. A temperature of 101 caused more confusion in a diagnosis than clarification. Lily looked up at Stephanie as she removed the blood pressure cuff. "Any medical conditions not listed on the form? Anything we should know about?"

"No," the father said. "There's nothing."

Lily directed the next question to Stephanie. "What medicines do you take, Stephanie?"

The girl shook her head. "None."

Lily thought about the kind of medications that teenagers didn't tell their parents about. Especially fathers. She made a mental note to check again when the father wasn't in earshot.

"Is there anything else you can tell me about how you're feeling? Stomach pains? Sore throat?"

Stephanie shook her head again, curling her legs onto the chair and resting her head on her folded arms. "I just want to sleep."

Lily completed an Emergency Severity Index evaluation and set Stephanie at a three. Sick but not that sick. The ED had an available bed. Lily could get her set up in a treatment bay and keep an eye on her, start an IV, and get Visser to take a look.

"Anyone else at home sick?" Lily asked.

The father shook his head. "It's only us. Her older brother is in the army, and her—" His mouth fell closed as his gaze dropped to his hands.

Stephanie lifted her head and glanced at him. "My mom died a few months ago."

"I'm sorry," Lily said, thinking of Iver's mother, who was now in a care facility in Fargo, Iver with her. Cathy Larson, her boyfriend's mother, had suffered a stroke six days ago and been transported immediately. Today was the first Sunday in years that Lily had gone to church without Cathy and Iver, then eaten dinner alone. The thought that Cathy might not make it stole her breath. Cathy and Iver were the closest thing Lily had to family.

Lily blinked hard and checked Stephanie's paperwork. "Okay. Let me go see about getting you into a room. I'll be right back."

The evening without Iver and Cathy and Iver's sweet mutt, Cal, had been lonely. Sunday dinners at Cathy's house were occasions Lily had never taken for granted. Family dinners weren't something she'd experienced. Or if she had, they were in the distant past . . . before her own mother's death, before her dad's drinking, before she was kidnapped and held captive, before she lost her memory. The time she and Iver referred to simply as "before."

As the doctors had predicted, her memories returned. Not all at once but in single notes and sometimes refrains, like a song buried somewhere deep. At first, what she recalled were odd images and memories from her time in Arizona with her aunt or when she had studied nursing. Her aunt's heart attack and death, for instance, had come back in vivid detail that first spring. But few other pieces had returned with such clarity. Over time, the memories were just there. A blouse on someone at church brought to mind an item of clothing she had once owned, and then she recalled a girlfriend, a shopping trip. Or a patient reminded her of a teacher she'd had in school. And then she could remember the class, the other students, as though the memories had been there all along, waiting for a door to be opened so that they might file out.

Almost four years after the memory loss, only the sixteen months she spent in captivity during middle school were still absent. But those memories had always been lost to her. What surfaced of those months felt like dreams, no more reliable than the nights she dreamed of flying, except that visions of captivity left her bathed in sweat when she woke, then bled their terror into her waking hours.

Lily stopped at the desk where the admin who managed the ED sat. "Sandra, let's get Stephanie Krueger registered, and I'll come back and move her into an open bay."

As soon as the words were out of her mouth, a voice from the ambulance dispatch announced a "priority one incoming" over the intercom. Lily lifted the ED Dispatch line and spoke into the receiver. "What've we got?"

"This is AMR one. We're four minutes out with a fifty-seven-year-old male involved in a high-speed MVA. Patient complaining of severe neck pain."

Lily started writing.

"Pulse one hundred ten, BP one hundred over sixty, respiratory rate eighteen."

"Got it," Lily said.

Lily returned to the Kruegers, laying a hand on Stephanie's arm. "We've got a critically injured coming in, so hang tight, and I'll be back as soon as I can."

Stephanie nodded, idly scratching at a spot on her arm through the sweatshirt.

The father's eyes went wide, his gaze frantic. "Wait. She's sick."

The girl did appear peaked. It might have been something she ate or seasonal flu come early. Whatever was going on with the girl, the car accident took priority. "As soon as I can. I promise."

With that, Lily exited the waiting area. As she passed through the emergency department doors, the on-call ED doctor, Charles Visser, emerged from a treatment bay where an older patient was complaining of chest pains. The other nurse on duty that night was Alice, who adjusted the cannula delivering oxygen in the patient's nose. Brand new to the department, she moved in jerky, uncertain motions under Visser's appraising watch. Lily remembered what it was like to be new, pinned constantly by Visser's intense gaze. The doctor paused at the door. "Administer nitroglycerin and one aspirin. Run a cardiac panel and watch his oxygen sat and BP."

Alice nodded, her eyes barely meeting Visser's. The girl seemed deflated, folded into herself. Lily made a note to talk to her when they had a quiet moment. The job was hard, and Lily knew that better than most. She'd been new at it twice, the second time after her accident and memory loss. She had known how to do the job—one of the few things she'd remembered was her training—but her sense of self had been destroyed. Visser had read her lack of self-confidence as ineptitude, the same as he was now doing with Alice.

"I've got it, Dr. Visser," Alice assured the doctor again.

He gave a brief nod and lifted his phone to his ear, giving Lily a single finger. "Airway's clear?" Visser put the phone on speaker, holding it faceup. She could hear the whine of the ambulance siren as Visser spoke to the paramedics.

"He's talking," the paramedic responded. "Good breath sounds, both sides."

Visser ended the call and walked purposefully through the emergency doors and out to the ambulance bay. As soon as they stepped out into the cold, the shriek of the ambulance grew louder. Three or four blocks away, she guessed from the volume. She bounced on her toes while Visser stood ramrod straight, unmoving. With gloved hands clasped in front of him, he might have been standing in church. He wore only scrubs with bare arms, not even a doctor's coat, but he didn't seem cold.

As soon as the ambulance bumped into the parking lot, Visser's stance relaxed, as though the arrival of a trauma relieved some of his tension rather than increasing it. The ambulance came to a halt, and the driver's door swung out almost before the wheels stopped moving.

The driver nodded to Lily and Visser as a second paramedic emerged from the rear of the ambulance. The two men moved with efficiency, unloading the patient. The gurney looked light in their hands. These were guys she knew, faces she'd seen laugh and joke. But not now. The gurney hit the ground with a clack, and the wheels whirred as they jogged toward the hospital doors, Visser at their side. Lily ran behind, picking up the exchange—the man had been drinking, ran his truck off the road, and hit a telephone pole.

Sundays were supposed to be quiet in the ED. Not this Sunday.

CHAPTER 3

Hannah

A gasp fell from Hannah's mouth; a sob caught in her throat. She imagined little Tiffany in her bassinet, only two feet away. But surely the killer was gone. Why would he come back? Unless . . . had he heard the baby?

Tiffany's shrill cries escalated into a high-pitched vibrato.

God, no. Hannah squeezed her eyes closed. *Please let him be gone.*

Tiffany let out another wail.

Stay quiet. Hannah clamped a hand over her own mouth as though muffling herself would make Tiffany stop crying. Her parents were dead. Did the baby sense that loss? Hannah fought to pull herself together, to form clear thoughts. Adam was right—these pills were stronger. She'd taken too much. She needed to think. To be clearheaded.

Wait. Be patient.

She felt a blanket of warmth, the coat beside her as soft as velvet. Breath filled her lungs. She thought of her phone. She'd turned it off earlier when her brother had been pestering her about her plans for the night, but she would call 911 and stay in the closet until someone came and took her home. She could go home and sleep in her bed. Hug her mother and call her father.

If only he was gone. If Tiffany was safe. If . . .

The screech of the screen door cut through the baby's crying.

Tiffany went momentarily silent.

No. That wasn't the door. The house was empty. The man was gone. Then came the thud of the screen door closing. Hannah fisted her hands, leaning forward to peer through the open slot beside the hinges of the closet door.

Across the room, Hannah spotted Ben's face—his lips parted, his tongue visible and eyes wide open. A single boot sounded on the kitchen floor.

She dug her fingers into her cheek, the pain seeping past the numbness.

Another boot step followed the first, then another.

A shadow passed through the light that cut into the closet. He was close.

Tiffany let out a piercing wail, and Hannah tensed. Would he shoot the baby? She wanted to cover her ears, but she didn't dare move. He was too close. If he checked the closet, if he opened the door . . .

The killer stepped into her line of sight, his back to her. The navy T-shirt he had been wearing was now tucked in his pants pocket, the fabric hanging down to his knees. Where she had remembered him in sweatpants, he now wore jeans, and he'd replaced his coat. She couldn't tell if he was wearing a shirt beneath it. As he leaned down to Tiffany's crib, Hannah's pulse raced like a train, a heavy thumping that felt far away through her high.

The man reached a hand into the bassinet.

Oh God. He was going to smother the baby.

Hannah held her breath, forced tiny sips of air to stay silent.

Tiffany let out another wail, and the man made a strange sound. He lifted the green pacifier from the bassinet and pressed it into Tiffany's mouth. "Shh," he whispered. "It's okay, little girl."

Hannah flinched. That voice. Her own pulse beat in her temples and through her ears.

"Shh," he said again.

Tiffany went quiet.

"There you go," the man said. "I don't want to come back for you, sweet girl."

Hannah knew that voice. The shadow shifted, but Hannah didn't move. She was afraid to look. Afraid he would see her. The drug saturated her limbs with warmth and softness while his voice hacked at its lightness like a machete. She searched her mind for a face to match that voice. A man. Younger than her father. Older than Adam. One of Adam's friends? But no. It was from somewhere else. School, maybe. Or the hospital.

She saw her father's face. Did the man know her father?

"Good girl," the killer whispered. "You stay nice and quiet. Don't make me come back."

Was the shooter a doctor? Someone on the hospital board? She tried to think where she'd heard that voice before, but her thoughts moved like scattering clouds, impossible to hang on to.

The door to the closet shifted, and Hannah froze. He was going to open the door. He was going to find her.

But the door only shifted a couple of inches, then stopped, like he'd bumped it. Next came the sound of his boots crossing the floor again, followed by the short screech of the screen door. The thump of it closing brought a rush of hope. Then she thought of that voice.

In the quiet, Hannah tried to picture his face, this killer that she knew. She could identify him. She could help the police find the killer.

But a terrifying realization slashed right through the thought—if she knew him, that meant he knew her, too.

Call the police. Find a way home.

Gripping her phone tightly, Hannah counted to one hundred. She had to be sure he was gone.

Her finger hovered over the phone's power button as she planned out what she would say. How she would explain what she'd seen. How she would explain how high she was. Could she hide it? Would they test her? Would anyone believe her if they knew she had taken drugs?

She imagined that voice and her father's together, the two of them talking at her house. Was the shooter someone her father trusted? Hundreds of people came into the hospital—not only patients but doctors, nurses, paramedics, the police . . . last month, an officer had visited the house to talk to her dad about a woman her dad had seen in the ED. She had been assaulted.

Hannah stared at the phone with a renewed rush of terror. What if the killer was a police officer? What if she called the police to the scene and the killer was the officer on duty? What if he tried to pin it on her? Say that she'd gone on some crazy murder spree. He would blame the drugs.

Oh God.

She had to call the police.

But she couldn't call the police.

Tiffany began to cry again. Soon, the cry escalated to a scream in that tiny angry voice.

He was gone. He had to be.

Hannah rose. Her legs were asleep, needles in her feet. She used the doorjamb to support herself as she climbed from the closet and stumbled to the bassinet.

The drugs made her feel loose, clumsy, and she imagined dropping the baby. She shook her arms out, clenched and unclenched her fists to gain control of her hands. As she reached in to lift Tiffany, Hannah caught the back of her hand on the bassinet. The hard wicker sliced her skin, drawing blood. Hannah tucked Tiffany into the crook of one arm and studied the blood on her hand.

Get out. Hannah spun toward the door and caught sight of a bright-pink backpack on the floor beside the bassinet. The pack was unzipped, a blanket spilling out onto the floor. Crouched, Hannah dug through the contents with her free hand. There was a water bottle, a blanket, diapers, and several long packages that said Similac. Baby formula, it had to be. Shouldering the pack, Hannah crossed into the kitchen and loaded the breast milk from the refrigerator into the bag.

As she carried Tiffany through the living room, a dark object on the floor caught her eye. The gun lay beside Ben's outstretched hand, as though Ben had been holding the gun and it fell free. But Ben never had the gun. Why would the killer leave it?

The room swayed, and she fought to stay upright. *Get out of here now.* She switched Tiffany to the other arm to grab her own pack, then turned for the door.

Standing in the entry, Hannah drew a breath, the baby making a sucking sound in her ear as she opened the door. Heart pounding, she crept out onto the front porch and stared at the dark night, the quiet street. Then she remembered. They were miles outside town, much too far to walk. She scanned the darkness. There was nowhere to go from here.

The sensible thing was to call the police. Wait for help.

But you're high.

She was so high.

She backed into the house and stood, trying to sort her thoughts. The killer was someone she knew. Someone who knew her father. What would he do to her if he realized that she'd seen him, that she was alive . . . ?

You can't stay here!

But how . . . Nadine's purse sat on the entryway table. Already her arms ached from holding the baby and two packs. She adjusted the straps on one arm to reach into Nadine's purse for her keys. Holding them in her fist, she stared at the purse. Questions of where she would go, how she would pay for food and gas . . .

Without another thought, she gripped the purse by the handle and slipped out the front door. In the cold night air, Tiffany cried out a single piercing shriek that made Hannah want to vomit.

Trembling, Hannah aimed the key fob at the car. A sob of relief broke from her lips at the chirp of the car doors unlocking.

CHAPTER 4

Kylie

Detective Kylie Milliard stabbed her fork into the last bite of banana-cream pie. Pie from Hagen Diner, where her best friend, Amber, worked, was Kylie's standard compensation for babysitting Amber's four-year-old son, William. Not that payment was required. Kylie loved William. Both Amber and Kylie understood that. They also both understood that Kylie would never turn down banana cream.

The truth was, Kylie appreciated the visits and time with William and Amber more than she liked to admit. After she'd lived with the mother and son for more than two years, her own house seemed unnaturally quiet. She even missed William's habit of waking at the crack of dawn and making his way to Kylie's room so she would tell him about the work she'd done the day before. Her detective job, which he pronounced "'tective."

Amber returned to the kitchen. "He's out like a light," she said, settling across the table from Kylie. Her gaze traveled to the plate that had been filled, almost end to end, with banana-cream pie. What remained was a thin line of yellow, creamy goodness. Kylie had to resist the urge to run her finger across the porcelain to collect the final taste.

Amber grinned at the empty plate.

Kylie followed her friend's gaze, trying to quantify how much pie she'd actually consumed. But then she thought better of it. In her defense, it was a salad plate, not a dinner plate, and she hadn't eaten much earlier in the day. She had a habit of forgetting about food until she was ravenous, then eating everything in sight until she was stuffed.

"Another one bites the dust," Amber teased.

"You have to stop bringing home extra pie when I babysit."

Amber laughed. "That wasn't what you said on Friday."

"Well, don't listen to me on Fridays. I'm an idiot on Fridays."

"Or was that Thursday . . ."

Kylie waved her off. "Fine. I'm an idiot about banana cream. It's a disease." She rose from the table and carried her plate to the sink.

She started to wash it, but Amber called to her to stop. "I'll do it later. You have time for a beer?"

Kylie shook her head. "I've got to get to the station and finish up a few things before the week starts."

"Sunday night at the station? Sounds like you're working too hard."

"You know me. I like the quiet."

"Sure you do," Amber said as Kylie took her keys from the table and headed out the door.

On the drive to the station, Kylie made a quick mental list of what she would accomplish that night with Amber's comment bouncing in her head. Kylie had always thought of herself as someone who relished her private time, but the transition to living alone again had been as strange as it was necessary. She was a thirty-four-year-old single woman and a detective, a little old to be living with a roommate. Her mother had been on her to move out of Amber's almost since she had moved in. Both of her older brothers were married with children. Hell, her nieces and nephews were almost grown. Long gone were her mother's days of having infant grandchildren or even grandchildren who required chauffeuring or meals. Which meant the grandkids were too old to keep Kylie's mother busy. Now the woman's sights were set on Kylie.

Never mind having children, Kylie would have liked to hang out at a restaurant with friends or go on a date once in a while. She'd done neither since moving to Hagen. And moving out of Amber's house hadn't improved her social life. It was possible that she was spending too much time alone. She just didn't know what she could do about it. If you weren't heading to the bar or Hagen's single movie theater, there wasn't much nightlife in town.

The department parking lot was quiet at this time of night, so Kylie parked her cruiser in the first empty spot. She entered through the doors and shook off her coat as she passed the front desk.

Marjorie was on Dispatch. If anyone spent more time at the department than Kylie, it was Marjorie. Never married, Marjorie had one son who lived an hour north of Hagen with his wife and two young boys. Other than work, the only thing Marjorie did was spend time with her grandsons. But their mother, Marjorie's daughter-in-law, was a stay-at-home mom and didn't need the help Marjorie offered. It was clear the situation was hard on her. Her response was to spend more time at the station. Sometimes Kylie wasn't sure the woman slept.

"Evening, Detective," Marjorie said, standing from her desk. "You mind sitting here two minutes while I use the ladies' room and refill my tea?"

"Sure thing," Kylie said, hanging her coat over an empty chair. "Will you pour me one? Anything with caffeine."

"Will do. Be right back."

Marjorie took off down the hall with her mug, and Kylie made the mistake of scrolling to the news app on her phone. Bad news, all of it. The economy was in the tank, or it was thriving, depending on the station. Same with whether the folks leading the country were brains or blockheads. Reading the news was almost enough to make her wish she had social media. She was about to open *Candy Crush* when the Dispatch line rang.

Kylie set down her phone and answered the call. "911. What is your emergency?"

There was the sound of someone choking, and Kylie froze. "Hello?"

"He s-shot them," came a small, scared voice. It sounded like a child.

Kylie yanked the chair out from the desk and sat quickly, grabbing a pen. "Slow down. Are you safe?"

"Wh—yes. He . . . he left."

"What's your name?"

"He just walked in the front door." Her voice gained volume, maybe a woman's voice after all, though the words were broken by hiccuped sobs.

"Who walked in?" Kylie asked.

"I hid in the closet . . . he shot Nadine, then tied Ben to a chair . . . neckties . . . and put the gun . . ."

Kylie wrote, *Ben. Nadine. Shot.* "Okay. I'm going to get someone to you as soon as possible. Tell me where you are."

The voice said nothing, and Kylie heard the low rumble of an engine. "Are you alone?"

No answer.

"Are you there?" Kylie repeated.

"It was at their house."

"Whose house?"

"Ben and Nadine Garza. On Bear—" The voice was breathy, older sounding now. Early twenties, possibly late teens. Kylie needed her name. But the location first.

"Garza," Kylie repeated. "Can you spell that for me?"

Marjorie had come up behind her, and Kylie put a hand over the receiver to tell her, "Shooting. Ben and Nadine Garza. I'm getting the spelling."

"G-A . . . ," the girl on the phone said.

Marjorie leaned over the keyboard and typed in the name. A listing appeared for Benjamin S. and Nadine G. Garza. "One three six Bear Root Crossing," Marjorie said, reaching to take the phone so Kylie could leave.

Kylie hesitated but handed it over. "Tell her we're on our way."

Grabbing her coat off the chair, Kylie sprinted for the door. She got into the cruiser and started driving as she put a call out on the radio. "A possible ten thirty-two, multiple shots reported. Requesting all available units to one three six Bear Root Crossing. AMR response requested."

Kylie dropped the radio as she yanked the seat belt across her chest and turned onto Main Street, her lights flashing and siren blaring. Her radio lit up with responses. Sullivan. Dahl. Gilbert. Smith. All headed to the Garza house. She gripped the steering wheel with both hands and thought about the caller. Why had she been at the Garzas' house? And how had she ended up hiding in a closet?

The engine noise told Kylie that the woman had called from a car. Which meant she'd left the crime scene. Kylie realized then that she never had gotten the woman's name.

CHAPTER 5

HANNAH

Instinctively, Hannah had crawled into the driver's seat, her arms loaded with backpacks and the purse and Tiffany cradled against her chest. Her limbs buzzed with the sensation of cold water, as though she were being bathed from within. It had to be the drugs. Ignoring the strange chill, she shifted the packs onto the passenger seat before starting the keyless ignition. It was only as she reached for her seat belt that she realized she couldn't hold the baby and drive. For long, panicked moments, she stared around the car, trying to decide what to do with the baby. She shoved the packs onto the floor, then laid Tiffany on the passenger seat.

As soon as she set the baby down, the drunk driving video they'd watched in PE, the one of the crash dummy slamming into the windshield, played clearly in her head. *You can't leave a baby on the seat.* The baby needed a special belt. What did a baby seat belt even look like? She knew this, but she couldn't conjure the image in her head.

God, she was high. Too high to do this.

Sobs choked her throat as she lifted the baby again. Headlights shone through the windshield. He was back. She cried out, hunching down in the driver's seat. Tiffany's foot kicked at her leg as the baby resisted her hold. "Shh. It's okay." The words, echoing those of the man who killed Ben and Nadine, rang in her head.

The headlights grew brighter. Her breath came in shallow pants. Her heartbeat was a painful nail hammering against her ribs.

And then the car passed.

She let out a cry, and Tiffany, too, called out in her little cat voice.

When the car was no longer visible, Hannah lifted Tiffany from the seat and opened the driver's door to crawl out. With the rear door open, she surveyed a plastic mount on the backseat. It had to be a baby thing, but Hannah couldn't see how the baby could sit there. God, why couldn't she think? *Find something. Move.* A coat lay on the seat. Hannah yanked it onto the floor and laid Tiffany on top. The baby bounced her arms and legs in her happy dance. Hannah closed the door carefully and climbed up into the driver's seat again. She couldn't crash. Crashing would kill the baby.

Kill.

Like Ben and Nadine. The engine was already running. Where was the key? Had she turned it on? No key. It was keyless. She gripped the gearshift and struggled to find drive, passing into neutral, then up into reverse, before finally settling it into gear. She pressed the gas, and nothing happened. Swiping the tears from her cheeks, she saw the bright-red brake light. It took several seconds to locate the release under the steering wheel. She yanked and heard the thud as the car lurched from the curb. She hit the brake, too hard. The car screeched to a halt. She twisted in her seat to check the baby, her legs still bouncing.

Face forward, Hannah gripped the wheel and drew a breath.

Stay calm. Drive. She eased her foot off the brake and tried to tap gently on the accelerator. The car moved down the dark road. She blinked hard, unable to see the road. Why was it so dark? She felt the car leave the asphalt as the road bent, cranked the wheel back toward the center of the street. She squinted out the windshield. Lights. Her lights weren't on. She stopped, lurching again. Panic burned in her chest, followed by a stabbing pain in her stomach. Where was the calm of the drugs, the soothing waves?

Instead, the drugs only made it harder to see, to concentrate. *Come on.* She found the lights on a lever beside the steering wheel, turned it until they shone brightly on the dark street. She almost cried out at the shift in her vision. She could see. She could do this.

You have to do it.

She drove slowly forward, both hands on the wheel. Though she'd driven with her brother dozens of times, she wasn't very good at it. Certainly she didn't feel confident, and it wasn't like she had a license. Or a learner's permit. Adam had asked her to take the wheel twice when they'd been high together, saying he was too messed up to drive. Both times, she'd told her dealer she didn't really feel like it. She wasn't about to tell him she was too young. Really, she didn't love driving the times she'd done it. There was too much that could go wrong.

"Hannah, relax," her brother had told her. Chase was always saying that. Like she had any control over being so uptight. She tried to loosen her shoulders now, to drop them the way Chase told her to. To hold the wheel with soft hands. But her fingers clenched like a vise grip, and she failed to find a way to loosen them.

At the freeway intersection, a police car whipped by, lights swirling. She stopped the car, her body frozen as she waited for the police car to circle around and pull up behind her. Blare at her through their bullhorn to come out with her hands up.

At almost that same moment, Tiffany let out a wail that made Hannah jolt upright in the seat. A porch light came on at a house to her right, and a man stepped onto his front porch in boxers and a T-shirt. Hannah drove forward, keeping her head turned to hide her face. Tiffany wailed again, and Hannah reached back to try to calm her. But her hands were shaking too hard, and she could barely concentrate on the road.

The panic swelled in her chest, pressing down on her lungs as she stomped on the brake. Sweat and tears in her eyes, she was paralyzed. She had watched a man murder two people. She'd stolen a baby. She was high on—she didn't even know on what. With the car stopped in the middle of the road, she reached into her pocket for her phone. It was still off, the screen dark.

A sob broke from her chest. Her mother. She could call her mother.

Her thumb moved to power the phone on when she heard his voice. *I don't want to come back for you, sweet girl . . . you stay nice and quiet.* That voice she knew. She pushed her fists against her temples and took hold of her hair, gripping it between clenched fingers and yanking. Who was he? Why couldn't she remember?

She let out a howl. And then she sensed someone approaching.

A man was crossing the street, walking toward her window. She shrieked and punched the gas, launching the car straight out into the two-lane highway. At the last minute, she gripped the wheel and cranked it to the right, toward town. She waited for the impact from a car behind her, but none came.

Her toe extended, the pedal on the floor, she didn't check the rear-view mirror. She wanted to put distance between herself and the scene. Get as far away as possible, so she held the pedal down and gripped the wheel. When she pried her gaze off the road, the number 92 shone on the dash in bright white numbers. The edges of the letters created crystals of light that bled across the dash, growing the longer she stared. What was ninety-two?

Her gaze on the dark road, the number appeared across the blackened sky every time she blinked. Ninety-two. It made her think of school. She was a good student, focused when she had to be. It was a requirement for a Visser. Her father was successful, her brother, too. She would follow in their footsteps, medicine or business. She would be a *good little Bean*, as her father used to call her. It was understood.

Or had her parents given up on her now? The way they'd given up on each other.

She passed a house with a bright front porch light. The light stretched out to touch her as she sped by. Sped. Speed. Ninety-two. She glanced at the number. Ninety-six now. Speed. She eased her foot off the gas and searched the rearview mirror. This stretch of highway was known for its speed traps. She could not get pulled over. The police. That voice again. A police officer?

The number on the dash dropped to seventy-three, then sixty-eight and fifty-six, and then into the midforties. She focused on the car and the road. Pressed gently on the accelerator, though her leg was a mass of trembling muscles that she could not control. The car lurched forward again as tears filled her eyes. Town was fast approaching. What was she going to do? Go home high? With a baby?

Her mother would not be home until tomorrow. She was over in Billings for some party at her brother's showroom. But what would she do with a baby? A few hours maybe . . . but all night? She stretched a hand to touch Tiffany, a bundle on the floor behind her seat. Her fingers found the blanket, the warmth. The baby had gone quiet. Was she still breathing?

The killer had left the baby unharmed. What if Hannah managed to kill her in the backseat? Just then, Tiffany let out a long, low wail, a tired cry. Hannah sobbed in relief, blinking against the bright lights as they reached the edge of town.

She needed to get the baby somewhere safe, leave her with an adult.

She stopped at the intersection of Main Street and Highway 1804. The police station was one block to the left. She squeezed her eyes shut against the image of Ben Garza that painted itself inside her mind. His face half-missing, bits of his head strewn across the carpet.

Hannah couldn't breathe. She choked on the spit that filled her mouth. Dropping her head, she tried to catch her breath. But her lungs failed. White bubbles swam through her vision as the world grew black. Her pulse throbbed behind her temples; she was desperate for air.

She clenched one hand and wrapped the other over it to create one large fist. Drawing them in hard, she punched her own abdomen, right below her ribs. Air rushed out of her lungs. For a moment, she was dead, airless, empty. But then her lungs filled. She gasped, drawing deep breaths.

She pictured her living room, filled with friends of her parents, colleagues, fellow board members. They were Hagen's city leaders and doctors and police officers. Fifteen or twenty people—mostly men—in suits or uniform. Was that where she'd seen the killer?

Headlights shone in her rearview mirror. The light was blinding, the rays stretching, digging into her eyes.

A horn blared.

She glanced toward the police department and turned in the opposite direction. Toward her house. Toward the hospital. Her father was working tonight. He would be there. She hadn't seen him since he moved out. Hadn't talked to him in more than a week. But he would be at the hospital. She would find him. A car swerved from behind her with a long, angry bleat. The driver raised a hand at her, his face obscured by the bright light still etched on her lids.

She fought the nausea, fumbled to roll the window down. Let the cold air blow in her face and tried to breathe. She passed the turn to her house and drove toward the hospital. She would leave the baby at the hospital.

What place was safer than the hospital?

CHAPTER 6

Kylie

Kylie reached Bear Root Crossing in under eight minutes. As she came around the corner to the Garzas' address, another cruiser was speeding from the opposite direction. The two parked in front of the house on opposite sides of the street, leaving space for the ambulance at the curb. Where the hell was the ambulance? Kylie grabbed her Kevlar vest off the passenger seat and stepped out of the car, pulling it over her head.

Carl Gilbert and the newest officer in the department, Dahl, jogged toward the house in their protective gear, guns drawn. Gilbert appeared steady. Dahl, whose first name she could not bring into her head, was clearly terrified.

"Suspect inside?" Gilbert asked.

"According to the 911 caller, no," Kylie said. "But we clear first."

"You want me to lead?" Gilbert asked.

"I'll go," she told Gilbert. To Dahl, she said, "You cover the outside in case he comes out the rear." She watched Dahl's rounded eyes. "You okay for this?"

He nodded, and Kylie looked at Gilbert.

"Watch your fire, Dahl," Gilbert warned. "No rookie mistakes."

Kylie strode down the path to the door, scanning the large front window for signs of motion. The interior was brightly lit, the curtains parted, presenting a clear view of the living room. A TV hung on the far wall, a couch beneath the window. No one in sight.

On the front porch, she paused until Gilbert was tucked behind her. One hand in the air, she counted down—three, two, one—then kicked the door open. Paused a second in anticipation of a response, then stepped inside, sweeping her gun left toward the hallway and the bedrooms, then reversing course toward the great room—the dining area straight ahead and the living room to the right.

No suspect was visible, but two victims lay on the floor near the dining table. Kylie took a glance—both looked dead—before returning to her sweep. She stepped to the left of the door, shoulder to a short wall as she pivoted into the corner of the house. An empty coat closet and, beyond that, a half bath. She cleared both, the barrel of her gun aimed slightly below center. Prepared to adjust and shoot.

Gilbert swept behind her. "Clear," she said and pointed a finger down the hallway. A lot of Hagen homes built in the early eighties—single-level starter homes—had the same design as this one. To the left were the bedrooms. Beyond the dining room would be the kitchen. In slow, even steps, she covered the carpeted hallway, Gilbert over her shoulder, and cleared the first room. A bedroom. She covered Gilbert as he crossed the hall and cleared another bedroom, then the bath. Finally, at the end of the hallway, they entered the master bedroom and bath. Clear.

There was no sign that the shooter had been in those rooms at all. Retracing their steps, she and Gilbert swept past the bodies and into the kitchen and a small laundry room off that. "All clear," she called.

"All clear," Gilbert echoed behind her.

A moment later, there was noise at the back door. Kylie swung in that direction. "Outside is clear," Dahl shouted, and Kylie exhaled through the pounding of her pulse.

In the distance, the ambulance shrieked its approach.

Kylie holstered her weapon and returned to the living room.

Gilbert peered down at the man who had once been Ben Garza. "Jesus," he whispered.

Dahl had barely been inside ten seconds when he saw the body and made a retching sound.

"Outside," Gilbert said. "Don't blow chunks in a crime scene."

The sound of Dahl's footsteps pounded across the linoleum floor, and the screen on the back door screeched open as the new cop bolted outside.

Kylie squatted beside the woman, who lay facedown. The carpet was spongy with blood as Kylie reached to feel for a pulse. She had assumed there would be none, but when her fingers touched the woman's neck, she felt a slow flutter. "She's got a pulse," Kylie shouted. "I need gloves."

Gilbert ran, and Kylie rolled the woman onto her back. The front of her yellow blouse was soaked with blood. An abdominal wound from the look of it.

A few seconds later, Gilbert returned, letting out a cry as he dropped beside Kylie. "Nadine."

Kylie pulled on the nitrile gloves and lifted the woman's blouse. "We need to slow the bleeding." She grabbed a coat from the carpet, balled it up, and pressed it to the wound.

Nadine flinched; her eyes flickered open before falling closed again.

"Where the hell is the ambulance?" Gilbert said.

Outside, the wail of the ambulance grew louder.

Kylie glanced up to speak to Gilbert, but the expression on his face stopped her. Kylie and Gilbert had a checkered past, and he had tended to be closed off to her. In that moment, though, he was an open book. The devastation was carved in his features.

"You know her," Kylie said. There was no need for a question. His face said it all.

He nodded, using a gloved hand to push the hair off the woman's face while Kylie did her best to keep pressure on the wound. "We dated for about a year. She broke up with me for Ben." His gaze tracked momentarily to the dead man on the floor; then he blinked and stared up at the ceiling, trying to collect the tears before they spilled over.

"I'm so sorry."

"Nadine," he said, whispering to her. "Stay with me, you hear?"

Another mumbled word. The woman's eyes remained closed.

The ambulance came to a screeching halt outside. Seconds passed in a long, agonizing wait until the paramedics bounded into the room. Kylie almost tripped to get out of their way while Gilbert shifted to keep pressure on the wound. The first paramedic checked Nadine's pulse, then listened to her airway, while the other tried to get an IV in her arm. Nadine's skin was tinted an unnatural gray, as though she had been coated in a thin layer of ash. The veins in her arms were flat. The paramedic tied a blue rubber tourniquet on her left arm, but there was little change to the vein there.

Kylie stood by, waiting to be called to do something. To help in some way. But knew she would not. When the paramedic took over for Gilbert, the officer remained on his knees, whispering to the dying woman.

It was all done in a flash as the paramedics loaded her up and the ambulance left. Kylie eyed her knees, where blood had saturated through the canvas material. The scene was destroyed, evidence contaminated by the presence of the officers, the paramedics.

Moving slowly to her feet, she fought to slow down, regroup. See what they could find out from the scene. The killer was at large.

"Dahl," she called out, and the rookie opened the back door. "We need booties in here."

"Yes, ma'am."

Carl Gilbert stared at the blood on the floor, on his gloves. So much blood. His expression was thoughtful but distant.

"She's in good hands," Kylie said.

Gilbert looked up at her with a furrow in his brow, like he didn't know who she was talking about. "Why don't you and Dahl go talk to the neighbors," she said, and he nodded, rising to his feet. Suddenly moving like a much-older man, he crossed the carpet in silence and disappeared out the front door.

Kylie remained where she was, standing in a pool of Nadine Garza's blood. Any movement would track it across the carpet. It wasn't Dahl who returned with booties but Doug Smith, one of their senior officers and one of the two Hagen officers trained for crime scene analysis. Tall and long legged, he stepped across the carpet and placed a bootie-covered shoe outside the line of traffic to bring them to her.

"Should I get my kit?" he asked.

"Please," she said, pulling the booties over her bloodied shoes. He was smart to bring her two sets. It was a lot of blood. She removed the gloves, folding them inside out to trap the blood inside. Still in the center of the room, she dialed Milt Horchow, Hagen's coroner.

"Yes, Detective," he said as though he'd been sitting by the phone awaiting her call.

"We've got a victim here—gunshot wound to the head. 911 caller saw the shooting. Looks like it might have been self-inflicted, but the caller said there was an assailant. Wife went to the ED with a GSW to the abdomen . . ." She started to say something about Nadine's chances but held back.

"Text me the address, and I'll be on my way in ten," Horchow said.

Kylie texted the address as Doug Smith carried his ActionPacker into the entryway and nodded over one shoulder toward the street. "We've got three cars out here. You want to tell the men what you want done?"

She had told Gilbert, but she took a cautious step onto a section of clean carpet, checking to make sure she didn't track blood. She deposited the gloves on the concrete step outside the house and peered up at the street, where Dahl stood on the curb with two other officers. Gilbert was nowhere in sight. Before she could wonder where he'd gone to, he walked along the side of the house and joined the others. "We're heading out to talk to the neighbors," he said.

Her gaze instinctively tracked in the direction he'd come, but she didn't ask. "Call me if you learn anything."

Gilbert gave her a nod and herded the group together to provide instructions.

Inside the house, Doug Smith squatted beside the large plastic bin that held supplies for evidence collection. In one hand he held a stack of numbered orange markers. "Where do we start?"

"Here," she said, pointing to the living room. As she scanned the space, she caught sight of a petite black-and-red square fabric pad on the floor. There had been one like it in Amber's house when William was a baby. Above the black-and-red fabric was an arc where little plush toys hung.

Kylie spotted a pink blanket hanging over the back of the couch, a lavender doll-size sweater on the floor near the hallway. "There's a baby," she said.

"What?" Smith asked, still crouched beside his ActionPacker in the entryway.

Without pausing to answer, Kylie raced down the hallway, retracing the steps she'd taken to clear the house. She started in the master bedroom, scanned the queen-size bed with its white damask coverlet pulled smooth across the surface. The same kind of comforter her mother always favored. Across the top was a collection of pillows. The one in the center read, *Home is where the heart is.* On a striped chair in the corner was a stack of neatly folded laundry. No baby. Kylie studied the stack of clothes—adult ones but little-girl ones, too. Baby size. Returning down the hall, Kylie ducked into the second bedroom, where a double bed was neatly made, several large prints hung on the walls. A guest room. At the last door, she inhaled. Had she missed a dead child when they cleared the house?

She opened the door and stepped inside, her stomach heavy with fear.

A desk on one wall, neat stacks across the surface, a laptop computer. But under the window was a small wooden crib, the newly painted surface bright white. It was empty.

"Smith?" she called out as she came out of the bedroom.

He was standing in the hall, staring at her. "What's going on?"

"There's a baby."

His gaze took in the crib.

"Where the hell is the baby?"

CHAPTER 7

Lily

Lily and Dr. Visser had stabilized the patient. His MRI showed a cracked C2 vertebra, and his treatment would require a neurosurgeon, which Hagen didn't have. The closest one was in Bismarck, three hours away. Heavily sedated, the man was loaded into an ambulance for transport to the airfield, where a helicopter would fly him to Bismarck. Only one helicopter serviced a three-county area, and Lily hoped it was available. Otherwise, he'd have to wait. Their little ED could handle a lot, but spinal injuries always had to be transferred.

Once the ambulance drove away from the bay, Lily returned inside. She had to get back to Stephanie Krueger, get the girl checked in. She'd been plotting a quick stop in the break room for a cup of coffee when Dr. Visser caught her eye. Standing at the nurses' station with a phone in hand, he waved her toward him. He turned, and the phone's long spiraled cord stretched taut over the counter. He covered the mouthpiece. "Incoming GSW. She's two minutes out." He asked into the phone, "What are her numbers?" His expression told Lily they weren't good. He lowered the phone again. "And we need blood."

"Which bay?" Lily asked.

"One," Visser answered.

"I'll get it hung and meet you outside." Moving quickly, Lily donned a fresh pair of blue latex-free gloves and pulled three liters of O-negative blood from the hospital's bank. With the first bag hung on an IV pole, she set the other two on the table, then headed outside to wait.

Visser was already there.

"Blood's ready." The patient would come with IVs in place, and the paramedics would have hung fluid.

Visser turned to her as though to address her when the wailing of the ambulance pierced the night. Visser closed his mouth, hands gripped in front of him, his calm preparedness once again both surprising and admirable. There was a rumor that Visser had planned to be a surgeon, but he had developed an essential tremor during his last year of medical school. Concerned it might worsen and make performing surgery impossible, he had switched to emergency medicine in the final months of school. In her time working with him, Lily had only noticed the tremor once, on a case where he was trying to intubate an infant. If she hadn't known he had a tremor, she would have chalked it up to nerves. Except Dr. Visser didn't get nervous.

The ambulance entered the hospital parking lot and drove straight to the emergency bay, the rear door swinging open at the same moment the vehicle stopped.

"Patient is late twenties, early thirties, with an abdominal gunshot," Visser said. The paramedic nodded. This was Visser's way. He liked to talk out loud, to repeat what they knew. "Stats?"

The driver joined him, and the two paramedics lifted the gurney out of the ambulance. "Pulse is one fifty-eight. BP's gone. Palp only and no femoral pulse at all," the paramedic reported, a sheen of sweat on his face reflecting in the bay's lights.

The two paramedics, Lily, and Visser moved as one organism to wheel the gurney to the first bay. As the paramedics spun the gurney around, Lily saw the victim's face for the first time. Nadine Garza. Lily felt the pang of fear, an emotion that had no place in the ED. Certainly not for those working it. There was no place for any emotion here. Lily didn't know Nadine well, but well enough. The woman had undergone an emergency C-section in OR room four and had given birth to a baby girl.

That was only two or three months ago. Where was that sweet baby now? And her husband. "Ben?" Lily asked the paramedic, who shook his head. Ben was dead.

Nadine appeared to be trying to stay awake. Sound came from her lips, an inaudible whisper. A moment later, "Tiffany."

Visser pressed the endotracheal tube into her mouth to intubate, and Nadine turned her head.

"Nadine, it's Lily. I need you to hold still for me."

Nadine quieted as Lily lifted her chin up and back to make intubation easier, and Visser slid the tube in without issue. Her pallor was ashen. She'd lost a lot of blood.

Working with practiced movements, Lily attached Nadine to the monitor. Her pulse was now 164. Blood pressure was still at zero. Lily started the blood infusion into the big-bore IV lines while Visser studied the monitor, waiting to see what the transfusion did to her pressure.

"How much fluid has she had?" Visser asked.

"Two liters en route," the paramedic said. "And we gave her an ampoule of bicarb."

Nadine's dark curls were flattened against the gurney's limp pillow. Her face was gray, dark around the eyes. She opened them then and shook her head, struggling to speak past the ventilator.

Lily took her hand. "You're okay, Nadine. Just stay still." Lily wanted to feel hopeful at Nadine's momentary alertness, but victims often experienced a brief period of clarity after receiving blood. Already Nadine's heart rate had started to slow. It was 130 now and dropping fast.

"She's bradycardic," Visser said.

The paramedic stepped away, his job done.

"Get a thoracotomy kit," Visser called.

Lily sprinted to the supply room, where she retrieved a metal tray from a stand. Inside was everything Visser would need to open Nadine's chest. In the treatment bay, she set the kit on the metal stand and ripped off the protective blue wrapping while Visser donned a surgical gown. It was only Visser and Lily now.

Lily pushed her arms into a surgical gown of her own and quickly tied the string around her neck. It hung open in back, but there was no time to waste. Needing no instruction, Lily prepped the surgical site.

As soon as she stepped away, Visser was there, scalpel in hand. With a steady hand, the doctor made his initial incision. Nadine's face showed no expression. The shock would prevent her from feeling the pain. One small mercy.

As soon as Visser's scalpel perforated the chest wall, blood sprayed from the wound, leaving a slash of red across their gowns. Neither one paused for the mess. Lily hung a fresh bag of O negative as Visser worked his gloved hand into the opening in Nadine's chest.

Eyes open, Visser gazed at the white ceiling as he snaked his hand between Nadine's ribs. The presence of the blood prevented him from being able to see what was going on inside the cavity. The doctor would have to identify the problem by feel. Lily blinked hard, a burning behind her eyelids, and thought of this woman's baby.

Several seconds passed as Visser explored the chest wound.

Lily held her breath.

"No blood in the pericardium," Visser said, commenting to himself. "Nothing compressing the heart." His hand shifted. He frowned. The silence in the treatment bay swelled to fill the space.

"No cardiac activity." Visser glanced up at the monitor, then down to Nadine again. "Clamp," he directed, taking it from Lily. Clamp in hand, he returned his hand inside the chest cavity.

On the monitor, the pulse line rose and fell in lazy motions, the electrical pulses continuing, even though the heart muscle was not pumping. "Clamp's in place," Visser said. His hand remained inside Nadine while they watched the monitor.

Nadine's blood pressure rose from 80/60 to 110/70, but her pulse was slowing. Though the clamp improved her blood pressure, the heart's natural pacemaker was failing. A tiny shake of his head told her it wasn't working. "Prep one cc epi," he directed.

Lily removed a vial of epinephrine from the crash cart. Moving swiftly, self-assured, she drew one milligram and inserted the needle into the port of the IV. "Ready."

Visser withdrew his hand from the chest.

"Go ahead," he said.

Lily pushed the plunger, forcing the epinephrine into the IV.

The pulse on the monitor ticked upward once, then again. But Visser didn't move. His hand hovered over Nadine as they waited. His gaze held the monitor, the flat line of his lips grim.

For twenty or thirty seconds, they watched the rhythm of Nadine Garza's heart on the monitor. The peaks were normal only for a few seconds. Then they dropped lower, then farther apart. Lily imagined the feel of Nadine's heart in Visser's hand. She'd once heard a doctor describe the sensation as holding a baby bird . . . as it died.

The line on the monitor was flat again.

Visser laid his bloodied palm flat on Nadine Garza's leg. His gaze remained on the ceiling. Lily looked away, focusing on the flat line of the monitor, desperate to shut it off but waiting for Visser's call.

"Time of death, nine thirty-nine p.m." He yanked the surgical gown off his shoulders and balled it up.

Lily had known it was coming, but still the words took her breath. With Visser's sharp eye on her, she moved with purpose and without emotion as she removed the breathing tube from Nadine's throat and wiped the excess blood from her chest, then disconnected the IV and gathered the waste around the new mother's remains.

Visser left without another word. Only the thwack of the trash can's top closing over his disposed gown and gloves confirmed that he was gone, leaving Lily alone with Nadine.

CHAPTER 8

KYLIE

Kylie darted past Doug Smith to the living room. The baby. Where was the baby? Only then did she notice the bassinet beside the front hall closet. She drew a breath and marched toward it, terrified of what she might find. But it, too, was empty. A pink sheet with tiny white angels covered the cushion. A baby girl. A missing baby girl.

Had the shooter taken the baby? Or had someone hidden her to keep her safe? A live baby would make noise. She stopped moving and listened. Smith seemed to intuit what she was doing and froze beside her. But the house was silent. Too silent.

Then Kylie remembered the 911 call. The woman's voice as she described the scene. The man had walked in the front door and shot Ben and Nadine. That woman had the baby. She had to. So where the hell was she? Kylie drew out her phone and called Dispatch. Marjorie answered.

"Our 911 caller on the Bear Root shooting, did we get her name?"

"No," Marjorie said. "She didn't stay on the line after you left."

Kylie drew a breath. "Did she mention a baby?"

"What?" Marjorie sounded like she was choking. Children—especially babies—were hard for everyone.

"The Garzas have a daughter—a baby. She's not here."

Marjorie was quiet a moment. "She didn't say anything about a baby."

"No one's come to the station with an infant?"

Marjorie let out a gasp. "No, but let me check outside."

Before Kylie could speak, the phone clattered down onto the desk. Smith eyed her. "You think the 911 caller was here when it happened?"

Kylie nodded. "She said she saw it. She watched it happen, which meant she was hiding somewhere."

A moment later, Marjorie returned to the line, breathless. "No sign of a baby anywhere."

"And you didn't hear one in the background of the call, right?"

"No, but I can play the recording. Listen again."

"Do that and call me if you hear anything," Kylie said, ending the call. Returning the phone to her pocket, she studied the house, trying to imagine where someone could watch the murders and remain unseen. The living and dining spaces made up one open area. The kitchen was around the corner, the bed- and bathrooms down the hall. There was no way the caller could have been in one of those places and seen the shootings. Her gaze trailed to the front door. To the right was a small coat closet and a half bath. "She had to be in one of those," Kylie said, pointing. "Stand by the table," she directed Doug as she crossed to the bathroom and opened the door with a gloved hand.

The space was tight, a pedestal sink and a toilet with nowhere to crouch or hide. The door opened inward and swung to the right, toward the toilet and sink. Inside the door to the left was nothing but wall, no place to stand that would enable a view of the main room. Kylie left the door cracked and tried to see through the narrow opening beside the door hinges. That angle only showed the far living room wall with the television.

"You think she was in there?" Doug asked when she emerged.

Kylie shook her head. "I don't think so. Almost impossible to see anything." She walked to the coat closet. A line of boots at the rear of the closet was tidy except for a place where two boots were on their sides, knocked out of line. Where someone had been crouched, hidden. "She was in here," Kylie said.

With her back to the room, Kylie peered into the closet through the narrow opening on the hinge side of the door. The caller could have seen the bodies from inside the closet. As she stepped closer, she saw a flash of blue tucked in the folds of a fallen coat. "There's something here."

Doug approached, and Kylie drew the flashlight from her belt and shone it down. The blue was a small ball of fur with a little metal ring on one end.

"What the heck is that?" Doug asked.

Kylie knew exactly what it was. Amber had a neon-green one on her key chain, a way to locate the keys she was forever misplacing. "It's part of a key chain, I think." She stepped away so Smith could photograph and collect it as evidence. Kylie stood back as he worked. The ball might have belonged to their caller, but it wasn't going to be much help. No chance of fingerprints or DNA and almost impossible to narrow down to a single person. It wasn't like she could put an APB out for someone who had a blue puffball key chain.

"Let's print the door, too," she said. "Hopefully we'll get something usable off the edges or the inside knob."

Smith nodded, though it would be tricky. Doorknobs were rarely good for prints. Not that the metal didn't hold them. It did. The problem was that too many people handled them to make any one set clear enough for prints.

Spinning in a slow circle, Kylie scanned the room. The large spot of Nadine Garza's blood was turning dark as it oxidized. Ben Garza's lifeless body lay untouched, the gun beside his outstretched right arm.

From the placement of the bodies, the most obvious theory would be that Ben had shot Nadine first, then himself. Like a marital dispute that had escalated. A typical setup for murder-suicide, which most often involved the husband killing his wife and then himself. But that wasn't the case here. There had been a shooter; the caller had confirmed it.

If the killer had intended it to look that way, he wouldn't have taken the baby. Which returned Kylie to the theory that the caller must have her.

Smith bagged the blue puffball and wrote on the plastic bag with a black marker. Kylie tried to imagine where the witness had been when the shooter entered. The white bassinet was on the wall feet from the closet. The woman had likely been standing close by when the killer broke in. Was she holding the baby? A babysitter, maybe? Noticing a shadow on the bassinet's white paint, Kylie stepped forward. It was not a shadow but a streak of red. Blood. And from the look of the bright color, it was fresh. "There's blood here." She prayed it didn't belong to the infant. "We need to collect it and get it to the state lab. Now."

Kylie pictured her friend Amber making the sign of the cross the way she did when she heard anything upsetting. Kylie found herself imagining the sign now, too, for Amber and herself. For the missing infant.

Then she took out her phone and sent a message to Sarah Glanzer, her friend at the state crime lab. She needed DNA run on this blood. And she needed it now.

CHAPTER 9

Lily

Lily put a sheet over Nadine Garza's body and bowed her head. The urge was strong to clean the woman's skin, to gently remove the traces of her violent death and leave her with some final beauty. But Nadine Garza was no longer Lily's patient. She belonged to the orderly now, then to the Hagen coroner, and after that the state medical examiner, where all Hagen homicides ended up. Lily allowed herself a short prayer for Nadine.

For we know that if our earthly house of this tabernacle were dissolved, we have a building of God, a house not made with hands, eternal in the heavens. 2 Corinthians 5:1.

Then Lily forced herself out of the treatment bay. Her eyes stung as she moved from the treatment bay, discarding her gown as well as her gloves and booties, which were now soaked with blood. Taking a detour, she ducked into the lounge to replace her scrubs with a clean set. One look in the mirror confirmed she appeared as frazzled as she felt, but busy nights in the ED always made her look like this. But she felt okay. Steady. And the clean scrubs helped. She pulled the hair tie from her head and redid her bun, smoothing the loose hairs behind her ears. Better.

On the board, she noticed Stephanie Krueger had not yet been admitted. Damn it. Lily was sure Alice would have gotten to her by now. Dr. Visser emerged from bay three, the new nurse with him. They both glanced in Lily's direction, so she wasted no time heading toward the waiting room. Something on the floor outside bay four caught her eye, and she slowed to study the whitish blob. It might have been a bit of food. There were always two or three staff who rotated through the ED and the ICU, cleaning through every shift, but who knew where they were now.

Across the hall, Visser watched her. She wondered if the new nurse had brought food into the ED. Visser was a stickler for that sort of thing. With a nod to Visser, Lily ducked into the nearest treatment bay, grabbed an exam glove from the box by the door, and used it to scoop up whatever was on the ground. Her back to Visser, she removed the glove inside out, trapping the food inside, tucked it in her scrubs pocket, and headed for the waiting area. The last thing Alice needed tonight was more heat from Visser. Sandra at the desk gave her a wave to indicate that no new cases had come in that needed to be triaged ahead of Stephanie.

The teenager was in the same spot, curled up on a chair, head in her father's lap.

Her father appeared to be dozing as well, but as soon as Lily's shoe squeaked on the linoleum, he was erect and facing her. "Thank God," he said. "I think she's getting worse."

Lily drew her thermometer from her pocket and ran it across Stephanie's forehead. One hundred one point eight. Her temperature was rising. Stephanie moaned, shifting her head in her father's lap.

"Stephanie?" her father said, shaking his daughter lightly. "Honey?"

Without opening her eyes, the girl reached out and put an arm around her father. As she did, the V of the hoodie gapped slightly, exposing a small triangle of skin.

Lily's breath caught in her throat. "Stephanie?"

The girl sat up, half-asleep but her expression alarmed. Her father practically jumped up from his chair. "What? What is it?"

Lily spoke slowly, calmly, pointing to her own chest. "I thought I saw something on your skin. Do you have a rash?"

Stephanie nodded. "Yeah." She freed one arm from her hoodie and tugged it over her head. She wore a gray ribbed tank top, her full arm exposed along with a semicircle of her high chest and neck. The skin there was peppered with tiny red pinprick marks called petechiae, similar to the kind that occurred in the eyes of a strangulation victim.

"What do you think it is?" the father asked.

Lily knew exactly what it was. But she hoped like hell she was wrong. "I'm going to get the doctor to take a look right away."

"What's wrong with me?" Stephanie said, her voice cracking with panic.

"Hang tight, Stephanie. I'll be right back." Lily jogged through the ED doors, forcing herself not to run as she scanned the halls for Visser.

Alice was making a note on the board.

Lily grabbed her arm. "Where is Visser?"

"He was here . . ."

"We need to find him," Lily said. "Now."

Alice took off toward the corridor that housed the operating rooms while Lily ran to the doctors' lounge. No sign of Visser in the lounge or in the kitchen or in either of the sleep rooms. Where could he have gone? She sprinted to the bathrooms and pushed open the door to the men's, standing on the threshold. "Dr. Visser?"

From the farthest stall, a man cleared his throat.

"Is that you, Dr. Visser?"

"Good God, Lily. What is it?"

"Nineteen-year-old in the lobby with a fever of one hundred two and a red petechial rash on her upper trunk."

There was the sound of the toilet flushing, and Visser emerged, still zipping his pants as Lily turned away. He moved to the sink, washing his hands with purpose. Without pausing to dry them, he crossed in front of her and out to the waiting room.

Visser took one look at Stephanie's rash and called for a wheelchair. Lily was ready. Stephanie's father helped his daughter into the chair, and the four of them moved through the automatic ED doors, Mr. Krueger spouting off questions like a *Jeopardy!* contestant.

"It's possible that your daughter may have meningitis," Visser told Mr. Krueger.

Krueger seemed almost knocked backward. When he recovered, the questions flew like darts. "How did she get meningitis? What's the treatment? Is she going to be all right?"

Visser put a palm up to the father in a kind but firm gesture and shifted his focus to Lily. He gave her instructions for the meds they would need. High-dose antibiotics were Stephanie's best shot. Lily went to the pharmacy while Alice set up the IV. When Lily returned, she started the antibiotics as Visser pulled Mr. Krueger into the conference room to talk.

Visser had prescribed a low dose of sedative to be added to Stephanie's IV, and after asking a few questions of her own, the girl was quickly asleep. Lily watched her rest. That was a blessing. Meningitis was an extremely painful disease, and Stephanie would need all the rest she could get before the disease took hold.

Her father seemed to have aged ten years in that consult, and when he entered the hospital bay, Lily showed him how the chair in the treatment bay reclined so he could sleep beside his daughter's bed. Alice brought a pillow and blanket as well as a pitcher of ice water and two cups.

Krueger shook his head when Lily asked if he needed anything else, so Lily showed him the call button and left the bay. There was little else to be done until the antibiotics had a chance to work. Even then, Stephanie Krueger's prognosis would be unknown for days if not weeks.

With a moment of quiet in the department, Lily settled at a desk to write up her case notes. Often, she did case notes at home, the nights in the department too jam-packed to allow her time to complete them between cases. But now, she entered the information about Nadine Garza. At thirty-one, Nadine had been just two years older than Lily. Only ten weeks postpartum. Lily thought again about Nadine's face when she'd held that little girl for the first time. Only ten weeks old, and she would never be held by her parents again. Where was the baby? The paramedics hadn't mentioned that a child was killed. God, the thought was sickening. She could not go there. Forcing herself back to work, Lily checked in on Stephanie, who was still sleeping, her father watching.

Had the petechiae been there earlier? Before Nadine came in? Had Lily missed it? When she had entered the initial information on both patients, she made her way out to the reception desk. Two patients remained in the waiting room, both regulars. One man would be seeking meds and the other complaining of general lethargy and some dull aches—lonely, most likely. If only they had been the cases waiting when Stephanie Krueger came in. Lily sighed quietly.

Sandra touched her hand. "I heard about Nadine Garza."

Lily said nothing.

"Take a break, Lily," Sandra said, tilting her head toward the two older men. "They'll still be here in fifteen."

Lily hadn't had a single drink of water or eaten anything since the start of her shift. A little fresh air would do her good.

"Go," Sandra said again.

"I'll be back in ten."

Sandra only waved her hand.

Quickly, Lily returned to the nurses' station for her water bottle and a granola bar. The outside air was cool and fresh, a little moist with a light breeze that made it feel like she was being sprayed with a fine mist.

In these moments, in the stillness between actively caring for patients, in the moments when all she could do was wait and see, the ED was perhaps the saddest place Lily had ever been.

All the effort to preserve, to save, to fix or extend, had been exerted, and now it was a waiting game . . . to see if it worked, to accept that they hadn't been able to save Nadine Garza, to wait until the next emergency arrived.

CHAPTER 10

KYLIE

Hagen's coroner, Milton Horchow, knelt in Tyvek pants on the carpet next to Ben Garza's body. Planting his gloved hands on the carpet, Horchow shifted his body weight to study the victim's head wound. Kylie sometimes wondered about Horchow's life. Never married, no kids, he lived in a house that was connected to the morgue he owned and ran, inherited from a bachelor uncle. He loved food and red wine and was a connoisseur of game meats, according to rumor. Built like a brick, Horchow moved like a turtle on the ground, slow and with purpose. What he lacked in physical prowess, though, he made up in mental acuity. Smart and thorough, there was little that got past him when it came to death.

Kylie shot off emails and text messages as she waited for Horchow's assessment while the four officers—Larry Sullivan and Mika Keckler, another new recruit, had also joined—canvassed the area and talked to neighbors and Doug Smith continued his evidence collection. Meanwhile, Kylie had a running list of things to do: Pull vehicle registrations for the Garzas in case they owned cars other than the two parked in the garage—a Subaru and an old Dodge truck. Connect with the Garzas' employers about issues at work; pull their finances to check for indications that they were in trouble or owed money; reach out to statewide law enforcement with a BOLO for someone traveling with an infant.

That last one was sticky. Whoever had taken the infant would likely not have all the relevant accessories—a car seat, diapers, bottles—but the last thing she wanted was for North Dakota troopers to start pulling over a bunch of new parents.

From the floor, Horchow grunted and sat up on his knees. "Your caller sure saved us some heartache."

Kylie stopped typing on her phone. "How do you mean?"

"Be easy to assume this was murder-suicide." Horchow sat back on his feet and waved a hand at Ben Garza. "One thing I've seen plenty of in my day, it's suicide by firearm."

It was true. The oil booms and busts of the last thirty years had left their town a hotspot for suicide. While the national average suicide rate was about fourteen in every one hundred thousand, for the past fifteen years, Hagen's had been close to twenty. Harsh conditions and a depressed economy did that to a place. And Hagen was still on the downside of the latest boom, which meant the numbers would likely be higher this year than last.

"Now that I know there was a witness, the signs are obvious that it wasn't murder-suicide. I guess it's a reminder to this old guy to look before I go jumping," Horchow said.

Kylie let the last part go. Horchow liked his idioms, and more often than not, he got them slightly wrong. "Tell me what you see."

The coroner removed his gloves and worked his way to his feet, using a chair to assist. Slightly breathless, he brought a red laser pointer from his kit and aimed it at the entrance wound on Garza's head. He waved Kylie closer. In his free hand, Horchow held what looked like a tongue depressor. "First off, the muzzle of the gun was resting right behind the temple. I've never seen a suicide entry wound in this location." Using the flat wooden stick, he demonstrated by pressing it to the side of Kylie's head behind her temple, high on the rounded bone above her ear.

"Feel that?" he asked.

She nodded.

"Not where you'd shoot, right?"

She fingered the hard knob of bone with one hand. If she were going to shoot herself in the head, she'd put the barrel to the soft spot at her temple. "Right. I'd shoot here," she said, pressing a finger there to demonstrate.

"Exactly," Horchow agreed. "Suicides tend to be intraoral—in the mouth—at the temple, or under the chin. Also, the bullet track in this case goes back to front. See how the exit wound is between his left eyebrow and his ear?" He handed her the tongue depressor. "Imagine holding the gun at an angle to shoot toward your eyebrow. It's awkward; try it."

He was right. The angle required shifting her shoulder back. Not a solid position to shoot from.

"The victim probably moved as the guy was taking his shot," Horchow said.

Kylie studied the pool of coagulating blood where Nadine Garza's body had been. If her husband was about to be shot, Kylie would have expected Nadine to be moving—running away or toward—and yet the blood was confined to a single area. But maybe the shooter had threatened Tiffany.

She imagined what Amber would do to protect William. Hell, what *she* would do to protect William. Her throat tightened as she gave the scene her full focus. If Nadine was shot first, how had the killer subdued Ben? "Any other contusions on him?"

Horchow lifted Garza's arms one at a time and studied his hands. "No defensive wounds on his hands. Nothing visible under the nails, but I'll scrape in case he took a swipe at his attacker. My guys should be here for transport in the next fifteen minutes."

"Can we remove his shirt and check his torso before you go?"

"Be my guest."

Horchow handed her a fresh pair of gloves from his kit, and Kylie pulled them on as she squatted beside the body. As she unbuttoned the shirt, she saw bits of flesh and brain matter that had sprayed across the fabric. As soon as she exposed the flesh, the answer to how the killer had managed to subdue Ben Garza was obvious. She pointed to the red mark on the skin, what looked like a beesting with a short curve at the base. Like a comma. From a barb. Spreading the shirt open across Garza's chest, she located a second mark below the nipple on his right side.

Horchow leaned down to study the mark more closely. "That would keep him down."

The marks were, unmistakably, from the barbs of a Taser.

CHAPTER 11

LILY

Lily sat on the short retaining wall along the side of the ambulance bay and took a long drink from her water before ripping open the granola bar. Eating at work was a matter of ingesting enough calories to keep up her energy. From her spot, she could see the high school's football field and the rear of the school itself on the next block. The parking lot around her was dark and mostly empty.

To someone unaware of what happened in the ED—the pain and death, the adrenaline and sorrow—it might seem almost peaceful. Especially in the middle of the night.

Lily balled up the wrapper and stood, ready to return inside, when she noticed the glow from a car in the far corner of the lot. The inside dome light was on, something she'd done herself, parked in this same place. It had been a bitter February morning when she came off her shift to find her car battery dead. She could at least save someone the trouble of needing a jump when they emerged from the hospital. Phone in hand, Lily walked toward the car to take a picture of the license plate so Sandra at reception could send out a page.

Lily halted when she realized the car wasn't empty. A shadowy form sat in the driver's seat, shifting to face Lily. From the size, Lily thought it was a woman.

Embarrassed to interrupt a quiet moment, Lily raised a hand in apology and turned back to the hospital, chastising herself for not considering that someone might be in the car. It wasn't uncommon to find people sitting in the parking lot. For most, the hospital was not an easy place. Folks came outside to wait for word about a loved one or to seek refuge from the endless hours of watching a clock that brought no news.

The sound of a car door opening made Lily look, with that unshakable sense that someone might be coming for her. She sometimes wondered if she'd always been a little jumpy or if the rush of adrenaline that came now with every unexpected event was the result of being held captive for sixteen months as a teenager. It was odd to consider that her brain had assimilated the experience and used it to alter her reactions even though the memories of that time were lost to her.

Lily glanced back again as a small hooded figure emerged from the driver's seat and opened the rear car door. As she ducked into the car, the woman called out, "Wait!"

The voice was reassuring to Lily. Statistically speaking, women were rarely attackers. But Lily didn't stop, assuming the woman was talking to someone in the car. The cold sank its teeth into her bones as she made her way across the lot. Why hadn't she brought her coat?

"Wait," the voice called again. "Nurse!"

Now Lily did turn.

The car doors closed, and the woman stood beside the car, wearing a jacket with a sweatshirt underneath, its hood tied tight around her head. A pink backpack hung off one arm, and she carried something in her arms. A bundle. The way she hugged it made Lily think it might be a child. The woman swayed as she walked as though she were drunk or injured. Lily moved toward her.

"Stop!" the woman cried out, her palm thrust in front of her.

Lily stopped. "Are you hurt?"

The woman shook her head, the motion exaggerated. But as she walked, her motions seemed too smooth for someone who had been drinking. Maybe she wasn't drunk. "You need to take—" Her voice cut off as she lifted a pink bundle.

"What is it?" Lily asked.

But the woman didn't answer. Head down, she walked closer, her pace slowing when she was within twenty feet. Though the woman was smaller than Lily—tiny, really—the way she approached was unnerving. Lily stepped away. "What is that?"

"Baby," the woman said.

Lily halted. "What?"

The word *baby* drove her forward, but the woman shouted, "Stop!" Lily froze. What was happening? Was it really a baby? Or an explosive of some sort? There were so many versions of terror these days. Lily took a step away, studying the woman as she approached, weighing how to proceed.

When the woman looked up, Lily saw the furrow on her brow, a moment of confusion. She was young. "It's a baby," she repeated as she lowered to one knee and laid the bundle on the asphalt. Rising again, she set the backpack beside it and moved away.

"Wait!" Lily called out. Trepidation made the blood run hot through her veins. A baby? A sick baby? But a baby. She approached the bundle and saw it really was a baby, wrapped in a pink blanket. Her brown eyes were open wide, her fists shaking in the air. The blanket was too thin, the air too cold. Lily moved closer as the woman edged away. "Wait! Is she sick?"

The woman turned around, and Lily squinted at her face in the dark, trying to make out the details under the shadow of the hood. "No."

Lily picked up the baby, wrapping the thin blanket over her bare head, tucking her tiny form into the crook of her arm. "Is this your baby?"

The woman didn't answer but retreated another step.

"Whose baby is this?" Lily called, rocking slightly to keep warm. To warm the baby.

"He left her," the woman said.

Lily scanned the parking lot, searching for another person. "Who? Who left her?"

The woman continued backing away. Her fingers gripped the neck of the jacket, holding it closed. Her fingernails were dark, or maybe it was a shadow. Lily wanted to go to her, but she could feel the woman withdrawing. Fear, she thought. The woman was afraid.

"Please," Lily called out, holding her place. "Who left her?"

A moment passed in silence, the woman's attention shifting. Then she seemed to jolt herself back. "He leaned over her and shushed her."

Lily took a step toward the woman. "Who are you talking about?"

"There's food," the woman called out. "In the . . ."

The blare of sirens erupted in the distance. An ambulance was incoming. The two women stood momentarily motionless. Lily had to get inside—see what was coming in. She gazed down at the baby. Wide eyes searched her face as though asking a question. *Where am I? What happened?*

"The backpack," the woman called. "She has . . ."

The wail of the ambulance drowned out the words. Lily lifted the bag onto one shoulder. "Wait!" She moved toward the woman. "What's her name?"

The building was washed in waves of red as the ambulance entered the lot. Another ambulance was on its heels, followed by two patrol cars. Headlights were momentarily blinding, a rush of them like searchlights in the distance. Then suddenly the bay buzzed with activity. Officers rushed from their cars. The ambulance doors sprang open, and paramedics unloaded patients. One and then two and a third. Visser stood in the bay, hands on his hips. Alice hurried out behind him. Another nurse, Beth, and two other doctors emerged behind Alice, one still tying the pants of his scrubs. They'd called in surgical backups. Something big had happened. Multiple victims.

Guided by instinct, Lily moved toward the hospital.

"Baker!" Visser shouted. "We've got—" He stopped when he saw the baby. "Is that a baby?" His gaze traveled beyond her, to the car in the lot.

Then Lily remembered the woman. As she checked the lot, the car was driving away, the headlights off. Lily searched for the license plate number, but the rear bumper was in shadow.

"What the hell," Visser said, but his attention shifted immediately to the patients.

"Three teenagers involved in a high-speed accident," the paramedic said, and Visser eyed Lily, who ran alongside the gurney as they entered the department, clutching the infant girl to her chest.

She didn't want to let go of the baby, but she turned to Alice and handed the infant over. "Check her vitals and strip her down; make sure there are no injuries." Lily thought of Sandra at the ED's desk. She had children. "Ask Sandra if you need help making a bottle, and have her call the police."

"Give the baby to Sandra," Visser said. "She can handle it. Then meet me in bay two," he directed Alice. "And make it quick."

Lily handed the baby and the bag to the terrified-looking nurse and donned a fresh pair of gloves. The treatment bay was cool, and Lily's arms were coated with shivers from her time outside. But the warm spot on her chest where she'd held the baby seemed to radiate heat through her.

Lily pushed thoughts of the strange woman and the infant from her mind and turned her attention to the first young man as the paramedics counted to three and transferred him off the gurney and onto the hospital bed.

CHAPTER 12

Hannah

Hannah steered the car away from the hospital slowly, choking down the sobs. The closer she had gotten to the hospital, the more she had longed to talk to her father. To tell him what she'd done, confess to taking the drugs. To stealing money from her mother, stealing drugs from Adam. She felt the plastic baggies through the light fabric of her jacket, four of them. A hundred dollars' worth she'd stolen on top of what he'd given her. She would tell her father all of it, and then she would share what she'd seen and tell him that the shooter was someone he knew.

He would help her identify the man, talk to the police. He would hold her and call her Bean and tell her everything would be okay. The way he had always done. She thought of the picture she'd found in the dining room credenza when her mother sent her to get the steak knives. At the back of the drawer was a silver frame, in it an image taken at the cabin of her dad with his arm around her. He was watching her, a huge grin on his face, and she was smiling, too, holding a tiny fish in her hands. That look—when had he last looked at her like that? How could she make him do it again? How she longed to be his Bean.

But the longer she'd sat in the hospital parking lot, the more the fear crowded out every other thought. She was so high. If she walked into the hospital, could her dad be fired? Could her mother be kicked off the board? Her mother always told her that first impressions were forever. And what if the man was there? What if he was a doctor? Or a nurse? Or what if they sat down with the police and they thought she'd done it? That was what her father had always talked about—how drugs made people into monsters. Could her own father think she might be capable of murder?

She would find the shooter, identify him.

But then, it would be his word against hers.

"Hannah is prone to drama," her mother always said. What if her own mother didn't believe her?

She pictured the shooter inside the house. Had he touched anything? Her own prints would be all over—the bassinet, the closet, the door. And the gun had been left there, dropped beside Ben's body. She'd stopped to look at it. But she hadn't touched it, had she?

The fear became like white water, rushing all around, threatening to drown her.

And then the nurse had come outside and offered Hannah a simple solution to get Tiffany to safety without anyone knowing her identity or seeing how high she was. For those few minutes, Hannah had struggled to act sober, together.

Hannah had hurried into the car, and safe from view, she'd watched her father come through the hospital doors in his scrubs, surrounded by the people he worked with, the people who admired him. And she could imagine his disappointment.

All those times he had warned her about drugs, about what he'd witnessed in his work at the hospital. When she'd seen his face, Hannah's insides had tied themselves into a hard, painful knot. She'd had no choice but to drive away.

She had no idea how long she'd been driving when she turned off the highway some fifty miles from her hometown. Her sobs had finally stopped, but she longed to be at the cabin where her father had taken her as a kid, to curl under the old flannel comforter and sleep. She had imagined driving all the way there tonight, but her exhaustion was overwhelming. Her eyes burned, and her neck seemed too weak to hold up her head.

Two miles off the freeway was a sign for a trailhead, and Hannah drove down the dirt road almost four miles to its end. There was a posted sign that prohibited overnight camping, and the trailhead parking lot was empty, the hillside dark. She parked beside a maintenance building and shut off the engine. Knees to her chest, she wrapped her arms around her legs, dropped her head. Made herself as small as she could be. As though she might be able to fold into nothing. But there was no escaping what she'd done.

An urge to claw open her own chest gripped her. The desire to climb out of her own skin, to make it all disappear. To die for a few minutes. She thought of the pills, and her fingers found the zippered pocket, the baggie Adam had given her—her prize for the favors he enjoyed from her. The memory of it still made her sick. Sick that she'd done it, that he'd asked her and then paid her in drugs. The extra bags she'd stolen as a way of punishing him when it was herself she most despised.

Three pills remained in the bag he'd given her. She longed for the sensation of floating away, the same one she'd had standing over Tiffany's bassinet before . . .

With effort, she pressed the images from her mind and opened the baggie. She tipped it, and two pills tumbled into her hand. Maybe she should only take one.

Her backpack was on the floor, the water bottle sticking out of one side. The pink floral bottle Adam said made her look like a kid. Because she was a kid, and he was too stupid to realize it. Not entirely his fault. She'd never told Adam how young she was. He'd never have sold to her if he knew she was fourteen, and her body was its own form of deceit. An early bloomer, Hannah had gotten her period at ten and her breasts at twelve. The moment she'd entered the tiny middle school that abutted the high school, Hannah had attracted attention from boys who were five and six years her senior.

She grabbed the water bottle and put both pills in her mouth, then drank until her empty stomach churned with the liquid. The bitter aftertaste on her tongue, she wondered if two more pills so soon after the first ones might kill her.

Would that be so bad?

Closing her eyes and never waking up? No more of the constant stomach pain that no doctor could find a cause for. The pain her mother swore she invented for attention. No more fear. She pictured Nadine and felt a wave of shame. What would Nadine have given to wake up, to be with her daughter? That man should have killed Hannah and let Nadine live. Nadine had a reason to live, but what reason did Hannah have?

No. That wasn't true. She had her parents, her brother. Her friend Emily. She had reasons. She drew a breath and told herself to wait until the drug hit her blood, let it wash this feeling away. For a little while at least, she would feel no pain.

Before long the drug worked its miracle. The first sensation always felt, to her, like being on a boat, the gentle waves carrying her, the rush of heat and light. The sensation of magic in her fingers and toes, the warmth in her belly. She could breathe—not normal, shallow breaths but deep, massive ones that filled not only her lungs but her entire body, like she was a balloon. And the air floated through her, painting every cell in an explosion of yellow and fresh-cut grass, and she felt total peace.

With the seat reclined until it was nearly flat, Hannah lay down on the soft leather. She remembered the puffy coat from the backseat and yanked it forward. Smells of woodsmoke and sweet tobacco were buried in the worn fabric—scents that evoked her father and the cabin. Curling herself tightly, she imagined herself there now.

She slid open the panel that covered the sunroof and stared out. The sky above was bright with stars, the moon nowhere in sight. The white spots started to dance, and she heard Mary Poppins singing in her head. Fingers pressed to the glass, she imagined floating up out of this world to join them. With the gentle sway of the drugs rocking her to sleep, she let her eyes fall closed.

Her thoughts drifted to her mother, and Hannah saw her, seated in the entryway as she'd been the day her father left. Hannah had been so angry at her. Furious about some comment her mother had made that morning. She searched her memory for what it was. A criticism—her grades, her appearance, the way she sat and walked and chewed and . . . there were so many these days. As though her mother had just started to notice how perfectly awful Hannah was.

Hannah had entered the house from school, ready to climb directly to her room. Surprised her mother was home, shocked to find her sitting in the chair in the entryway. No one ever sat in that chair. Hannah didn't know why it was there other than that she always took off her shoes there and stored them beneath it. The chair was where her backpack lived on nights when she didn't take it upstairs.

But that day, her mother sat there. She had been dressed up—Priscilla Visser was always dressed up. She wore black slacks and a cream silk blouse, a long string of pearls around her neck. On her feet were black leather flats, their toes adorned with bows and little gold plaques where a designer's long name was etched in cursive. Some Italian designer for old people.

Hannah had been startled. But then she'd closed the door, crossed to the stairs, and sat down to untie her shoes.

"Your father has moved out."

Hannah's insides had gone cold. She turned slowly and studied her mother. She noticed the wrinkles in her mother's blouse, her missing belt. She imagined crossing the room and hugging her, the two of them holding each other for comfort. Their mutual loss. But her mother's posture gave her pause. Her mother sat ramrod straight in the chair, almost unfamiliar in her hard edges. Hannah saw her brother, Chase, in her mother's shoulders, in the set of her jaw. Chase, who had always been standoffish to people he didn't know, a trait Hannah always thought he had gotten from their father.

Hannah's gaze lifted to her mother's perfectly smooth face. The brow that never rose, never fell, never furrowed was suddenly screwed in on itself. It was as though her mother was breaking through the wall of whatever had been injected into her face to freeze her expression into one of permanent neutrality. A single blue vein pulsed in her forehead. Her dark gaze was narrowed on Hannah.

"Mom," Hannah had whispered, trying to find a way to comfort her. "I'm so sorry."

"Just don't make it harder," her mother had said. "Try to be easy for a change."

The words struck Hannah like a physical blow. Her eyes watered as though she'd been slapped. But her mother was too far away to have hit her, still seated upright and rigid in that stupid chair. Hannah had only come through the door from school minutes earlier. Her backpack was on her shoulders, her Chuck Taylors still on her feet. She stared down at them, the laces undone.

Was this somehow her fault? Had her father found out what she'd been doing? About the vape? About Emily and the pills? Hannah forced her chin up, ready to apologize, to make it right. She would call her father. She would explain.

"I have to get out of here," her mother had said, rising and snatching her purse off the floor in a single motion. There was a slur to her words. Her mother rarely drank more than a glass of wine and never during the day. She yanked her coat from the rack by the door without pausing to put it on. Had she been drinking?

Hannah had never asked. And when her mother had returned, the conversation was over. They didn't speak of her father's departure. They barely spoke at all.

And now . . . no, Hannah couldn't go home now.

Shivering in the cold car, Hannah drew the jacket tight across her shoulders. The stars were blurry through her tears, and she blinked them away, searching for the quiet space in the drugs. Surely it would come and she could escape this night, this life.

A crack of thunder boomed in the distance, blasting through the numbing effects of the pills and her exhaustion. She checked her surroundings, shivering as she pressed the door-lock button and heard the comforting click. Then again. And one more time.

She closed her eyes and felt herself begin to float. She saw Nadine's face, in the moments after the man had entered the house. The pain on her face as she eyed her baby. The yearning in her expression. Nadine would have done anything to keep Tiffany safe. Hannah imagined telling her, *He didn't hurt Tiffany. Tiffany is okay.* Nadine's face appeared in her mind, a sad smile as she blinked back the tears.

My baby's okay?

She's okay.

Relief washed over Nadine's face, and Hannah blinked. *I'm okay, too,* she told Nadine. But Nadine's face was replaced by her mother's, her expression stern and pained in comparison.

Hannah blinked and blinked again, trying to conjure Nadine again. Her chest seemed to cleave in two. She imagined reaching toward Nadine. *Take me. Let me be yours, too.*

If Nadine had been Hannah's mother . . . if she'd had a mother like that.

How different her world would be . . .

But Nadine was dead, and Hannah was not her child. She belonged to Priscilla, who hated her.

CHAPTER 13

Kylie

With Horchow and Ben Garza's body both gone, Kylie helped Doug Smith finish collecting evidence from the house. The blood evidence from the bassinet was en route to the lab in Bismarck, and Gilbert was doing a drive through the neighborhood, checking for any security signs that might indicate someone had cameras that faced the street. Working alongside Doug Smith, Kylie was his second set of eyes as he processed each room. They spoke little, and Kylie enjoyed the quiet focus, which gave her space to work the pieces in her own head.

Most people didn't appreciate quiet these days, but she did. As an army brat, she'd spent a lot of time alone as a kid. Her two brothers were four and six years older, leaving her a natural straggler. With pressure from her mother, Kylie had made friends at each of her new schools—five of them between kindergarten and ninth grade. But constantly being the new kid was exhausting, and the older she got, the more Kylie sought time alone, even if it regularly meant hiding out so that her mother couldn't badger her to assimilate with kids in the neighborhood.

With the knowledge that the case was a homicide, Smith worked with intensity and focus. Like her, Smith was a believer in Locard's exchange principle—anyone who entered a scene would leave something behind and take something with them. What they needed was to locate that something. So far, aside from the blue fur ball and the blood on the bassinet, the only obvious evidence was a series of shoe impressions on the carpet that appeared to be from a men's size eleven. That was larger than Ben Garza's foot and substantially larger than Nadine's or what Kylie would expect from the woman who had called in the murder. The flat sole and pointed tip suggested a cowboy boot. A half dozen people had been in and out of that room since the murder, but none had worn cowboy boots.

In an effort to record every detail of the boot print, Smith collected the tread multiple ways—using several types of photography, utilizing an adhesive on the kitchen's linoleum floor, and finally spraying one print with a chemical to create a blue glow that allowed the tread to be photographed in better detail. With the smooth surface of a cowboy boot, identifying any distinguishing marks—loose stitching on the sole, uneven wear, a scratch or mark—would be critical to finding its match.

While Smith processed the tread, Kylie went outside to check on Gilbert. Though the other officers had gone home, Gilbert had insisted on staying until she and Smith were done. He was sitting in his patrol vehicle, typing up the notes from conversations with the neighbors, when Kylie came out to check on him. She opened the passenger door and eased down onto the seat, happy to sit for a moment.

"Hang on," Gilbert said. "I'll lose my thought."

"Take your time," she said, checking her phone, something she'd already done four dozen times. She was still hoping that Sarah Glanzer would wake up in the middle of the night and see Kylie's text messages.

After her first murder case in Hagen almost four years ago, Kylie had formed a friendship with Sarah Glanzer, one of the state lab's senior criminalists. The two women had worked exclusively via phone and email in that first case, but on one of Kylie's trips to Bismarck for evidence training, they'd finally met in person. Close in age and similarly unattached and ambitious, they had a lot in common. Also an army brat, Glanzer had spent her high school years in Bismarck. Where Kylie relied on instincts, her insights stemming from what she had learned of human nature, Sarah was bookish and serious, confessing to being awkward around strangers, though Kylie never saw that herself. Or maybe she was equally awkward.

What had started as a quick drink after a full day of work and training had ended in a long night where they'd shut down the Bismarck bar that folks from the crime lab frequented after work—where they "coagulated," commented one very odd male lab tech who seemed keenly interested in Sarah. When Kylie didn't laugh at his joke, the tech shrugged and turned to Sarah. "Not everyone gets blood humor, I guess, eh, Sarah?" he asked conspiratorially.

"Guess not, Roland," Sarah had responded, dryly.

That had made Kylie laugh. Kylie had never before shut down a bar, and this was not a drunken fog of flirting and dancing. Instead, Sarah and Kylie, though they'd had a few drinks, had spent the evening in a corner booth, engrossed in conversation and effectively ignoring everyone else. Explanations of lab processes that normally would have driven Kylie insane from boredom became engrossing with Sarah at the helm. Kylie listened as her new friend explained how tread could be altered, how the consistency of dirt could lead to a conviction. Likewise, Sarah was enthralled by Kylie's stories of crimes in small-town Hagen and what it was like to be the town's only detective.

After that night, the two women stayed in regular contact, Sarah sharing stories of cases and Kylie giving Sarah tastes of the life of a detective in Hagen. While no case had been as dramatic as that first one, Sarah had processed a few of Kylie's crime scenes over the years, including the murder of a woman by her husband, which was headed to trial in a couple of months.

With this new case, Kylie was anxious—almost desperate—for Sarah's input. And she wanted it now. But it was almost two in the morning and the senior criminalist was obviously asleep. Kylie reminded herself that, even if Sarah were awake, she'd still only be waiting for the blood evidence to arrive in Bismarck.

Gilbert closed the laptop and rubbed his face with both hands. When he lowered his hands, Kylie saw the haunted expression was still there—in the hollows under his eyes and the thin set of his mouth. "I uploaded the report, so it's in the system."

"You want to summarize it for me, or you ready to get home?" He clearly needed sleep. "I can read it," she said.

"No," he said. Firm, unyielding. "We didn't get much, but I'll come back tomorrow." He pointed through the windshield, straight ahead. "Number two twenty-seven around the corner has an alarm system. No one home there now, and it looks armed. Maybe there's a camera. That might be our best bet.

"The little boy in one twelve"—he pointed across the street as he continued—"saw a girl get out of a car in front of this house, right after seven p.m."

"He said a girl?" Kylie stared at the darkened house.

"Yeah. I guess Dahl talked to him for a bit, and the way the boy put it was that the girl was older than him but younger than his mom." Gilbert shrugged. "He's only six."

Kylie thought about that. "A babysitter, maybe."

"Would make sense. They were dressed to go out." Gilbert went quiet a moment, and Kylie wondered if he was seeing Nadine in that yellow blouse, covered in blood. There had been a bottle of wine on the dining room table. Could have been a hostess gift. She made a note to find out who babysat for the Garzas.

"And one eighty-eight said he saw a gray Corolla fly by his house at about that same time—few minutes past seven. Recognized the driver from around town."

"He know the guy's name?"

Gilbert shook his head. "But he volunteered to come in tomorrow and work with Marjorie, see if they can come up with a workable likeness. Maybe someone will recognize him." One of their Dispatch officer's newest hobbies was a software program for creating facial composites. In a town of fewer than a thousand people, the chances were pretty good that they could locate the guy with a decent artist rendering. Though this would only be Marjorie's third or fourth attempt, and the earlier attempts didn't leave Kylie with great confidence.

Gilbert sighed. "That's basically the best of what we got."

"It's promising," she said, and when he didn't answer, she cracked the door and stepped out of the car. "You should head home, try to get some sleep."

Gilbert nodded, though she sensed he wouldn't be sleeping that night. She left him and returned inside. Smith was still at work, collecting the things they'd marked, so she walked through the house on her own, taking pictures on her iPhone without knowing either what she was looking for or what she was capturing. There was always the hope that some realization might strike her when she viewed the images later.

"I'm done," Smith said an hour or so later. "The blood evidence on the bassinet is the best lead we've got. Tread will be helpful if we find those boots."

When she checked her phone, she was surprised to discover that it was now almost three in the morning. Sarah would be up in a few hours. With the state crime lab's Rapid DNA machine, Sarah could have results in under an hour and a half.

Once she was awake.

By 9:00 a.m., Kylie might have a name to go with that blood.

If the DNA had a match in the system.

At the front door, Smith stowed the last of the evidence bags into his ActionPacker, and Kylie took a final look around the room for any orange markers he had missed.

A thought occurred to her then. "Have you seen Nadine Garza's purse?"

"I haven't."

It wasn't in either of the cars or visible anywhere around the house. Kylie wondered if Nadine Garza was one of those women who only carried a wallet. But Kylie hadn't seen a wallet either. Ben Garza's wallet had been in his back pocket. "I'm going to make a last loop of the house," she said. "Banner should be here soon." The officer would sit on the house until the morning.

"I can wait," Smith offered.

"You should head home, Doug. Get a little sleep."

"Don't think I could," he said honestly.

"I hear you," she said.

Her own plan was to find Nadine's and Benjamin Garza's families. Next of kin notifications had to be made. Once that was done, she'd shift her attention to their records, see if they had any enemies.

She'd get whatever support she asked for. She knew Sheriff Davis would see to it that she had what she needed. No case since Abby Jensen's murder almost four years ago would be as high profile as this one.

A silver lining, she thought with a twisted gut—in the world of crime, working to catch a man who had killed a couple in cold blood was trumped by little else.

CHAPTER 14

Lily

It was only while Lily was entering her cases into the hospital records system at quarter to six the next morning that the reality of the night started to sink in. Sundays were rarely so busy. She couldn't remember one as chaotic as last night. A gunshot wound, a case of meningitis, two different high-speed accidents, at least one spinal injury . . . the night had felt like working a shift in a very different hospital.

She was already imagining crawling into bed as her cell phone buzzed from the purse at her feet. She dug it out and saw *Detective Milliard* on the screen. She should have changed the name to Kylie. The two women were friends now. Sort of. And in spite of how much time had passed since Abby's death, the detective's name on her phone made Lily's stomach twist in an awkward lurch.

"Hey," Lily answered.

"Hi," Kylie said. "Are you at work?"

"Just finished my shift."

"Sandra said a woman gave you the Garzas' baby."

Lily replayed the scene in the parking lot. "I'd gone outside for a few minutes when a woman got out of a car with the baby in her arms."

"What woman?"

"I don't know. I don't even know if she was a woman—she might've been younger. Late teens, maybe. She was wearing a hoodie and hiding her face. At the time, I assumed she was drunk or high, abandoning her baby." Cool air blew from an overhead vent, and Lily tucked the phone under her chin to pull a cardigan over her scrubs top.

"But when you took the baby, you must've been close enough to see her face. Was she young?" The detective's voice was tense, her agitation clear.

Lily glanced at the computer screen, where her notes were only half-finished. She really wanted to go home. "I didn't really see her face. She set the baby down and backed away."

"Down?"

"On the asphalt," Lily said, remembering that she had wondered briefly if the pink bundle was a bomb. "I was never closer than ten or fifteen feet."

There was a moment of silence before Kylie said, "Damn." A beat passed as Lily saved her progress on the file for Stephanie Krueger, their young meningitis patient. "You think she could've been a teenager?" Kylie asked.

Lily replayed the voice in her head, pictured the woman's narrow frame. "It's possible."

"What about the car?" Kylie continued.

Closing her eyes, Lily worked to retrieve the memory of first seeing the running lights on the car. The effort of trying to remember felt stressful. After a time with no memory at all, followed by months of recollections returning at random while some seemed forever lost, the notion of memory was now coupled with pressure. She sometimes thought her ability to recall her own past might be permanently weakened, as though in her brain's effort to forget the trauma, she forgot most things, even now. But it wasn't true. She could picture the running light on that car, the dull red. "It was white, I think. Or could've been tan or silver. Light colored, though. An SUV. Ford, I think. Or maybe Chevy. I don't think I got a look at the emblem on the grille."

"And no license plate?"

A wave of defensiveness swelled in Lily. She'd thought of the license plate. Of course she had. Even though the woman came after the first motor vehicle accident, after the gunshot wound. Lily had taken the baby, kept her safe. A torrent of responses filled her head, and Lily suppressed the frustration that rose through her tired bones. "I looked, but her lights were off. It was too dark."

"What about hair color? Eyes?"

"I couldn't see. She never got that close. At first, I thought she might've been drinking, but when she started walking toward me, she didn't seem drunk . . ."

"Not drunk but maybe something else?"

"Maybe," Lily agreed.

"Anything else you can remember? Any little detail?" There was desperation in the detective's voice. "We think she might be a witness to the shootings."

"Witness to the shootings?"

"Yes."

"That makes sense. She seemed scared." Lily stared out into the quiet ED, the strangeness of the previous night swept away in the warm light of day. "I remember thinking she was small—like five two or three and thin. Athletic, but it may have been that she was just young. She had a little nose—or not a big nose, anyway. It looked like she'd been crying, but that was all I saw of her face. She wore a hood pulled tight around her cheeks, and her hair was under that, so either short or tucked back. I don't know."

"Okay," Kylie said.

Lily sifted through the interaction, searching for something helpful. "When I asked about the baby, she said, 'He left her.'"

"Who left her?"

"I don't know. I asked, but she never answered. That's all she said: 'He left her.'"

"The shooter," Kylie said aloud.

A man had killed Ben and Nadine and left the baby. Because the baby couldn't tell anyone what she'd seen. If the baby had been a toddler instead of an infant . . . or if the shooter had known there was a witness. Lily crossed her arms, suddenly cold despite the sweater.

"Did you see Nadine Garza?" Kylie's question dragged Lily from dark thoughts.

"Yes," Lily confirmed. "I worked on her with Dr. Visser."

"I know she didn't make it," the detective said.

"No, she didn't," Lily confirmed.

The two women were silent a moment. Lily pictured Nadine's gray complexion, her half-lidded eyes. She'd been too far gone. She thought again of the Garzas' baby, wondered if they had family nearby.

"Was Nadine conscious when she arrived?" Kylie asked.

"Yes, but barely." Already Lily knew what Kylie was going to ask. "She didn't say anything except a name . . ." Lily tried to remember what it was. She had assumed it was her daughter's name.

"What name?" Kylie asked, intensity in her tone.

"A girl's name," Lily said. "I think it was her daughter."

Kylie sighed over the line. "Tiffany?"

"Yes. That's it." Lily had seen a lot of dying people in her time in the emergency department. Not a one had let out any sort of secret. It wasn't like in the movies. She wished it was. Had Lily asked Nadine to name her killer, could she have done it? Probably not. Even if she had known his name, she'd been too weak. Her mind would have started to detach from reality to protect her from the pain. Plus, Lily would never have asked. Her focus had been on saving Nadine. But had she known that Nadine would die anyway . . . Lily brought herself back to the conversation. "Did you ask the paramedics?"

"I've got a call in to them," Kylie said. "I suspect they're sleeping at the moment."

Lily thought about Nadine's arrival at the hospital. "She was still breathing on her own when she arrived. If she was talking, the paramedics would've been able to understand whatever she said."

"That could be promising," Kylie said with a sigh. "Thanks for the help."

"I'll text if I think of anything else about the woman who brought in the baby," Lily said.

"Please," Kylie said, the desperation clear in her voice as she ended the call.

No wonder Kylie wanted to find the woman who had dropped off Tiffany Garza. She was a witness, maybe the best chance at solving the Garzas' murders. Possibly a teenager. How terrified she must be. Could Lily have said something to convince her that she was safe?

And where was she now?

CHAPTER 15

HANNAH

"Miss! Hey, miss!" Someone was pounding on her bedroom door. Who was that? Where was her mother? It was always her mother who woke her when she overslept.

Hannah's stomach was cramped, her throat was dry, but she had no saliva to swallow. Her head ached, as did her shoulders and her neck. She shifted against the hard surface and opened her eyes.

"Miss! Wake up! You can't sleep here, miss!"

She pushed the covers off and sat up. A man peered in at her, his face pressed to the window, inches from her own. She jerked away, striking her spine on the console. Outside, the sky was bright. Daylight. Morning.

And then it all came rushing back. The Garzas, the man, the baby.

She scanned the empty trailhead, remembering the deep exhaustion that had come over her. She had been driving toward the cabin, the place where the picture had been taken of her and her father together with the fish. The place he used to take her when she was his Bean. But she'd had to stop, too tired to drive farther. Told herself she'd sleep a few hours. Then she'd crawled over the middle console into the passenger seat because the hard curve of the steering wheel had been digging into her hip. And now . . .

"Miss!"

Hannah focused on the man outside the car. His brown uniform, the brass name tag. He turned his head and spoke into a microphone clipped to the shoulder of his jacket.

A police officer. Adrenaline roared in her ears.

"Step out of the car," he said.

There was nowhere for her to go. Even if she could drive away, he would follow. He would call for backup. She would be brought to the police station. An image in her head. The tattoo on her father's arm with the two snakes twisted around a thin pole. From his time as an army medic. She almost never saw it. He kept it hidden, ashamed. "Something I did when I didn't have any sense," he'd told her once. "Be smarter than I was, Bean."

But she'd seen that same tattoo somewhere else. The vision of it broke away like a plume of smoke dispersing in the wind.

More knocking. "Step. Out. Of. The. Car."

She raised a hand in surrender and pressed the unlock button before cracking the handle and opening the door.

"I need to see your license, miss," the officer said.

She smoothed her hair and shook her head as she stepped out onto the gravel. Her lips were plastered to her teeth, her mouth dry as she tried to form words. "I don't have a license." Did she seem high? Was she still high? Standing so quickly had made her light headed and dizzy. Her stomach churned, and she breathed through her nose, trying not to be sick.

"You don't have a license?" The officer narrowed his gaze at her and motioned to the car.

"I-I don't drive," she said, the words tumbling from her mouth. She clenched her fists against her stomach.

"Then how did you get here?"

She glanced across at the empty driver's seat, grateful that she had crawled to the passenger side. That might have saved her. He couldn't prove she'd been driving. But then who was driving?

"Miss?"

She spun back, the motion ending in a wave of nausea.

He eyed her. "I said, how did you get here?"

"I—" She spotted the brown trail sign, the wood cracked and worn. Had an idea. "My dad's here. He wanted to stop for a hike. I decided to sleep." She pointed to the trail sign behind him.

The man consulted his watch. "How long ago did he leave you?"

"I don't think it's been too long," she said. "An hour maybe."

"Where are you headed?"

She swallowed the bile in her throat and shoved her hands in the pockets of the big puffer jacket she'd found in the car. "Montana."

The officer peered through the window of the car, and she prayed he didn't notice Nadine's purse. "Where in Montana?"

She thought of her mother and Chase at her brother's showroom last night. "Billings?" she said with a shrug.

Her mother hated her shrugging, told her it made her look like a surly teenager. She *was* a surly teenager. Or she had been. Now, she was a terrified one.

"You don't know?" he clarified.

"Not really. My dad's got a cousin there."

"You're not in school?" he asked.

Then she realized it was Monday. She was supposed to be at school. Would someone have called her mother? Did anyone know she was missing? The officer studied her, his gaze a vise that held her still. A stabbing pain pierced her stomach. The pain was always worse after the drugs wore off. She needed food. Or more pills. Her finger found the cuticle of her thumb and started to pick. She reminded herself to breathe, but the rapid beating of her heart only added to her nausea.

"You okay?" he asked.

"Actually, I don't feel very good. It's why I didn't go—" Acid flooded her throat. She spun toward the car and bent over, vomiting beside the tire.

The officer made a disgusted sound.

"Sorry," she mumbled. She spit several times and pressed the back of her hand to her mouth as she gagged. She had hoped it would be over, but another wave overtook the first. She vomited twice more, the officer backing farther away with each release. If she kept vomiting, maybe he'd leave.

"You have any ID?" he asked.

She shook her head. "No."

"School ID? Anything?"

"No," she repeated. "I left my wallet at home." She lifted her head to look at him, the sweat on her face cool against the outside air.

The officer took a step closer. "What's your name?"

"Hannah," she said.

"Hannah what?"

She thought again about the shooter and her father. The image of the twisted snakes. As the officer shifted, his shirt sleeve rode up, displaying tattoo ink on his forearm. The man she'd seen at the Garzas' had a tattoo like her father's. She had seen that man's tattoo. Not in the Garzas' house but somewhere else.

"Hannah?"

She looked up at him. "Sorry?"

"What is your last name?" he repeated.

Her breath was trapped in her throat, and she had to cough out the name. "Garza. G-A-R-Z-A."

He was watching her. He didn't believe her. She thought about Nadine Garza's purse in the car. But she'd said her father was here, so why would she have her mother's purse? She was sick and a minor. Without ID and without a parent. He was going to take her in. She couldn't go in. She had to get out of there, get to the cabin. *Think, Hannah.*

"Maybe you should—"

"There's probably something in the glove box with our name," she said, cutting him off. "I can check."

"Sure. Good idea," the officer said.

Her hands trembled as she dug through the contents of the glove box. A pack of baby wipes, another packet of formula, papers. She found a thin leather trifold pouch with the words *DeVries Insurance* embossed on the front. Inside was a AAA card in the name of Ben Garza. She climbed out of the car, closing the door behind her, and handed the card to the officer.

He held it in one hand and motioned to the insurance folder. "Mind if I see that?"

"Sure," she said, giving it to him.

"Stay here, and I'll be right back."

Hannah stared after the officer as he returned to his truck, which was parked behind the Garzas'. It was a light green. Not a police officer. A park ranger. Could a park ranger arrest her? If only she had driven farther. If she'd made it all the way to the cabin. She would have built a fire and slept in a bed . . . she'd be asleep now.

Safe.

She clenched her opposite elbows and held tight.

Play along. Stay calm.

As soon as he opened the door and climbed into the truck, Hannah crawled into the Explorer. Checking that the ranger was still in his car, Hannah hid Nadine's purse on the floor of the backseat and glanced at the base to Tiffany's car seat. She pictured Tiffany's wide brown eyes. Where was she now? At the hospital? Had someone taken her home?

Home. Tears needled behind her eyes. She missed the baby. Getting Tiffany to safety had given her a purpose. But Tiffany hadn't been in danger. Not really. The shooter wasn't going to kill a baby. Tiffany had been safe all along. Unlike Hannah.

That man would kill Hannah if he knew about her.

Hannah stared back at the ranger's truck, the officer still in the front seat. He was holding a white piece of paper and talking to someone. His lips moving, his gaze lifting to her car, then down again. Why had she given him the Garzas' name? They were dead. Would he link her to them? Arrest her?

Whatever he was doing took forever. Her teeth chattered, another effect of the drugs. The shakes and sweats, the sharp pain in her gut . . . how badly she wanted more pills. The pills. What if he searched her car? By the time the ranger was getting out of his car, Hannah was trembling.

The ranger closed the door to his truck and gazed up at the trailhead before walking toward the Garzas' car. Hannah cracked the car door open again, struggling to sit still. His gaze found hers, steady and serious and impossible to read. As he closed the distance between them, she was certain he knew. He knew she was lying. That the Garzas were dead.

He reached out, the blue insurance folder in his hand. "You have a cell phone?"

"Yeah."

He handed her the insurance folder and a business card. "Good. You should have decent cell service here," he told her. "You call that number if you need anything or if your dad isn't back soon. The trail only goes about three miles, so he shouldn't be gone too long."

Hannah nodded. "I'm sure he'll be here any minute."

Then the ranger turned toward his truck. As he passed the backseat of the Explorer, he leaned into the window, cupping one hand on the glass. It was a brief pause, but Hannah felt certain in that moment that her heart would explode. She pressed a fist into the painful emptiness of her belly, held her breath.

But after a moment the ranger stood back, gave the SUV a pat like it was a good horse, and walked to his truck.

Hannah waved as he drove past, and only when he was gone did she close and lock the car door. She spent several long minutes catching her breath as she drew out the bags and emptied the last blue pill from the first bag into her palm. Then she took one from the second bag as well and swallowed them down with the rest of the water from her bottle.

She let the empty bag drop to the floor and thought about the remaining pills. Fourteen pills left. She'd taken six in the past twelve hours.

She needed to slow down.

But more than that, she needed to remain calm and not be found until she could get to the cabin. And she couldn't imagine doing that without the drugs.

As far as she could tell, the pills were the only thing holding her together.

CHAPTER 16

Kylie

Seated at her desk, Kylie took a swig of lukewarm coffee and fought to keep her eyes open, still replaying what Lily Baker had said. A petite woman—or a teenager—in an SUV had set the baby down in the parking lot of the hospital, diaper bag and all. She didn't have a big nose, was athletic, Lily had said. Unless they could narrow her age, the description matched a third of the women in Hagen. Kylie was on her third or fourth cup of coffee, and despite her efforts to muscle through, she was dead on her feet. But she wasn't going anywhere until she heard from Sarah Glanzer at the state lab. She woke the screen of her phone and read Glanzer's text message again. I've got the sample. Heading into the lab. Will call ASAP.

The time stamp of the message was 7:11 a.m. The time was now 7:57. It was dangerous that Kylie knew Rapid DNA could be done in as little as forty-five minutes because it meant she'd been watching the clock in anticipation of the forty-sixth minute. Dangerous and frustrating. She kept reminding herself that Sarah hadn't started the test at 7:11. She had only arrived at the building then. She had to boot up her computer and start the DNA machine. Who knew how long that thing took to warm up. Hell, the department copy machine needed an hour before it could function.

Groaning internally, Kylie returned her focus to the computer, where she was compiling a list of known associates of Benjamin and

Nadine Garza. Friends, work colleagues, neighbors. She'd already gotten a partial list from Gilbert, written in his long, lean print, a mirror of his physical build. Kylie had tried to ask how he was, but he only shook his head in response. He was at his own desk now, his back to her, and she wondered what he was thinking about. He ought to go home and rest, but she was much too smart to suggest that to him.

Both Nadine and Ben had grown up in or around Hagen. As far as she could tell, Ben Garza had never left. From high school, he had gone straight to work for Belt Construction Company. A year younger, Nadine had gone to the University of Iowa on a scholarship and studied business. They'd been married in 2016 and bought their house the following year. Their finances were unremarkable, no outstanding warrants or priors. No records of any disputes, no lawsuits. They were a normal couple. And someone had assassinated them and attempted to make it look like a murder-suicide.

Kylie thought about the baby. At first, the baby had seemed like a possible motive. But the baby—Tiffany—was safe. Unharmed. If the couple had been killed for the baby, the baby would be missing.

The phone on her desk rang, and she snatched it up, praying for Sarah's voice. "Milliard."

"There's a Priscilla Visser up here," said the officer manning the front desk. "She says her daughter is missing."

Kylie stifled a yawn. "How old is her daughter?"

"Fourteen."

Pressure built behind Kylie's eyes. She was not going to make it through the entire day without catching a nap somewhere. "And the last time she saw her?"

"Not since early yesterday."

Twenty-four hours. "And she tried all the girl's friends?"

"Yes, and her phone is shut off."

"Okay," Kylie said. "Bring her on back to the conference room. I'll meet her there." The detective grabbed her notebook and recorder and made her way down the hall. She had only just set her things on the table when she heard Sheriff Davis's voice in the hallway.

"Mrs. Visser," he said. "How are you?"

Kylie listened.

"Hannah's gone missing, I'm afraid," the woman said.

The front desk officer interrupted the conversation to tell them Kylie was waiting in the conference room.

"I'm sorry to hear it," Davis said. "Come sit down and tell us what happened."

A moment later, a rail-thin brunette with flawless ivory skin stepped through the door. Her wool coat was heavy and buttoned to her neck, its camel color rich. Expensive. Davis stepped in beside her, and a beat passed before another man joined them. Tall with dark hair and light eyes, the man was attractive; he wore a jacket and slacks, the pant crease no longer clean, as though he'd been in them for hours already. When he turned toward the sheriff and smiled, a dimple appeared high on one cheek, a strange asymmetry that made him seem less perfect.

"Chase," Davis said, reaching out a hand, and Kylie saw the twist of awkwardness in the sheriff's smile. The two men were approximately the same age, but there was something between them. Maybe it was old teenage drama. She'd seen it all in this town. Kylie's gaze returned to the woman. She was beautiful. Only the soft wrinkles around her eyes suggested her age.

Kylie rose from her chair and introduced herself. The woman's grip was loose, her hand angled to one side as though Kylie might kiss it rather than shake it. The man's grip was firm, his eyes direct as he repeated his name. "Chase Visser."

The name Chase Visser rang a bell in Kylie's head. Nadine Garza's employer was Chase Visser. She was one of three accountants for his high-end building-supplies business. Headquartered in Hagen, Chase Visser Interiors had showrooms in seven or eight cities. Nadine had worked for him for almost seven years. The same man. It had to be.

Davis glanced in her direction, then back at Chase. She shook her head. No one had informed Chase Visser about Nadine Garza's death. At least, no one in the department. And he didn't look like he knew.

She studied Chase as he pulled out a chair for Priscilla. "Sit here, Mom," he said, a hand on her arm.

Kylie tried to hide her surprise. The woman didn't look more than fifteen years his senior. His mother. His sister was missing. His employee was dead. She watched him closely, scanning for a sign of his involvement in either. Or in both. But Chase sat beside his mother and let his jacket flap open. He blew a strand of hair off his forehead and shrugged out of his coat. Gave Kylie his attention.

Sheriff Davis shut the door behind them and took a seat opposite Chase.

Priscilla gave her son a little nod.

"Jack, we'd like to keep this from getting out all over town," Chase said to Davis. "With Dad's position and all."

Dr. Visser was the current medical chair of the hospital. But it was Priscilla Visser who was everywhere in Hagen. Kylie had seen her name in the minutes of city planning and finance meetings, in local articles about the school board and the mayor's reelection campaign. Kylie wondered whether the request for discretion was really for Dr. Visser's career or for Mrs. Visser's. She said nothing. If she had a missing fourteen-year-old child, her priority would not be on keeping things quiet.

"My sister is a little adventurous," Chase said with a tired smile. "She doesn't always think things through."

"Chase," his mother said with a little shake of her head. Priscilla clearly did not want their dirty laundry aired.

"And you've checked with all her friends?" Davis asked.

Chase's mouth twisted a bit, but it was his mother who answered. "She doesn't have a lot of friends," the woman said, her shoulders hunching slightly, out of sadness or disappointment, Kylie couldn't say. "Only really one that I know of—Emily Carpenter. And," she said, turning to Davis, "I spoke to Emily's mother this morning. Emily hasn't seen Hannah since school on Friday."

"Do you have a recent photograph of Hannah?" Kylie asked.

Priscilla seemed to soften. "Of course."

Kylie watched as the woman went through her phone, her long nail clicking on the screen as she scrolled for an image of her daughter.

"In this sort of case, we'd like to learn as much as we can about Hannah and her habits," Kylie explained. "How she is at school, who she hangs out with, her activities, where she likes to go. We'll want her social media accounts and access to them if they're restricted."

Priscilla frowned. "Charles and I don't have social media accounts." She picked at an invisible speck of lint and added, "Hannah isn't supposed to have any either." She glanced sideways at her son.

"Hannah does have a private Instagram," Chase said. "I can give you the handle." He lifted his phone. "And I've got a picture from last week. It's pretty close up. I can text it to you?"

Davis reached out. "I can enter my number if that's easier."

Chase handed over his phone without hesitation. Whatever awkwardness had been between them was gone now. Both were focused on finding the girl.

"Great," Kylie said. The next request was tougher to say. She leaned forward, trying to be delicate. "A sample of Hannah's DNA would be helpful as well."

Priscilla's eyes went wide. "What are you saying? Why would you—"

"In case we find another match," Kylie said carefully. "It's standard in a missing persons case."

But Priscilla Visser still looked terrified. "Her DNA," she repeated, her manicured fingers tugging at the cuff of her blouse.

Chase eyed his mother, their fear clearly shared. Matching DNA brought bad connotations.

"I know that can sound scary," Davis said. "We have no evidence that something has happened to Hannah. We ask for the DNA as a matter of course," he said with a look in Kylie's direction.

It was not how she would have phrased it, but it was true enough. They did ask for DNA as a matter of procedure. There had been a change in Davis in the past few years, an increased effort to keep things smooth. He had been a good leader when she had joined the department—sharp and willing to step on some toes to get to the truth. But he'd gotten softer. Midthirties and remarried to a beautiful blonde five years his junior after his first wife left him, Davis had a two-year-old boy and a second on the way. Some shift with fatherhood—or maybe the new wife—had made him more cautious, more worried about what people thought. Sometimes at the expense of the truth.

Kylie didn't understand the shift, but it made her respect him less.

"We want to make sure we pursue every angle," Kylie said. "The more we know about your daughter . . ." And here she paused. "The more we know exactly what she's been up to, the better the chances that we can find her."

"I sent the picture," Chase said.

"I'll forward it to you as well," Davis said to Kylie.

"Thank you." She folded her hands and spoke to the Vissers. "We understand the request for discretion. It is never our intent to broadcast other people's business." She glanced at Davis, then back to Priscilla Visser, holding the woman's gaze. "But we'll do whatever is necessary to find Hannah." She paused. "That is what you'd want, I'm sure."

"Of course. Of course," Priscilla said as though giving herself a pep talk. To her son, she added, "Oh, your father is going to be so angry."

Kylie noted the reference to Charles Visser. Was Priscilla Visser afraid of her husband?

Chase placed a hand on his mother's shoulder. "Don't worry about Dad right now," he said. "We have to find Hannah first. And the police are going to help us, so let's give them whatever they ask for."

Priscilla smoothed the sleeve of her coat. "Of course." She turned to Davis. "I can get those items for you immediately. If you'd like to come by the house . . ."

"I'd be happy to come by for them," Kylie said. A look at the house of a missing kid was never a bad thing. She checked the time on her phone. Hearing from the crime lab on last night's shooting was her first priority. But surely Sarah would have results soon. "Would eleven a.m. work?"

Priscilla nodded. "That will be fine."

Just then, the text from Davis flashed on Kylie's screen. Hannah was only fourteen, but this was a young woman's face—delicate features, the face thin and mature. Kylie's thoughts veered in a different direction. Nadine Garza worked for Chase Visser. Was it possible? "Does Hannah ever babysit?"

Priscilla frowned.

"Sometimes," Chase said. "She's taken care of the infant of one of my employees."

A strangled sound came from Davis, and all three looked at him.

"Is it possible she was babysitting last night?" Kylie asked before Davis could speak.

Priscilla shook her head. "I don't know. We were out of town last night—Chase and I—at a design show at one of his stores."

"Maybe," Chase said. "I was texting with her before the show, but she doesn't always answer the questions I ask." A beat passed; then Chase sat upright in his chair. "Wait. Why are you asking?" His voice was thick with tension, his eyes narrowed as though he sensed the impending news.

Kylie watched Davis, who seemed to be weighing their options. But then she studied the Vissers, pausing to focus on Chase. "Nadine and Ben Garza were shot and killed in their home last night."

Chase's mouth fell open as his mother gasped beside him. "Oh my God," he whispered.

"Shot?" Priscilla Visser said, pressing a manicured hand to her mouth and shaking her head. "I don't understand. What does this have to do with Hannah?"

Chase wrapped a hand around his mother's shoulder as though to steady her for what was coming.

"There was a witness to the murders," Kylie said. "She was hiding when it happened. She called 911 but didn't leave her name."

"You think that was Hannah?" Priscilla asked.

"Where is she now?" Chase added.

Kylie shook her head. "We don't know that it was Hannah, but we could find out. If you'd be willing to listen to the call."

The Vissers agreed, and Kylie called the front desk and requested that Marjorie pull the recording.

While they waited, Chase struggled to sit still in his chair. "What else do we know about the caller?"

"Only that someone—and we believe it was the same person—dropped the Garzas' infant daughter at the hospital and drove off," Kylie said.

"Oh God," Priscilla whispered at the same moment Chase said, "Drove?"

With a glance at her son, Priscilla Visser expelled a rush of air as though relieved. "Chase is right. It can't be Hannah. She doesn't drive. She doesn't have a license."

"She drives sometimes," Chase said after a beat, looking at his mother. "I've been teaching her."

"But what car would she be in? She doesn't have a car," Priscilla said, as though her logic made Hannah's involvement impossible.

"It may have belonged to Nadine and Ben Garza," Kylie said. "We found a Subaru and a truck in the garage, but—"

"The Explorer," Chase said. "They've got a new white Ford Explorer. It's actually a company car. We got it a few months ago."

Kylie nodded. "That car is also missing."

Marjorie appeared at the door and passed a handheld recorder to Davis, then left, closing the door behind her. Davis held it up. "You ready to hear this?"

"Just play the beginning," Kylie said. "If it's Hannah, they'll know."

Davis set the recorder on the table and pressed play.

Kylie's voice filled the room. "911. What is your emergency?" The choke of someone crying, and then Kylie again. "Hello?"

"He s-shot them," came the small voice.

Chase let out a choked sob, and Priscilla gasped as Kylie's response played in the room.

"He just walked in the front door," the voice on the recording said.

"That's her. That's Hannah," Chase said, breathless.

Davis ended the recording.

"What does she say? Who shot them?" Chase asked.

Kylie shook her head. "She didn't say. I don't think she knew."

"Where is she?" Priscilla said, her voice cracking. "Where is Hannah?"

CHAPTER 17

Lily

With her notes finally finished, Lily gathered her things and headed out of the emergency department toward the front parking lot. She paid little attention to the man standing at the reception desk with Carmen, the a.m. registration attendant, though there was something vaguely familiar about him. Lily found herself giving the desk a wide berth. A familiar face always brought a wave of anxiety. The time when she couldn't remember anyone, including herself, was like a scar that still ached in certain weather.

"What is the name?" Carmen asked the man.

"Hannah Visser."

At the name Visser, Lily looked up. Studying his profile, Lily realized there was a younger version of him in a photograph on Dr. Visser's desk. That was why he was familiar. The man was Visser's son.

"Any relation to Dr. Visser?"

"She's my sister," he said. "Is she here?" He was easily six two or three and broad shouldered, but the way his voice pitched high at the end of his question made Lily recognize fear in his voice. She studied his face, a single dimple high on one cheek and the soft smile that was clearly an effort to combat whatever anxiety he was feeling.

Lily recalled the girl in several pictures on Visser's desk. In one, she'd been no more than three or four. In another she was maybe in middle school, standing on the bank of a river. Lily had never seen it that closely.

Carmen typed something, then looked up, shaking her head. "No. There's no patient by that name."

"She wouldn't be a patient," he said. "I'm wondering if she might've come inside, if she could be in one of the doctors' lounges or sleeping in one of the rooms."

"No," Carmen said. "Anyone going back would have to be escorted. Unless your dad took her?"

He shook his head. "Definitely not." As he said that, his chin lifted, and she sensed his gaze heading toward her. Not wanting to be caught watching, Lily kept moving, her steps slow as she opened her purse to search for her keys. Should she intervene? Return to the department and see if Dr. Visser was still in the hospital? He was the on-call physician. He'd have known if his own daughter had been admitted to the hospital.

The man's voice dropped then, and Lily heard only whispered words: *drugs, treatment, kids*.

"No. I'm afraid we don't have anything like that. You might—"

"Okay," he said, cutting her off as he walked away. Then his tone softened as he said, "Thank you."

"Have you spoken to the police?" Carmen called after him.

Striding down the hall, he raised a hand in acknowledgment but didn't turn back. Lily wondered where he was going, if he planned to check every department. Any patient who was admitted to the hospital last night would have come through the ED. The only other department that admitted patients outside of office hours was labor and delivery, and surely Hannah Visser wasn't having a baby. Plus, why not ask his father? Dr. Visser could view patient information from his personal computer or his phone.

"Did you hear that?" Carmen asked.

The attendant stood with her arms crossed over her stomach as though she were cold. "I did," Lily said. "That's Dr. Visser's son?"

"Chase," Carmen confirmed. "He was asking about his sister, Hannah." With a glance down the hallway, Carmen rounded the desk and approached Lily. "I wonder what happened."

"Dr. Visser was on call last night," Lily said. "If his daughter had been in this hospital, Visser would have cared for her. We all would've known."

"Right," Carmen agreed, arms still crossed. "But did you see his face? He looked terrified, poor guy. He thought she might've gone into a room and fallen asleep. I wonder where she is."

He had looked worried. "But she's an adult, right?" Lily asked. Visser's son had to be in his early thirties.

"No. The girl is much younger than him—maybe fifteen or sixteen." Carmen leaned in and whispered, "I heard from my sister's kids that she's kind of a druggie. The Vissers' surprise baby," she added. "Can you imagine? I'm sure his parents were done parenting, Chase grown, and then, bam, they're starting over."

But Lily's thoughts kept returning to Dr. Visser. "But why wouldn't he ask his dad about Hannah? He was here the whole night."

"You know Dr. Visser sent Chase to that military school in Minnesota for high school. Or maybe it wasn't military, but it was intense. Chase didn't want to go. It was a big thing. When he graduated, Chase started his business in Montana. He didn't want anything to do with his father. Don't know why he ended up back here—his mom, probably," she went on, talking to herself. "Long and the short is the Visser men don't get along very well." Carmen waved a hand in the air. "I did hear he's been dating . . ."

Lily's mind drifted as the woman went on about Chase Visser's love life. Her own thoughts stuck on Visser.

But when Carmen grabbed Lily's arm, Lily was jerked from her thoughts. "I wonder what the girl got herself into," Carmen went on. "Maybe I should call over to the police, see what Marjorie knows."

The phone on the desk rang, and Lily was grateful for the distraction. "See you later," Lily said as she shouldered her purse and walked toward the door.

Put on the whole armour of God, that ye may be able to stand against the wiles of the devil. Ephesians 6:11.

Phrases from the Bible, uttered by her aunt during the years Lily had lived with her, still popped into her head unbidden. She knew very little about Dr. Visser's personal life. He was married with two kids. He had a tremor that she'd only ever seen once. She didn't know if he fished or hunted, rode a bike or ran or skied. He wasn't one to share, but he'd always been a fair boss to her. She hoped his daughter was all right.

The desk attendant might have been right. Maybe Dr. Visser *was* unreasonable with his kids. He was certainly strict in the department. But the idea that Chase wouldn't call him when he thought his sister might be in real danger? That seemed extreme.

Whatever was going on, Lily was too exhausted to try to puzzle it out.

Inside her car, Lily pulled out her phone and hit the favorites tab. She dialed Iver's number and, when the call went to voicemail, left him a quick message to say good morning. She and Iver always spoke when she was off shift and headed home. Though they would normally be together ten minutes later, that early call helped Lily unwind from her shift and alerted Iver to the fact that she would soon be home. It had been their routine since the day they moved in together, more than three years earlier.

Until now. She wondered how his mother was doing.

So much time had passed since Lily had lived alone, and it held no appeal now. She and Iver had been dating six months when Iver moved his things into her house. Cohabitation likely would have happened sooner, but they'd been trying to decide which house to live in. In the end, they had opted to rent Iver's, which had been updated and maintained, while they fixed up Lily's, which she had inherited in a state of disrepair from her father. The last time her house had seen a fresh coat of paint before Iver, Lily was almost certainly still in grade school. After her mother had died, her father had let the house go. Along with everything else. And then there was Lily's abduction . . .

Iver was handy in a way that Lily would never be, and he enjoyed the project. It rounded out his days of substitute teaching and working on his master's in counseling. Eight months and he'd complete his degree. He was already writing grants to get funds to provide addiction counseling through the hospital, the school, and the local VA.

Between the proceeds of the sale of the bar he'd inherited from his dad and renting his house to Kylie Milliard, he made enough money that the two of them lived comfortably. A nurse and a counselor, they were never going to be rich. But Lily felt rich. Since she'd been with Iver, they had created a lifetime of memories. She had a home and a good job and a man she loved. They talked about having kids someday, but that could wait. "If we have one, we have to have two," they always said. Both of them were only children, and neither wanted to put that lonely burden on their own child.

Driving toward her house, she hoped Iver would be home soon, but the doctors had warned that his mother's recuperation could take months, maybe longer. Lily refused to think about how they would survive so much time apart. She would go home, eat something, and crawl into bed.

She ought to have been famished, but what she wanted most was to talk to Iver. He was her sounding board, and she longed to share the strangeness of her shift with him.

Without someone to help her untangle the events, she imagined her dreams would be plagued by them—Nadine dying on the table, her daughter's name the last word she uttered, followed by the appearance of the terrified young woman in the parking lot who had set the baby on the asphalt rather than allow Lily to get close to her.

And perhaps the eeriest of all, the appearance of Dr. Visser's son that morning. Chase Visser seemed willing to do anything to find his sister . . . except speak with his own father.

CHAPTER 18

Kylie

At her desk, Kylie studied the notes she'd written up from the meeting with the Vissers. She and Davis had run Priscilla and Chase through dozens of questions about where Hannah might have gone, but it was a fruitless interview. They were unfocused and in shock. Priscilla fretting aloud about what her husband would say while Chase seemed to sink into a state of deep worry that set him as rigid as a block of ice. Kylie would go by the house in a few hours to pick up a sample of Hannah's DNA and try to get a chance to speak to Chase alone. Maybe he could tell her something that would help locate the girl.

She stood from her desk, considering the intelligence of yet another cup of coffee over making herself drink some water, when her cell phone rang. Sarah Glanzer from the state lab. "You have something?" she asked before Sarah could speak.

"Yes," Sarah said. "You sound like you're running."

"What did you find?"

"We matched your sample," Sarah said.

There was a hesitation in her voice, and Kylie felt it in her gut. Something was wrong. She considered that the blood could belong to one of the dead people in the house. Or a grandparent. That it could be useless. Kylie opened her mouth to ask when Sarah added, "It's a single-source DNA."

Single source meant the sample was from blood that was not a mixture of DNA. It had been identified as from a single person. That was good. It meant the results were solid. "You matched it in CODIS?" Kylie asked. The Combined DNA Index System, or CODIS, was a database that housed DNA from crime scenes, suspects, and offenders, allowing crime labs to compare DNA profiles electronically.

"Yes," Sarah said. "Although not in the place I would have expected it. The match came from CODIS(mp)."

"MP? What's that?"

"It's another name for the National Missing Person DNA Database," Sarah said. "The match is to a missing persons case."

In her head, Kylie was already searching for missing persons cases in the Hagen area. Her thoughts returned to Hannah Visser, but her mother had only just come in to report her daughter missing. She wasn't in the database. It had to be another case.

"It's a match to the Derek Hudson kidnappings," Sarah said without waiting for Kylie to ask.

The air rushed from Kylie's lungs. She realized she was still standing and sat down hard. Derek Hudson had kidnapped and held five girls in a cabin for sixteen months, a nightmare that had ended almost fourteen years ago. Four of those women were now dead. Kylie herself had nearly been killed while working that case. Derek Hudson had been hiding in plain sight. And he had almost gotten away.

Sarah was talking, but Kylie's brain was still spinning. Hudson was in prison, where he would remain for the rest of his life. But his DNA . . . before the thought was fully absorbed, her fingers typed his name into the state prison system. Location: North Dakota State Penitentiary. "What? How?" Kylie interrupted Sarah. "Hudson's in prison."

"That's what I was saying," Sarah said. "The DNA isn't a match to Derek Hudson."

Kylie rubbed her face. *Slow down.* "Sorry. You said it matched a missing person. Who?"

"You know it's standard protocol to collect samples from the victims after that sort of crime," Sarah explained in her slow, thoughtful way. "That way we're able to eliminate their DNA in the course of the collection of evidence—from the cabin where they were held, in this situation. And of course, the girls were all reported missing by their parents, long before they escaped. The DNA found at the Garzas' home is a close relative of—"

Kylie was shaking her head. "For God's sake, Sarah," she interrupted. "This is me. Why the hell are you hemming and hawing. Just tell me. Whose DNA does it match?"

Sarah's long exhale was audible over the phone. "Lily Baker's."

The moment the words were out of her mouth, Sarah said, "Hang on. I've got to take this. I'll be right back." Two seconds later, Kylie was listening to bad elevator music.

Her thoughts spun circles. There was no way Lily Baker could be a suspect in the Garzas' murders. She had been in the ED last night. She had been in the parking lot when the Garzas' baby was dropped off.

But the idea that her blood was at the scene. No. Not her blood. Sarah had said the DNA matched a *relative* of Lily's. But what relative? And why Lily? Hadn't she been through enough already? Kylie had heard that Iver was up in Fargo with his mother, who'd had a stroke. So Lily was home alone.

God, what a mess.

The elevator music ended, and Sarah returned. "Sorry that took so long."

Kylie paused only a second. "Both of Lily's parents are dead. She doesn't have any siblings. I don't think she *has* any relatives, so how can—"

"Kylie," Sarah interrupted with a laugh. "Have you been perched over the phone, waiting to say that?"

Kylie let out her breath. "Probably. But you know what she's been through," she said, still trying to figure out what relative of Lily's might have left blood at the Garzas'. A cousin, maybe? Hell, when people in Hagen started to talk about family, it sometimes felt like the whole town was related. "Can you tell how close a relative?"

"I can," Sarah said. "But I have to explain it to you. Or I can write it up and send it so you can read it, if that's better."

Sarah was nothing if not thorough. As a senior criminalist, she was required to create a report comprehensive enough that no defense attorney could poke a pinhole in her work. At times like this, it made Kylie want to scream. But that was on Kylie, not Sarah. She let out her breath. "I don't want to wait for the report."

"Okay," Sarah said slowly.

"You're asking if I can be patient and listen," Kylie said.

Sarah laughed. "Exactly."

"I will certainly try my hardest."

Sarah sighed. "This is going to happen at Sarah speed, not Kylie speed, okay?"

"Fine. I'll be patient." But already, Kylie was antsy in her chair. She opened her notebook to take notes. She focused better that way.

"Okay," Sarah began. "So everyone is born with two copies of the twenty-two autosomal chromosomes, one copy from their father and one from their mother."

"Got it," Kylie said, trying to take notes. Immediately, she was stuck on how to spell *autosomal*.

"The chromosomes don't show up in the exact same order in the offspring as in their parents," Sarah went on. "Instead, the little building blocks of chromosomes, called nucleotides, get remixed into a new chromosome in the child. Still with me?"

"I'm pretty sure I failed biology."

Sarah laughed. "All you need to know is that there are little snippets of these building blocks that get inherited together. Those are called short tandem repeats, or STRs."

"I don't know if I need the official names."

Sarah ignored her snarky comment. "Imagine a necklace made of beads, strung with different patterns throughout. If the necklace got broken and was restrung, some of those little patterns would end up together again. Does that help?"

"So much." Kylie wrote *broken beads restrung, some patterns same.*

Sarah pressed on. "The more of those little patterns that are found together between the two DNA sequences, the more closely the two donors are related. With enough of those patterns, we can figure out exactly how related the two people are. The probability of recombination between the two nucleo—the two necklace snippets—can be measured as their genetic distance in centimorgans, where one centimorgan is a one percent probability of—"

"Sarah!" Kylie interjected. "A centimorgan? Really?"

"This stuff is so cool, Kylie. It's literally changing the way we solve crimes. Cold cases from decades ago are now being solved with a few weeks' work."

"Sarah, I promise the next time we're together, you can show me the PowerPoint, and I'll learn every little detail. I'll even buy the drinks."

"Okay," Sarah said. "Basically, the more of these short tandem repeats—"

"STRs," Kylie interjected.

"Yes!" Sarah was much too excited that Kylie had picked up a single thing from the explanation. "The more matching STRs we identify in the two samples, the closer the relationship between the two sets of DNA."

"Great," Kylie said. "So how many matches between the DNA at the Garzas' house and Lily Baker?"

"Three thousand six hundred."

Kylie shook her head. "Is that only a little or a lot?"

"It's a lot," Sarah said with un-Sarah-like emphasis.

"So the DNA is a close match to Lily?"

"Very close."

Kylie shook her head. "Is there any way it could be Lily herself?"

"That's not possible."

"I don't know who it could be," Kylie said, stumped. "Like I said, her parents are both dead. She was an only child." Lily had regained all her memories from before she was abducted. Or she thought she had. Was it possible that Lily had known about a half sibling before the accident and that knowledge hadn't resurfaced? Was there any way Lily might be related to the Garzas? But surely someone would have mentioned that. But a half sibling somewhere . . . maybe. "I suppose it's possible her dad had an affair that ended in a pregnancy. Or her mother had a baby before Lily came along and gave it up for adoption or something. If they did, she doesn't know about it."

"This is not a half sibling, Kylie."

"Then what is it?"

"The DNA sample," Sarah said, "is from a female offspring."

"A female offspring," Kylie repeated. "Wha—"

"Lily Baker's female offspring," Sarah added, drawing out each word.

Sarah's words were slow to sink in. The blood at the Garza house matched Lily Baker's female offspring. And then it struck her.

Lily Baker had a daughter.

CHAPTER 19

Lily

Lily woke to the sound of her phone vibrating on the bedside table. Sitting upright in bed, she pushed the sleep mask off her face and squinted in the bright sunlight. Iver's face on her screen gave her a little jolt of energy as she answered the call. "Hi."

"I woke you up," he said.

She leaned against the headboard. "It's okay. I'm glad to hear your voice. How's your mom?" She felt her breath hitch, praying that he'd say Cathy was well enough to come home, that their separation was coming to an end.

"She had another stroke last night," he said. The catch in his voice told her more than the words.

"Oh God. I'm so sorry, Iver. I wish I was there." She thought about her schedule the next few nights. The ED was already short two nurses—one out with a shoulder injury and another on maternity leave.

"Me, too," he said.

The two sat in silence as Lily searched for the right thing to say. Their conversations had always been so easy. Right from the beginning. "How are you doing?" she asked finally.

"About like you'd expect," he said. "How are things there?" His tone shifted, and she imagined him packing away his fear, sealing it into a footlocker where it couldn't bother him. If they were together, she would have urged him to lay it out, to give it air. But they weren't.

He was up in Fargo, staying with old friends, spending his days hoping that his mother got better rather than worse.

"Busy night last night?" he asked as though sensing she was going to circle back to his mother. And warning her not to go there. These little unspoken dances they performed—walls raised and lowered, lowered and raised.

The events of the night flooded her with an exhausted sorrow. She longed to share them with Iver, to tell him how her heart hurt for Nadine, how holding that baby had affected her. About the strange interaction at the registration desk with Chase Visser and his missing sister. Instead, she thought of Iver and his dog, Cal, and wished they were home. "Yes. Kind of a crazy one." And before he could ask for details, she said, "I miss you guys."

"We miss you, too. Cal keeps putting his head in my lap."

She smiled. That was what Cal always did with her. "He wants you to rub his ears."

"You working tonight?"

"Yep. Tomorrow, too. Then off Wednesday and back on Thursday. I could come up Wednesday morning. I'd love to see your mom."

"I'm sure she'd love that," he said, and Lily tried not to feel slighted by the fact that he hadn't mentioned how much he would like it. "You guys are going to get some snow, so you should probably get your snow tires on before you drive up. I think they're in the back of your garage, but check because I might've taken them to my garage last spring to get them out of the way."

"Okay. I'll check now and try to get to the tire shop." How easily they drifted into talk of life's minutiae.

"I'm heading to the hospital. I'll try to call before your shift."

"Give your mom my love," she said.

"I will."

"I love you," she said at the same time he said, "Bye." A beat passed, and he said, "Love you, too." And then he was gone.

Lily glanced at the screen of her phone. The call had lasted two minutes and forty-one seconds. The conversation with Iver had left her feeling off, and she longed for a diversion from the laundry list of all they hadn't said. She changed into sweats and a fleece, started the coffee. Iver was distracted, worried about his mother. She was, too, of course. They were fine. They were solid.

In her bare feet, she passed through the laundry room and out to the garage. It was easily twenty degrees cooler out there, the smell of dust and engine oil and damp concrete hitting her nose as she flipped on the halogen lights. After a half dozen flickers, the lights powered up, casting a stark white glare on the space. The concrete floor was icy on her feet as she stepped inside. There was another smell behind the first ones. She scanned the garage, Iver's weight set in the center of the space, their bikes hanging upside down along the far wall. Beyond those was his workbench, the tools on a pegboard behind it, their shapes outlined in black Sharpie like dead bodies at a crime scene. The smell grew stronger as she walked toward the corner. It seemed to be coming from the large metal cabinet where Iver kept paints, cleaning supplies, gardening tools. It turned her stomach, the smell, some combination of wet wool and a chemical she couldn't identify.

The inside of the cabinet looked like it always did. Rows of neatly organized items—paints and turpentine and seed packets and trowels and pots and cleaners, a bin of paintbrushes, another of putty knives and sandpaper. And on the bottom shelf, a wool picnic blanket. She saw then that it was stained at the center, felt the moist wool and noticed a bottle of leather cleaner tipped over on the shelf above it.

She yanked the blanket from the shelf and spread it across the garage floor. The smell rained around her as the wool drifted down through the air, landing with a muffled whap on the concrete. And when she blinked, she saw him as clearly as if he were standing beside her.

Greasy hair hung across his face, revealing only half of his scrappy beard, dark against pale skin. His hand was huge and moist, clamped around her wrist as he yanked her down the hallway. The man from her nightmares was always Derek Hudson, but this man was not Hudson. He was taller and leaner than Hudson, harder edged and stronger. He towered over her, his breath some mixture of skunk and cheap whiskey. He was red around his nose like the man who had gone to their church in Arizona, the one her aunt said drank too much. The proof was on his face, her aunt declared, though the man had never seemed drunk to Lily.

Rubbing her wrist, Lily took a step backward from the cabinet as though she might distance herself from the memory's onslaught. She tried to rally images of the church in Arizona, of the time living with her aunt. Anything to get away from whatever was coming.

But the image of his face was there when she blinked and when she opened her eyes again. Blood trailed along his pale jaw, dripping on her. The neckline of her dress was dark from it.

The blood was her fault.

Somehow she knew she had done that. She had made him bleed. He didn't seem bothered by the blood, but she wanted to turn her head away from him, imagining with horror that it might drip into her mouth as he leaned over her.

He made an almost gleeful hissing noise, exposing a row of bottom teeth. They made a straight line of white squares interrupted by one black one. Not a tooth, she realized, but an empty place in the line, the inside of his mouth visible through the space.

He smiled at her, almost kindly, right before he stabbed her.

Lily clutched her stomach, the pain there momentarily vivid. Above her head, the lights flickered, and she imagined she was having a seizure. She gripped the door to the house and twisted when the lights went out. She shoved open the door and scurried into the house. Spun around, half expecting to find the man from her memory standing in the garage.

The lights came on, and the garage was returned to its previous state. Innocuous, tidy, exactly as Iver had left it. Lily peered toward the corner where Iver thought her tires might be. She couldn't see the tires from the door, and she couldn't bring herself to go back out there.

Instead, she shut the garage door and twisted the dead bolt, trying to force the man's face from her head. *Move. Keep moving.* Across the kitchen, she reached for her coffee mug with a trembling hand, then set it on the counter. Coffee was the last thing she needed.

She went into the yard. Her feet padded across the dew-soaked grass, and the air cooled the heat in her cheeks as she fought to dissipate the terror that had saturated her limbs.

The motion was calming, so she continued to walk a small circle in the yard. Rarely had she remembered anything so vividly. Or was it a memory at all? It might have been a movie she'd seen. And yet she had felt responsible for the man's bleeding face. She had hurt him. Then he had stabbed her.

She halted. No. A palm pressed to her abdomen, she realized that she hadn't been stabbed. Her fingers pressed against the unmarred skin of her belly.

She had no scars, so surely it couldn't be a memory.

Or could it?

CHAPTER 20

Hannah

With some distance between herself and the trailhead, Hannah began to relax. The blue pills were doing their part, too, their buzz like a river that swept through her and washed away the pain in her stomach, freed the fear that corked the base of her throat and made each breath tight and vaguely uncomfortable.

She drove in the direction of the cabin and stopped at a gas station for chips, a couple of candy bars, and a large bottle of water. The older woman at the register watched her carefully, coming out from behind the counter as though suspecting Hannah would steal something. Hannah thought about the clothes she was wearing, the oversize coat. Could the woman tell she was on drugs? What did she look like high? She'd always felt calmer but in control. Unless she was talking. Words were hard to come by, clumsy on her tongue. She said nothing to the woman, only nodded her thanks as she paid with cash she'd taken from Nadine's purse.

A few miles from the gas station, Hannah parked on the side of the road overlooking a slow-moving creek and ate and drank. She hadn't realized how hungry she'd been until her stomach was full again. The sound of the gurgling water and the slightly fishy smell of the creek were soothing. She closed her eyes, imagining the cabin and the days when she'd had her dad all to herself. She fell asleep, and when she woke, the sun was in a different spot in the sky. She took another pill, only one this time. She wanted to get to the cabin, and for that, she would need the ability to focus.

Back on the road, the names of the towns that she drove through were only vaguely familiar. Years had passed—three or four at least—since her last visit to the cabin, but even without knowing its exact location, she could feel herself getting closer. The flatlands around Hagen gave way to craggy slopes of striated towers, their colors terra-cotta and gold, amber and ash. The ground that she remembered as lush and green was brown and dormant with the approach of winter.

She crossed over a metal bridge, and her father's music filled her head. The bands with their twangy voices and string-picking tunes. Music she never heard at home, where her mother preferred classical or light jazz. But mostly, her mother preferred silence. Along the way, Hannah stopped twice to pee on the side of the road, took two more pills, one at a time, though she hadn't paid attention to how many hours had elapsed. Had it been one hour or five?

One of her favorite things about the drugs was the way they made time feel unimportant. She didn't feel rushed or late. Even when she *was* late, it no longer seemed to matter. The sensation was so freeing.

Down a slow incline, she arrived in a tiny town, huddled at the base of the hill. As she turned onto Main Street, she spotted the wooden sidewalks and let out a squeal of joy.

She had been here. This was where her father had stopped each time they came to the cabin.

A motor home honked behind her, and she pulled to the curb and shut off the car, scowling at the driver as he passed. She remembered how annoyed her father was by the RVs and motor homes with their out-of-state license plates. He had always cherished this little town as an escape, a quiet place for locals.

Main Street only stretched three blocks. Parked on the first block, Hannah took another blue pill and was surprised to find it was the last one in her second bag. The empty plastic gave her a shot of panic. She'd be out before she knew it. But not yet. Not today. If she remembered correctly, the cabin was only a ten-minute drive from town.

And she was going to find it. She considered taking another pill, letting the high take over, forgetting where and who she was. She ought to wait, draw out this high. But then she had a memory of the night before. The gunshot blast, the spray of Ben's blood and brains.

She fumbled to open the bag and took another pill. Nine pills left. That would last her until she found the cabin. Surely there would be some medicine there she could take. She was about to tuck the bag of pills under the driver's seat, then changed her mind and zipped them into her coat pocket before climbing out of the car. She crossed the street and walked along the sidewalk. The sidewalks were quiet, only a few tourists bundled up against a cold wind. Children pushed in strollers piled high with blankets.

A woman in a long wool coat gave Hannah a wide berth as she passed. Hannah stopped to peer into a store window and saw her hair was a ratty halo around her head. With both hands, she combed it down and twisted it into a single tail, which she tucked over her shoulder. She rubbed her face with one palm, wishing she'd checked herself in the car mirror.

Behind the glass, the shop woman approached the window, using a hand to sweep her along. Embarrassed, Hannah hurried down the street. She used two fingers to smooth her eyebrows, checked that her hands were cleanish, and pinched her cheeks to bring color into them the way her mother sometimes did on her own face.

Then, setting her shoulders back, she tried to walk with confidence. The street reminded her of her father, of his laugh and the woodsy smell of the cabin. She couldn't wait to be there.

She passed the post office with its log cabin facade. And then the bank and a mercantile store, their exteriors a nod to times past. The farther she walked, the more familiar the place was. There was a diner that served the best doughnuts, as well as the candy store. Hannah thought of the sour gummy treats—peach and cola—that she always picked out. Her father let her fill the bag much higher than her mother would have, and each time, she ended the day with an aching stomach and sores on her tongue. She felt a wave of desperation to be in that store, with her dad. To return to the days when candy was her worst vice.

As she crossed to the next block, she saw the saddle store where her father had once bought himself a hat. He'd been so happy then, his joy rubbing off on her. The contrast between then and now caught her off guard.

Life at home was so dreary. Every day the same things—school, homework, dinner, bed, broken up by the occasional interaction with someone at school or a parent. She streamed endless shows to distract herself from the monotony. But when she'd been young and her father had brought her here . . . she had felt real joy. A few weekends in this little town held more good memories than years of being in her own house. Passing the saddle store, she searched the window for the hat her father had bought all those years ago.

And then she searched for faces, too. As though her father might be in that store, shopping for his hat again. A man stood in the window, browsing a selection of felt Stetsons, a half smile on his lips. She imagined the smell of leather and aftershave, the way her father strode down these streets in his cowboy boots, his gait both bigger and slower, as though the air here transported him to a different body. She tapped on the glass, and the man looked up, surprised.

In that moment, he was no longer her father but a stranger. Heat seared her cheeks, and she spun away, hurrying toward the Garzas' car. She needed to get to the cabin and call her father.

He would keep her safe.

CHAPTER 21

Kylie

Kylie had spent the last few hours trying to focus on the reports coming in on Ben and Nadine Garza while fighting the constant whirring in her brain caused by Sarah's news that Lily Baker had a daughter. And her daughter had been at the Garzas'. Hannah Visser had been at the Garzas'. Had the DNA been on the bassinet before Sunday night? Or had someone else been there with Hannah? A friend?

Or . . . was it possible that the DNA was Hannah's?

In which case . . .

But wouldn't the Vissers have mentioned if Hannah was adopted?

Unsure how to go about finding an answer to such an indelicate question, Kylie had turned to Marjorie. Off duty, Kylie had called her and been unsurprised when Marjorie answered the phone on the second ring. Marjorie had thought Hannah Visser was her parents' biological child, but she promised to dig into it and get back to Kylie.

No word yet.

Kylie filled her coffee cup with water, the first of the day, and carried her notes into the conference room for their afternoon staff meeting. At the table, Sullivan sat at the far end with Mika Keckler on his left and Rich Dahl on his right. Both men were new recruits in the past six months. Both hardworking and smart, both tall and broad—Mika with the dark coloring of his Native American ancestors and Rich Dahl with the fair coloring of his Dutch ones. Carl Gilbert sat beside Dahl.

No one had been home at the Vissers' when Kylie had dropped by to pick up Hannah's DNA sample, so Davis had gone back to try again. She left an empty chair for him by the door in case he returned in time to join them.

Kylie took the lead, updating the group on the next of kin notifications and Tiffany Garza, who was in the hospital, unharmed and awaiting a relative or child protective services to step in for her care. Then she announced to the team that Hannah Visser, local fourteen-year-old, was their 911 caller and their witness. The room erupted in a back-and-forth about the Vissers. Kylie had already known that Charles Visser was practically a town celebrity, but she hadn't realized that Priscilla was active in a number of nonprofit organizations in addition to her board positions. Or what Hagen termed organizations—some of which were likely a half dozen constituents meeting at the diner.

"My mom's on a few, but Mrs. Visser's on *all* of them," Richard Dahl said, the reference to his mother making Kylie feel old. "Literacy, clean water, organizing the annual trash cleanup, updating the school computers . . ."

"Not sure how any of that would relate to the Garzas' murders," Gilbert cut in, and Dahl went silent.

Kylie nodded. "But we need to find Hannah Visser if we can. If she saw the murders, it stands to reason that she saw the killer."

"Any idea where she would've gone?" Keckler asked.

"Not yet. Davis went to speak to the family, and I've got a BOLO out on the Garzas' Ford Explorer, which was the car Hannah Visser was driving."

"I thought she was fourteen," Dahl said.

"She is," Kylie said without elaboration. Then to the group, she asked, "What else do we know?"

"I ran their finances and talked to their workplaces," Gilbert said. "Both Garzas have been with their respective employers for years—Nadine for seven and Ben for ten and a half," he said, leaning over his notebook as his free hand quieted the carabiner of keys he wore on his belt. The clinking sounds would have made Kylie crazy, but she never said anything about the keys. Not since her first Hagen murder case. And after Gilbert's reaction at the Garzas', she had done her best to tread lightly. She, too, had lost someone to murder once, though she'd been a teenager then. The way Gilbert had stared at Nadine when she was bleeding out on her living room floor had softened something in her. It made her look at Gilbert differently than she had before. Let him jingle if he needed to.

"Nothing in their financial records implies any trouble. Mortgage is up to date, no big deposits or withdrawals," Gilbert went on. "No large purchases. We've requested bank and credit card statements for the past four months. That'll probably take a few days, but there might be some clue in those."

"How about life insurance?" Davis asked from the doorway.

Kylie hadn't heard him come in.

"They each had a small policy through work," Gilbert said. "His was twenty-five thousand. Hers was fifty. They've had them for a few years, and they were each other's beneficiaries. No changes, no increases. Nothing suspicious there either."

Davis entered and sank into the chair, his expression unreadable. Kylie studied him, offering him the opportunity to share what he'd learned from the Vissers, but he only shook his head.

Pushing aside questions of what had happened with his visit, Kylie moved to the next item on her list. "Evidence from the house."

"We're waiting for the results on the DNA from the bassinet," Sullivan said with a glance at Kylie. She had yet to tell anyone about the familial match to Lily Baker. Not until she'd spoken to Lily. "We've got some good tread images and imprints," Sullivan went on. "We're looking for a cowboy boot, Roper's brand, size eleven."

Ropers size eleven. The news was crushing.

"Hell," Gilbert said, pushing away from the table to lift one of his boots. "I've got that very boot on my foot right now."

"It's common," Davis agreed.

"There is some good news," Sullivan said. "According to the state lab tech working the tread, our shooter shows signs of excessive supination."

"What's that?" Dahl asked.

"It means he walks on the outsides of his feet. Some folks tend to walk on the insides of their feet—pronated—while others walk on the outside—supinated. According to the tech, fewer folks are supinated than pronated." He looked up at Kylie, then at Davis. "Might help us ID him when we've got some suspects."

"That's good," she said.

"Doug Smith did the real work," Sullivan said.

Smith had worked through the morning, but when Kylie caught him cross-armed and dozing at his desk, she had convinced him to go home and get some sleep. Of Keckler, she asked, "You follow up with the paramedics?"

He gave a single nod, then shook his head. "Nadine didn't say anything in the ambulance."

It had been a long shot. She made a check mark in her notebook and moved on. "What about their computers?"

"Still haven't located hers," Gilbert said. "It wasn't in her house or the cars—possibly it's in the car Hannah Visser has. The secretary in Visser's office said Nadine normally took the computer home on the weekends. Ben Garza's laptop is with the lab in Bismarck. Should get word in a day or two if there are any leads."

Kylie made a note in her book. The computer might be in the missing car. But if it wasn't, its absence could indicate that Nadine Garza was the target. "Anything new from the neighbors?"

"The boy across the street matched the picture of Hannah Visser to the woman who got out of the car at the Garzas'," Gilbert said. "But we already knew that."

"Any luck with the others?"

"The neighbors at two twenty-seven Bear Root Crossing with the alarm system still aren't back in town, and I'm not having any luck reaching them. I've got a few more calls to make."

"What about the neighbor who saw the gray Corolla?"

"Number one eighty-eight," Gilbert said. "He got called in to work today, but he'll be in first thing tomorrow to sit down with Marjorie and do a composite."

"Good. Once you've got a usable image, pass it around."

Gilbert nodded.

The meeting was adjourned soon after, and Davis remained, the two of them waiting until the room emptied out.

"You talk to the Vissers?"

He shook his head. "No one home, and neither Chase nor Mrs. Visser is answering their mobile numbers."

"You think they found Hannah? Or they went to find her and are out of cell range?"

"Would've been nice if they'd told us," Davis said.

"What about Charles Visser?" she asked.

"I talked to the hospital. He's not on call, and according to the hospital CEO, if Visser's not working or sleeping, he's usually fishing. I left messages with the hospital and on his cell phone."

Kylie exhaled. "What next?"

He checked his watch, and Kylie eyed the clock on the wall. It was almost 6:00 p.m. On a normal day, she might have been close to packing it up by this time. But this was not a normal day. She still had a hundred pages of reports to go through, searching for some piece of information that might illuminate a next move. Because without Hannah Visser, they had no easy way to identify the shooter.

She had yet to tell Davis about the DNA match. Lily deserved to hear the news first, and Kylie didn't want to approach her without first reading Sarah Glanzer's full report to understand how the science had come to that conclusion. That would be hours from now.

"I'm going to the Vissers' again tonight," Davis said with a sigh, stirring Kylie from her thoughts. He stood from the chair. "I'll text you as soon as I get in touch with someone. Let me know if you hear anything."

Kylie stood as well, closing her notebook. "Will do."

Starving, Kylie walked down to the public cafeteria next door and bought a Pepsi and a bag of Cool Ranch Doritos to hold her over until she could get home and cook something healthy. Stress made her ravenous, but it also made her distracted. Her father used to point out that whenever the family moved to a new town, Kylie ate sporadically and not particularly healthily. Not much had changed other than her metabolism had slowed a bit. But the busier she was, the thinner she got and the worse she felt.

Part of the tremendous ebb and flow of her workload came with being a detective in a town like Hagen. Small town meant a low tax base, which translated to limited resources. Though the city had recently added two new officers in Keckler and Dahl, only two of Hagen's active force of twelve officers were trained as official crime scene techs. Four of those twelve were only part time. The officers, Kylie herself (the only detective), Marjorie at the front desk, two Dispatch officers, and the sheriff made up the whole team, which meant she did a lot of the initial investigative work on her own.

At her desk, Kylie saw an email notification from the crime lab. The other blood samples from the Garza scene had been processed. Kylie double-clicked the file and read the summary. Other than the blood on the bassinet that was a familial match to Lily Baker, the rest of the blood in the Garzas' house came from two sources only—Ben and Nadine Garza.

Kylie wondered if Marjorie had learned anything about whether Hannah Visser could be Lily's daughter. Kylie pictured the two women in her head—the photo she'd seen of Hannah and a mental image of Lily—but she didn't see a resemblance. Kylie reminded herself that there was no evidence that the daughter was Hannah Visser.

And sending Marjorie on a wild-goose chase might have been in vain. Maybe when Kylie asked, Lily would say yes, she'd had a child. She had to have the conversation. But where would she even start? What would she possibly say? *Hey, Lily, it's Kylie, just checking in. I hope all is well, because I'm about to ask you whether you had a child. And if you didn't, I'm going to tell you that yes, you did.* Kylie knew the baby's gender—a daughter. Did that piece of information make the situation better or worse? But that was all Kylie could tell her definitively. Not who was raising her. Or who her father was . . .

Or anything.

That was jumping ahead. Kylie knew better than to do that. It was entirely possible that Lily had given birth in Arizona and found adoptive parents in Hagen. That way, the girl would be close if she wanted a relationship with her biological mother. The doubt seeped in again. A story like that in Hagen, after everything Kylie knew about Lily Baker . . . surely someone would have mentioned her baby.

Kylie forced the thoughts away and dug into the report on the DNA.

When her phone buzzed again, she was surprised at how long she'd been focused on the report. The text was from Amber. Kylie had texted to check in earlier, while she was waiting to hear from Sarah.

Crzy am. ok to come now. Prmse xtra BCP.

Amber had a strange habit of shortening every word in a text message, though, to Kylie, it seemed like the autocorrect function of the phone should have made this impossible. Amber still managed. For years, Kylie had been deciphering her old roommate's abbreviations.

Her exhaustion was obvious when she couldn't think of what Amber meant by BCP. And then it hit her. Banana-cream pie.

But Kylie had to talk to Lily Baker, and even banana-cream pie wasn't going to make that conversation any easier. She silenced her phone and returned her attention to the report, forcing aside the growing concern over the circumstances that had led to Lily Baker's motherhood.

CHAPTER 22

LILY

The hospital was quieter than it had been the night before, and Lily spent the extra time restocking the rooms and checking inventory, things the nurses always handled on their own in the small department. The other nurse took the lion's share of the patients who came in, the normal Hagen fare—a finger sliced while field dressing a deer, a broken collarbone from a fall off an ATV, a kitchen burn. Dr. Bruce Reade was the attending. Younger than Visser and much friendlier, Reade was constantly chewing bubble gum and making jokes. He often showed Lily pictures of his three daughters, petite things all dressed in tutus and baby-pink leotards. He joked that if they had their way, he'd be in a tutu, too. The image made her laugh.

Reade had also grown up in Hagen, though he was old enough that their paths had never crossed before the hospital. Reade had done his residency and internship in Chicago, and the rumor was Reade's wife had come into the ED with a friend who had broken her wrist on Rollerblades, and she'd fallen hard for the young doctor. The same rumor had it that his wife's family was Chicago royalty and her father none too happy that his daughter had fallen for a lowly doctor.

Reade himself had joked on more than one occasion that his wife had only agreed to live in North Dakota if she could have as many babies as she wanted. "Seems like a fair trade, right?" Because Reade had still been in Chicago when Lily returned from Arizona and started at the hospital, he was one of the few people she worked with who hadn't been in Hagen when Lily's past had come to light again.

There was no question that he'd heard about it—everyone had—but there was comfort in knowing that it was only a story to him. A horrible thing that had happened to someone else. Lily found herself dividing the people she encountered by the subtle distinctions of where they were four years ago when she had woken without her memory, in a stranger's car, about to go off the side of an overpass. The less someone might know firsthand of that time, the more comfortable she was around them.

At her first break of the night, Lily went down to the ICU to check in on Stephanie Krueger, her meningitis patient from the night before. She was sleeping soundly when Lily entered the bay, her father in the chair beside her, reading the *Wall Street Journal*. The terror in his eyes had settled into fear. "She's responding well," Lily told him, and he folded the paper to look at his daughter. "She's a fighter," he said. "Like her mother."

Lily smoothed the covers around the girl and checked her IV and her pulse oximeter to make sure everything was attached correctly. As she left, Harrison Krueger called out to her.

"Thank you," he said.

"Of course," she told him and made her way back to the ED.

It was not yet ten o'clock when Lily got a page from reception. Sandra was off that night, and the woman in her place had a high-pitched voice that made her sound perpetually nervous. "There's a Detective Milliard here to see you," she announced. In the background, Lily heard the detective say, "Just tell her it's Kylie. Can I have the phone, please?"

And then Kylie was on the line. "Lily?"

Lily felt her pulse race at the sound of the detective's voice. Clearing her throat, she said, "I'm here."

"I know you're at work, but I need to talk to you," the detective said. "Any chance you've got ten or fifteen minutes?"

Last night, Lily would have had to say no. There had been no extra minutes. But tonight was quiet. She had the time. The only question was if she *wanted* to sit down with the detective. But this was about the Garza baby. Or Nadine's gunshot wound. What else would it be about?

"Lily?"

"Yeah," she said. "I think so."

"Is there somewhere quiet we can talk?"

The detective's tone made her uneasy, and she had to remind herself that it was nothing new. Kylie Milliard would forever remind her of Derek Hudson, and that would always be accompanied with a wave of fear. "Let me check things back here, and I'll be right out."

Lily explained to her coworker that the detective had some questions about the Garzas and she needed to duck into the conference room for five or ten minutes.

"No problem," he said. "I'll come grab you if any big cases come in, but things are pretty quiet."

Lily thanked him and went to reception, where the detective stood at the desk, cell phone in her hand. The sight of the sheriff's department emblem on her jacket brought a memory of being in Iver's house that first night, almost four years ago. It was weird that Kylie lived in that house now and Iver lived with her. "Kylie?"

The detective looked up, and Lily saw a flash of fear. For a moment, Lily wanted Kylie to ask her questions right there. But a woman approached the desk, complaining of stomach pain, and Lily motioned toward the hallway while the front desk attendant handled the new patient. In the conference room, Lily sat in the chair closest to the door, the best seat in case she was called to a case. That was what she told herself.

But there was more to it.

The tight sensation of panic was there in her chest, jabbing lightly, like fingers under her ribs. Only two fingers, she thought, but there nonetheless.

Sitting across from her, Kylie slipped her phone into her pocket and zipped it closed. "Sorry to bother you at work. I tried your phone."

"I don't have it on me when I'm working." Lily laid her palms on the arms of her chair, then folded them across her chest. She wished she had her water bottle or a can of soda, something to hold in her hands.

"I figured," Kylie said.

Lily folded her hands in her lap, forcing them to still. "This couldn't wait until tomorrow?"

Kylie leaned forward and folded her own hands on the dark wood table. "No."

"I assume it's about the baby?" The question came out hopeful. But what else could it be?

Surprise flashed across Kylie's face, lasting only a moment before sliding away. "You mean the Garzas' baby." She shook her head. "No."

Lily shoved away from the table, a sudden jolt of energy in her legs. She stood, terrified. She didn't have her phone. The detective had tried to call. Suddenly, she was certain there had been an accident. She pressed her hands to her chest, trying to draw breath. "Is it Iver?"

Kylie rose, too. "No." The detective circled the table and took hold of Lily's shoulders. "No. It's nothing like that. No one's hurt."

"There wasn't an accident?"

"No one is hurt," Kylie said, settling Lily back into her chair. "I promise."

Lily swiped her face, surprised to find tears. "What is it, then? You're scaring me."

Kylie's eyes were moist, too. Like she might cry. "It's a hard thing to ask. And it's none of my damn business," Kylie said. Then her voice dropped and she said, "But I have to know. For the case."

The fear closed on Lily's throat, raised the hairs on her scalp. "Know what? What is this about?"

"We found blood at Ben and Nadine Garza's house—on the baby's bassinet."

Lily tried to follow what she was saying. Blood at the Garzas' house. She pictured Nadine on the gurney, her blouse saturated. Of course there was blood; they'd been shot.

"Blood other than Nadine and Ben Garza's blood," Kylie continued as though reading Lily's mind.

"Whose blood?"

The detective's gaze held on a spot over Lily's shoulder, her eyes no longer moist but clear, pointed. "It's a familial match to you."

"To me?" But the word that Lily heard was *family*, and a ping of hope rang inside her. She had family? "Who is it?"

Kylie took Lily's hand, but Lily yanked it back, shaking her head. She did not want to be comforted. Not by the detective. Not in the middle of her shift while she was trying to do her job. Not when the detective was dangling some idea of family in front of her. Her family was in Fargo. Her family was Iver and Cal. "I don't have any family," she said.

Kylie returned her hands to her own lap, sat up straight, and drew a slow, audible breath.

Lily felt every muscle tighten until she was spring-loaded. What had happened? She was ready to scream when the detective spoke.

"I need to know if you've ever had a baby. A daughter."

CHAPTER 23

Hannah

The road beneath the car was pitted and bumpy, and the sky had long since gone dark. At a grocery store a few hours earlier, she had bought more water and a turkey sandwich that, when she opened it, stank of rancid meat. She tried to eat a few bites of the bread, but most of it had gone in the trash. Now she was hungry and a little sick to her stomach, anxious for another hit of the drugs. Without them, she felt twitchy and nervous, every thought like a brick piled on her chest. Where the hell was the cabin? She'd been so certain that she could find it on her own. How many times had she sat in the front seat and stared at these roads?

She'd had the thought that maybe it had burned down. The cabin could have been gone and she was searching for something that no longer existed.

But there would be remains, the burned-out foundation.

She remembered when the house down the block from them had burned down. The squeal of fire trucks had woken the house. Chase had been home visiting, her parents not yet separated. The four of them had stumbled out of the house and onto the street. Hannah had stood next to her father, who held her close, as they watched it burn. "If they bring out Mr. Salater, I'm going to go help," he'd told her.

She nodded, relishing the sensation of his arm around her. She knew how important he was. He would save Mr. Salater when the firemen brought him out. He would run down the street in his navy pajamas and his leather slippers, and he would get down on his knees the way he had when Mrs. Olsen collapsed in church. He had saved her, too.

But the firemen never brought Mr. Salater out of that house. Hannah had assumed he wasn't home. It was days later that she learned he'd still been in his bed. She'd asked her father if it would hurt to burn to death, and he'd explained that Mr. Salater would have died from breathing the smoke before the fire ever got him. He didn't tell her if that would be better than burning. She didn't ask.

Mr. Salater's house had smoked for three days after the fire was put out, and Hannah had trouble sleeping, worried that the smoke would travel down the block and burn her house down, too.

When she cried out in the night, it was her mother who came to her room. Her father had been at work.

"That smoke isn't getting anywhere near this house, Hannah," her mother had promised. "And none of us are dumb enough to smoke, let alone in bed, so we're safe." And then she'd planted a kiss on Hannah's forehead and left.

Hannah remembered thinking that she wasn't dumb. That she was smart. That they were all smart. But Mr. Salater hadn't seemed dumb either, even if he did fall asleep with a lit cigarette in his hand. Later, Hannah had thought it an unkind thing to say about a dead man. But her mother was often blunt about people—even people that the rest of them liked. Like Nadine and Ben.

When Nadine and Ben had come to dinner last winter—Nadine early in her pregnancy and not drinking—her mother had criticized the couple as soon as they were out the door. Ben was a lowlife, she said, and Nadine too nosy for her own good. Hannah had barely given it a second thought. Was Ben a lowlife? How so? Was that what had gotten them killed? Had he done something to that man? Stolen from him?

Or had Nadine poked her head where she wasn't welcome?

The thought of the shooter brought back the panic, the pressure on her chest. Hannah pulled out the bag of pills and studied the little blue pellets. She had intended to wait to take any more until she found the cabin.

But maybe just one . . .

CHAPTER 24

Lily

Lily searched the detective's face, replaying the words. Kylie had said "had" a baby. But the detective must have meant *been given*. Kylie already knew this; they had talked that morning. Lily stood up, then sat down. "You mean the Garzas' baby? The one that woman brought me . . ."

Kylie was shaking her head. "No. Did you have a baby? Your own baby? Were you ever pregnant? Like while you were in Arizona in school?" The detective's tone was hopeful, her eyes wide and their expression seeming to plead with her.

But Lily shook her head. "No. I've never had a baby. I've never even been pregnant." She blinked and felt her hands stretched across an expanse of belly. The skin taut, the shape firm. Bubbles rising inside her. Memories she'd never had before. They weren't real. She was imagining it. She rubbed her face, shook off the sensations. But they felt as though they were inside her, rising from her own experience. Memories. "Never," she said again as though she could usher out the doubt with one forceful word.

Kylie rose from the chair and retreated to the far wall before speaking again. "I'm so sorry, Lily."

"No." Lily stood quickly, blood rushing from her head. Her hands gripped the table to hold herself up. "No," she said again, unwilling to hear whatever the detective was saying. It was wrong. She turned to leave.

"Lily, wait!"

Lily held the door handle. Stopped. If she walked out, Kylie might follow. Lily did not want another person to hear this conversation. Not Dr. Reade and not the other nurse. She thought of Iver, but he was worried about his mother. She would deal with this alone. Figure it out. Fix it. Surely, there was a way to fix it. To unlearn this piece of information. How desperate she was to unlearn this news. But it wasn't true. It couldn't be true. And yet . . .

"I can't imagine what this is like for you," Kylie said, her voice low.

Lily was surprised that the detective was standing beside her. She dropped the handle and crossed her arms. She was suddenly so cold.

Kylie clasped her hands together, stared down at them. "I was r—" The detective drew a slow breath. "I was assaulted my freshman year of college—"

"No," Lily cut her off. "No, no, no." She wanted to shove the detective away, to push her down. The detective was telling her about an assault. "I'm sorry," Lily said. "I'm sorry for what you went through." She stiffened her spine, tried to pull everything into her chest. "But that didn't happen to me. I've never been pregnant." A baby. A child. Her. She thrust the notion from her head, shoving with all her might as though the idea were a boulder she could send off a cliff.

"Okay," Kylie said, taking a step away. "Maybe it's an error."

Lily exhaled in a fast rush, unaware that she'd been holding her breath. She studied the detective, searching her face. Kylie wanted to believe her; that much was obvious. But Lily could also see that she didn't believe her. Her eyes told Lily she thought this information was correct. For whatever reason, Kylie thought Lily'd had a baby. Lily thought about her time with Derek Hudson, those lost months—sixteen of them. All that she'd done to get through that experience. To move past it. "Hudson," she whispered, her mouth filling with bile.

"It's not," Kylie said.

Lily shook her head, not understanding.

"The DNA isn't a match to Hudson. The father is someone else."

Lily frowned. The police always believed that Derek Hudson had worked alone, though they'd found another man dead at the cabin, the one Hudson told Lily she had shot. But she hadn't shot him. Her memories of that last day were clear now. Derek Hudson had shot that man as Lily had run and Abby followed. The man who had set them free, the man whose identity Hudson had stolen and used when he returned to Hagen. That man had been from North Carolina, only passing through. Could he have fathered Lily's child? Or maybe the results were erroneous. If the DNA wasn't a match to Hudson, then surely it couldn't match her either?

She had tried to chisel at those memories, the ones deep in the hard rock layers of her mind. None of that time had ever surfaced in her memories. Just the strange dreams, clusters of images and what felt like short clips from movies in which she starred.

In one, she was drunk and high, walking along a gravel road under the stars, Abby singing beside her. Hudson kept telling them that they were going to a party. He warned her not to tell anyone about where she'd been, about where she came from. "You mention that you're staying with me in the cabin, and I'll kill the others. All of them," he'd said.

Staying with me in the cabin. That had been Hudson's euphemism for keeping her a prisoner.

That night, Lily recalled being in a dress with no sleeves and had the sensation that she should have been freezing cold in the night air. Instead, the air felt like warm silk on her skin. Pills, Hudson had said. It was the booze and the pills.

In another, a man held her hand and swung her around in a dance she wanted no part of. When he released his grip, she flew backward and landed in the divot of a lumpy mattress.

Now she searched for the man's face, and it was there—as clear as in the vision that had come to her in the garage. The same pale skin and scrappy beard, the same bleeding face . . .

He had stabbed her. Stabbed her belly. That was how she remembered it. A knife stabbing her. She gasped at the realization. What if he wasn't stabbing her? What if . . .

She spun from the door, grabbing hold of the closest chair.

"Lily," Kylie cried, catching her.

But Lily recoiled from her touch. Away from the door and the chair until she had reached the far corner of the room. There, she pressed her back to the drywall as though it might yield and take her in. *Please. Please take me.*

Her mind had walled off memories of that time. Iver's theory was that her brain was protecting her from whatever had happened. This was what he'd meant. She thought about the dream of the man stabbing her. The blood on his face. The stabbing pain in her abdomen.

He had been stabbing her, but not with a knife.

She had been raped.

She trembled, sobs choking her breath. That pain she'd felt. That was rape. She tried to draw a breath, to fill her lungs, but it felt like sucking against a vacuum. Rape. But not a baby. Surely she would know if she'd given birth.

She imagined the fear she would have felt giving birth in that cabin, a prisoner. Her brain couldn't possibly have blocked out such a massive event. She thought of Abby and wanted to fall to the floor. Instead, she leaned against the wall, the painted surface cool on the nape of her neck. She closed her eyes. "I can't. I can't be a mother."

"Can I take a DNA sample, Lily?"

Lily opened her eyes, stared at the detective. Kylie wanted to run a test. To check this theory that would turn Lily's entire life upside down.

"That way we can be sure," Kylie said.

Lily felt frozen. She didn't want the lab to be certain. She wanted the lab to be wrong. She wanted Kylie to disappear and erase the last ten minutes.

But that was not a choice she could make.

She drew a shaky breath, pressed her palms to the wall, and forced herself upright. *Take the test. Get it over with.* Before she lost her courage, she nodded.

Kylie unzipped her coat and drew two medical swabs from an inside pocket, lifting them slowly.

Three and a half years Lily had spent rebuilding her life after Derek Hudson. Creating a new life, one free of those memories. She had a good job, a relationship. She knew who she was now.

Or she had.

"I'm so sorry," Kylie said, her words accompanied by the hushed sound of ripping plastic.

Lily closed her eyes and opened her mouth. The first swab reached the back of her mouth, and she gagged at the sensation, pulling away.

"Sorry. Sorry," Kylie said.

Eyes open, Lily took the swab from the detective and scraped the inside of her own cheeks, one side, then the other, before sliding the stick into the protective plastic. Then she repeated the same with the other swab, never making eye contact with the detective. Once it was done, Lily didn't wait for Kylie to speak. She crossed the space and darted out of the conference room, turning toward the corridor of medical offices, locked up and dark this time of night.

She followed the hall to its end and ducked into the family bathroom there, locked the door. Pressing herself into the corner, she squatted down and held her face in her hands. She focused on the bright ceiling light, fighting away the images that returned with every blink.

She forced her eyes open, but new memories continued a steady assault: Abby on the floor in front of her, her face between Lily's knees as she urged Lily to push. The waves of terror brought back the intensity of the pain and pressure as Lily bore down and . . . what?

But she knew the answer.

She had given birth to a baby girl.

CHAPTER 25

Kylie

Kylie woke to the sound of banging on her front door. According to her cell phone, it was barely 6:00 a.m., and she'd spent much of the night tossing and turning. But she was up in seconds, her fight instincts kicking in as she yanked her pants on and pulled her department coat over the long-sleeve T-shirt she slept in.

On the front doorstep was Marjorie, wearing a heavy fleece jacket with the sheriff's department emblem on the breast, jeans, and boots. In her hand, she held papers, which she was waving in the freezing morning air. "I found proof," she announced. "About Hannah. She's definitely the Vissers' child."

Kylie stared at the street behind Marjorie. From the knocking, she had expected a battalion outside her door. "I need coffee," Kylie said, moving toward the kitchen. She started the machine, which, mercifully, she'd set up the night before, and turned to face Marjorie, who looked ready to explode with her news.

"What proof?" Kylie asked.

"Connie at the library dug up this—"

Marjorie shoved two stapled pages at Kylie, who took them and blinked hard. She glanced over at the coffee, where the liquid was collecting in the pot, and wished it would hurry up. The front page was a photocopied newspaper article. *Power Couple Teams Up for a Healthy Hagen.* On the right was a shadowed image. Kylie pulled it close and squinted to make out the Visser family, standing in front of a hospital. Priscilla held a baby—Hannah, presumably—in her arms while Chase and Charles stood on either side of her. Kylie scanned the text, which talked about Charles's efforts to grow the hospital's services—emergency as well as preventive—and listed a number of philanthropic endeavors that Priscilla had launched and spearheaded in the two decades of their marriage.

"What am I looking at? She's holding the baby, but it doesn't mean—"

"Next page," Marjorie said, reaching out to turn the page for her.

Kylie pulled away. "Okay. I can do it." She turned the page slowly, glancing up at Marjorie. "How long have you been awake, anyway?"

"Since four," Marjorie admitted. "I don't sleep anymore. I had gone to the library yesterday to search for articles on the Vissers, something that would mention Hannah's parentage. My friend over there—Connie—said she'd check the archives. She sent this at one in the morning. Don't get old, Kylie. I tell you . . ."

Kylie had stopped listening. On the second page was another image, a close-up of Priscilla Visser propped in a hospital bed, a bluish-gray gown with tiny flowers snapped over one shoulder. Her complexion free of makeup, perspiration dampening the hair around her face, she looked both exhausted and joyful. In her arms was a tiny baby wrapped in a pink blanket. The only things absolutely Priscilla-ish in the photograph were the dangly diamond earrings she wore.

The caption under the image said, *Priscilla Visser, 42, welcomes the Vissers' second child, a healthy baby girl at the Billings Hospital.*

"That's Hannah," Marjorie said. As if it weren't obvious.

Kylie set the pages down and poured a cup of coffee, then offered one to Marjorie, although it seemed like a bad idea to make her any more energetic than she already was.

"No. I can't do caffeine. I'd never sleep."

Kylie took a sip of the liquid and burned her tongue. It was worth the pain for the buzz that came from the first drop of caffeine. Kylie thanked Marjorie for the good work, and the older woman left, leaving Kylie to wake up and focus on what the article meant.

But the meaning was obvious—Hannah Visser wasn't Lily's daughter. Which meant there must have been another girl out there somewhere, one who would be about the same age. It was almost fourteen years ago that Lily had escaped from Derek Hudson, so Lily's child would be the same age as Hannah. But there was no indication that Hannah had a friend with her the night of the murders.

Did the Garzas have another babysitter?

Once the caffeine had worked its magic, Kylie showered and drove to the department, where she sifted through emails and lab reports. Other than the supination evident in the shooter's tread, the cowboy boots weren't traceable. They could be matched once they had a suspect . . . if they found a suspect. The state lab had done their preliminary scan of Ben Garza's laptop and come up with nothing that was flagged as a possible motive. They were now working with Chase Visser's cloud provider to gain access to Nadine's files since her laptop still hadn't been found.

In the interviews Smith and Sullivan had conducted with the community, there was nothing but praise for the Garzas. They were well loved at church and work, had friends they'd known since grade school as well as others they'd made recently. There was literally nothing noteworthy about them.

Which made Kylie wonder if perhaps they weren't the target at all. Was it possible that the shooter had been after someone else and made a mistake?

Or had he been after Hannah Visser, and she had somehow eluded him? What could Hannah have done to make someone want to kill her? Plus, she had taken the baby after the shooting was over. She said she'd seen it. She'd been hiding in the closet. Surely if the killer had searched for her in that house, he'd have found her.

Could she have left and circled back? The more this case went on, the more Kylie felt like Hannah Visser was at the center of it.

At the very least, the fourteen-year-old held the key.

A text from Amber pinged on her phone. Amber had texted last night, too, as Kylie was arriving home after visiting Lily at the hospital. r u ok?

Kylie started to respond but couldn't find the right thing to say. Amber was her best friend in Hagen, but there was no way she could talk to Amber—let alone sit across from her—and hide the devastation she felt at what was happening to Lily Baker.

After leaving the hospital the night before, Kylie had been furious with herself for mentioning her own assault. What had she been thinking? She'd never shared that story with anyone in Hagen, not even Amber. Only a few people in the world knew about it.

But somehow, she'd thought it would help Lily to hear. *Hey, we're both part of this shitty club. Let's go get #metoo tattoos.* Damn it.

Her response to Amber had been vague, citing work, and Amber had texted back right away. 1 qwk slc? Amber text for one quick slice. Kylie didn't respond. For the first time she could recall, banana-cream pie held no appeal.

Instead, she'd come home and made peanut butter toast, eaten it with a bottle of beer before showering and climbing into bed. It was hours until she fell asleep, only to toss and turn most of the night, alternating between feelings of guilt for having to confront Lily Baker and fear over what she'd discovered. Things were no different now.

Lily Baker's DNA sample had gone to Bismarck early this morning, and Sarah at the lab was expecting it. Unlike the earlier anticipation Kylie had felt about the results on the blood from the bassinet, what she felt now was mostly dread. Errors were rare in the state's DNA records system, which meant the DNA on that bassinet was very likely a match to Lily Baker. Which meant Baker had probably given birth in captivity.

What that meant—to Lily, to her recovery, to her life—was beyond Kylic's ability to calculate. What it meant to their case, too, was hard for Kylie to quantify. Harder still because she was overtired. Two nights with little or no sleep. But Marjorie's news this morning meant there was another person they had to account for—if they could identify her.

Kylie carried her mug to the department kitchen and refilled it, adding cream and, because she needed a little extra boost this morning, two cubes of sugar. Davis entered the kitchen as she was about to leave. He lifted his mug in greeting and crossed to the coffeepot as Kylie moved out of his way.

"You have a minute?" he asked as she headed for the door.

"Of course," she said.

He was quiet a few moments, and she wondered what he was going to say. Had she done something wrong? Did he know about the DNA match to Lily Baker? She could explain that. But she stayed quiet, taking a sip of coffee. The fake cream and sugar coated her tongue, and she wished now that she'd left it black. She felt like she, too, was coated in something distasteful.

Davis ran his hand down his face as though wiping off rainwater. His beard was a day or two grown out, unusual for him. There were bags under his eyes. Maybe the pregnancy was hard on Emily and she wasn't sleeping. Or maybe their son was up in the night. These were things Davis might have told her a few years ago, but they barely spoke about their personal lives now. Barely spoke about much at all.

"I never heard back from Priscilla Visser," she said, breaking the silence.

"I got the DNA sample," Davis said. "I stopped by about eight o'clock last night, caught Dr. Visser coming out of the house."

"Hopefully, we won't need it now," Kylie said. "Since Hannah Visser isn't missing but on the run."

"Or the killer tracked her down."

Neither said anything for a moment. A fourteen-year-old up against a violent killer was not good odds.

Davis stared at his coffee. "I left voicemails at the hospital and on his cell, but Dr. Visser didn't seem to know Hannah was missing until I saw him. And he definitely had no idea she'd witnessed a shooting."

Kylie shook her head. "How could he not know?"

"I get the impression he's not living at the house," Davis said.

It seemed odd that a doctor wouldn't regularly check his voicemail. Or had Dr. Visser lied? But why? Where was the urgency about finding their daughter? "Where were Priscilla and Chase?"

"No idea about Chase. Maybe at his house, but Priscilla was at a city planning board meeting."

"A board meeting? While her daughter is missing and a killer is loose?" Who were these people?

Davis shrugged. "They were voting on a temporary replacement for Ben Garza."

"Garza was on the city board?" Ben Garza had been a project manager for Hagen's largest construction company, Belt.

"He headed the planning committee," Davis said.

Kylie shifted the piece of information like a puzzle piece. "And he worked for Belt Construction. Isn't that a conflict of interest?"

Davis didn't answer.

"But you never heard back from Priscilla Visser or Chase?"

He shook his head. "No. But when I explained about Hannah, Charles—Dr. Visser—gave me Hannah's hairbrush and her toothbrush."

She tried to imagine why Priscilla and Chase hadn't told Charles that Hannah was missing. Even if Priscilla and Charles weren't together, surely he had a right to know about his daughter's disappearance. "What did he say?"

"Almost nothing," Davis admitted. "But he was visibly distraught."

Priscilla Visser seemed more and more a mystery and less and less likable with every encounter. "A fourteen-year-old girl witnessed a murder, and now she's missing," she said. "If it was your daughter, wouldn't you want every available person looking? Including her father?"

Davis rubbed his face again as though wanting to move away from her, from this conversation. But he was the one who had wanted to talk. So what wasn't he saying?

"What's the deal with you and Chase Visser?"

Davis looked up at her, surprised. "What do you mean?"

She waved a hand through the air. "The two of you, the weird energy . . ."

"What?" He dismissed her with a wave of his hand. "That's nothing."

"Were you two in school together?"

"Yeah. He's a year younger."

"But you weren't friends."

Davis hesitated. "No. But that's all ancient history."

"What is?"

"Last year or two of high school, he went to a boarding school in Minnesota, some fancy place. It wasn't his idea, but after that, he always acted like he was better than folks here. He was a good-looking kid, but he came back dressed all in black with long wavy hair, like he was going to model in Europe." A beat passed, and Davis added, "We all thought he was a rich ass—" He clapped his mouth closed, the adult he was now filtering the kid he'd been then. "A jerk," he corrected. "I imagine Chase didn't like us much either."

Kylie nodded. It didn't seem relevant to the case, but she was grateful for the honesty. This was the most personal, candid conversation they'd had in months. "And Hannah's DNA, where is it now?"

"I sent it up to the state lab this morning."

With Lily Baker's DNA, she thought.

Davis seemed to be gathering himself to make an announcement, and the muscles in her arms and back tightened in anticipation of the blow. "A call came in on Friday, on my number here," he said finally. "There was a missed call on my cell phone, but I didn't recognize the number. And there was no voicemail. So I didn't get the message until last night."

"What call?"

Davis stared at a point on the wall somewhere over her head. "From Ben Garza."

Kylie lowered her mug to the counter. Ben Garza was dead. He'd been dead since Sunday. "He called you on Friday?"

"To report an incident on the job," Davis said. "The new project Belt is working on."

"What project is that?"

"The hospital annex building."

Since Kylie had arrived in Hagen, Belt Construction had won the contract for every city construction project. They won most of the private contracts for commercial buildings as well. But now that she knew Garza had been head of the planning committee, it made sense. Had someone killed him over a construction contract? But stopping Garza wouldn't stop Belt. "What incident? You think it's related to their murders?"

"I'm not sure. It's on my office line." Davis set his full mug of coffee in the sink as though he'd lost the taste for it and led her into his office.

He shifted the phone to the center of the desk and pressed a button. There was a ringing sound, and Davis punched in his password. After a few clicks, Ben Garza's voice filled the air.

"Hey, Jack. It's Ben Garza . . . long time, I know," the man said, discomfort clear in his tone. His voice was calm and deep, the speed of his words indicating he was organized and thoughtful. "Someone in corporate hired a new guy, Cory Brunt. He's been here about a month, an okay worker, but he's got a nasty streak. This morning, he and one of my senior guys got into it over pouring some foundation. Ended in a fistfight. Brunt left the other guy pretty well pummeled, but he's not the type to press charges. The way the laws are, I can't dismiss Brunt without jumping through a lot of hoops.

"I told him to take a few days to cool off, but he was talking some serious shit, Jack. Haven't had one like that since that tweaker who jumped off the second floor of those apartments in 2018." Ben Garza exhaled in a loud, deep sigh. "Sorry for the long message. Give me a call when you can."

Davis pushed the button, and a mechanical voice said, "Message saved." When he met her gaze, his eyes were round, their gaze soft. And she realized what she saw there. Sorrow and guilt.

He was wondering whether, if he had gotten that message on Friday, he could have saved Ben and Nadine Garza.

CHAPTER 26

Hannah

Hannah woke in the unfamiliar car, her stomach in a painful knot. The small fishing inlet was empty as she crawled out and squatted to pee in the dirt. She was dizzy as she stood, nausea coming so fast that she barely managed to avoid her own shoes as her stomach heaved its meager contents.

She dropped to all fours as her empty stomach was racked in waves. She thought of the remains of the last candy bar, the empty water bottle in the car, the blue pills. For hours last night, she'd followed the river and driven along dark dirt roads in search of the cabin. Without luck. She had no address, no cross streets, only the memory of a gravel drive that curved left for a long bit and then made a sharp right. For almost an hour after she'd given up the search, she held her phone in her hand and considered powering it on and calling home.

But by then, it was almost one in the morning, and the pain in her stomach was unbearable. Trembling and crying, desperate to ease the pain, she had taken two more pills. They hit quickly, a relief considering she had to be building up some tolerance. And then she'd found this little turnout, hidden from the street by a grove of aspen trees, and she had parked to sleep.

Still on all fours, she gagged and heaved a tiny stream of bile. When was the last time she'd had real food?

She imagined one of her mother's meals—a pork chop and potatoes and salad, so much food that Hannah felt like there ought to have been a dozen people at the table rather than only three. Two now that her father was gone. What was her mother doing in that moment?

She was down to six pills.

She had to find the cabin.

Crawling away from the bile, Hannah rolled onto her back in the dirt. Her hair slid across her face, and she inhaled the ripe scent of her dirty scalp, the stink of her unwashed body. She wanted to go home. She longed to see her father, to have him hold her shoulders and look her in the eye the way he did when he was proud. "You did good, Bean," he used to say. When had he last said that?

It hadn't been that long. It only felt that way . . . didn't it?

Was her mother right that she made it harder? Was it her fault that her father had left? If she was really to blame, how much worse were things now that she'd stolen a car and run away?

She curled her knees to her chest and gripped them hard, the earth solid beneath her. The pain in her stomach was so much worse now. She needed real food. Water. She needed to stop taking those pills. The thought came to her even as her fingers found the zipper of her pocket, removed the plastic bag.

The sensation of the hard little pellets in plastic showered her in relief. One in one bag, five in another. Six of . . . it took her a moment to do the math. She'd had twenty on Sunday evening. Today was . . . she stared up at the blue sky, the sun still hidden behind the trees that surrounded her. She had no idea what day it was.

She walked down to the creek bed. There, she put one pill between her teeth and bit it in half. With one hand, she scooped the icy water and drank it down. Her empty stomach balked at the water, and she stopped drinking. A moment too late. The water came back up, a rush of clear liquid that was quickly swept into the stream.

She reached out for it, her fingers searching for the partial blue pill. She couldn't lose it. There weren't enough left.

But the pill was gone.

Tears streamed down her face. She wanted to take another but didn't dare risk vomiting it up, too. Five and a half pills wouldn't last her the day the way she'd been taking them. What then? She'd had hard days, days when she'd run out of pills, when she had to face home or school without that buzz. But she'd never taken so many so fast.

How would she be able to manage coming off them?

Don't think about it.

Leaning down, she pressed her face into the cold water. The icy temperature stole her breath as she tilted forward, letting the water rise past her ears and then over her head. How easy it would be to simply fall in and let the cold take her.

To give up.

As she tried to sit up, she lost her balance and tipped into the creek. She reached out and felt a rock under the water. Its surface was slick, and her hand slid off. She pitched forward. The icy water struck her chest and thighs. Her arms were completely submerged. She screamed beneath the water, scrambling for purchase. She managed to get a foot into the water and stand.

As her face reached the surface, she cried out and gulped for air. The shock of the cold left her gasping as she pedaled backward, out of the water and onto the rocky shore. Water ran from her hair onto the few remaining warm bits of her. She shifted her head to let the icy water drain onto the ground, but it was too late. She was drenched. And a moment later, a cold wind carried the chill to the very core of her bones.

Shivering, she hurried to the car, started the engine, and cranked the heat to its highest setting, then turned on the blower. Frigid air blasted her face as she bent over the passenger-side floor and wrung out her hair over the plastic mat. She shrugged out of the jacket, then her hoodie, kicked her shoes off, and sat, teeth chattering, as she waited for the air to heat.

The drugs would warm her, she thought, desperate for another pill, despite the pain that still cramped her stomach. She thought of the water and remembered the last pills in the jacket pocket, suddenly terrified that she'd lost them. She yanked the wet jacket into her lap. The zipper was closed, and she felt a shimmer of relief as she worked her stiff and frigid fingers around the clasp.

Inside, the bags were still there, the remaining pills dry. A wave of relief was interrupted by the reminder that there were so few left. Not nearly enough.

She felt alone. But she was not alone.

The cabin had to be close. She would make it there. Shower, find something to help her sleep. Then, tomorrow, she would sober up and call her father. She would be honest with him about what she'd seen, the man she remembered. It would be okay. Or if he reacted badly, she'd call Chase. Her brother would help her, too.

Tomorrow, this would all be over.

The air was finally hot, and she tilted the vent toward her face, combing her fingers through her hair as the numbness retreated from her hands. The car issued a high-pitched ding, and the gas tank warning light came on. The screen announced a range of thirty miles. She was at least three times that far from home. Plus, the range wouldn't be thirty miles for long if she stayed right there, running the heat.

But she couldn't be outside, not as wet as she was. Despite the taste of bile that lingered between her teeth and the knowledge that she was running out of pills, Hannah took the blue half pill out of the plastic bag and put it in her mouth. Rather than swallowing it, she chewed, the bitter chalky taste wiping away the taste of vomit.

Then she sat back in the seat, letting the hot air blow. She hoped the half pill would be enough to ease her anxiety and settle her stomach.

Until that happened, she was staying right there. To hell with the thirty-mile range.

She was too far gone anyway.

CHAPTER 27

Lily

Palms flat on her belly, Lily Baker stared at the ceiling of her bedroom. She'd only stolen moments of sleep since returning home from work. She was exhausted, but closing her eyes brought no peace. Instead, she saw things—memories, as the rape crystallized in her head. Images from a cabin with leather furniture and a narrow hallway, a wool blanket beneath her, wet from spilled alcohol. Her stomach roiling while her mind traveled somewhere else, the drugs making her fly high above the man who held her down.

Through the fog of drugs, she had fought, bucking and kicking as she tried to roll herself out of the mattress's massive divot. Her hands scrambled across the bed, connected with something hard and square—a clock? A book?

She had thrown it at him.

A look of shock on his face as it connected with his eye. Then blood dripped down his cheek, the skin open on his face. A flash of rage passed over his features as his fingers tightened on her wrists. His laugh was sharp as he pinned her down. Then a whoop of triumph, like the winner of a hog-tying contest.

There had been noises from down the hall. Abby's laugh or a cry? Men shouting, riling each other up, as Lily was dragged under. Then somehow he was naked and Lily was floating, as though watching from miles away. She studied a bright-red bruise on his thigh, wondered how he'd gotten it. Had she done that, too? Like the injury to his face.

Then time shifted and the voices were quiet, the room still except for his panted words. "You like it?" he'd asked. "Is this how you like it?" Over and over, never waiting for her response.

Questions but not questions, so she hadn't answered. She'd closed that part of herself off and waited for it to be over.

Thoughts swirled like a rising storm. She'd been raped. She'd had a child. No. She *had* a child—a fourteen-year-old child. Or could her daughter be older? She did the math. If the rape had happened in her first weeks of captivity, the girl would have turned fourteen in late May or early June. How rarely she considered having children, and now she had one, almost fully grown.

Most twenty-nine-year-old women had an idea about whether or not they wanted children, but Lily was not most women. Let alone most twenty-nine-year-old women. She had spent the past three and a half years—the past almost fourteen years, really—rebuilding a life that had been shattered. The idea of raising a child when she hardly knew herself was bewildering. Add to that Iver's injuries from Afghanistan and his alcoholism, and matters were more complicated.

Their conversations about kids had been purely hypothetical, more a way of confirming that they wanted to be together for the long run rather than an actual decision about what a family might look like. Iver struggled with the relationship he'd had with his father, worried he would re-create the dynamic with a child of his own. Lily had few strong emotional recollections of her own parents and so almost no guide on which she might base her own parenting.

And now there was a chance that she had a child already. Not a child she would have to raise, she told herself. The job had been done for her. At least fourteen years of it. But having a child in the world was significant. That realization itself shifted the axis of her world. Had already shifted it.

Slow nights at the hospital usually meant she had an easier time falling asleep when she arrived home in the morning. But nothing about the past twelve hours had been normal. Inside the quiet house, she had showered and gone straight to bed without eating. Her stomach was quiet, uncomplaining, and she imagined a pulse deep inside. A drumbeat, a tiny human. *Her* tiny human. Not so tiny anymore. She squeezed her eyes closed and felt the burn of them. The lack of sleep, the tears she had shed. She blinked, but no more came.

She had cried them out last night in the shower, the heat almost unbearable. Only there did she give herself permission to let herself go. After Kylie had left, Lily had hidden in a bathroom, allowing herself a few minutes to cry before forcing herself back to work. The shift had passed in a strange fog, and she was grateful for the low-adrenaline cases. There had been no high-speed car accidents, no serious injuries. Lucky for her, because had she been faced with a case that required her to be especially sharp, someone might have died. Shifts with few accidents normally inched by, but last night had passed in a blink. Her mind, fully occupied by the what-ifs of the detective's news, had barely noticed the time passing.

She glanced at the clock on her bedside table, the room now bright with sunlight. It was 10:00 a.m., and she'd slept at most an hour or two. She would have to work again at eight tonight. She could not make it through another shift without sleep.

That was a problem for later.

She checked her phone for messages, though she had been checking it regularly all morning. Nothing. No word from Iver. No word from Kylie Milliard. How long would it take to complete the DNA testing? She hadn't thought to ask. Would she be waiting, in limbo, for weeks?

But she wasn't in limbo. Not if she was honest with herself. As soon as the words were out of Kylie's mouth—even with the assurances that there might be an error—Lily knew. She had not known before. She might have lived her entire life without knowing. But once the words were in front of her, Lily knew in her gut that she'd had a baby. She'd had a baby in captivity. As a teenager.

She thought about her father's decision to send her to Arizona, her aunt's strict religion. *He that believeth and is baptized shall be saved; but he that believeth not shall be damned.* Mark 16:16. How often had her aunt preached about being reborn or restored? Had that been her way of saying Lily could move past not just her captivity but also a rape and a birth? Was there any chance of being saved after that?

But if her father had known about the baby, then Lily would have been the one to tell him. She couldn't see how else he could've known. A pregnancy was nowhere in the reports—not the police ones or the medical ones. She had gotten access to her own records following Abby's death almost four years earlier. She knew everything that was in them. But she couldn't imagine telling her father any such thing. She thought about her father's best friend. He was the only one who she could imagine her father might have confided in. But how could she ask? *Hey, I found out I had a baby fourteen years ago. Did Dad ever mention that to you?*

There was still so much she couldn't remember. *So much you won't remember.*

One of the neurologists she had first consulted almost four years ago after her memory loss had suggested she work to unearth the memories that her subconscious had so carefully buried. "Whatever is there will almost certainly surface," the doctor had warned. "Usually in a time of high stress. It's always best to find those memories in a safe environment, like therapy."

A time of high stress. Back then, she had wondered what situation would create more stress than what she'd already experienced. Surely she'd been through the most stressful circumstances of her life. Or so she had thought then.

Forcing herself out of bed, she went to the kitchen to brew coffee. As the machine clicked and hissed, she found herself listening for the familiar sound of Cal walking down the hallway. The dog always rose when they started the coffee. Five a.m. or five p.m., Cal got up and made his way into the kitchen, with his slow, steady pace, nails clicking on the wood floor. She shivered now in the cold space.

Taking her coffee, she returned to the bedroom and dressed. She gave a passing glance at the overflowing basket of laundry that spilled out of the closet. The unmade bed, the mail stacked on the dresser. With nothing better to do, Lily carried the basket into the laundry room, set her phone to the Kenny Chesney station, and dumped the clothes on the floor. She sorted lights from darks, checked the pockets, and tossed the lights into the washer. One of Iver's T-shirts, a pair of his jeans. She considered calling him and decided she'd wait until lunchtime.

She lifted a maroon scrubs top from the pile and felt something in the front right pocket. A purple exam glove. She remembered the piece of food she'd seen on the floor of the ED. She'd ducked into a treatment bay for a glove to scoop it, not wanting Dr. Visser to see it. Now, on her way to throw it in the kitchen trash, she noticed a smear of red on the glove. Almost black. Blood?

She carried it into the kitchen and brought down a white salad plate, where she dropped the contents of the glove. To her, it still looked like food, but the dark drop definitely could have been blood. A memory, a pleasant one this time, took shape in her mind. Her father and his best friend seated around this very table, talking about all things related to death. Her father had been a civil servant, a clerk in the city's treasury office. But his best friend, Milt, had been the town's coroner. Still was.

Lily would come home from school and hear the two men talking. "You wouldn't believe how much it smelled like roast pork," Milt had told her father about a man killed in a house fire.

But one time the coroner had been over for breakfast, and Lily, home after her captivity, had come out of her bedroom to find them staring down at their scrambled eggs. "Brain looks just like that," Milt had said. "Whiter, though. Like those newfangled eggs they serve without the yolks."

Lily wondered now if that was what she was looking at—brain from the floor of the ED. They hadn't treated any patients with open head wounds that night, though. Maybe she was wasting time.

But going to see Milt would give her a chance to ask about what her father had told him of her time in captivity. And it would provide the one thing Lily needed most—a distraction.

CHAPTER 28

KYLIE

Kylie stared between Davis's phone and the sheriff's face. Ben Garza had called about a Belt Construction employee. Then two days later, Garza was shot in his own home. "You think Cory Brunt might have killed the Garzas?"

Davis rubbed his face with one hand and pushed a short stack of pages across the desk with the other. "It seemed far fetched until I pulled his sheet."

Kylie spun the papers around to face her and read from the top. Cory John Brunt, born August 31, 1994. The most recent entry was a charge for assault and battery, then several possession charges, and one possession with intent to sell. Before that, another possession charge and assault with a deadly weapon. Trespassing. Unlawful possession of a firearm. More possession charges. Attempted rape. Public endangerment. Kylie flipped the page and scanned the list of infractions, one after the other, dating back to 2012 with a sealed juvenile record.

"Damn," she whispered.

Brunt certainly had the résumé of a killer. Still, something about it didn't line up. People killed for all sorts of reasons, but the Garzas' deaths had been designed to look like a murder-suicide. That took planning, cunning. Brunt's rap sheet read like a guy with a restraint problem.

Either way, they needed to talk to him. "We know where he is?"

"I sent Sullivan and Keckler to his address." He glanced at his cell phone screen. "I haven't gotten word yet. I should have done this yesterday, but I didn't get to my messages until last night."

"It wouldn't have saved them," she said.

He met her gaze. "It could have if I'd heard it Friday."

She had nothing to say to that. Could-haves had little use in a homicide investigation. The conversation reminded her of the secret she'd been keeping. She should have come clean yesterday, too. Kylie was prepared to tell Davis about the DNA match to Lily Baker when the phone on his desk rang. She rose from his chair as he answered, a hitch still audible in his voice. "Sheriff Davis."

She opened the door and stepped out into the hallway without looking back. She was thinking about the newest suspect, Cory Brunt. Ben Garza had compared him to a tweaker. A tweaker who had planned a nearly perfect killing. It was unlikely but not impossible.

"Milliard," Davis called from his desk. He waved her into the office and pointed at the door. She stepped in and closed it as Davis said, "Hold on. I'm putting you on speaker, Luke." To Kylie he said, "Luke Thomas is a park ranger. You're going to want to hear this." Davis punched a button. "Okay, Luke, go ahead."

"Right," came the voice on the phone. "I'm a park ranger stationed out near Elkhorn Ranch."

Kylie pictured a tanned, athletic man in his early twenties.

"Our office just received the BOLO alert for a Ford Explorer registered to Benjamin or Nadine Garza."

Kylie shifted closer to the phone now. The Garzas' third car. "You located the car?"

"I drove into the Southfork trailhead yesterday morning and found a Ford Explorer parked in the lot. Looked like it had been there overnight. It's illegal to park at the trailheads overnight," Thomas continued.

Kylie said nothing but mentally urged him to talk faster. She thought of Hannah Visser, terrified and alone.

"There was a girl sleeping in the car."

"Sleeping?" Kylie repeated.

"Sound asleep. Took a bit to wake her up."

Kylie exhaled. "Alone?"

"Yes."

Kylie let her head fall back and took a slow breath. If Hannah Visser was at a trailhead near Elkhorn, then the killer hadn't caught up with her. She was safe, for the moment.

"You spoke to her?" Davis asked.

"Yes. She told me that her father had gone for a hike and would return soon. She said they were driving to Montana."

Kylie sat upright. Her father? Maybe she wasn't alone. Davis glanced at her, and she could see his thoughts following the same path.

"And you never saw the girl's father?" Davis asked.

"No. She seemed a little under the weather but okay. She said she was confident her dad wouldn't be gone much longer. I gave her my card and told her to call me if he didn't show. But I never heard. And as soon as I saw the BOLO, I sent a ranger to the trailhead, but the car's gone."

"And there was no sign of a second car?"

"None. And only one set of new tracks down that road," the ranger said. "I've alerted the NDHP and the sheriff's department about the car. We'll all be on the lookout."

Kylie was hopeful that the North Dakota Highway Patrol or one of the local deputies would spot the Explorer on the move again.

Davis thanked the ranger and ended the call.

Kylie didn't like the idea of Hannah out there alone. But was she alone? "What do you think?"

"Shooter might've been hiding, waiting for the ranger to leave."

"But the ranger said she was sound asleep. Be hard to sleep soundly if you were being held by a killer."

"Unless she was faking."

"But why keep her alive? Why risk it? If you killed two people and you found the one witness . . ."

"You kill her before she can talk," Davis said flatly.

Kylie nodded. And that was exactly what she was afraid of. She had to believe that Hannah Visser had been alone at that trailhead. Or at least not being held against her will. The ranger had been confident that there was no one nearby when he'd woken her inside the car. Which meant Hannah Visser had not been abducted. She was on the run. But why not come to the police? What would drive her to steal a car and leave town? Most likely it was fear—that the killer might come after her, that the police couldn't keep her safe in their small town. Those words echoed in her Kylie's brain. *Their small town . . .*

What if the killer was someone Hannah knew?

It couldn't be someone in her family. Priscilla and Chase Visser had been in Billings, Montana, the night of the shooting. Mika Keckler had called over to the Hampton Inn and spoken to the front desk clerk who was there when Chase and his mother checked in and also when they returned from the show at approximately 10:00 p.m. on Sunday. The clerk reported they had stopped at the front desk for some bottled water, then rode the elevator to their rooms on the third floor. And Charles Visser had been at work in the ED. Plus, what motive would the Vissers have to want Ben and Nadine Garza dead?

Still, there was more to the Vissers. Despite that family's beautiful facade and all that money, Kylie sensed something not quite right about them.

There was a knock on the sheriff's door, and Gilbert stuck his head in. "I talked to the neighbors at two twenty-seven Bear Root. With the security system."

Kylie sat up, excited. "And?"

He shook his head. "It's a fake sign. They don't have a system at all."

"Damn," Davis said.

So no footage of the street. She'd known it was a long shot . . .

"Also," Gilbert said with a sigh that announced more bad news, "Keckler and Sullivan are back from Cory Brunt's address. Place is empty. According to the leasing office who manages the apartments, Brunt left town on Saturday. Broke his lease and paid the five-hundred-dollar penalty in cash."

"Which leaves us where?" Davis asked.

It left them nowhere. Hannah Visser remained their only lead.

"Any word from the Vissers?" Gilbert asked as though reading her mind.

Davis shook his head. "Not a one."

"I had Dahl go to the house," Gilbert said. "No one's home. Or at least no one is answering the door."

"We know where Chase Visser lives?" she asked, trying to think where they might all be.

"He's got a place out off Millhouse Lane," Davis said. "But he'd be at the office now."

Gilbert shook his head. "I was just over there to return some files, and he wasn't there. Receptionist said she hasn't seen him since Friday. And I sent Dahl out to Chase's address, too. No cars in front, and no one answering the bell there either."

"You think they found Hannah?" Davis asked.

"If they'd found her, wouldn't they call us?" Kylie asked the two men. "Especially since they were so concerned about keeping her disappearance under wraps."

"Right," Davis agreed. "They wouldn't want us investigating."

"What now?" Gilbert asked, and both men looked to her.

"Let's get everyone in the conference room and regroup," she offered, which was as much positivity as she could muster.

Keckler, Sullivan, and Dahl joined her, Davis, and Gilbert. In a matter of minutes, Kylie updated the team on the Hannah Visser sighting and explained that locating the girl remained a top priority. "We believe she had to have seen something."

"Otherwise, why run?" Keckler commented.

"Exactly."

Kylie searched for an opportunity to mention the familial DNA match to Lily Baker, but it still didn't seem relevant. And she was reluctant to out Lily until it was absolutely necessary.

The conference room door opened in an explosion of movement. A grinning Marjorie stood on the threshold, a laptop cradled in her arms. "I've got something you guys might want to see."

"Bring it in," Davis said.

"Just finished working the composite with the Garzas' neighbor," Marjorie announced as she stepped inside. "We did a composite of the guy driving the Corolla, the one who dropped Hannah Visser at the Garzas'." With that, she spun the computer to face the group. On the screen was a computerized image of a male face.

Kylie leaned forward to study the face. Mid- to late twenties, the man had a scruffy beard, wide-set brown eyes, and a short forehead with a pronounced widow's peak. "Adam Blaney."

"Totally," Gilbert said.

Marjorie clicked a button and showed an image of Adam Blaney beside the composite. "It's so close, right? This program is amazing."

"Who's Adam Blaney?" Davis asked.

"I interviewed him after the OD case last spring," Kylie said. "He came from Minnesota with his father in the last boom, graduated high school here. Dad moved back to Minnesota, but Adam stayed."

"He's a small-time dealer," Gilbert added. "He's been picked up a handful of times, but we haven't managed to make any charges stick."

"So that's who dropped Hannah at the Garzas'?"

"Looks that way," Marjorie confirmed. "According to motor vehicle records, he drives a 2001 Corolla. Gray."

CHAPTER 29

Hannah

The half pill did almost nothing to settle Hannah's stomach. After a last-ditch effort to locate the cabin on her own, Hannah drove the Explorer back to Main Street. According to the car, she now had nineteen miles' worth of gas. Nineteen miles, five blue pills, and sixteen dollars.

She drove with the windows down, the cold air stinging her cheeks. But despite the temperature, she was bathed in a cold sweat when she parked on the block before Main Street. Her chest was uncomfortably tight, and it felt like she was getting sick. And she needed a bathroom—a real one, not the side of a road somewhere.

She tried to tell herself that there would be meds at the cabin. Surely, her father kept something there, in case one of them got injured. She just had to find that damn cabin.

But first, she needed food. Real food. It was afternoon, and she couldn't remember when she'd last eaten a meal. Her hair and clothes were still damp, and the smell coming off her was dank and fishy.

She'd never felt so hungry and disoriented. She couldn't think how long it had been since she'd left Hagen. How many nights she'd spent in the Garzas' car. But she was here now. She was going to find that cabin. But she would eat first.

Pocketing the sixteen dollars, she locked the car and walked toward the small downtown. On trips to the cabin with her father, they rarely stopped in town for more than a few quick errands. Her father didn't enjoy eating out the way the rest of their family did. He was impatient and seemed to find food more a necessary task, like filling a gas tank, than something to be relished.

On the corner of Main Street was a diner, the kind that served breakfast all day. Yellow Formica tables and chairs with rust-colored cushions beckoned. She thought of the Hagen diner, of their peanut butter pie. Clutching her stomach, she stopped and looked through the window. Spotted fluffy waffles on a woman's plate and felt the saliva collect around her tongue. She opened the door and stepped inside.

"Seat yourself, hon," the woman behind the counter said.

"I need the restroom first," Hannah said.

"Through the red door," the woman said, aiming a finger at the back of the restaurant.

Hannah hurried into the bathroom and locked the door. Her stomach clenched, and for a moment, she worried she was too late. The smell of her was more potent in the closed space, and after she'd used the toilet, she washed her hands and face with soap. Then she scooped soapy water under her arms and around her neck before using the toilet again.

Her stomach was a twisted knot of anxiety. She debated taking another pill. She'd be at the cabin soon. There would be more there. She reached for the bags in her pocket and took one from the last bag and swallowed it, washing it down with water from the faucet.

Four left.

She stared at her face, the pale skin, damp looking from sweat. The circles under her eyes. There was a knock on the door, and she hurried to wash up one last time before leaving.

In the hallway stood an older woman in a plaid button-down shirt and Carhartt coveralls, who watched Hannah carefully as she emerged and walked toward her table. Hannah chose a booth next to the bathrooms, shrugged out of the still-damp puffy coat, and tucked it beside her. Her hunger was so potent now it was almost painful.

"Coffee?" the waitress asked, coming by with two pots.

Hannah shook her head. "Just water, please."

The waitress gave a single nod and started to turn away.

"And can I have scrambled eggs . . . and bacon," Hannah called after her. "Oh, and a side of pancakes." She felt almost breathless. How long had it been since she'd said so many words at once?

The waitress looked back over, scanning Hannah. The memory of her own appearance from the bathroom mirror was sharp in Hannah's mind. Her damp and ratty hair, the circles under her eyes. Her trembling fingers, the sheen of sweat on her face.

Holding her breath, she unearthed the cash from her jeans pocket and laid it on the table beside the salt and pepper. The smell of food was painful as she sat, unmoving. She waited for the waitress to tell her that she needed to leave. To be called out for what she was—a druggie, a runaway, a thief.

But the waitress tapped her pen on her notepad. "Eggs, bacon, and pancakes," she repeated.

Hannah swallowed hard and forced a smile. Her lips felt like they might crack open, her tongue bloated in her mouth. "Please."

"You want maple syrup or blueberry?"

Hannah licked her lips. "Both?"

The waitress smiled. "Sure thing, hon, and I'll be right back with your water."

When the waitress set down the red plastic Coke glass, the same style as at Hagen's diner, Hannah's eyes filled with tears. "Thank you," she whispered and lifted the glass to her lips, drinking it down until she felt momentarily seasick. She had to force herself to stop, knowing that if she finished the water, she'd surely vomit again. She gripped the plastic, feeling the moisture on her hands and pressing them to her cheeks. Clean water.

Her food came within minutes of the water, almost as though the kitchen had known she was coming and predicted what she would order. Eggs, bacon, toast, and three enormous pancakes, two types of syrup. She dug her fork in and scooped a massive bite of eggs into her mouth, pressing a piece of toast to her lips to keep the food from falling out. She ate half the eggs, two pieces of bacon, and a slice of toast this way, shoving it in so quickly she was barely breathing. When she looked up, two older women seated at a table in the center of the restaurant were watching her, their mouths slightly open.

A flush of embarrassment flooded her cheeks. Hannah imagined her mother's face as she dropped her gaze. She lifted the napkin from beside her plate and wiped her mouth before setting it in her lap.

A few minutes later, she noticed the women were still watching, and Hannah considered everything she'd been through, what she'd seen. Embarrassment sharpened into anger. She stared back at them, narrowing her eyes in an effort to look fierce.

It did nothing to discourage the stares. Hannah snapped her teeth as though biting, and the women turned away, expressions of horror on their wrinkled faces. What would her mother do if she saw Hannah baring her teeth at strange old women? The thought brought an odd swell of pride. Why should she care what these women thought of her? They didn't know her. They didn't know what she'd been through.

Her hunger slowly ebbed, taking with it some of the stomach pain. Warning herself to slow down, she studied the remaining food and sipped her water until she felt confident she wouldn't be sick.

Rearranging the dishes, she brought the pancakes to the center of the place setting, where she drenched the right side with blueberry syrup and the left with maple, then proceeded to carve alternating bites. Nothing had ever tasted so good.

The waitress came by and filled her water glass from a pitcher she held in one hand. A pot of coffee was in the other. Leaning against the edge of the booth, she eyed Hannah's disappearing food. "You okay, hon?"

There was something in her tone that made the next bite harder to swallow. Hannah blinked hard without meeting her gaze. "Uh-huh."

"You don't look familiar. You live around here?" she asked, setting the water pitcher on the table.

Hannah felt her breath catch. She lowered her fork and lifted her gaze. Chin up, she shook her head.

"Didn't think so." Leaning forward, the waitress hitched a thumb over her shoulder and lowered her voice. "Don't you mind Ruth and Betty. They like to stare." She waved Hannah back to her plate. "You enjoy your food."

Hannah glanced up and saw the women watching her again. Did they recognize her? Was her face on the news? On a milk carton? She hadn't thought about what her parents would be doing to find her. But they would have called the police. Hannah felt a sudden urge to bolt. "Can I just get the check when you can?" she asked, uncomfortable with the attention.

"Sure thing."

As the waitress was turning away, Hannah said, "I used to come to a fishing cabin down near here."

The waitress gave her a nod. "Yep. Lots of folks come here to fish."

"With a man named Charles Visser."

The woman shook her head. "Can't say I know him."

"You have any idea how I might find it? The cabin, I mean."

The waitress gave it a bit of thought. "If this Visser fellow has a cabin round here, he probably visited Roosevelts." She pointed through the window, aiming a finger across the street and down the road. "It's one block south and three blocks east from here. Takes up near a whole block. You can't miss it."

Hannah couldn't imagine her father in a place called Roosevelts. "What is it? A bar?"

The woman laughed. "No. It's a sporting goods store—everything from bait to bullets, as they say. But folks like to hang out there, especially menfolk." She shrugged. "At least until the bars open."

Roosevelts. Hannah repeated the name to herself. Though she couldn't remember the place itself, her father *had* always stopped in town for supplies.

"Talk to Teddy," the waitress said, picking up the water pitcher again. "He's the owner, and he's always there. If your guy came around, Teddy would know him."

"Thank you."

The waitress left, her attention shifting to a table of men just seated across the room. Hannah looked down at the remaining food, suddenly unable to take another bite. The two old women had turned their attention to the newly arrived table of men, and Hannah thought about her sixteen dollars and wondered if there was an exit by the bathroom.

If she might sneak out.

She hated to leave the food, but if she could get away without paying . . .

Before she could make a decision, the waitress had returned. She set the bill and a brown paper bag on the table and left with a wink. Hannah stared at the bag without touching it, then fingered the bill. She tried to imagine what her meal might have cost. What if it was more than sixteen dollars? Was that possible? She had been so hungry she hadn't thought to check the prices on the menu.

She felt a wave of terror at what might happen if she was caught. Would they arrest her? Send her back to Hagen? And what then? She wished she could talk to her brother, wished Chase were there with her. Gathering her breath, she flipped the bill right side up. There were words but no numbers. She flipped it over, then over again.

Was she supposed to take it to the register up front? Without knowing how much it cost?

She fought against the trembling in her hands. Breathe. When she scanned the bill again, she recognized that there were words scrawled across the ticket. *Looks like you could use a break. This one's on the house. You take care. Kim.*

Hannah read it again, then one more time. Tears streamed down her face, and she could feel the two old women staring at her. Grabbing the bag, she lowered her head and hurried from the restaurant.

CHAPTER 30

Lily

The T. Milton Horchow Funeral Home was a large clapboard house on a corner at the east end of Main Street. The original Milton had chosen his location well, the house kitty corner from the Lutheran church. As far as Lily knew, Horchow's was the only funeral home in town, but its superior location would have made it difficult for competitors to get a foothold.

She parked on the side street and walked around the rear, where she buzzed down to the morgue. There was a bell that rang when someone entered the mortuary, a way of telling Milt he had customers, but that was at the front. Lily had only been through the front door once—on the day of her mother's service. And she never intended to do it again.

"Hello?" Milt's voice was scratchy through the intercom, like it was being pushed through several layers of empty potato chip bags.

"It's Lily," she said. And then when a beat had passed, "Lily Baker."

"Lord, girl, you think I don't recognize my own goddaughter? I'm old and fat, not senile," Milt responded. "I just had my hands full."

She tried not to imagine what he had in his hands. The buzzer went and the door released.

"Go into the kitchen and make yourself at home. I'll be up in a few."

Lily opened the screen and let herself in through the back door. The building housed both Horchow's work and his home, and the appearance of the kitchen always varied by whether or not there was a showing coming up. Today, though, the kitchen was tidy and bare. Faded yellow checked curtains hung on the windows, the lace fringe tattered. Lily thought she could remember when the yellow was marigold bright, the lace stiff and new, but she couldn't think of who would have made Milt new curtains when she was a child. He'd never been married, never even had a girlfriend that she'd heard. He'd grown up with her father, the two of them neighbors. Her father's house had been a block up, a two-bedroom bungalow, close enough that her grandfather could walk to the church where he was an assistant pastor and, later, the church's youth pastor.

The stairs from the basement groaned under Milt's weight, his own grunting louder than it used to be. A few seconds later, he emerged from the stairwell, red faced and sweating. "There's some iced tea in the fridge. Be a doll and pour some, would you?"

Lily got up and found two glasses in the cupboard, their surfaces dull and foggy from decades of wear and washing. Only Milt's wineglasses were regularly replaced. Milt loved his red wine, had installed a small cellar off the downstairs prep rooms. Now, she lifted a plastic pitcher from the refrigerator and poured two glasses of iced tea, the Lipton smell a reminder of all the years Milt and her father had sat together and talked. Before her mother had died and her father started adding something stronger to his tea.

Milt stood at the sink and washed his hands, humming the alphabet song. "That was my trick for proper handwashing before it was popular," he used to tell her.

He settled into the chair across from her and drained half his glass in a single swig. "Haven't seen you in a bit," he said.

She nodded. "Sorry I haven't been by."

He shook his head. "No worries. You haven't missed much," he said with a wave of his hand.

Barely a minute passed while she tried to find a way to tell him why she was there. "You got something on your mind," he said with a laugh. "Your mother used to make that same face."

She looked up. "What face?"

"Your eyebrows sink into a straight line, and you've got your cheek between your teeth. Left side, exactly like your mother did." He leaned back and crossed his hands over his substantial belly. "Out with it, then. Nothing my goddaughter can't ask me."

"There's a couple of things, actually," she said. "First, this . . ." She pulled the sandwich bag from her pocket and handed it over.

Milt patted his shirt pocket and found his reading glasses. With the spectacles balanced at the edge of his nose, he lifted the bag close to his face. "What you got here?"

"I'm not sure."

He studied it for several seconds before peering at her over the top of the glasses. "Where did this come from?"

"Found it on the floor of the ED."

He fingered the mass through the plastic. "Brain."

"Human brain?"

He shrugged. "I'd assume so, but I don't have much experience with animal brain, so I couldn't say for sure." He studied it again. "Probably came from the shooting." Milt was protective of his clients and his work, but Lily knew he had to mean Ben Garza.

"He never made it to the hospital."

"But she did," Milt said, setting down the plastic bag. "It's probably transfer."

Lily retraced the moments with Nadine Garza—out of the ambulance and directly into the first bay. She died there and would have been transferred to a body bag from the table, then wheeled to a storage room until she could be transferred to Milt's or straight to the state medical examiner's office in Bismarck.

"I never saw her," Milt said, reading her mind. "She went straight to Nelson," he said, referring to the state's ME, Craig Nelson.

Nadine never went farther into the hospital than the emergency bay. Yet the piece of brain had been outside the doctors' lounge. It could have been on their shoes—hers or Dr. Visser's—dropped when they were working on her. Except they'd both been in booties, which they had discarded before leaving the treatment bay. She didn't know why it bothered her, why she was still thinking about it. She didn't know exactly why she'd brought it over to Milt.

It was an excuse to come. That was why.

Milt slid the bag back to her and finished off his iced tea before rising slowly and ambling to the refrigerator for more. "Just brain on your brain, kid?" he asked, giving her a smirk. He brought the pitcher of iced tea to the table and refilled their glasses, then sank down into the chair.

As a kid, she had sometimes been embarrassed by how large her godfather was. By any medical definition, he qualified as obese at least a time and a half over. But he'd always been this size. Pictures of him and her father showed a squat, square-shaped boy and a tall, pencil-like boy beside him. She'd always assumed Milt would pass before her parents, but here he was, his heart still pumping, still working, while her own parents were both dead. Like judging a book by its cover, her mother used to say.

"What's going on, Lily?" Milt asked, his expression displaying a rare state of concern.

There was no easy way to ask, so Lily steeled herself and let the words out. "I was wondering if Dad ever talked about what had happened to me while . . ."

"Oh," Milt said, his lips forming a perfect circle. He reached for the glass of iced tea and moved it from in front of him as though clearing space for the conversation that was to come.

She waited.

"He barely survived the time you were gone," Milt said. "Slept a lot of nights on that couch," he said with a thumb hitched toward the brightly lit sitting room that was one of the only private spaces in Milt's house. He laced his fingers again and looked down at them, intertwined across his stomach. "I honestly didn't think he would. With you and your mom both gone, he didn't seem to have any will to keep going."

Lily had rarely thought about what that time must have been like for her father. Or her godfather, for that matter. She'd been a child in captivity and then a teenager recovering from it. Too much to handle, she was sent to Arizona. She'd assumed her father didn't want her around. She hadn't ever considered how traumatic it was for him.

"But then you were home. He called all the time, asking me what he should do. Talk about it, not talk about it. Hire someone. Medication . . . we didn't know as much about trauma then . . ."

"What about physically? Were there changes that he noticed?"

Milt narrowed his gaze. "You left a kid and came home a woman. You were too skinny, and you weren't the kid we remembered."

"There's evidence that I have a child, that I gave birth in captivity."

Milt sat slowly upright, hands dropping to his sides as he leaned forward.

"Did my father know?"

Milt reached across the table and gripped Lily's hand. "Oh, Lily."

Lily began to cry as Milt shook his head. "No. There's no way. There is no way your father knew that. It would've . . ." Milt stopped talking.

But they both knew what he was going to say.

It would have killed him.

CHAPTER 31

Kylie

Gilbert offered to drive, so Kylie sat in the passenger seat. In the bright light of day, Gilbert's naturally thin face appeared hollow, and the skin beneath his eyes was a sickly lavender shade. "You doing okay?"

He looked over at her, and she prepared for a suggestion to mind her own business. Instead, he shrugged. "Seeing her like that . . . it's a hard image to get out of my head."

"I'm sorry."

"It's ancient history," he said with the edge she'd been expecting. But then his shoulders dropped, and he added, "Or I thought it was . . . but I guess I still had feelings for her."

The words *I'm sorry* formed on her tongue again, but they felt pat, overused. And what words could possibly replace them? She didn't know what he was feeling, and yet she was filled with an unfamiliar fear of her own. Was it for Lily Baker, who had almost certainly had a baby while she was held in captivity? Or for the idea that, in this town, every murder was so personal, so intimate to them all? She'd never shared the story of Veronica, the friend who was murdered when they were juniors in high school. The friend who had stopped being a friend in the final months of her life.

Kylie thought about how she'd announced her assault to Lily, as though anyone would be comforted by knowing someone else had trauma, too. She'd learned her lesson on that one. Unable to find anything to say, she put a hand on his arm.

He glanced at her hand, then her face, and nodded.

She squeezed his arm and returned her hand to her lap, shifting her attention to the text from Marjorie with Adam Blaney's address. "We're heading out toward the Field."

Gilbert drove past the edge of town to the strip of farmland that had been purchased by one of the drilling companies and turned into a trailer park to house employees in the last oil boom, the place locals had dubbed the Field. As he drove, she recalled how strong his arm had felt in her hand. What was wrong with her? She shoved the thought away and shifted her focus to the cluster of ugly buildings in the distance.

Oil prices had dropped in the past couple of years, reducing the demand for drilling and its ancillary employees. Like many of the small towns in the Bakken Formation, Hagen was hit hard. The influx of outside workers had ebbed, the demand for housing had fallen, and crappy rentals that had gone for a thousand dollars a month back then were practically free now. This particular trailer park was one such area.

The patrol car was bouncing off the paved street and onto the long gravel entrance to the trailer park when Kylie's phone buzzed in her pocket. It was Sarah Glanzer in the lab. "Hi," she said.

"Kylie?"

"Yeah, it's me," she answered.

"You okay? You sound . . . off."

She was off, all right. "I'm on a dirt road. It's bumpy."

"Okay," Sarah said.

"You confirm that the DNA match was correct?" She felt Gilbert look at her out of the corner of his eye. She hadn't mentioned any DNA tests at the meeting. She hadn't mentioned them to anyone yet. She had to do that soon. Or maybe she wouldn't have to. Maybe it was a mistake.

"They're a match," Sarah said. "No errors."

Kylie exhaled, turning to look out the window to avoid Gilbert's gaze.

"And I got the DNA from the sheriff on the missing girl," Sarah said. "Which is actually why I'm calling."

Outside the car, dust swirled through the air like smog. She knew Sarah well enough to recognize when she had news. And suddenly she pictured the long dangly earrings Priscilla had been wearing in the birth picture. How bizarre it seemed to give birth in those things—that the earrings wouldn't catch on something and be torn out.

"Kylie?" Sarah asked. "You there?"

"The match is Hannah Visser," Kylie said before Sarah Glanzer could speak. "She's the daughter."

Sarah blew out her breath. "How did you know?"

Priscilla Visser had staged the hospital photos to make it look like she'd given birth to Hannah. But Hannah Visser was Lily's baby.

"Kylie?" Sarah prompted. "How did you know?"

"Lucky guess."

"You don't sound good, Kylie."

Kylie said nothing to that. How could she be good when she was the one who had to tell Lily Baker that the child she didn't know she had was being raised by the doctor she worked with? And that she'd recently gone missing? How much more could Lily Baker take?

"I'll send the report over now," Sarah said. "Keep me posted, okay?"

"Will do," Kylie promised. She ended the call and closed her eyes. How the hell had Lily Baker's baby ended up with Priscilla and Charles Visser?

"Hannah Visser is the daughter?" Gilbert repeated.

Eyes open, Kylie nodded.

"You can explain after," Gilbert said, motioning to a single-wide trailer, the yellow paint chipped and the undercoat of metal heavily rusted. "This one's his."

A piece of particleboard with *#15* spray-painted in orange leaned against the rusted stairs. Pieces of the trailer's front end had corroded so completely as to fall off. The gray Corolla sat in the gravel drive at an angle that suggested the driver must have been impaired when he parked it.

"Looks like he's home," Gilbert said, putting the patrol car in park. Kylie tightened the Velcro on her vest and waited for Gilbert to give her the go sign before the two of them emerged from the car.

Kylie had yet to open the car door when Adam Blaney sprang from the trailer, descended the stairs, and took off at a sprint, gripping a paper bag in one hand.

CHAPTER 32

HANNAH

Once outside the diner, Hannah chewed one pill as she opened the paper bag to see a sandwich, chips, and a Coke. Lunch. The gesture helped buoy her spirits as she followed the directions to Roosevelts, and when she found it, the green script sign, faded from years of sun, was instantly familiar. Her father had brought her here. As she opened the store's door, the smells of tent fabric and gun oil and rubber floated from her memories along with the clack of her father's cowboy boots on the hard floor, the squeak of her sneakers as she scurried to catch up. She had loved this place. How could she have forgotten it?

Between the food and the pill, Hannah felt more herself as she stepped inside and scanned the store. Guns were at the rear, camping to the left, sports and clothing to the right. The high shelves of gear, the round clothing racks, and behind them all, the mounts on the wall. Seeing the familiar sights felt like success, like she knew where she was going.

Because she'd been here. Which meant Teddy would know her dad and maybe—hopefully—the address of the cabin.

She paused in the doorway to shift the paper bag to her other arm. On the wall above her was the mountain goat. Mounted on an artificial cliff, he peered down at whoever entered the store. The animal had been terrifying the first time she'd seen it. Her father had told her to look, and she'd burst into tears, but now the bearded beast felt like an old friend. A reminder that she would find the cabin and be safe.

"Can I help you with something?"

She swung toward the voice, almost losing the grip on her lunch. The man in front of her was young—probably early twenties—with a bright smile and too-big teeth. His tongue darted out of his mouth and swept across them as though trying to hide the giant white squares.

"Uh." The chalky taste of the pill caught in her throat, and she coughed. "Is Teddy around?"

The man stared at her a moment, then looked up, scanning the store. "Haven't seen him, but he's usually here by now. Maybe I can help."

She considered him a moment. "Maybe. My dad and I used to come up here and stay at a cabin nearby. I wanted to find it . . ."

The empty space grew uncomfortable as the man stood silent. Hannah shrugged and added, "For old times' sake, I guess."

His smile faltered. He eyed the bag in her arms, and she held it closer. "Not sure how I can help," he said finally.

Tears filled her eyes, and she glanced away, blinking hard to quell them. She would not cry. The kindness of the waitress returned to her. "Kim told me Teddy might remember the address."

"Kim?"

"At the diner," she said, the words stilted, as though her mouth were full.

He nodded with another swipe of his tongue. "The address could be in the computer."

Hannah felt the drugs wash across her and fought to stand still and upright.

"I guess I could check in the back," he said.

She exhaled in a long, audible sigh. "That would be great."

"What did you say the name was?"

"Visser. Charles Visser." She spelled it out.

He headed to the rear of the store, and she hurried to catch up. Her feet felt slow, her balance off, like the linoleum floor had suddenly turned to sand. "We updated the computer systems about two years ago and . . ." He kept talking, but the words stopped making sense. Something about "migrating data" and "new system."

She just followed and nodded, trying to seem both interested and grateful.

When they reached the gun section, he paused and pointed to a swinging door behind him, saying something she missed. When he started forward, she followed. He pivoted and put a palm up to stop her. "You'll have to wait out here."

She felt a swell of dizziness as he waved toward the shoes. "You can look around if you want."

"Sure," she said, stepping away.

"I'll be right back," he said.

Unable to stand still, Hannah made a slow circle of the shoe section and strolled toward the fishing equipment, keeping an eye on the employee door. In front of a display of fly rods was the full-size grizzly bear. In her memory, the bear was as big as a car, and though he wasn't quite that size, he was still extraordinary. Upright, his head stood four feet above hers. She reached out to feel the familiar roughness of his fur, the way she had as a child. Like thin strands of wool yarn. But as she reached up, she noticed the sign on his neck. An addition since her last visit. **PLEASE DON'T PULL ON MARLA'S FUR. SHE NEEDS IT TO STAY WARM IN WINTER.**

Hannah read the sign again and found herself smiling. Marla. The bear was a girl, and she had a name. Had she known that when she was a kid? How could she have forgotten Marla? Sweet Marla, stuck in this store.

There was a bald patch on Marla's belly at the height where small hands could reach and tug. Hannah smoothed the fur in a failed effort to hide it.

"I found it."

Lost in thought, Hannah jumped at the voice.

"Sorry," he said, his tongue darting across his teeth.

He handed her a piece of lined paper with scratchy, almost illegible writing.

She took it and squinted down, trying to read the words. Wiping the sweat from her lip, she told herself she could read it later. She began to hold it up when he said, "My handwriting's pretty bad. That cabin belongs to the Sutton family . . . that's a big name down here." He paused as though waiting for her to explain. The Suttons were her mother's family, but she said nothing.

After a moment, he said, "But it's listed as Mr. Visser's address, too." He pointed to the paper. "Address is two ninety Crow Tower Road."

"Crow Tower," she repeated. Crow Tower. Crow Tower. She said it over and over inside her head.

He nodded. "It's probably three or four miles from here. Northwest on 48 about a mile, then a left turn on Old Coopers Mill Road. Crow Tower runs right off Coopers."

The long left, followed by a sharp right, she remembered. Hannah repeated the directions to herself. Northwest on 48, left on Coopers Mill Road. Three miles. She could be there in ten minutes.

There was a voice over the loudspeaker. "Darren, you've got a call on line two."

He pointed up. "That's me. I got to run. See you around."

And then he was gone. The lunch bag under one arm, Hannah folded the paper and tucked it in the front pocket of her jeans, though she'd already committed the address to memory. Three or four miles. She was so close. She imagined a shower, hot water and soap, the soft twin bed in the small back bedroom. A night there, and she could decide what was next.

Walking toward the front of the store, she approached the family tent pitched in the middle of the camping section. Her fingers touched the fabric with a whisper.

As a kid, she had always climbed inside the tent to wait for her father while he picked out flies, his last stop in the store. On his way out, he would swing his shopping bag in through the tent's zipper door and call out, "Bean, I've got the supplies. Time to go." And she would crawl out to meet him.

They would drive to the cabin, and he would open a beer and give her a Coke. The first night he always cooked sloppy joes with a packet of ground beef and seasoning, followed by s'mores over the little firepit in back. By the time the sky was dark, she could barely keep her eyes open long enough to make it to the bedroom. She never did brush her teeth out there, something her mother always commented on when she got home with a dry, clean toothbrush.

Would her father have brought her out here more recently if she'd asked? Had he offered and she'd rejected it as too babyish? Had she pushed him away as much as she felt he'd pushed her? How she wished her dad were here now.

Around the tent, she located the main zipper and ducked inside. It was not the same tent it had been on her last visit. In those days the tent was yellow, the color of the spicy mustard her parents liked. This tent was a steel blue gray. Inside were two full-size cots, made up with sleeping bags and pillows. Above her head, someone had hung a row of silver stars from the top of the tent, and they swayed as she moved.

Someday she'd own a tent, she thought. She'd never slept in one, but it had always seemed magical to her. Being outside but inside, too. She shifted the bag of food in her arms and stepped out of the tent.

She ran her fingers along the canvas one last time before turning for the door. A voice came from the other side of the tent. "I'm hoping you can help me."

She froze.

"Sure," came another voice. Not the man she'd talked to. Not Darren.

Surely she was mistaken. It wasn't that voice. How? But then he spoke again. "Have you seen this girl?"

It was him.

The killer was inside the store.

CHAPTER 33

Kylie

"Damn it," Gilbert said as Adam Blaney sprinted down the gravel drive and ducked between two trailers where the road curved left. Gilbert jumped into the cruiser as Kylie refastened her seat belt. Seconds later, he revved the engine and took off in a storm of dust and gravel.

"Where's he going?" she asked.

"Not sure, but they've got the road dug up for a broken water main, so he's probably not going far," Gilbert said as they came around the bend in the road. Blaney was slowing now, approaching the giant trench and starting to search for other ways out.

Gilbert gave the sirens a couple of long shrieks and called through the loudspeaker, "Adam Blaney, stop where you are."

Whether too tired to run anymore or realizing there was no way out, Blaney took only a few more steps and stopped at the edge of the trench, leaning forward momentarily before reversing course. Maybe he was considering jumping but thought better of it. Hands on his head, he walked slowly toward the patrol car, veering into the shade of a half-dead green ash. Kylie radioed for backup and requested a crime scene tech for Blaney's trailer while Gilbert approached Blaney. By the time Kylie joined them, Blaney was already feigning shock about Hannah Visser's age.

"I had no idea, I swear. She told me she was eighteen," Blaney said. "And I believed her." He walked a slow circle, winded from the short run. "We never had sex. Never. It was one blow job."

"Shit," Gilbert said.

The same thought entered Kylie's head. A fourteen-year-old girl and this slob. She hoped Lily Baker never heard about what Hannah had done with this creep. "Stop talking." The air was cold, and she zipped her jacket against the wind.

Blaney closed his eyes, his mouth hanging open as he gasped for breath. A skinny guy with ratty blond hair that hung in thin clumps, Blaney was flushed red from the roots of his hair. Beneath the red, his face was a sea of freckles and shiny with sweat. He pressed his hands to his thighs, then dropped to his knees and, finally, lay down in the dirt on his back. Like a dying dog. Like they were in the middle of a heat wave.

"What the hell, Blaney?" Gilbert said.

"I can't breathe."

Kylie hated to hear those words. "You need an ambulance, Blaney? You got some heart condition we don't know about?" Kylie asked. "I'll call."

"I'll probably be all right," Blaney said. "You know, just got to get on my feet. If you could help me to the trailer . . . I need to lie down."

Gilbert glanced at Kylie, who shook her head. Blaney looked fine to her. She scanned the area around them. "You had a sack in your hand. Where'd that go?"

Blaney rolled to one side and pushed himself up. Reddish dirt stuck to his sweaty neck. The mysterious illness seemed to have passed. "What? What sack?"

Kylie walked toward the trench, where a line of yellow caution tape was strung between orange cones, blocking the road. Beyond the cones, sitting on a mound of earth, was the paper sack. The color was almost enough to camouflage it. Almost. Kylie lifted the bag off the ground and shook it. "What's in here?"

"I've never seen that before."

Kylie unrolled the top of the paper bag and stared down at dozens of small plastic bags. Five round pills lined the bottom of each one, making a soft clicking sound as she shook it. "You sure?" she asked. "You were holding this bag when you came hauling out of that trailer."

"I found 'em," he said. "It's why I ran. I knew you guys would think they were mine. But they're not."

"Save it," Gilbert said. "We want to know about Sunday night."

"I was home." He licked his lips in a way that turned Kylie's stomach, though it was probably because his mouth was full of dirt. "Alone."

"Before that," she said, returning the pills to the paper bag. "You drove Hannah Visser out to Bear Root Crossing."

Blaney's eyes flashed wide, their whites red and a little yellow. He was rough looking for such a young guy.

"You're saying you didn't drive her to Bear Root?"

"I did. Just gave her a ride, is all. She doesn't drive." He put a hand up. "I didn't know it was 'cause she's not old enough. She always made it seem like she didn't like to drive, not that she couldn't." He wiped a hand across his face, spreading the amber dirt across pasty skin.

"Stop talking," Gilbert snapped.

"I don't want you to think that I'm into young girls or anything," Blaney continued, his mouth like an out-of-control train. "I swear on my mother, I didn't know. She looks—" And there he paused, the first smart thing he'd done. "Well, you know how she looks."

"Blaney," Kylie shouted. "Shut the hell up, or I swear I'm going to book you for statutory rape."

"You can't do that. I never—"

"Shut. Up. Now." The ash tree seemed to shiver at the words, kicking off leaves to the wind.

Blaney's mouth continued to move, but the words finally stopped.

Kylie squatted next to Blaney and pressed a finger to her mouth. "Not a word now, okay?"

He nodded.

"Just nod if I'm right and shake your head if I'm not. Okay?"

Another nod.

"On Sunday night, you dropped Hannah Visser at the Garzas' house on Bear Root Drive."

Blaney nodded.

"That was about seven o'clock?"

Nod.

"Did you see anyone else at the Garzas' house?"

Blaney shook his head.

"Did you go into the house?"

Eyes wide, he shook his head again quickly, left right left right, making his point. He didn't want them to think he had been anywhere near the shooting. If Hannah had seen Adam Blaney shoot the Garzas, she would have called the police. She would have told them. Plus, the neighbor had seen Blaney leaving the area. Drop off and leave. "Okay, now you're going to have to talk."

Blaney's mouth opened with a hiss like a seal being broken.

"But only to answer my question," Kylie said. "Just the question."

Nod.

"Did you give Hannah some of your drugs?"

Blaney froze like a deer in headlights.

"Answer the detective's question," Gilbert warned.

Blaney seemed to make some calculation in his head. "She had some pills, yes."

"Did she take them with you before she went into the Garzas'?"

Another nod.

"How many?"

"I told her it was strong stuff, not to take two of them," he said. "But she did it anyway. I swear—"

"Stop."

Blaney stopped.

Kylie shook the bag, the plastic and pills rattling inside. "What are they?"

A light in Blaney's eyes. A realization. He smirked and forced a shrug. "I found 'em, like I said."

Gilbert walked away a short distance. Then he turned and came at Blaney in two long strides. A burst of wind sent a flurry of leaves down around them as though Gilbert were creating the breeze on his own. "Two people are dead, Blaney. Answer the question, or so help me God, I'll see that your ass ends up in jail till you're fifty."

Blaney looked at Kylie, who said, "We need you to tell us everything you can remember about Hannah Visser that night. Was she worried about anything? Afraid of anything or anyone?"

Blaney licked his lips and appeared to taste the dirt on his face. He used the sleeve of his flannel to wipe his mouth. "Her parents were fighting. Her dad bailed, and her mom's a total bitch. She can't wait to move out, but that's all I know. I thought she was leaving next year, not . . ." And there he trailed off, as though it was too much strain to calculate how many years Hannah had left in high school.

None of what he said was news to Kylie. "Hannah took two of these pills before she went into the house."

He nodded.

"How many pills did she have?"

Blaney frowned. "I thought she had five total, one baggie full. Payment for the—" He snapped his mouth closed.

For the blow job. And again, she wanted to be sick.

"But she stole some more. I was missing four bags total, so . . ."

"Five in each bag, so twenty?" When Blaney nodded, Kylie asked again, "And what are they?"

"Oxy . . . I think."

Gilbert leaned over and yanked Blaney to his feet and spun him around. "Let's go on over to the station. See if you're more cooperative there."

"I swear, I don't know what it is."

"You sell it, Blaney. We know you do, so cut the crap."

Yet another nod. He was getting good at this.

"Who supplies it?" Kylie asked.

"A guy from somewhere east—Michigan or Illinois. Hell, I don't know. I get a delivery every other Sunday. Comes to my PO box in Felton."

"Where the hell's Felton?" Kylie asked.

"Twenty minutes east of Bismarck, give or take," Gilbert said. "And what about the cash?"

"Same thing," Blaney said. "Drop it at a PO box in Felton. I've got a key. I go every Sunday. Pills are a little different every week, so I'm never sure."

Behind them, another cruiser pulled to a stop, and Sullivan and Keckler stepped out of the car.

Gilbert transferred a complaining Blaney into the back of the patrol car as Kylie tried to find something useful in anything they'd learned. Blaney was part of some obvious drug ring in North Dakota, but Hannah wasn't involved in that, was she? Either way, Kylie couldn't see how the drugs linked to the Garzas. There was no evidence they were involved in running drugs, and their bank balances didn't suggest any extra income source.

When the shooter barged into the Garzas' home, Hannah had almost certainly been high—possibly very high. Was that why she was on the run? Because she was afraid of getting caught with drugs? But that was Sunday. It was now Tuesday—plenty of time to get sober and come home. Unless there was a situation at home she didn't want to face.

"You want us to take him in?" Gilbert asked, dragging her from her thoughts.

Adam Blaney sat in the patrol car, his mouth moving, though his words didn't reach her. With the door closed, they didn't reach anyone.

But that didn't stop him. All that talking, and he hadn't said anything that would lead her closer to an answer on the Garzas' murders.

"Give him some time and see if he tells you anything useful. And let's have Sullivan search the trailer. He have his evidence kit?"

Gilbert nodded. "He's heading over to the trailer now. What about you?"

"I need to talk to Priscilla Visser."

"I can drop you on my way to the station, then come back after I book Blaney," Gilbert said. "Unless you want me to come along?"

"I think Mrs. Visser will be more accommodating if it's only me," Kylie said and pulled her phone from her pocket, raising it to indicate she was going to make a call first.

"Meet you at the car," Gilbert said.

Kylie stared at Lily's phone number in her contacts. What words did you use to tell a friend that the daughter she hadn't known existed had been living with her boss for the last fourteen years? As though the right delivery might soften the blow. There was no good way. The call went to voicemail, and a flash of shame followed the relief Kylie felt at the sound of Lily's prerecorded message. And then Kylie left a message that she had results from the lab and requested Lily call her back.

She ended the call and thought about Iver up in Fargo, caring for his mother. Had Lily told him what was happening? Would she?

Since Iver was Kylie's landlord, he was in her contacts. It wasn't her business. Lily would tell Iver if she wanted him to know. But where Kylie couldn't help Lily, Iver could. Kylie was pretty sure that Lily would prefer to never see her face again. So she tapped out a quick message to Iver.

Lily just got some hard news. I'm not sure if she'll ask you for support, but she probably needs it. It's not my place to ask . . . She stopped typing, trying to figure out what to say. Coming up with nothing better, she typed, but I hope you'd want to know. I would. —Kylie

Kylie pocketed the phone and walked to the waiting patrol car. Now for a chat with Priscilla Visser. Kylie hoped like hell the woman was home.

CHAPTER 34

Lily

The brain tissue remained with Horchow, who promised to dispose of it properly. He had a cremation chamber for that sort of thing. The first time he'd taken Lily to see it, they had gotten no closer than the door. The chamber stood thirty feet away, the brilliant orange glow like staring at the sun. The heat stung her cheeks, even from a distance. Milt had joked that it was a pizza oven.

Still in the parked car on the curb by his house, Lily considered going back inside. She didn't want to go home and be alone. She longed to drive to Fargo and see Iver, but there wasn't time before she was due at work. Plus, the roads were slick, and she hadn't managed to get her tires changed. They were still in the garage with the smell of wet wool and the memory of the man's pale face, his greasy hair.

Even if she could get to Iver, what could he do? What could anyone do?

Her phone buzzed on the seat beside her, and she both hoped and dreaded that it was Iver. Instead it was a missed call from Kylie Milliard. The call meant news—something about her daughter.

Did Kylie know the girl's identity? Lily scanned the street, caught sight of a group of women emerging from the church doors. Did one of them know her daughter? Had one of them raised her? Heat burned her cheeks, and her chest tightened. How had she gone fourteen years without knowing she was a mother?

Her phone buzzed again. A voicemail.

She forced herself to push play. The detective's voice was hesitant, soft, almost unfamiliar. Not the Kylie Milliard Lily knew. The tone reminded Lily of the detective's admission in the hospital conference room—she, too, had been sexually assaulted.

"We checked your DNA against the sample on the bassinet. It's a match, Lily. You have a daughter," Kylie said. "There's more . . . call me."

Lily held her breath.

The line went silent. The message still had twenty seconds left. Kylie's voice was gone. Lily called her back, and Kylie answered on the first ring. The way the detective said her name made Lily want to scream. "Who is she?"

"Hannah Visser. Hannah is your daughter."

The car was suddenly a vacuum. Where was the air? Lily released the door and tried gulping the cold outside air. But it felt thin, her lungs weak.

"I'm so sorry, Lily," Kylie said. "I'm here if you need to talk."

But Lily could say nothing in response, so she ended the call and let the phone fall from her hand.

Hannah Visser. Her daughter had been raised by Charles Visser. Through the swirling thoughts, she realized Charles was a good father. Firm but steady. And he was well off. Hannah would never have wanted for anything. "Hannah." She said the name aloud, a sob collecting around the *H*s. Hannah Visser was her daughter.

What name would she have chosen? What would she have done if she'd come out of captivity pregnant? Or with a baby?

Anger and distress fused, synthesizing into the need for motion. Lily slammed the door and yanked her seat belt across her chest, tugging as it halted, then halted again. She screamed into the empty car and dropped the belt, sucked a heaving breath, and pulled the belt slowly until it reached the buckle and snapped into place.

Without knowing exactly where she was heading, Lily followed Highway 1804 out of Hagen. Drove too fast, felt the car lift off the bumps in the road and settle down again. Some ten or twelve miles away was a turnoff at the crest of the valley, the spot that offered a 360-degree view of the surrounding flatlands.

It had been her father's place. He had loved to gaze at the horizon, especially when the air was warm and the distance seemed to shiver in the heat. She was often his companion on those trips. Early on, he packed toys for her or a coloring book for entertainment while they sat with the windows down, the breeze hot and dusty.

Lily had come to find the view as hypnotic as her father had, the giant pumps rising and falling in the distance. Lily, too, had enjoyed watching those pumps, which reminded her of the old *Star Wars* movies and made her hometown seem otherworldly. She couldn't remember the last time she and her father had come here. It was certainly before her time with Hudson. Had her mother been alive then? Were those trips a way of giving her mother a chance to rest in quiet, her body fighting the spreading cancer? It would have been around that time.

Letting Hannah and Dr. Visser and Kylie drain from her mind, Lily sat in that spot for hours. Her only movements were to start the car to warm it when the chill grew unbearable. Around her, the sky bled orange, then pink, and finally violet to black as the sun set. She needed to eat something before her shift started. One hour. Dr. Visser wasn't working tonight. That, at least, was a blessing. She watched the horizon until the far hills and pumps disappeared into the shadow of the night, and then she drove toward the hospital. The last place she'd seen her daughter had been standing in the hospital parking lot—the only time she'd spent with her one on one.

No. Surely she'd been with Hannah when she was first born. Had they put Hannah in her arms before taking her away? She fought to draw those memories from whatever buried place they resided, but nothing came. As she drove into the hospital parking lot, exhaustion weighed on her. Could she really work a ten-hour shift? What choice did she have?

She parked her car and walked through the doors, through the lobby where Chase Visser had stood asking after Hannah. He'd thought she might have come here. He was partially right. Hannah had come to the parking lot to deliver the Garzas' baby. Her daughter had kept the infant safe. Lily felt a well of heat and tightness in her chest—pride and also longing. She'd missed so much.

She thought of the pictures on Visser's desk, the ones of Hannah. She had never given them much thought. Now she longed to study them. In the ED, she stood at the entrance to Visser's office and stared in. Diplomas on the wall, books on the shelves, but little of it felt personal. She walked to the desk and saw the picture of the family standing in front of a fireplace, dressed in holiday clothes. Hannah couldn't have been more than eight or nine. Lily longed to see a more recent picture. She'd thought there had been another picture on the desk, but it was gone now.

Did her daughter look like her? Would Lily recognize her movements? Would she feel familiar? As Lily came out of Visser's office, she turned for the cafeteria, passing the floor where the brain tissue had been. Her eyes were drawn to the spot with the thought of how different her life had been two days ago. Before she knew about Hannah.

"You okay?"

Lily glanced up and realized she was staring at the line of wrapped sandwiches in the cafeteria. She didn't remember walking through the main hall or coming past the cash registers. Beside her stood Noah, who had been a few years behind her in school. He worked in hospital security and had the pale skin of someone who spent too much time indoors. In Noah's case, he did—ten-hour shifts huddled in the tiny security office, managing the systems and keeping an eye on the cameras that filmed the hospital and its surroundings.

Lily's thoughts returned to Sunday night as she wondered whether Hannah had been in the ED. Why would she have come here? To see her father? Had Hannah talked to Dr. Visser and Lily just hadn't known? It might explain the brain tissue on the floor. It could have come off Hannah if she was a witness.

"Earth to Lily," Noah said.

She turned to him. "Do you keep the footage from the hospital cameras?"

Noah smiled from one corner of his mouth as he reached for a sandwich. "Why?"

"I'm wondering if there's a way to see if someone was in the hospital on Sunday night?"

He scanned her face like he was waiting for a punch line.

"I'm serious. I need to see if a fourteen-year-old girl was here on Sunday night. Inside the hospital."

"Can't you check patient records?" Noah took his sandwich and started for the registers.

Without looking at the contents, Lily grabbed a sandwich and followed. Suddenly, she was consumed with the idea that Hannah might have been in the ED. And the cameras would prove it. Maybe it would matter to the police, too, but what Lily wanted was to see her daughter in motion, watch her walking through this very building, only feet from where she had been on Sunday. "She's not in the patient system." Lily tugged the sandwich from Noah's grip. "Let me buy this."

He shook his head and reached to take it back.

"Please, Noah. It's important."

He checked his watch. "I've only got a twenty-minute break."

"Perfect. We'll be fast."

He opened his mouth to speak, then shook his head. "Fine."

She paid for their sandwiches and drinks and followed Noah to the security room off the main lobby. Despite two big fans blowing from the corners of the ceiling, the space was easily ten degrees warmer than the hall. A flat desk surface stretched the length of one wall, a single large monitor sitting at one end. On the wall above were eight TV panels, and on the floor below, four CPUs. Noah sank into the only chair. "We've got eighteen cameras in the hospital. I can run the footage fast-forward, but we need to narrow it down—either by time or location."

Lily tried to remember what time it had been when she'd seen Hannah in the parking lot with the Garzas' baby. After Nadine had died. "Let's start with cameras closest to the emergency department, sometime between nine p.m. and . . ." How long might Hannah have driven around before she returned? Sometime before Chase arrived. That was the end of her shift. "Six a.m."

Noah eyed her. "Nine hours?"

"Four a.m.?"

With a sigh, he started working, his sandwich and drink beside him, untouched. After several minutes, he pointed up to the screens. "These will be running at eight-times speed, so if you see anything, shout, and we'll slow them down. I'm going to run six at once, on these six screens." He pointed to a cluster of screens closest to them. "You ready?"

It felt like she was getting ready to play some intense video game. Shifting closer, she nodded.

The first screen showed a view of the ED bay. The ambulance carrying Nadine Garza sped to the curb. Doors swung open, and a second passed before Lily and Visser were sprinting alongside the gurney. On the second screen, Stephanie Krueger sat with her father in the ED triage room, waiting for Lily to notice the petechiae that signaled her meningitis. Yet another screen showed the ED nurses' station. She saw herself, the other nurse, Visser, all of them moving at superhuman speed, darting in and out of the treatment bays. The other screens showed different angles, and Lily scanned back and forth, watching the night pass. Lily saw herself walk outside, the memory catapulting her pulse. "Slow that one, can we?"

All six screens stilled, and Noah played the one of the ED bay exterior. Lily held her breath. On screen, she looked up and started forward. Approaching the car. She waited for Hannah to appear on the screen. Instead, Lily disappeared off the edge of the film. She was out of the camera's view. "Is there another camera that captures the lot?"

Noah shook his head.

Lily fought her disappointment.

"Keep them rolling?"

"Please," she said.

At the nurses' station there was a moment of quiet on the film, as she, Alice, and Visser had all hurried into different treatment bays. Bruce Reade strode in, wearing jeans and cowboy boots and carrying a duffel bag. She hadn't remembered seeing him Sunday night. Glancing away, she scanned the other screens, searching the faces as they rushed by. When she looked back, Dr. Reade was coming out of Visser's office. Something in his hand—a paper, a flash of green. He put it in his bag, all of it over in a heartbeat, and then he disappeared again.

Motion on another screen drew her attention, a woman being wheeled in by her husband. She gripped the rounded shape of her swollen belly, pain etched in her face. Her husband sprinted toward labor and delivery.

The other cameras showed familiar faces. Another ambulance; then the sky grew light. No sign of Hannah. The screens went black. "That's all from those six cameras."

"There are more?"

Noah sighed, and a minute later, the screens filled again. Two angles on the hospital lobby, the front parking area, the pharmacy, and two separate hallways. Faces passed, but none were Hannah. A few seconds in, a man entered the hospital, one side of his face stained red. A birthmark, maybe. But there was something about it. She looked away, scanned the other screens. No Hannah. On another screen, Bruce

Reade appeared again, walked down a hall, and ducked into the last room on an unfamiliar corridor. "Where's that?"

Noah paused the footage with a frustrated sigh. "Trash room. Is that who you're looking for?"

"No, sorry."

The tapes stopped at the six o'clock time stamp. No sign of Hannah. Without a comment, Noah started up the footage from the last cameras. Lily stood stiff, her shoulders aching as she waited to see Hannah's face. But the more time that passed, the more certain she was that Hannah hadn't been in the hospital that night.

When the screens went black again, Noah sat back in his chair and reached for his sandwich. "Thanks for the sandwich."

"Thanks for checking." Working to hide her disappointment, she let herself out of the small space.

The air was instantly cooler, and a fan over her head blew cold against the perspiration on her cheeks. Her shift started in a half hour. She had to pull herself together. Get some food in her stomach, prepare herself.

As she walked toward the emergency room, her cell phone rang. She yanked it from her pocket. *Please be Kylie. Let Hannah be safe.* But the picture on the screen was of her and Iver over the summer. She stared at his name, thinking of all that had happened since they'd last spoken.

She couldn't imagine how she could tell him. Certainly not before her shift started.

So she let the call go to voicemail.

CHAPTER 35

HANNAH

Hannah edged closer to a round display of hanging sleeping bags, hidden from the killer's voice.

"Can I see that picture?" the store clerk asked.

"Please," the killer said, and there was the crinkle of photo paper changing hands.

Hannah shuddered at the idea of the store clerk studying a picture of her. Looking at her face. Had he seen her enter the store? She'd walked around in full view for—what—fifteen minutes?

"We found her car right off Main, so we know she's nearby."

Hannah squeezed her eyes closed. The car. The Garzas' car. How did he know she was driving that car? And who did he mean by "we"?

"She's gone missing, and we're really worried about her," the killer continued. "I need to find her."

Find her. What would he do if she stepped into view? Would he shoot her right there? No. He'd have to get her alone. What if she screamed bloody murder? What if she told everyone in the store what he had done? She held her breath.

The photo shifted. "She doesn't look familiar to me."

Hannah covered her mouth. Water rushed in her ears, the sound deafening. It was blood, her pulse.

She was in plain sight. She couldn't stay there. *Move.* But fear made movement impossible.

Huddled close to the sleeping bags, she held her breath. Their puffy down reminded her of the coats, the coat closet, hiding. She wanted to run. She needed to run.

"She your daughter?" the shop attendant asked.

"Yeah. Been in some trouble with drugs. Sometimes doesn't even know me." A pause. "I'm just trying to set her right again," he added, a catch in his throat. There was no mistaking that voice. The shooter was here. Pretending to be her father, pretending that she had gone crazy.

So people wouldn't believe her if she said she didn't know him. That he was a killer.

His daughter. She tried to picture his face. Who was he? Was he friends with her father? No. He was a liar, a killer.

Desperate now, she slid behind a sleeping bag and stepped into the center of the circular carousel that stretched high above her head. She listened for noises of an approach. Heard nothing. She shifted until she could see a sliver of the front of the store.

The killer stood in a gray Cubs T-shirt, jeans, and a hat. Despite the low inside light, he wore sunglasses, his profile visible. He was disguising himself. Hiding so that they couldn't identify him after he . . .

"Wish I could help," the attendant said.

How had he found her? Did he know about the cabin? Had he tracked the car? Or followed it? She thought about sleeping at the trailhead, the ranger. Was it the ranger who had told this man where to find her? Or had someone else seen the Garzas' car?

Escape. She needed to escape.

And then the voice was so close she almost screamed.

"You mind calling me at this number if you see her?"

A moment of hesitation. "Sure thing, sir. What'd you say your name was?"

"Sam," he said. "Sam Jones."

She searched her brain, but she couldn't think of anyone named Sam.

She stole another peek and saw the ink on his forearm. The tattoo from her dream—with the snakes winding around a cross with wings. It was the same tattoo her father had from his time as an airborne army medic at the start of the Gulf War.

"Sure hope you find her."

"Me, too," he said.

And then the voices went silent. The store employee hummed to himself, and she shifted slowly to see him at a shelf of books, straightening the stacks. Hannah waited with the memory of that closet, of hovering in terror as Ben and Nadine lay dead on the floor, as Tiffany cried from her bassinet. And now she was doing it again. Hiding, praying. She counted to one hundred, losing track twice and starting over.

Finally, when she ached from the effort of standing completely still, Hannah shifted one of the sleeping bags and scanned her surroundings. Was he still in the store? Had he left, or was he talking to other employees? What if he showed her picture to Darren?

Hannah slipped out from the sleeping bags, keeping the carousel between her and the worker. She glanced at the front of the store, then turned toward the back.

No sign of the man, so she walked with the hurried pace of a little girl who had to use the bathroom. She remembered the sensation, fighting the tears, the way her body felt like a betrayal. Her father's frustration that she hadn't gone while he was shopping.

That memory brought her to the rear of the store, to the bathroom inside the stockroom. Past the bathroom was a rear entrance.

She pushed open the door, surprised at the fading daylight. She searched the sky as though some object might be blocking out the sun. But it was coming on evening now. It would be dark soon.

There was no using the car now. She had to go on foot. To get to the cabin before dark, she'd have to move.

CHAPTER 36

Kylie

Kylie studied the beautiful Victorian home from the curb where Gilbert had dropped her. Nineteen Dutch Street was probably the best-known house in Hagen, built by one of the town's founders as a way to try to appease the wife he had dragged there from New York City. The previous owners had let it succumb to time and the elements, and the Vissers had meticulously restored it to its former glory.

The house was a symbol of Hagen history and perseverance, a source of pride. Only now did it feel to Kylie like a house of mirrors, something dark and insidious billowing off the pristine exterior.

Sheriff Davis had finally gotten Hannah's DNA, but it had not come from Priscilla, as promised. Instead, he'd gotten it from Charles Visser. Priscilla didn't want to share Hannah's DNA because she knew it wouldn't match her own. And how could she explain that? Kylie rang the bell and listened to the sound of the house. Someone was definitely inside. She rang again, and the clack of heels on hardwood grew louder.

Priscilla Visser opened the door, a flash of surprise in her eyes. Another silk blouse, this one cream, with dark slacks. Black shoes with square heels. "The DNA," she said, a hand to her mouth. "I'm so s—"

"We got Hannah's DNA," Kylie interrupted.

Priscilla took several tiny steps backward as though the news was a physical blow. "What?"

"The sheriff got it from Dr. Visser last night."

"Oh," she said, lifting her chin and regaining her composure. "Good. But I don't think we'll need it. I—"

"Is Hannah here?"

"No. We haven't located her as of yet, but we—"

Kylie raised a palm. "Save it, Mrs. Visser. We need to talk."

The woman blinked twice as though she'd been struck.

Kylie didn't back off. She didn't care about Priscilla Visser's social status. "Here or down at the station—your choice."

A little shake of her head. "I'm afraid it's . . ."

"Mom? Is everything all right?" Chase Visser appeared in the entryway. Unlike his mother, Chase was dressed down in a sweatshirt and jeans. His hair was messy. He didn't appear to have shaved. He appeared genuinely worried about his sister. Maybe even losing sleep over it. "Is it Hannah? Has something happened?"

"Shall we talk inside, then?" Kylie asked, her gaze narrowed on Priscilla. "Or does the station sound better?"

The woman's mouth twitched up on one side, like Kylie had amused her. But the fear was evident in her wide eyes. A moment later, the door swung open.

"Let's sit in the living room," Priscilla suggested with a grand sweep of her arm to Kylie's left.

Kylie followed Priscilla Visser into a space that was at least half the size of the house she lived in. Two massive sofas faced each other across a square glass table. A grand piano hogged one corner, bordered on either side by a set of glass doors that led to a patio. On the opposite wall was an enormous fireplace.

Kylie sat down on the end of one sofa while Priscilla and Chase sat opposite her.

"What's going on?" Chase asked again. "Have you found Hannah?"

"We got a call from a park ranger who saw her early yesterday morning."

Chase sat upright. "Where? What park?"

Kylie shifted her gaze to Priscilla. "First, have either of you heard from Hannah since Sunday night?"

"No," Chase said, pulling his phone from his pocket. "I've been trying to call her, but it goes straight to voicemail. Her phone is off . . . or she lost it . . ." His gaze swept the room, and he closed his mouth as though unwilling to think of additional reasons why his sister's phone might go unanswered.

"Chase," Priscilla said. "Would you mind making some tea?"

"Mom," Chase snapped. "What's going on? Do you *know* where Hannah is?"

Priscilla winced, and Kylie spotted a flash of the woman's temper before the calm countenance swept back across her brows. Almost like a magic trick. "Of course not. I'm trying to help the detective find her." Then, with a wave of one hand, she added, "Please."

Chase stopped pacing. "This is my sister."

"Chase," Priscilla said. "Now."

The grown man was suddenly a teenager, caught between standing up for himself and doing as he was told. Kylie watched the internal struggle play out, on his face, in the stiffening of his shoulders, in the fisting of his hands.

Priscilla reached up and touched his arm. "Just for a few minutes," she said gently, and after a brief moment, Chase obeyed.

With the two of them alone, Kylie prepared to square off against Priscilla Visser.

"Where is my daughter?" Priscilla asked, crossing her arms.

"Why don't we start with *who* is your daughter?"

The flash in her eyes was gone so quickly Kylie almost missed it. Surprise and more fear. "I don't—"

"The state lab matched Hannah's DNA to an existing sample," Kylie said before Priscilla could go on. "A sample the lab was able to confirm is from Hannah's biological mother."

Priscilla didn't move. Not even her long, painted fingernails twitched against her black slacks.

"And that's not you," Kylie added.

Priscilla stared down at the giant diamond on her left hand. "It's true," Priscilla said, dropping her voice as she folded her hands in her lap and glanced toward the closed doors. "Hannah *was* adopted."

"And yet there's a newspaper article showing you in a hospital bed, looking like you'd just given birth."

"I don't believe there's a law against taking a photograph with a newborn," Priscilla said, her chin hitched a little higher.

Kylie sat straighter. "And I assume you have paperwork for the adoption?"

"No," Priscilla said smoothly. "It was handled privately."

Kylie removed her notebook from her coat pocket and opened it on her knee. "In the state of North Dakota—as in every state—a private adoption requires the involvement of multiple agencies. There would be paperwork."

Priscilla eyed the notebook and shook her head. "This was handled as an independent adoption."

"An independent adoption?" There was no process Kylie knew of in which a baby could be adopted without a legal process—at the very least, attorneys and someone to confirm the adoptive couple were fit to parent.

"Yes," was all Priscilla Visser said in reply.

In other words, the adoption was illegal. "How did you locate the pregnant mother?"

"A dear family friend—a nurse who had cared for me when I was a girl."

"The friend's name?"

"Amelia Brown. She was my nanny for almost ten years when I was young," Priscilla said, and she seemed to relax as she continued, "I struggled to carry a pregnancy to term after Chase. That was quite hard for me. Even sixteen years later, we were still trying, hoping for more children."

Kylie tried to follow Priscilla's story, measuring each part for fact or fiction. "And Amelia happened to know a young mother who was pregnant and wanted to give her baby away?"

"Yes," Priscilla said. "I saw Amelia over the holiday that year. I had mentioned that Chase had gotten so big that he no longer needed me." She straightened her chin. "The way boys do at that age."

"And voilà, Hannah."

Priscilla's gaze was hard when it rose to Kylie's. "It wasn't as simple as that. Amelia called me in January to say that a teenage girl in her town was pregnant. A good girl who had gotten in trouble."

The words filled Kylie with rage. As though Lily had gotten herself kidnapped and raped. "Where was this girl?"

"Down in Molva," Priscilla said.

The name of that town turned Kylie's stomach. "And the girl's name?"

"I don't know her name. I never knew it. I didn't want to," she added quickly.

Kylie leaned forward and set her elbows on her knees. "I find it hard to believe that Dr. Visser would agree to an illegal—"

"It wasn't—"

Kylie sat back and raised a palm to stop her. "Whatever you want to call it, if the court wasn't involved, it wasn't a legal adoption. Surely that would jeopardize your husband's medical career."

"No one knew."

Kylie watched her. "No one?"

Priscilla gave a single shake of her head. "Other than a few people in Molva, no one. Not Chase, not Hannah. Even Charles doesn't know."

Kylie blew out a breath and gave a little laugh. Did Priscilla really think Kylie would believe such utter bullshit?

"I was actually pregnant at that time," Priscilla said. "I'd had a few pregnancies that didn't take. The one before Hannah—that was the last. I lost the pregnancy about two weeks before I learned about Hannah."

"And you hadn't told Charles about the pregnancy? That you'd miscarried?" How had she kept that from her husband, a doctor?

She shook her head. "I'd gone down to stay with my sister in Molva. I was down there quite a lot then with Chase off at boarding school. Charles and I had grown apart, distant."

Not distant enough to stop having sex, Kylie noted. "So you let Charles believe you were still pregnant?"

"When I found out I was pregnant that last time, Charles did an ultrasound at the hospital. We saw the heartbeat together," she said with a shrug. "He'd seen the proof."

Proof. Like she was making a case. In her mind her husband had seen the fetus and that had convinced him the pregnancy was real. But a pregnancy was nine months long, followed by delivery. Charles hadn't checked the pregnancy or seen his wife naked for all those months? "Who was your doctor, then? Who was checking out this imaginary baby?" Kylie pressed.

Priscilla twisted her lips. "Because it was a high-risk pregnancy, I told Charles I was seeing a doctor in Billings. It was reasonable," she said, as though it were fact, not fiction. "I'd had five miscarriages—four before that one. And then I gave birth in Billings. My sister was with me. That's what I told Charles."

But she hadn't given birth in Billings. She hadn't given birth at all. Before Kylie could point this out, there was a knock, and Priscilla looked at her. "Please. He doesn't know." She called out to him, "We need a few more minutes, Chase."

But the door opened, and Chase entered with a tray that he set on the glass table. He studied his mother, then the detective, as though measuring how much damage Kylie had done to her.

"Thank you, Chase," Priscilla said.

"Would you like me to pour?" he asked.

She shook her head. "I think we can manage."

Chase hesitated.

"A few more minutes," Priscilla repeated.

Kylie watched as Chase left. As if a few more minutes could resolve the mess Priscilla had created.

What did she imagine would happen when her husband found out? And Hannah. And Chase. What would happen when Hannah's biological mother stepped forward? Kylie pictured Hannah. She didn't resemble the Vissers—certainly not the way that Chase took after his father. But she didn't resemble Lily either, at least not in a way that was obvious to Kylie.

Or the girl took after her father. The thought brought a chill. Who would be the one to tell Hannah Visser that she was a product of rape? That the father she probably looked so much like was a violent criminal?

"Hannah's biological mother," Priscilla said. "Does she know that we've raised Hannah?"

Kylie held Priscilla's gaze. "This isn't a secret you can keep."

Priscilla nodded, but rather than seeming resigned, she seemed to be thinking. Perhaps plotting how to soften the news that she was a liar. That she'd been lying to them all for fourteen years.

"Will you please tell me where she is now?" Priscilla asked.

Kylie relayed the information about the ranger in Elkhorn Ranch and watched as Priscilla Visser exhaled deeply. "Does that mean something?" Kylie asked. "Do you know where she's going?"

Priscilla's expression shifted as she gazed at the detective.

"Hannah witnessed two murders," Kylie reminded her. "She's in danger."

"I don't know why she would be near there," Priscilla said, and Kylie knew with total certainty that she was lying.

"Elkhorn is close to Molva. Could she be visiting your family?" Kylie asked.

"My sister's in Billings now," Priscilla said. "And my brothers are gone. There's no one in Molva that Hannah would know."

Kylie felt another wave of frustration. "It's crucial that we find Hannah, Mrs. Visser."

"I understand, Detective."

The wave of anger was channeled from her gut into her throat, and she had to bite it back. "I'd suggest that you not leave town, Mrs. Visser. And please answer your phone when it rings."

The hard line of Priscilla Visser's jaw was cut like a cliff beneath her well-preserved skin, but she said nothing.

Rising from the couch, Kylie glanced at the untouched tray of tea. "And I'll need contact information for Amelia Brown."

"Oh," Priscilla said, giving what Kylie assumed was her best sad face. "I'm afraid that won't be possible."

Kylie felt pressure in her lower back, a warning. She didn't want to ask why. She didn't want to hear the answer she feared was coming.

"She passed away about four years ago," Priscilla Visser said with a little shake of her head and a pout. "Cancer."

CHAPTER 37

Hannah

Hannah sucked in the cool outside air and surveyed the area behind the store. A line of cars was parked in the alley. She saw no faces. No people. Stepping outside, she pulled the hoodie over her head and ducked left, away from the restaurant and the Garzas' car.

Away, too, from the cabin. She tried to decide what to do. Since she'd left the hospital, her only thought had been of getting to the cabin. But would she be safe there now? If the killer had followed her here, then it was possible that he knew about the cabin, too. But where else could she go? Not back to the Garzas' car. Not to the police. He had told the store clerk that she'd gotten into trouble with drugs, that he was her father. Would anyone believe that *he* was the liar?

She needed to get away from town and call her brother. Surely Chase would know what to do. Maybe he'd know who that man was. That man knew her father. They had the same tattoo, but that didn't mean her father was involved. What reason would her dad have for killing the Garzas? What reason would anyone? Her mom and Ben Garza were on the city planning board together, and Nadine had worked for Chase for as long as Hannah could remember. They'd all gone to the hospital when Tiffany was born. Her mother had brought flowers and a whole basket of pink baby things.

No. Her father had nothing to do with the murders. Head down, Hannah walked several blocks east before turning north to cross Main

Street. Half a block away, she caught up to a family and walked with them, scanning for people or cars. The killer could be anywhere—driving by, sitting in his car watching her, or looking somewhere else; maybe she was safe. For now.

She continued past Main Street, relieved to be away from the thoroughfare. The night was getting cold. She had planned to be at the cabin by now, and she had no other place to go. Every time a car passed from behind, her heart pummeled her ribs. Walking between the houses and across blocks, she took the indirect route northwest in the direction of the cabin, telling herself she could hide nearby. She wouldn't go inside until she was certain no one was there.

When she hit a road dense with aspen, she ducked in among their narrow trunks until the road was no longer visible. The deeper she went into the aspen grove, the dimmer the light grew. Away from the headlights on the main road, it would be almost impossible to find the cabin. And even if she found it, the darkness would make it harder to see what was waiting for her there.

Or who.

Paralyzed, she felt fear crest like a wave and descend on her. Lowering to a squat, she removed the plastic bag from her pocket. She took one blue pill. She had to conserve them. She had to be sober. She chewed and winced at the bitter paste in her dry mouth. She had no water.

Only sixteen dollars and two pills. And her phone.

She thought again of her brother and pulled out her phone. The car keys tumbled out into her hand, the dark fob like a giant beetle on her palm. Could someone track her from the fob? Was she leading the killer right to her? In a wave of panic, she pitched the keys into the woods.

Hands trembling, she powered on her phone. Watched as the white apple appeared and a line moved slowly across the screen. "Come on." Tears burned in her eyes. Something rustled. She jumped, heart pounding as she scanned the dark. She was alone . . . wasn't she?

Finally, the screen came alive, and she saw the image of Lizzo. Her lock screen. The image of the musician was almost like a friend, and tears leaked down her cheeks. She punched in her code and waited for the phone to come alive. As soon as the phone was unlocked, it vibrated with alerts. Forty-three text messages. Twelve voicemails. Missed Snapchats. She clicked on the Snapchat icon, wondering who the messages were from.

The list loaded, and she'd gone to click on the first message, from Emily, when the phone went black.

She tried to start it again, but the screen only glowed a dull gray, the icon of an empty battery at its center. She thought about the charger. It was in the car. With her backpack and her water bottle.

Dropping to her knees, Hannah felt as though she were the only person on the planet. She was alone. She thought of all the times she'd felt alone. In her bedroom, in her house, with her parents, even sometimes with Chase. But she'd had no idea what alone really was. A man wanted her dead. And he was here—he might be anywhere.

The sensation of someone watching sent shivers like electricity down her spine. She scrambled upright again, stumbled as she caught her foot on a limb. Finding her balance, she scanned the woods. Her pulse climbed up her neck, echoing in her throat and mouth as though to choke her. *One step at a time,* she thought. *First, breathe. Second, get to the cabin, where you can call Chase. Walk along the main roads, but keep out of view.* With her phone back in her zippered pocket, she swiped the tears off her face.

She could do this. She had to do this. Her fingers felt for the pills in her pocket. Two more. She stared at the two blue pills. So small. So powerful. She could take the last three. Drown the pain, drown herself. Maybe they would even kill her. She felt a wave of nausea and leaned down to press her hands into the cool earth, dropping her head and breathing slowly.

She didn't want to be sick. She needed the food in her stomach. That was all the fuel she had. When the nausea dissipated, she pushed herself to her feet slowly. She opened the bag and dumped the last two pills into her hand. Breathing slowly through her nose, she gathered her nerve. She had to be sober. *That man wants you dead.*

Eyes closed, she hurled the pills into the woods.

CHAPTER 38

Lily

Lily sat in the doctors' lounge with her sandwich and ate without tasting a bite. When the sandwich was gone, she looked down at the plastic wrap and thought it might have been ham and cheese. Pieces of it stuck in her teeth, and she tried to suck them free. Fifteen minutes until her shift. She folded her arms on the desk and lowered her head. *Rest for five. But not sleep. Don't fall asleep.*

The security footage replayed in her mind. The uninterested expression on her face as she'd walked toward the car and vanished from the camera's view. Then she imagined the tightening of her brow and thinning of her lips—the trepidation she'd felt when Hannah had carried the pink bundle closer. What if she'd known then that Hannah was her daughter? How would that have changed things?

What a strange job Noah had, sitting in that hot, closet-like space, watching other people come and go about their business. Dr. Reade coming in to work, and the man with the birthmark walking toward—where had he been going? A port-wine stain, the mark was called. Another birthmark came to her—not a port-wine stain but a raised cluster of blood vessels on the skin. Dotted like the petechiae on Stephanie Krueger's torso. The shape was like a hand, the fingers closed. She imagined a thin thigh, dark hair, and that birthmark. In a rush that felt dizzying, she was on her back, the room blurry and spinning. Dark hair, blood. Then, if she lowered her eyes, the thigh and the mark. The air was tinged with the scents of campfire and brown liquor. Her throat burned from it, that and the pills Hudson had put in her drink, the bitter taste she'd only noticed once she'd swallowed. On her back in that strange place that smelled of wet wool and chemicals . . . and also something else. Something warm.

Memories from her rape.

She sat upright and scanned the space, confirming that she was still alone. Pressing her palms flat to her eyelids, she searched the dark place beneath them. Where was his face? What did he look like? Blood on his cheek and hair over his other eye were like place markers. She knew they were there, but they lacked clarity and detail. His left eye was visible above the trail of blood. There was something familiar.

A face flitted across her vision and vanished. The food heavy in her stomach, she checked her watch. Six minutes until the start of her shift. The face was gone. Even with her eyes closed, she couldn't draw the memory out. Her heart pounded with a dull, heavy thumping. A sound from behind startled her. Charles Visser at the door. When he saw her, he stepped back, startled, as though he had walked into the wrong room.

Lily rose slowly. Her thoughts were like a jumble of wires, crossed and twisted, sparking in one direction and then another. She held on to the table as she stood. "You're not working tonight. Dr. Reade is on call."

"He requested the night off, so I came in." Visser scanned her face. "Are you all right?"

She shook her head, and he approached, one hand out as though to catch her. Had he ever touched her? They had stood shoulder to shoulder, but his hand? She stepped away. "Hannah," she whispered.

Visser halted. "What's happened?"

Lily clawed at the tightness in her chest.

"What's wrong? What's happened to Hannah?" He spun to the door. "Is she here?"

"No."

He studied her, searched her face. "What are you saying?"

I gave birth to her. I carried her. I was raped. I was drugged. "She's mine."

Visser shook his head. "What's yours? Dear God, Lily, what are you talking about?"

"You raised my daughter," Lily said.

Visser stepped toward her, and Lily backed away. "Are you sick, Lily? Do you feel febrile?"

A fever? She shook her head. "She's my daughter, Charles."

"What is going on?" He spun toward the door. "Is that meant to be a joke? A sick joke? She's missing. She may be injured, and you want to tell me—"

The door swung open, and Kylie Milliard barged in, breathless. The detective eyed them both as Visser came at her. "What's happened to Hannah? Where is she?"

Kylie shook her head. "I don't have any news. She was seen by a ranger down by Elkhorn Ranch."

Something crossed his face.

"Why would she be there? Where would she be going?" Kylie asked, but Lily pushed toward the detective.

"Tell him, Kylie. Tell him about the DNA."

A shake of her head. "Lily, you should go home. Let me do this."

Lily stood her ground. "I'm not leaving." She glanced at her watch. "My shift starts in two minutes."

"No," Visser said with alarm. "Take the night off." He drew out his phone and started texting.

"You have to tell him," Lily said again.

"I think she's ill," Visser said.

He'd barely returned the phone to his pocket when a nurse cracked the door. "We can stay, Dr. Visser," the nurse said. "How long?"

"A half hour, maybe forty-five minutes?" he said, a hitch in his voice that spoke to his desperation. "I need to call in another nurse."

"No," Lily said. "I'm fine."

The nurse scanned their faces—the detective's, Lily's—and nodded. Did the nurse suspect that something had happened with Hannah?

"Please," Visser said, the word coming through a locked jaw.

"Of course," the nurse said and, after a last look at the three of them, left.

"Detective," Visser said. "Let's go talk in my office."

"I'm coming," Lily said.

Visser shook his head. "This has nothing to do with—"

"Let her come," Kylie said. "Let's go, and I'll explain."

Visser hesitated, realizing that something was very wrong. One hand pressed to his stomach, he led them from the room.

"Let *me* explain," Kylie whispered to Lily before the two women followed him.

At the entrance to his office, Visser let the women pass, motioning to the chairs across the desk before closing the door behind them. The doctor settled in his chair, though he remained upright and stiff. He shifted his torso to face Kylie. "What is going on? Where is Hannah?"

"I don't have any news on Hannah since she was seen yesterday morning at a trailhead near Elkhorn Ranch."

"Elkhorn Ranch?" Visser repeated.

"Do you know where she's going?"

Visser said nothing, and Lily studied him. Why would Hannah be running away? Had he done something to her daughter? Lily found it almost impossible to sit still. As though anticipating that Lily was growing impatient, the detective put a finger out to stop her from interrupting.

"Elkhorn's on the way to Molva," Kylie said.

"I know . . ." Visser paused. "That's where Priscilla's family is from, and she—Priscilla, I mean—used to go all the time. I took Hannah to their family's fishing cabin a few times before I bought the place up by Knife River. There's no one in Molva now. Priscilla's sister is in Montana, and both of her brothers are dead."

"Would Hannah think there was someone down there? Can you think of any reason she would go there?"

"I can't imagine that she'd remember those trips; it was so long ago." Visser looked at Lily, and she leaned forward, refusing to be shut out of this conversation.

"Kylie," Lily said.

Visser glanced at her, then back to Kylie. "Lily said something about Hannah, about . . ." *About her being my daughter,* Lily thought. But he didn't speak the words out loud.

Here, Kylie closed her eyes momentarily as though what she was about to say was excruciating. What about when she had told Lily that she was a mother? That she'd had a baby with her rapist? A baby she didn't remember? Had never met? Had Kylie felt pain then? Lily caught herself. Of course she had. This was not easy for Kylie either.

Kylie nodded at Lily as though sensing her growing angst. "We sent Hannah's DNA to the state lab. We'd found blood at the crime scene—at the Garzas' house. It came back as a familial match to someone already in our system."

"Blood at the scene?" Visser repeated with alarm.

"Just a small amount, but the DNA matched the female offspring of a victim in the database."

Visser's gaze shifted to Lily.

"Your wife confirmed that Hannah was adopted."

"She was *not* adopted!" Visser pounded the desk, and the floor shook beneath her chair. He launched to his feet. "No. I did the ultrasound myself. I confirmed the pregnancy. She's my daughter."

Lily waited for Kylie to apologize, to take a step back, but instead the detective pressed forward. "Earlier today, Priscilla confessed that she lost that pregnancy shortly after the ultrasound you did. She went to be with her sister in Molva. Told you she was seeing a doctor in Billings."

"That was real," Visser said, his voice only slightly softer. "Hannah is our child."

"Actually," Kylie said, the words soft but firm, "she's Lily Baker's daughter."

Again Visser glanced at Lily, then around the room, as though the answer might be written on the walls. "It's impossible." But the words fell flat; doubt shone in his eyes.

Lily studied his face. "You really didn't know?"

Visser's jaw clenched twice in quick succession, the muscle twitching under the skin. A quick shake of his head. He lowered himself to the chair, his entire frame seeming to deflate. "Priscilla wouldn't let me have anything to do with the pregnancy after that initial ultrasound," he said. "She'd had four miscarriages after Chase and thought she was cursed. Or that I was cursed. Or maybe she blamed the hospital.

"She stayed in Molva most of the pregnancy." He was quiet a moment before continuing. "She said she felt good, but she rarely shared anything about it—certainly she never let me get close to her. She acted like it was superstition—journaling everything she ate, how much weight she'd gained. She was completely devoted." His gaze flitted toward Lily, but he didn't meet her eye. Like he couldn't. "Priscilla can be manipulative, but that kind of deception . . ." He reached across the desk, but his hand paused in midair, and he inspected its surface. "Where's the picture of her?" He stared at Lily. "Where's the picture of Hannah?"

Lily sat back, startled by the anger in his voice. "I didn't touch it."

"Dr. Visser, there's a picture right there," Kylie said, pointing to the family image on the corner of the desk.

"No. The other one." He patted the wood surface. "It was right here." He ducked his head to check under the desk, then crossed to the bookshelf. After a moment of shuffling, he pulled something from behind a book. "This is the frame." He started shifting the books onto their sides, moving them around. "Where is it?"

Then Lily remembered. "Green."

Visser spun to face her. "Yes. She was wearing a green dress."

"I think Dr. Reade had it," she said, remembering the footage. "He was in here on Sunday night."

"I worked Sunday," Visser said.

"I know, but Reade came in."

"You saw him in here? In my office?"

Lily shook her head. "I saw the security footage. Noah showed me."

"Footage?" Kylie repeated.

Heat traveled to her cheeks. "I wanted to see Hannah up close. To see if she looked like—"

"Hannah wasn't here on Sunday."

Lily thought about the Garzas' baby, the pink bundle. Visser didn't know that Hannah had brought her.

The detective was suddenly upright, wildly alert. "What was Reade doing here? What did you see?"

"He came into the department," Lily said, trying to understand the detective's distress. "He was wearing jeans, carrying a duffel bag. He walked into this office and came out with something that he put in his bag. It was about the size of a photograph, and I saw a flash of green."

"Reade? Why would Reade take a picture of Hannah?" Visser asked.

"Lily," Kylie said, the word short, tight. "Are you sure it was Dr. Reade?"

"It's on the video. He was in here; then he left. He paused outside the door, right at the entrance to bay four." Bay four. The whitish blob on the floor. She gasped. "He stopped right where I found the piece of brain."

"Brain?" Visser asked. "What brain?"

The pieces seemed to be falling together, but Lily had no idea what the puzzle was. Only that it included her daughter and maybe Bruce Reade . . .

Kylie took hold of her arm, halting her. "Where did you see this? You need to show me. Take me there now."

Lily was barely up from her chair before the detective was out the door.

CHAPTER 39

Kylie

Kylie followed Lily down the hall, phone to her ear. Lily had just shared the news that Reade was supposed to be at work tonight, but he'd requested the night off. But surely Reade wasn't a killer. Why would he want the Garzas dead? Bruce Reade hadn't come up in their research into the Garzas at all. They were almost out of the department when a pager went off in the ED and Visser was called to assist. A tractor accident. "You two go on. I'll try to catch up when I can." He hesitated then and touched Lily's arm, as if he was extending some kind of olive branch. "Please let me know if you find Hannah."

"Of course," Lily said, and the two women left. Lily led them through the waiting room en route to the security office.

The phone rang again in Kylie's ear. "Come on," she whispered.

Another ring, then the coroner's voice. "Horchow."

Kylie quickly explained what she'd learned from Lily about the tissue on the hospital floor.

"I saw it," Horchow said. "It's brain tissue."

"Human?"

"I'd guess so, but no way to be sure without a microscope. Not really my area of expertise."

"Any way to match it to Garza?" she asked, knowing it was a long shot.

"Not without a DNA test. But Ben Garza's the only open head wound I've seen in Hagen since the wreck last spring."

Kylie thanked him and hung up as they rounded the hospital's main desk. "What was Reade wearing?"

"Jeans and a jacket," Lily said.

"On his feet?"

"Cowboy boots."

Same as the shooter. Same as four-fifths of the men in Hagen. But why had Reade taken a picture of Hannah from Visser's office? If he'd taken it. Maybe Lily had seen it wrong. And why wasn't he at work tonight? There could be a million reasons for taking the picture, for not being at work. Well, probably not a million.

Lily stopped at the door past the hospital's front desk and knocked twice before pulling it open. "Noah."

The man in the closet-like space was young, dressed in a plaid shirt unbuttoned with a Metallica T-shirt beneath it. From the wear, it might have been vintage.

"I need to see the footage from the ED Sunday night."

Noah eyed Lily. "We already checked. We never found the girl."

"We're not looking for her. We want to see Dr. Reade," Lily explained.

Kylie displayed her badge, and Noah eyed it, then Lily. "What the hell—"

"Go to the part where Dr. Reade is in the ED. It was the third or fourth camera," Lily said, pointing to a screen on the wall. "I saw it there."

Noah grunted and started typing. Kylie texted Gilbert to send Dahl or Keckler to the hospital. She didn't mention Reade. Not yet. Crying wolf wouldn't serve anyone. And without a motive, none of it made sense. Above her head, the screens flashed black before Lily, Dr. Visser, and another woman appeared on a single screen, clustered in a hallway.

"Fast-forward?" Noah asked.

"Until we see him," Kylie said.

Several seconds passed before Bruce Reade came through the department doors, his movements jerky in fast motion. "There," Lily said, and Noah slowed the footage to normal speed.

Like Lily said, he wore a jacket, jeans, and cowboy boots and carried a black duffel. He went through one door—not Visser's office, though.

"That's the locker room," Lily said before Kylie could ask.

Reade returned a moment later, still carrying the bag, wearing the same clothes. What had he been doing in the locker room? Picking something up? Leaving something?

With a quick scan of the hallway, Reade ducked into Visser's office. He vanished from the camera's view, visible only as a shadow on one wall of Visser's office as he moved around. "Can we slow it down when he comes out?"

Noah grunted. Must have been a yes, because the playback was sluggish as Reade slipped out of Visser's office. Two steps from the door, he paused.

"That's where the brain was," Lily said, touching the screen where Reade stood. The film quality wasn't good enough to see any detail on the floor. In his left hand was something roughly five inches by seven. It might have been a picture, but Kylie saw only white.

And then his hand shifted, and the front of the item appeared. "Stop there," Kylie said.

The video halted, Reade's hand hovering above his unzipped duffel bag, a face and a green dress visible on the image in his hand.

"It's Hannah," Lily said.

"Keep playing," Kylie directed, and Reade was moving again. His hand vanished into the bag, the picture disappeared, and then he left the department. Kylie looked at Noah. "Where does he go from there?"

"No idea," Noah said.

"I saw him in another hallway," Lily said, shifting toward the screens. "On this one. In the second set of cameras."

A beat passed before Noah nodded. "Camera eleven."

Kylie had no idea what they were talking about, but a moment later Reade appeared on the same screen. "Where's he going?"

"He goes to the last door," Lily said. "It's the trash room."

At that moment, Reade pushed through the last door in the hallway.

"The trash room," Kylie repeated. "Can we see that?"

"I'll take you," Lily offered.

A second later, the screens returned to live feed, and Noah leaned over his keyboard as though they'd already left. Outside the small room, Kylie found Rich Dahl waiting.

"Gilbert sent me over," he said.

"Follow us."

As they walked, Kylie caught Dahl up on the past hour—most of it, anyway. She left out the information about Hannah Visser being Lily's daughter. For the moment, that piece felt like it belonged to a different puzzle.

Kylie scanned the hallway's linoleum floor as though she might be able to isolate Reade's boot prints on the floor. Two days had passed. There would be no evidence of him here.

At the end of the hall, Lily pushed open the door, and the three of them stepped inside. Lined along one wall were five large plastic trash bins—two blue and three gray. Alone in a corner was a red plastic can, a slit opening in the top. That bin was locked with a padlock. "This one?"

"Sharps," Lily said.

Kylie peered through the slot. "How often do we think this is emptied?"

Lily joined her to look. "No idea, but that's got to be more than a week's worth there."

Would Reade have put something in the sharps container? She pulled a glove from her back pocket and slid it onto her hand to lift the lid of one of the gray trash cans. There was almost nothing in it. "These've been emptied."

Had Reade come here to dispose of something from the Garzas' shootings? His clothes? The Taser? And now it was gone . . . she'd missed it.

On the far wall of the room, she noticed now, was a steel door. "And what's this?" She twisted the knob and pulled it open, revealing a metal chute.

"That has to be the incinerator," Lily said.

Kylie balled her free fist.

"For any bloody clothes, soiled material. Human waste on clothing . . . that kind of thing," Lily went on.

Bloody clothes. Was that why Reade had been there? Kylie stared down the dark chute. "Hold this door, Dahl, will you?"

Officer Dahl took hold of the door as Kylie used the flashlight on her phone to try to see down.

"Use this," Lily said, offering her a heavy-duty flashlight off a red plastic clip by the door.

The steel chute bent and disappeared from view. She stepped away. "Dahl, text Sullivan and Smith and tell them we need someone over here. Maybe there's still something down there. Or maybe Reade touched it. They'll want to check the sharps container, too, but my money's on the incinerator."

"On it," Dahl said, and Lily took hold of the steel door as Dahl pulled out his phone to text.

Up on her tiptoes, Kylie leaned forward into the chute, wondering if someone ever cleaned the walls of the chute. Was it possible that there was evidence still on the metal surfaces? Dried grime whose origins Kylie did not want to consider ran in hardened rivulets along the metal. She had expected to see bits of things stuck along the way, but aside from the streaks, there was little there.

Sighing, she'd turned her head to back out again when she caught sight of a wad stuck on the wall below her, an arm's length down. "Dahl, give me your camera."

"What?"

Shifting the flashlight to her left hand, she waved her fingers for him to hurry. "Your phone, the camera. I found something."

Dahl handed her his phone, and she leaned into the chute and angled the phone toward the wad. Gum. Behind her, the officer seemed to be holding his breath.

"I won't drop it."

"I know," he said defensively, though she could tell he wasn't totally confident.

Kylie took a dozen images of the gum, shifting the light and the angle of the camera. Chain of custody for evidence meant documentation. She returned the phone to Dahl, who took it happily. "There is a chance that this evidence will fall into the incinerator before the crime scene techs arrive," she announced. "So I'm collecting it now."

With her gloved hand, she reached down and pried the gum off the wall, trying to be gentle. Could they get a dental match from gum? There would be DNA, of course. She opened her palm, revealing the lump of pink bubble gum.

"Oh, that's Dubble Bubble gum," Lily said. "Can you smell it?"

Kylie didn't particularly want to smell chewed gum that had been in a chute with bloody clothes and human waste.

"Dr. Reade chews that stuff twenty-four seven," she went on. "Keeps a tub of it in the ED supply closet."

"You think Reade spit his gum into the incinerator?" Dahl asked.

"Maybe," Kylie said. "Or it might've fallen out if he was throwing things down there." Kylie pulled out her own phone and dialed Gilbert. Before he could utter a word, she said, "We need to put out an all-points bulletin on Bruce Reade." She stared at the piece of gum in the palm of her gloved hand. "I might be wrong." She hoped she was. "But I think he could be our killer."

While Gilbert processed that information, Kylie lowered the phone and said to Lily, "Can you show me what's in the locker room?" Maybe there was evidence there to prove Reade's guilt.

Or his innocence.

But she wouldn't put a bet on the latter.

CHAPTER 40

Hannah

Visible through the scattered breaks in the trees above, the sky was a deep violet as Hannah made her way along the route Darren had told her would lead to the cabin. She avoided the roads and stuck to the woods. At least there she'd be harder to find. She was coming down hard from the high, her stomach cramping painfully. Plus the nausea. Her hand kept moving to the jacket pocket as though of its own accord. Empty. She'd thrown the last pills away.

Why the hell had she done that?

She tried to imagine the high, to fill her brain with those sensations, to trick herself. But every step twisted the knife in her gut. She had to take regular breaks, bending over to compress her stomach or leaning back in an effort to stretch the pain out. Nothing worked. Now it was getting colder, too. Hannah clenched and unclenched her fists to stay warm. And alert.

Just get to the cabin. Maybe there would be something there to hold her over until . . . until what? Her father wasn't going to get her more drugs. But surely, when she told him, he'd prescribe medication to help the pain of detox, wouldn't he? He wouldn't make her suffer. Adam crossed her mind with a strange affection. If she called him, would he come down here? If she agreed to sleep with him, probably. What would he give her for sex? More pills? Or she could steal them. Had he missed the extras she'd taken?

Keep moving.

Twice she found herself at the end of a gravel street and had to backtrack. No sign of Crow Tower Road. On the third attempt, she found it. Riddled with bullet holes, the sign for Crow Tower Road hung at a forty-five-degree angle from its perch. What was left of the words read OW OWE D. No wonder she'd missed it. She was lucky there were only so many options, or she'd have been looking all night.

After the sharp right turn in the road, the cabins appeared—small, A-shaped buildings constructed of logs. Each had a square concrete porch, a shingle overhang above the front door, and two front windows, one on either side of the entry. Every one of them was shuttered, some fastened with padlocks. The fishing season ended at Labor Day, the fish having made their way to other places. Without insulation, the cabins were uninhabitable in the winter. The quiet was like a cemetery, and she shivered as she slid between two empty cabins and walked along the woods.

A thin tract of land separated the cabins from the woods, and she made her way inside the tree line, her steps quiet on the moist ground. Overhead, a sprinkling of stars dotted the sky between the high pine trees. Majestic pines. Had her dad said that?

The closer she got to the cabin, the stronger the scent of the trees. Four houses down, she spotted the familiar back porch where she and her father roasted marshmallows by a fire. The cabin was dark. Empty? She winced at the stabbing pain in her stomach. She needed help. *Get there and make your call.*

Picking up the pace, she hurried toward the cabin, breathing through the pain. She was close enough to see the paver stones, the ones she and her father had redone on one of her first trips out there. The two had worked to find the best pattern for the stones, covering the most area with the fewest stones.

"It's math," her father had said.

"I hate math," she had replied.

"You shouldn't hate it, Hannah. You're good at math."

She'd basked in his approval. Her mother's had always felt mercurial, attaining it a fluke of the right outfit, the right words. But her father's affection had been consistent, if not effusive. He was on her side. She'd always felt that way. Until this past summer, when he'd left her. She recalled that day with the paver stones, the way they had worked together, the surprising realization that she *was* good at math. It must have been third or fourth grade.

She was no longer good at math. Or anything. And she couldn't remember the last time they'd had that kind of conversation. A conversation about something real, not simply to relay information. *Dinner is there. Mom said this.* How she longed for him to stop and talk to her. Most kids her age wanted to be ignored by their parents. She wanted to be seen by hers.

The cabin was dark as she approached. Of course it was dark. It was good that it was dark. And yet the darkness brought on a new terror. Somewhere in her mind, she'd had the thought that someone would be there, that once she arrived, she would no longer be alone.

The darkness of the cabin repelled her. To give herself time to build her courage, she eased into the trees and crouched in the shadows, imagining the open field where her father had tried to teach her to cast. She could feel her father's hands on hers, the arc of their motion as they drew the fly rod back, then cast it forward. Farther down the hill was the place where her father would cast for hours, his arm a rhythmic flow, the line dancing through the air like a dragonfly.

It was time to go inside the cabin. Call home. She retraced her path and cleared the trees. As she approached, the moon reflected on the sliding door, creating strange angles in the glass. Was the door open? Or was it an optical illusion? She recalled how her father used to crack the door to let the breeze in while he was working in the kitchen or reading in the living room. Cautiously, she moved closer, drawn by the need to end the pain, the loneliness.

She reached the firepit, where leaves had collected in their absence. Moving slowly, she climbed the steps and felt the weight of exhaustion. She imagined the tight room in the back of the cabin, the stall shower. It felt like being home. Or what being home used to mean.

As she stepped through the open door, something crunched under her foot. Her eye caught the reflection of light on the tiny pieces of crystal there. She lowered herself and grabbed for one, yelping as it cut through the skin on her finger. A thin trail of blood trickled toward her palm. She brought her hand to her mouth and pressed the wound to her tongue.

Why was there glass? And then she saw. The coffee table was broken. One of the chairs was on its side and shoved into the middle of the room. The place was torn apart. The groan of weight on the old floor traveled from somewhere else in the house. Was someone there?

Hannah ducked behind the couch, feeling deep grooves along the back. It was like something with claws had taken them to this couch. Suddenly she imagined the killer not as a man but as some sort of beast, like Wolverine, with long metal knives sliding from man-like hands. What had she been thinking, coming here? How had she been so stupid? The cabin wasn't safe. Her father wasn't here. A thump echoed from the bedroom. Hannah measured the distance from the couch to the door. She had to run.

The crunching of boots on glass grew closer, and the dim light in the hallway flickered on. *Go. Go.* She leaped up and ran, tripping on the threshold and catching herself with a thunderous bump. Tears burned her eyes as she jumped down the four stairs and raced toward the woods. Once she was in the trees, the moon vanished, the high pine trees cutting off the light. Though she hadn't been here in years, her body knew this land.

"Hannah!" the killer shouted as she slipped on the soft ground, landing on her side. She clawed at it, the wet earth tearing the skin under her nails as she righted herself.

"Hannah!" Her name was like a roar, and she longed to cover her ears. But she kept running.

From somewhere near the house came a high-pitched squeal, like a child's scream. She grabbed hold of a tree and used it as cover, glancing back at the dull glow of the house. A shape scurried on the ground, a large cat or a small dog, maybe. A gun exploded in the darkness. The animal shrieked, its beady eyes glowing in the dark. A raccoon. Another shot was followed by a piercing squeal as the animal lunged, then dropped to the ground, one leg pedaling in a frenzied circle.

Hannah was still watching the animal suffer in the darkness when she heard the crunch. A boot on twigs and leaves. She stepped away from the tree, keeping it between herself and the house for as long as she could, before spinning and sprinting deeper into the woods.

"Come back here, Hannah!" the man shouted.

She continued in the direction she swore would bring her to the creek. It felt like she should have been there already. Suddenly, the hill grew steep and the terrain was foreign. From the cabin, she'd always come through the trees and across the pasture to the second forest. But that pasture was nowhere to be seen now. She paused a moment, scanning the darkness, listening for the sound of water. The undergrowth was thicker here. Gone were the twigs and leaves, and she could no longer hear the killer behind her. But he was there. She was sure of it. Her pulse was its own living thing, drumming its terror in her ears. She wasn't sure where she was.

Light exploded on the horizon, and she blinked at the brightness. She stumbled backward and spun away, up a short hill. She made it only six or seven paces before she stepped into thin air. For several seconds, there was nothing below her. She imagined falling off a cliff, hitting rocks. Instead, she landed on an awkward slope with a thud, twisting her knee. Her breath was knocked from her chest as she tumbled down the hill, landing a few feet uphill from a pile of downed logs.

Above her, the cabin and the killer were gone from view.

"Hannah?" His voice was a whisper, still far away. He must have returned to the house for something. Then she saw the light.

As she tried to decide what to do, the light crept steadily closer up the hill. She could hear the distant hiss and pop of the fire. A torch.

She got to her feet, right knee tender. The glow from his torch cast sufficient light to illuminate the creek in the distance as she calculated the growing brightness of the light and the time it would take to reach the creek, which was still ten or fifteen feet away. She'd have to cross it and get through the open land on the other side before she could find cover again. She imagined the blast of that gun, the animal's pained shrieking.

It was too far.

She scrambled down to the pile of trees and climbed over the first trunk, then under the second. There was a gap large enough to hide in, but he would find her here. Surely. As she ducked into the dark cavern created by the upturned roots of two giant trees, she had an idea. She palmed the ground, searching for a rock. But the ground was only twigs and soft plants. Stooping to one knee, she yanked her right shoe off her heel, then rose to stand between the logs.

Behind her, the light glowed past the crest of the hill above.

She studied the creek, the shoe in her hand. It had to reach the water. It was her only chance to send him in the wrong direction.

With a deep breath, she hurled the shoe toward the creek, then ducked down between the fallen trees.

A moment later, she heard a splash. Hugging herself in a tight ball, she held her breath and prayed.

CHAPTER 41

Lily

When they returned to the ED, Visser was in one of the bays, attending to a patient, and Alice was at the desk. At the sight of Lily, she stood quickly, suddenly awkward. "Dr. Visser said you weren't well. That's why I came in."

"She's going home," Kylie said. "She's just helping me for a few more minutes."

The idea of going home to that empty house settled like wet sand in her limbs. For two nights, Lily had barely slept. She needed the rest but was afraid of what sleep would bring. What nightmares would come to her. But they weren't nightmares. Worse, they were memories that had started to break through her walls. What had triggered their onset? Memories of the rape had always been more dreamscape than reality.

Were the new memories somehow attached to the arrival of Hannah with the Garzas' baby? Had something in her subconscious connected Lily to Hannah Visser? But she'd seen the girl before. She and Iver had been to the Vissers' house for the hospital's annual picnic in June, and no memories had surfaced then.

Or was it the infant that had beckoned the old memories? Had the sensation of a tiny baby in her arms triggered memories of her own pregnancy and the event that had caused it?

"Lily." Kylie's voice, a hand on her arm, dragged her from the thoughts. "Are you okay?"

Lily nodded, less as a real answer than as an instinctive response. "Fine." An outright lie.

Officer Dahl stood behind Kylie, studying Lily with a look of suspicion. Lily averted her eyes from his gaze.

"I need to see Bruce Reade's locker," Kylie said. "Are you up for showing me?"

"Of course." Relieved to have a task, Lily led them to the locker room and knocked loudly on the door. The space was small and coed, and it was custom to offer a warning when entering. But there had been no hesitation or knock from Bruce Reade when he'd entered this space in the Sunday-night footage. Had he known it would be empty? It usually was. Or had he been in too big a hurry to wait?

When no one answered, Lily pushed open the door. The space was about twice the size of the security room they'd been in earlier and easily fifteen degrees cooler. The rear wall was covered by a row of old, drafty windows, overlaid with an adhesive layer that made the glass opaque for privacy. Beyond the windows was a courtyard. Down the center of the space was a row of lockers with benches on either side. Men tended to go left, the area more visible from the door. Women occupied the right side.

"Which one is his?" Kylie asked.

Lily walked along the lockers, imagining where she'd seen Dr. Reade standing the last time they were in that room together. She paused in front of a cluster of three. "It has to be one of these." None were locked. It was rare to see a padlock on any of the lockers. People rarely stored anything of value there—a change of clothes, maybe a hairbrush and some deodorant. Lily opened the first one and scanned the empty interior. Then the next, also empty. The third try was a win. Hanging on the metal interior hook was a white jacket with blue script stitching that read *Bruce Colin Reade, MD.*

Kylie pulled on a fresh set of gloves, her face unreadable as she removed the medical coat, patted the pockets, and set it on the bench behind her. Next a button-down on another hook and finally a pair of tennis shoes. These she drew out, one in each hand, and flipped them over. She turned to the officer. "Look."

Dahl moved forward to inspect the worn tread on Reade's running shoes.

The shoes were old but clean. Nothing in the tread—no blood or brain tissue—that Lily could see. "What is it?"

"Supination," Dahl said.

"I need a bag for these," Kylie said.

"I'll get one," Dahl said and left the room.

Lily was still staring at the shoes, which Kylie had set on the bench beside the shirt and coat. Her attention on the locker, the detective was shining her phone light into the metal box. Maybe searching for some additional evidence.

"Supination?"

Dahl returned before Kylie could answer. "Sullivan's on his way, and he's in touch with the janitor about the trash room."

"Bag this stuff up."

Dahl went to work as Kylie addressed Lily. "We have to go. Will you be okay?"

Lily considered offering to come along. She wanted to follow the case until Hannah was found. She didn't want to be alone.

"I'll check in later," Kylie said. Dahl was already heading for the door.

Lily grabbed hold of her sleeve. "You'll let me know? As soon as you hear any news?" She forced her fingers to unclench the fabric. "About Hannah, I mean."

"I promise," Kylie said.

When they were gone, Lily sank onto the bench and stared up at Bruce Reade's empty locker. There was no reason to stay here now. But she dreaded going home to wait for . . . what? For the police to find her daughter so that she could introduce herself? "Hi, I'm actually your mother." And what did she expect of a fourteen-year-old? What did she want from Hannah Visser? It was much too late to step in and mother her.

The fact that she had a daughter was only a sliver of what Lily had to process. She'd been raped, had given birth. It wasn't as though injecting Hannah into her life was going to make all that go away. And she knew better than most that pushing things into the recesses of the mind wasn't an effective tactic either.

Her back and legs stiff, Lily collected her things and walked past the nurses' station, grateful that the corridor was momentarily empty. Exactly like Bruce Reade had found it on Sunday night. Only minutes after she had been outside with Hannah. Ironic that the person Reade had been hunting had been so close. What if Lily hadn't gone out for a break? Would Reade have been the one to find Hannah and the baby?

Lily walked into the cool air and stared at the place where Hannah had been parked. Hannah here and Bruce Reade inside. The fact that those two things had happened simultaneously felt wrong, but her brain couldn't quite make the connection.

She felt drunk from the nights without sleep, the emotional exertion of the past two days leaving her discombobulated. It was impressive that she was still upright.

But not for long.

Go home. Eat peanut butter toast or cereal with milk. Sleep. She had turned the key in the ignition and was leaning across to pull her phone from her purse when there was a tapping on her driver's-side window. She jumped at the noise, spinning to see the window was blocked by a shape. Its silhouette was dark and shadowy. She shrieked, jerking away from the window.

As the object outside the window shifted, she saw what it was. Flowers. White flowers. And behind them was Iver.

He smiled at her and tried to open the door. “It’s locked.”

It took her a moment to find the button to unlock it.

He pulled open the door and knelt beside her. “I’m sorry,” he said. “I didn’t mean to scare you.” He leaned in and kissed her head.

As his fingers touched her cheek, she covered her face and sobbed.

CHAPTER 42

KYLIE

Kylie sat at the conference table with Davis and Dahl, brainstorming next steps. They knew everything she did now—the DNA match between Lily Baker and Hannah Visser, her meetings with Dr. Visser and Priscilla, the video of Reade in Visser's office, the gum evidence in the trash room, and the supination evident from Bruce Reade's tennis shoes. They'd contacted the departments within a hundred miles of Elkhorn Ranch, and Kylie had been trying to reach the Molva department herself. She'd left two voicemails but had no response. The APB was out. If they had news, they would have called. Wouldn't they? She thought about driving down there herself. Four hours there and back. What if it was a wild-goose chase? Those weren't hours she could afford to lose.

Smith was collecting evidence at the hospital; Sullivan was in the bullpen at his desk, making phone calls to Chicago in hopes of learning something helpful about Reade; and Keckler and Gilbert were out checking every location in Hagen where Bruce Reade had ever been seen. No answer at his house. No sign of his car, and his phone went to voicemail. Smith had already submitted a request to the cellular provider for his records, but the soonest they'd see that would be tomorrow. If they were lucky.

If Hannah was lucky.

The conference room door opened, and Sullivan stood in the doorway, holding his laptop. He looked tired. She didn't even know what time it was.

"Got something on Reade," he said. "Or it might be something."

Davis waved him in, and Sullivan sat in the closest chair. Without preamble, he started in. "Reade's wife is the youngest daughter of Max Lotari. Lotari's originally from New York, been in Chicago about twenty years. Runs a distribution business—mostly high-end bathroom and plumbing fixtures."

Kylie tried to imagine what toilets had to do with anything.

"The business has three times been the target of federal investigations into drug smuggling—pharmaceuticals, almost exclusively. The FBI's been watching him for money laundering for over a decade."

"This is Reade's father-in-law?"

"Right."

"We have anything to connect Reade to the drug business?"

"Not a thing," Sullivan said.

Kylie blew out a breath. Adam Blaney had been at the Garzas' that night. Blaney had said the drugs he sold came from Michigan or Illinois. Was it possible that the person Blaney sold drugs for was Reade's father-in-law? But what did that have to do with Nadine and Ben Garza? Blaney said he'd never gone into the house. He'd dropped Hannah and left. Had he been lying?

"Anything else?" Davis asked.

"Some news about Reade's time in Chicago. He spent five years at a hospital in the city and was served with a malpractice suit the year before he left. During the five years he was there, there were almost a dozen complaints registered with the hospital board."

"Drug related?" Kylie asked.

"I don't know. I've been in touch with an ex-ED doc who worked with Reade, but she didn't have all the details. She referred me to Reade's ex-wife, who lives in upstate New York now. I'm trying to reach her."

Kylie didn't know Reade had been married before. But nothing about that fact was a helpful lead.

"We know what happened in the malpractice suit?" Davis asked.

"No details," Sullivan said. "Patient died. Suit was brought the next month. Three months later, the whole thing vanished—complainants dropped the charges; hospital cleared Reade of any wrongdoing. Four months after that, Reade interviewed with Visser for the position here. That was three years ago. And according to our hospital HR, Reade's record was squeaky clean when they checked his references. I'll keep digging."

Kylie thought about Adam Blaney. She couldn't see how his selling drugs by the baggie could get Nadine and Ben killed. "I'll—" She covered her mouth and tried unsuccessfully to stifle a yawn.

Davis pointed at her. "You need to get some sleep."

"I—"

"If we hear anything on Reade, we'll call." Davis rose from the table, and Kylie didn't argue.

It was almost midnight, and her limbs felt unnaturally heavy. She couldn't remember the last time she'd eaten—had she eaten? She thought about the diner, wondered how Amber was. They rarely went more than a few days without seeing each other. Kylie could hear Amber telling her she looked like shit. "When was the last time you ate anything with protein? And water? Are you drinking water? You look like dried death."

The sound of Amber's voice—even inside her head—brought Kylie comfort as she drove home to her quiet house. She stopped in the kitchen long enough to grab a handful of Triscuits and a string cheese—a snack she'd started eating while living with a toddler. Kylie ate as she undressed, then drank down two large glasses of water, brushed her teeth, and climbed into bed.

She couldn't imagine falling asleep. She plugged her phone into the outlet and tucked it under her pillow. Kylie thought back over the day—the call from the ranger, the conversation with Priscilla Visser, Lily at the hospital, the evidence that had led them to Bruce Reade. If only they'd found it a day earlier. Reade had been in the ED for his previous shift, but he'd called for a replacement tonight. Why?

Had he realized he was close to being caught? But how could he? It was a fluke that Lily had seen the footage from the hospital. She closed her eyes and reminded herself that she needed whatever sleep she could get. The right steps were in place. A three-state alert for highway patrol and TSA personnel had been issued for Reade. She'd cast the net as wide as she could.

Now she hoped that Bruce Reade stepped in it.

Before he found Hannah Visser.

CHAPTER 43

Hannah

The glow of the torch cast shadows all around her. The hiss and crack of the fire from its lit end felt close enough to burn her skin. Something tickled her ear. Hannah reached up and felt a moving creature. Swallowed a scream and flicked the bug off her skin. Her hand struck a log with a thud. She held her breath, feeling an army of invisible insects crawl over her. Spiders. Probably venomous ones. She remembered her father warning her about black widows, how they liked dark, damp spaces.

The killer passed the cluster of logs, heading toward the water's edge, swinging the torch as he scanned the area. He breathed in heavy grunts as he moved. From her hiding place, she took tiny sips of air. A broken limb dug into the small of her back. Another branch into her thigh.

Something slid down her neck. Clenching her mouth closed, she tried to flick it off. But it was thick and moist, its epicenter painful. Blood, a cut.

At the river, the killer paused before stooping down and lifting her single Converse from the water. He held it up to the light, then stood upright and peered into the darkness on the other side of the creek. Dropping the shoe, he waded across.

Her chest swelled as he moved away from her. The shoe had worked. But the joy was short lived. Halfway across, he stopped and stared back.

His gaze seemed to land directly on her hiding spot. His head swiveled as he peered across the river, then toward the place where she hid, some calculation happening in his brain.

And then he started toward her again. His steps were slow, deliberate, as he scanned the landscape. The torch cast a gruesome light on his face. His open mouth, his eyes like black holes, while his cheeks and forehead looked lit from within by the flames.

He turned his back to her, and she sipped another breath. Her stomach tensed, a shooting pain ripping through her gut. She fingered her belly, expecting to find a wound there. But the pain came from deep inside. The withdrawal from the drugs combined with hunger and thirst. She fisted her hand and pressed against the pain. The killer took another dozen steps away from her, down the slope of the river, without crossing.

Again he stopped. The torch extended, he swung it in a circle, illuminating an area of fifteen feet in every direction. Sparks escaped the torch and floated off in all directions. She watched them as they went black in midair.

When he had made a full turn, he came at her again. With purpose this time. Closing in. Forty feet and then thirty-five—he was heading for her.

She imagined herself in that tiny closet. If he'd found her then, this would all be over. Or if she'd gone to the police. To her brother. To her mother or father. They would have helped her. She would be home, safe now. Or she would be dead. Either was preferable to this—waiting for death to come get her.

She wished she'd had a chance to tell her father how much she loved him, how much she missed him. To hug her mother, to be enveloped in her stiff embrace. To smell the bouquet of her perfume and hair spray, hear the jangle of her gold bracelets as she ran her nails through Hannah's hair. Asked her when she'd last brushed it. How those things had annoyed her. But now . . .

The killer was fifteen feet away now. Closing in. Then he halted and cocked his head to one side. Like he'd heard something. Then Hannah heard it, too. A man's voice, calling out in the distance. Hope sparked inside her as the killer stepped behind a tree. He lowered the torch as though to hide the glow.

From above her on the hill came a second glow. Someone was coming. Was it someone else who wanted her dead? She imagined Nadine's face when he'd shot her. The surprise. Had it hurt? For how long?

But the killer did nothing to make himself known. Maybe it was someone who could help. Her throat burned. Her pulse seemed to beat through her stomach and against her fist.

Words rang into the night, caught and muffled by the trees. "There?"

The killer moved, his steps quick as he retreated from the tree toward the creek. The torchlight on his expression was different now. She saw fear.

When he reached the creek, the killer lowered the torch into the water. The fire was extinguished in a loud hiss. Smoke billowed around him as he stood at the edge of the water.

"Who's out there?" The voice cut through the darkness.

Hannah dug her fist under her ribs.

The killer hesitated only a moment before crossing to the far side of the river. He stepped gingerly, trying to be quiet. She watched as he receded from the growing light and her hiding place. Relief was a rush of warm water. She shifted her position away from the branches that stabbed her. But she remained in her hiding spot, watching as the killer arrived at the far side of the river and crept across the lowland. He was still visible when he reached the patch of woods on the far side. His dark form paused as he hesitated, glancing back.

The glow crested the hill, and the round beam of a flashlight cut through the trees. "Who's out here?"

The killer froze where he was.

"You see anything?" another voice called out, coming up behind the first. A second circle of light appeared.

"Not yet. Might be they took off," the first man said.

Hannah didn't move as the two lights bounced across the trees. When she scanned the woods across the creek, the killer had vanished. She studied the dark, watching for motion. Had he moved to another tree? Was he watching the men? Would he shoot them, then come for her?

Other than the sounds of footsteps coming down the hill, the woods were quiet.

She scanned the darkness for the killer, listening to the sounds of the two men approaching. The first to come into view was heavyset and breathing in noisy puffs. He held a flashlight in his left hand and a gun in his right. He had a holster around his waist and wore heavy work boots with slacks and a jacket. On top of his head was a wide-brimmed hat like the ranger wore. The darkness made it impossible to make out the details of his clothes, but she guessed he wore a uniform. Local police, probably. The man behind him moved more fluidly. Leaner and taller, he wore jeans and a heavy flannel. Work boots, too. Without a gun or holster, he didn't look like a police officer. The two men approached the creek and shone their lights across the water and into the woods where the killer had been.

"What do you think?" the lean one asked.

"Weren't a bear," the other answered. "That mess was human."

The word *bear* made her think of the marks on the couch.

"Have to come up tomorrow and board the place up. Whoever tore it apart must've been on drugs or something," the deputy said. "Ain't like the Suttons to leave it open, but Lizzie's over in Montana now, so maybe no one's watching over the place."

"Be a shame," the lean man said.

She listened as they talked about her mother's family. She'd only ever been to the cabin with her dad. She had assumed it was his place.

Would it have occurred to him to find her here? Days she'd spent trying to get to this cabin—her dad's cabin—and it didn't even belong to her dad.

Why hadn't she called her dad? Why hadn't she walked into the hospital that first night and told him? She swiped her face and pushed the thoughts away. She could step out right now, tell these men about the killer.

The deputy took his hat off and wiped his brow with the sleeve of his shirt. "Must've been the girl," he said. "If she's got half a sense, she's gone."

Hannah stiffened. Did they mean her?

"Darren sure it was the missing girl he saw in the store?" the lean man asked.

"Says he is. And the girl asked about the Suttons' cabin, so I believe it's the same girl."

The beams of their flashlights swayed left and right up the creek. Hannah felt an urge to stand up and run to them. Tell them to take her to her father. She would explain about the shooter, what she'd seen in the Garzas' house.

"How old her father say she was—fourteen?" The lean man addressed the deputy. "What the hell's she doing out here shooting raccoons?"

Hannah froze. Her father? They had to mean the killer. He had told the store clerk that he was her father. *Stand up. Tell them.* But something inside her froze.

The deputy said nothing for a moment; then he turned to the hill and shrugged. "Hell if I know. He said the drugs made her hallucinate. She was paranoid, making up stories."

Making up stories. He had told them she was a liar.

"Guess we ought to call Sam, tell him we haven't had any luck finding his kid. Imagine what that must be like, a kid taking off like that."

Sam Jones. That was what the killer had called himself in Roosevelt's. But his name wasn't Sam. It didn't feel right, and she was sure she'd known it. She knew it.

It wasn't her father they were talking about. It was the killer.

"You meet the dad?" the lean man asked.

"Nah. Hasn't been by the station," the deputy said. "Not like the girl's gonna turn up there."

Huddled in the dark, she pictured the killer's face, and suddenly she recalled where she'd seen him. He had been at her house in June, for the hospital picnic. He had the same tattoo as her father, and they'd been talking about their time in the army, Hannah barely containing her boredom. Bruce was his name, and then Hannah remembered his beautiful wife was newly pregnant with their fourth, his three little girls all in matching brightly colored dresses. Bruce Reade. And now these men were going to call him, the man who wanted her dead. Her heart pounded in her ears, so loud it seemed impossible that the two men couldn't hear it.

Would they believe her if she told them he was a killer?

"It's all those damn video games," the lean man said. "Rotting kids' brains."

"Amen," the deputy said. "Poison, those things."

And with that, Hannah tucked herself tight in a ball and waited for the men to leave.

CHAPTER 44

KYLIE

The vibrations woke her immediately. Kylie grabbed the phone from under the pillow and answered. "Milliard."

"It's Carl."

Gilbert. "You found him?"

He exhaled, and Kylie felt the air release from her own lungs. "Sorry," she said. "What's up?"

"Sullivan found Reade's other house. I'm coming from there now."

She sat up. "You're there now? You went without me."

"I thought you'd be sleeping," he said softly. "But if I'd known what that place was like, I'd have brought you. It's insane."

She didn't care what Reade's house looked like. "Did you find Reade?"

"He's not here. But his wife—his very pregnant wife—and three daughters were there. Mrs. Reade wasn't too happy that I showed up at two in the morning. They've got an early flight."

"Flight? Where are they going?"

"Chicago. That's where her family is from."

"Right." The name Max Lotari came back to her—Reade's drug-smuggling father-in-law. "You sure Reade's not with them?"

"Pretty sure," Gilbert said. "He could've been hiding somewhere, but she was convincing that she hadn't seen him. Said he left for work Monday after lunch and hadn't returned. The older girl had come out from her bedroom by then, so if that wasn't the truth, I'd have expected to hear the girl say something."

"How do you mean?"

He laughed. It was a nice-sounding laugh, and she found herself wanting to smile along with him, but instead, her muscles were clenched with anticipation. "Put it this way," he said. "They're not good liars at that age. But he might have come home after they went to bed, so I've got a Bismarck car watching the mansion."

"Mansion?" she repeated.

"I don't know what else to call it. It's got to be ten thousand square feet. Looks brand new, built right into a damn cliff. A massive barn with glass doors. Saw a restored 1972 Bronco in there through the glass doors. A beauty."

"A Ford Bronco?"

"Not just any Bronco, Kylie. This thing was a work of art. Restored like that, they go for north of a hundred K."

"How much money does a small-town ED doc make?" she asked.

"Not that much," Gilbert said.

"So he's selling drugs. Or it could be a gift from his father-in-law."

"Yeah," Gilbert agreed. "Sullivan's looking into it. I'm almost back in Hagen now. I've got unmarked cars coming from Bismarck to follow them to the airport, see if Reade shows. I've also got the Bismarck airport readied if Reade arrives. The wife has four tickets booked on an eleven fifty direct to Chicago. In her name and the girls'. No Bruce Reade, but we're watching closely."

"And if they don't end up in Bismarck?"

"Keckler's been in touch with the private airfields. Nothing on the books for Bruce Reade. But his photo is out at all the locations."

Kylie swung her feet onto the wood floor and held her head in one hand. The clock beside the bed read 2:42 a.m. Suddenly, she felt wide awake. For several moments, they sat in silence on the line. She thought of his reaction to seeing Nadine Garza, his old love, dead in her own home. She occasionally forgot that most people in Hagen had known each other from childhood. Their lives were interwoven with the threads of family and school and home. So much history. "Carl?" It felt strange to say his first name out loud.

"Yeah?" His voice was gravelly and low. He sounded exhausted.

"What if it's not him?"

"Then he'll be embarrassed but innocent."

"I'll be embarrassed," she said.

"It's a solid lead, Kylie. The shoes, the gum, the stolen picture of Hannah—it all points to Reade," Gilbert said. Then a beat passed before he said, "You should try to get some sleep."

"I don't think I can sleep."

"I feel it, too. Something's going down," Gilbert said, and Kylie felt the twist in her gut.

"But where?"

"Wherever Hannah is," Gilbert said.

Hannah was gone. Now Reade was gone, too. But he'd been in town after Hannah's disappearance. He'd worked at the hospital Monday night. If Lily had watched the footage earlier or Kylie had seen Reade's tennis shoes, they might have connected him sooner, caught him before he went—where had he gone?

"What are you thinking?"

"I'm wishing we'd caught Reade sooner," she admitted.

"That would have been nice."

After several quiet beats, Kylie said, "Do you think Reade knows where Hannah is? How could *he* know but not her family?"

Gilbert said nothing for several moments. "Her family told you that they had no idea where she might've gone?"

"Priscilla said she had no idea. And Charles—" Kylie thought back to the conversation with Charles and Lily. Had he even answered the question about why Hannah might be down near Elkhorn Ranch? He'd said it was where Priscilla's family was from, that they hadn't been there in years. "He didn't know either," she said after a pause. "If your kid was missing, you'd be able to list off a half dozen places she might be. Right?"

"If someone was trying to kill her, I'd sure as shit try," he said.

His engine noise shifted, the sounds of slowing down.

"Where are you?"

"About to turn onto Main Street."

"What are you going to do?" she asked.

"Head to the station, I guess. See what else I can dig up. Sullivan's working on Reade's past, and Smith's working through Hannah and Chase's social media accounts, searching for any spots that the family might have visited."

Kylie stood. "Places Hannah might be."

"That's the idea."

"Brew a big pot of coffee, would you? I'll be there in fifteen."

"You should sleep."

"So should you," she countered.

"I'll brew the coffee," he agreed.

CHAPTER 45

LILY

Lily Baker had fallen asleep in Iver's arms and woke sometime after midnight to the comfort of his warmth beside her. Two hours earlier, he had cooked eggs and toast, and all she could think about was the rape and the baby. Seated across from him, she'd been unable to hold his gaze. The truth felt like this barrier between them. It was Iver who urged her to talk. "What aren't you telling me?"

So much, she thought. But how to start? And then she was talking. "There was blood evidence, at the scene of the Garzas' murder."

Iver frowned but nodded at her to continue.

"The blood is a match to mine."

He had reached across the table and interlaced his fingers with hers. *I'm here,* the gesture told her. *We can weather this.* "A familial match," she continued. His brow furrowed, but he said nothing. "They can tell the relationship from the blood," she explained. "How close this person is related to me, I mean."

Iver waited, his hazel eyes steady. Cal nudged at Iver's leg, but he didn't respond, his full attention on her.

"This blood belongs to a female offspring, a child." She wanted desperately to look away, her own shame at what had happened brimming in her. "My female child."

"I don't understand."

"I have a daughter," she said. "A daughter I never knew about. And the only way that's possible is—"

Tears filled his eyes. "Derek Hudson."

"Yes. Only he's not the father. The DNA didn't match Hudson, so there must've been—" The words caught, and she had to force them from her throat. "There must've been someone else."

"Oh, Lily." She had barely blinked when he had rounded the table and pulled her into his arms. He said nothing as she cried, and then, when the tears were drained from her, he asked if there was anything he could do.

"You're doing it," she told him. "There's more . . ." There was so much more—that her daughter had been raised right here in Hagen, raised by her colleague, was now missing . . .

"Tell me," he whispered.

She glanced at the food on the table.

"Or we can eat now, and you can tell me later?" he said.

"Eat," she'd said.

Over food, she had told him about Stephanie Krueger, the teenager with meningitis, and about the night Nadine Garza had come in. About the brain she'd found and seeing her godfather.

He had questions. She could see it in the way he studied her, in the pull of his brow and the shape of his lips. But she was exhausted. Maybe they were wrong about Dr. Reade. Dozens of people had been in the hospital that night. She thought about the confrontation with Dr. Visser, the grief in his expression as he realized what his wife had done, how she'd lied. Eventually Lily stopped talking. Instead, she shifted the talk to him. She asked about his mother, longing to focus on something other than the memories and her past.

It had been Iver's mom, Cathy, who had convinced him to return to Hagen. "Go take care of our girl," she'd told him, and he had described how she'd been lucid for the first time in days, how she'd struggled to say the words, slow and slurred from the stroke. Lily was so relieved to hear that Cathy was improving, and the words . . .

Our girl.

Iver had told her that part twice. Each time brought a fresh onslaught of tears. Hearing what Iver had been through made her wish she'd gone with him. It had seemed easier at the time for him to stay with friends, to avoid the expense of a hotel, but she should have insisted. She could have taken the time off, asked for leave. She hadn't taken a sick day in years, and she had plenty of vacation.

There was so much to share that it took everything out of her. All she wanted then was to go to bed and hold him.

As they were lying together, he had asked if she wanted to talk about her daughter.

Her exhaustion felt like lead in her bones and sand in her eyes. "Tomorrow?"

He had kissed her then, and for the next little while, she had managed to let all her thoughts drift away.

In his sleep, Iver twitched beside her. Easing away, she gave him space and watched his expressions. Every emotion seemed to cross his face—from fear and anger to determination in the way he set his jaw. It was hard to watch his dreams, which she knew were memories from his time in Afghanistan, dark and haunted.

Not unlike her own dreams.

She drifted in and out of a light sleep but woke in the pitch black to the sound of her cell phone vibrating an unfamiliar two-buzz tone. The screen showed a text from the hospital system, requesting backup in the ED. Lily took the phone into the bathroom and closed the door, reading the message in its entirety. They needed an additional doc. She'd taken the night off, and now they were short staffed. She didn't want to go in. She probably shouldn't anyway. She hadn't gotten enough sleep to be effective, and the ED was not a place to take those kinds of risks. Still, she found herself calling the ED desk.

"It's Lily Baker," she said when Sandra, who was on call, answered. "What's going on in there?"

"It's actually quiet," Sandra said. "But Dr. Visser had to leave. Some family emergency out of town." She lowered her voice and added, "I heard him on the phone, and I think he said he's going to Molva. That's where his wife's family is."

The name of that town sent a wave of nausea through her. She immediately thought of Hannah. His daughter. Her daughter. "What kind of emergency?"

"I don't know. He didn't say anything to us about why he was going," she whispered. "I just happened to hear him. Dr. Anthony arrived and Visser left about ten minutes ago."

Lily thanked Sandra and ended the call. She stared at the screen, searching the depths for some memory that would unveil the missing thing in her mind. Was Visser's trip to Molva about Hannah? Was that where Hannah had run off to?

Lily opened a new text window and addressed it to Kylie.

Visser is on his way to Molva. Any connection to Garzas? She read the words again and deleted them. She wasn't a police officer. She was a nurse. But then she thought again. She had missed the chance to stop Reade and try to help Hannah. Could she take that risk again? Lily retyped the message and added a last line. Maybe I'm going crazy . . . but I'd rather say too much than not enough.

She hit send and set the phone down to splash her face with cold water. It was three o'clock in the morning, but she felt awake. She patted her face dry and picked up her phone, surprised to find it buzzing in her hand. She swiped across the screen and brought the phone to her ear. "Kylie?"

"When did you get the news about Visser?" Engine sounds and the echo of Kylie's voice made it clear that the detective was in her car.

"Where are you?" Lily asked.

"I was heading to the station, but now I'm going to Visser's. See if I can catch him before he leaves."

"What's going on?" Lily pressed.

Kylie paused only briefly before saying, "I don't know, but I need you to trust me that I'll tell you as soon as I can. Okay?"

Lily agreed because there didn't appear to be any other option. And she did trust Kylie.

"I need to know how you heard about Visser," Kylie said.

Lily explained about the text alert from the hospital and shared what Sandra had told her. "Do you think this is about Hannah?"

"Maybe," Kylie said. Then a beat later, "Probably."

"Then isn't it about me, too?" Lily asked past the sensation of something clamping tightly on her throat.

Kylie said nothing. Only the engine sounds confirmed the detective was still on the line.

"She's my daughter," Lily whispered.

Kylie exhaled. "Lily."

Lily had never heard her name spoken with so much pain. Empathy or maybe pity. But whatever it was, Lily heard it as a call to action. Almost fourteen years had passed since she had escaped, but Molva still had its hooks in her.

"I'm coming to Molva," Lily said.

"Absolutely not," Kylie said. "You can't be anywhere near this case, Lily. You know that."

But Lily wasn't listening. It was no longer a choice. "I have to come," Lily said and ended the call before Kylie could respond. She paused only a moment to decide whether or not to wake Iver. Then she headed into the bedroom.

CHAPTER 46

Kylie

Kylie wished she'd lied to Lily about Molva. The last thing she needed was to worry about Lily while she was trying to find Bruce Reade and Hannah. But she didn't have time to think about it. She dialed Gilbert, who answered his cell phone on the first ring. After she caught him up on the hospital text and her call with Lily, they made a plan to meet at the Vissers' home. "He's not living there now, so I'm not sure we'll find him," Kylie added.

"Then we'll get Priscilla to tell us where he'd be going in Molva," Gilbert said, determination in his voice. "I'm there in five."

Kylie called Marjorie at the front desk and told her to get in touch with the deputies down in Molva. "I've been trying to reach them since eight o'clock," Kylie said. "Someone has to be down in that town."

"I'm on it," Marjorie promised.

It would take two hours to drive to Molva, much of it through areas that lacked cell coverage. If Reade was already there, she needed someone to find Hannah and keep her safe.

The Vissers' grand house on Dutch Street was lit up like midday when she arrived. A new black Cherokee was parked on the curb, lights on and engine running. Kylie parked across the street and down a few houses, shutting off her car and rolling down a window. The air was cold, carrying a winter chill, though it was only October.

She listened for sounds coming from the house, but it was quiet. Something had to be going on. Who left a car running on the street in the middle of the night? Even in Hagen, which had few automobile thefts, there was no way that car had been sitting there for hours. Someone would have taken it, if only some kids for a joyride.

A few minutes later, Gilbert drove up behind her. Kylie got out of her car and winced at the chirping sound her Honda made when she armed the lock.

As she approached the patrol car, Gilbert reached across to open the door. She climbed in and closed the door as quietly as she could. Gilbert had shut off the engine and the lights. The glow of the dashboard painted his face a ghostly white. "What's going on?" he asked, motioning to the house.

"I haven't seen anything other than the car."

"That's Charles Visser's car," he said.

"You sure?"

"Positive," Gilbert said. "Chase drives a Porsche, and she drives a Lexus. I heard he bought that up in Fargo. Pissed off Smitty."

Alan Smit owned the only car dealership within fifty miles of Hagen, and he tended to price his vehicles according to what he thought folks could afford rather than by the manufacturers' recommendations. It meant people, especially people with money, often went elsewhere.

"Sullivan's gathered some additional information on Reade's father-in-law," Gilbert said.

"Max Lotari."

"That's the one. You know his legitimate business is in distribution of plumbing fixtures."

Kylie nodded.

"Sullivan got hold of a partial list of his trucking routes. He's got a lot of customers across the Dakotas. Chances are he's in Hagen, too. Or his reach is."

"But Reade is a doctor—it's not like he deals in distribution." They were quiet a moment before Kylie asked, "It's possible that Belt Construction or Visser Interiors received shipments through Lotari's company, but what does that have to do with Bruce Reade? Unless he's involved with his father-in-law's business?"

"It's possible." Gilbert paused, then added, "They did find the charred remains of a computer in the hospital incinerator."

"Nadine's?"

Gilbert shrugged, still watching the house. "We think so, but it's on its way to the lab in Bismarck to see what they can find."

Kylie noticed he kept his eye on the house when she mentioned Nadine. She wondered how he was doing but didn't dare bring it up. Kylie felt like there was some piece they'd overlooked, but she had no idea what it was.

Gilbert reached behind his seat and brought up a large green-gray thermos. It was heavily dented with areas of rust, well loved. "There's coffee here if you need it."

She was about to take him up on the offer when the front door of the Vissers' house opened. Shouting filled the air. "I said no!" Dr. Visser sailed out the door. In his hand was something approximately the size of a book but triangular in shape. The pattern made her think it was a scarf folded up, but she couldn't make sense of it.

Mrs. Visser ran out the front door in a long white nightgown. "You will wait for me, or I swear . . . !"

He spun to face her. "Swear what, Priscilla? That you'll take me for everything I have?" He waved at the house. "Do it. File for divorce already. I don't care about any of it."

Gilbert glanced at Kylie, who cringed.

"Charles!" Priscilla shrieked the name, ducking back into the house.

Dr. Visser strode to the car, and as he came around to the driver's-side door, Kylie got a better glimpse at the object in his hand. "It's a gun case."

Gilbert nodded. "Revolver, probably."

Visser held the padded zipper pouch to his chest as he opened the car door. He was sliding into the car when Priscilla Visser bolted from the house. A long coat pulled hastily over her nightgown and a pair of tennis shoes gripped in her hand, she sprinted barefoot down the walkway.

Seeing her coming, Charles Visser revved the engine and started to drive away. But Priscilla launched herself in front of the car. "I'm coming with you!"

Charles blared the horn and reversed the car.

Priscilla followed, staying close to the bumper of the car. "Let me in."

Kylie held her breath. For a moment, she expected Visser to charge forward and knock her down. Instead, he honked and yelled, "Hurry up."

Priscilla hesitated a moment as though it had just occurred to her that he might run her over.

Charles honked again. "Hurry up, for God's sake!"

Keeping her hands on the vehicle, she made her way to the passenger side and opened the door with a hard yank on the handle. Before her door was even closed, Visser sped off.

Gilbert waited a beat and started his engine. Then he made a U-turn in the quiet street and followed.

"Guess we're going to Molva," Kylie said, buckling her seat belt.

"Looks that way." He motioned to the thermos of coffee on the console between them. "May need to pour some of that."

Kylie opened the thermos and poured hot black coffee into the mug in the cup holder.

"There's another mug on the floor back there," he said. "Clean, if you want some, too."

Gilbert made a right turn onto Highway 1804, the red taillights of Charles Visser's car visible on the road in front of them.

Kylie reached back and found a white mug that said *10-4 Coffee That*. The first time she'd pulled that one out of the department cupboard, she'd laughed. But she couldn't find the humor now. What she felt was the same sensation she'd had that January day when she'd driven to meet a deputy in Glendive, Montana, to see the murder site of one of the women held captive by Derek Hudson.

It was fear.

Kylie poured herself some coffee and watched Visser's glowing taillights. She pictured Priscilla Visser in her white nightgown running down the walkway, her thin form visible as the fabric blew against her in the cold night air. A far cry from the way she'd looked at the police station—buttoned up, in control. Then she thought about Chase. How his mother had shut him out of the conversation about Hannah's adoption.

Chase Visser hadn't seemed keen to leave his mother's side. So where the hell was he now? While his parents were racing toward Molva, was he at home, fast asleep? Or was he already on the way to Molva too? Perhaps even ahead of them?

Kylie texted Marjorie to send a patrol car out to Chase's residence. But she had a feeling there wouldn't be anyone home.

CHAPTER 47

Hannah

Hannah woke in the dark with a rush of adrenaline and an overwhelming need to vomit. Disoriented, she scrambled upright and slammed her head into a tree trunk. Crying out, she turned her head to the ground and emptied the meager contents of her stomach. Then she remembered earlier that night—the killer, the men at the creek, her hiding place. She covered her mouth, bile sour on her tongue. Had she given herself away? Was anyone out there?

Her pulse was a painful throb in her skull that barely distracted her from the pain in her belly. Her back ached, and her feet were asleep, but she didn't dare make any noise. Bathed in sweat, she was freezing cold and trembling. Soon she'd be in full withdrawal. Her heavy eyelids tugged her toward sleep. She longed to drift back, to wake when this was all over. But she didn't dare.

Shifting carefully, she listened for sounds. All she heard was the gurgling of the creek and the wind that made the trees groan like old bones. Nothing human.

The sky was still dark, and without her phone, she couldn't tell if she'd been asleep for hours or only minutes. She rubbed her head, feeling the tacky sensation of blood and a rising bump. A painful electricity flowed into her feet as she moved them. She couldn't stay there. In daytime, she'd be visible, and she had no idea how soon daybreak would come.

Moving stiffly, she climbed out of her hiding place and scanned the area. With only one shoe, she crept along the uneven ground, avoiding the spiny pine cones that littered the area. At the creek, she searched for her shoe and found it on the far side of the water. She removed the other shoe to keep it dry and crossed the stream. The water flowed across her feet, which ached in the cold. The sharp rocks were painful on her stockinged feet, and her stomach twisted with every motion. She drew slow breaths and kept walking.

She made it to the far side and sat on the riverbank to check the soles of her feet for cuts. She retrieved her shoe and stared down at the river. Her mouth was painfully dry, and it hurt to swallow. "Never drink the river water," her father had always told her. But the need was too great. Lowering herself, she scooped water to her mouth. She drank until her stomach felt full, splashed her face to wake herself, then crossed the river again.

Seated again, she discarded her socks and pulled on her Converse, the canvas hard against her bare, wet feet. Through the woods to the east, darkness leached from the inky sky. It would be morning soon. And then what? Where would she go now? Where was the killer?

The landline at the cabin still seemed her best bet. She would call Chase's cell phone, one of only two numbers she knew by heart. The other was her home phone. But she wasn't going to call home. She would call Chase, and when he arrived, they would call the police.

She considered what she would do between the time she reached him on the phone and when he could get here. It would be hours. She could go back to that diner, sit in broad daylight. If the killer came in, she'd tell everyone what she had seen him do. Would they believe her? The fear that he would tell lies about her, that people might believe them, gripped her. She would tell them every detail. She would talk until Chase arrived.

In her coat pocket, she felt the absence of the pills, her fingers still hunting for them. Her mind longed for that escape. But it was better that they were gone. Despite the sweats and stomach pains, she was alert. That mattered more than the relief they had brought.

Pushing cold hands into the jacket's pockets, she started up the hill toward the cabin. Even in the frigid air, she was sweating. Halfway up the hill, she paused to catch her breath, though she'd walked no more than thirty yards. The trees were thick around her, and the feeling that she was being watched pressed down like a weight. Her gaze swept her surroundings, half-focused to sense movement. There was only the gentle sway of branches high above her head.

Would the killer be waiting for her in the cabin? Or had the appearance of those two men scared him away? What choice did she have? She had to go there, at least for the phone. If there was any sign of danger, she'd return to the woods. Or better yet, head for the main road. She could get there and wave down a car. But first, the cabin.

From the edge of the woods, she studied the cabin's sliding glass door. The night sky had grown violet, the horizon magenta as the sun pushed its way upward. Still protected by the cover of trees, she spotted the dead raccoon. Blood coated its belly where it lay dead, legs outstretched. The cabin looked exactly as it had the night before.

She hesitated to walk into the open. If the killer was watching her, he'd have a clear shot as soon as she took two steps. Backing away a few feet, she scanned the ground for a weapon. She found a thick tree branch with a sharp end and imagined plunging it into his gut.

He had a gun. She'd never get close enough to stab him. Still, the weight of it in her hand was comforting as she gathered her nerve to continue forward.

The branch tight in her fist, she crouched and emerged from the woods. She ran, her shoes rubbing at raw spots on her feet, to the firepit. There, she spotted a long two-prong toasting fork abandoned in the embers and exchanged the branch for the metal weapon.

When she reached the house, she stopped, pressed flat against the log exterior, to catch her breath.

The strip of magenta on the horizon spread, the sky growing light. There would be no more cover from here. To get inside the cabin, she had to cross in front of the sliding glass doors with nothing to hide her. She should have approached from the other side of the house. Panic building, she rounded the house away from the glass doors to get a glimpse into the windows.

The first set of windows—the ones in the kitchen—were too high off the ground to allow her any view. There was nothing to stand on, no way to climb up. She tried to wedge the toe of her shoe between the logs, but the wood was slick with dew, and her foot slid right out. She considered dropping the toasting fork and trying to lift herself up, but she didn't want to let go. And she wasn't strong enough.

Instead, she moved along the house toward the front of the cabin. At the window of the second bedroom, she peered inside. The bed was unmade, sheets twisted at the foot, but no one was visible. Had someone left it that way? Or had the killer slept there last night?

She considered turning around, ducking back into the woods and heading toward town. Finding a big crowd. She could borrow a phone at the diner. What was she doing coming to this place?

Shoes crunched on gravel, and she froze. Someone was at the front of the house. A car door opened, then closed. She crouched low against the house and held her breath. She was in plain view. If anyone came from either side, she was dead.

From the distance came the sound of another car, the rising pitch of the engine a half second before the driver shifted into a higher gear. Hannah felt a spark of elation as the noise grew closer. It sounded like Chase's car, the high whine of his Porsche. But it couldn't be. She hadn't called him.

A car door opened again as the sound of tires chewing gravel reached the street. There were two cars out there now. If neither of them was Chase, she would have little chance of getting away. She eyed the cabin next door and calculated how long it would take her to get there. They were too far apart. She'd be exposed for at least thirty or forty seconds, even if she sprinted as fast as she could. Too far. Unless there was a distraction. At the corner of the house, she peered around to the front. The killer stood beside a black Audi SUV, the door open. Back to her, he was less than twenty feet away.

The road was thick with dust as the second car stopped in front of the cabin. A navy Cayenne. It had barely stopped when the door swung open and Chase emerged. He wore sweatpants and a T-shirt.

Hannah leaned into the house, tears flooding her eyes. Chase was here. Her brother had come to save her.

She wanted to jump from her hiding place. Call out.

"What've you done, Reade?" Chase shouted as he climbed from the car.

"Back off, Visser," the killer said. "This is your fault."

Hannah shifted back against the house. How did Chase know the killer? What did he mean, it was Chase's fault?

"Screw you, Bruce. You're lucky I'm helping you at all," her brother said.

"Like you're doing me some favor. We both know you couldn't run that business of yours without something on the side. You'd have gone under the first year."

The words made no sense. Chase and the killer didn't work together. The killer was a doctor who worked with her father. Chase sold home finishes. Was this about her father? Confused, Hannah was ready to call out to her brother when she spotted the gun. Hidden behind the open car door, the killer held it in his hand.

Chase had no idea it was there. The toasting fork was no match for a gun. He could kill them both and be gone before anyone saw him.

"Where's Hannah?" the killer asked.

"We'll find her," Chase said.

Hannah shrank away from them both.

Chase's words made her think maybe she didn't want her brother to find her after all.

CHAPTER 48

Lily

Sitting upright in the passenger seat, Lily gripped the door handle and watched the dark road. Every once in a while, she sensed Iver watching her. The question still hung in the air, the one he'd asked when she woke him and told him that she needed to go to Molva. Back to the place where she'd been held captive for sixteen months, where the worst of her nightmares—and also her child—had been born.

"What are you going to find in Molva?" Iver had asked when she'd told him that she wanted to drive there in the middle of the night.

"I think she's there," she'd said.

And he'd understood without her saying the word. Daughter. Her daughter. And that was the truth; she did believe Hannah was in Molva. But she also suspected that Hannah's presence wasn't the only reason for her need to return. It was the police's job to find Hannah Visser. Lily couldn't help with that, and yet she felt an undeniable draw to the town, along with a strong repulsion. She could not understand the pull Molva had on her since the last time she'd ventured there, she'd been abducted, drugged, and thrown in a trunk.

With each passing mile, the fear inside her ballooned. The scars on her back from the cutting she'd suffered during her captivity suddenly itched. Unfamiliar smells filled her nose. The dankness of wet wood, the smell of sweaty bodies huddled close together, the taste of powdery, stale mac 'n' cheese. Her bare feet on gravel, the pulsing of her heart as she pumped her arms and sprinted, the taste of dirt in her mouth and the dust in her eyes. A man on top of her, sweaty and boozy, his weight pressing her painfully against a scratchy wool blanket. Her thoughts unclear, the memory of drugs and alcohol. Abby had called it a party. Of the girls, only Lily and Abby had gone. Before they'd left the cabin, they'd drunk cups of bitter brown liquor laced with drugs. Lily had felt outside her own body as they walked through the cold night to the other cabin. A room full of people, laughing and drunk, the music loud as that man pulled her down the hallway, laughing and teasing like it was a game.

And raped her.

Had she screamed? Had Abby heard her and let it happen? Had the others known what was happening to her?

The urge to tell Iver to stop and turn around swelled to fill her chest. Her breathing grew short, shallow. What was she thinking?

She had sworn she'd put that all behind her. But it was still here, rearing its ugly head. When would it end?

As though sensing her anxiety, Cal pressed his muzzle into her leg from the seat between them, and she rubbed his head as he made little sounds of pleasure at her touch. The purring noise and his soft fur soothed her as she stared out at the passing road, not daring to look at Iver, who would see clearly the fear in her eyes. The indecision. *Why put yourself through this again? Why go back there?*

Or maybe he would understand it. He'd often spoken about returning to Afghanistan, of what it might mean to be able to see it again, the place where his friends had died. And he hadn't hesitated when she'd asked him to come with her. "Of course," he'd said. "I'll drive." He had gotten out of bed and dressed, quickly brewed a pot of coffee, and climbed into the truck with her.

He knew how that place haunted her, how those memories she couldn't find always felt like a bomb ready to detonate. But the memories were coming up. The man's face—Hannah's father—seemed to grow clearer all the time. Hazel-green eyes and long lashes. She had noticed that her rapist had beautiful eyelashes. Did her daughter have beautiful eyelashes? If only she'd gotten closer in the parking lot. What she wouldn't give now to have seen Hannah up close.

She thought of the picture Bruce Reade had taken from Dr. Visser's office. At the same time Hannah had been outside.

Iver took her hand and lulled her from her thoughts. She drew a full breath and let it out. Last night, she'd felt better than she had since Iver left. He was home. For her. He loved her.

His fingers gripped hers, and she spun to face him. He glanced over, gave her a little smile. "You want to try Kylie again?"

Lily lifted her phone off the seat and stared at the screen. No new messages. "She hasn't answered the last four calls."

Iver squeezed her hand. "We're better than halfway there. Another forty-five minutes." He didn't ask the question at the end of that. Where were they going? Molva was a tiny town, but she needed to know where specifically they were heading.

Lily lifted the phone and composed a text message. Iver and I will be in Molva in under an hour. At least tell us where to go.

The three dots appeared on the screen, and Lily clenched the phone. Kylie was responding. But when the words appeared, they made Lily want to throw the phone out the window.

Find an all-night coffee shop. I'll be in touch.

She could not let this all unfold without trying to help. She was the one who had led them to Bruce Reade. She'd seen him taking that picture out of the office on Sunday night. Sunday night. Something shifted in her brain, and she realized what had bothered her about the timing.

How had Reade known to take the picture of Hannah on Sunday when no one else knew she was a witness to the murders until Monday?

CHAPTER 49

Hannah

Hannah pressed herself against the side of the house, her grip tight on the toasting fork. The pain in her stomach brought tears to her eyes. She couldn't remember it ever being so bad. Fear and withdrawal from the drugs were making it worse. She wanted to curl up, to cry out, and yet concern for her brother, for herself, kept her upright. For the first time in days, her head was clear and focused. That, in spite of the pain, gave her strength.

"She's my sister, Bruce," Chase said. "My baby sister."

Bruce laughed. "Really? Now you want to play that card?" He shook his head, the barrel of the gun shifting upward as Chase approached. "You're the one who texted me that she was at Nadine's that night, Chase. If I'd gotten your text thirty minutes earlier, your sister would no longer be a problem. She'd be in a ditch somewhere."

Hannah fisted a hand against her stomach. Chase had told the killer where she was? Her own brother. She had the urge to back up, to turn and run.

"Where was the brotherly concern then?" the killer asked.

"Seriously, Bruce. I gave you the coordinates for the cabin so you could come get her, not hurt her."

Not hurt her. Of course Chase wouldn't hurt her.

"Then you should've come yourself," Reade said.

Chase took a step forward, and Hannah bit back a cry at the shift of the killer's gun. "I couldn't leave town. It would've been too obvious. Now, where is she?"

The killer shook his head. "I haven't found her. Yet."

Hannah watched the gun. He was going to shoot Chase. She shifted her grip on the fork to hold it like a spear as she dropped to her knees. Awkward on two knees and one hand, she crawled along the line of the porch, where she could remain hidden from Chase's view. She didn't want him to give her away. Taking little swallows of air, she tensed her body, ready to attack if the killer looked in her direction. She reached the end of the porch. From there, she'd have to run. If he heard her . . . no, when he heard her.

She crouched low and didn't blink. As she took it all in, her surroundings felt hyperfocused. She couldn't remember ever seeing so clearly. Whether from adrenaline or the drugs leaving her system, she felt certain she could do this. She could save Chase.

"We'll find her together," Chase said. "Then we'll deal with what's next. We'll get the business squared away, reschedule those deliveries. Lotari never needs to know. Okay?"

Hannah remained frozen against the house. What was next? What did Chase mean? Who was Lotari? She clenched the fork tighter in her fist.

"What's next is that I tie up the loose ends." The killer slammed the car door closed and lifted the gun to aim at Chase.

Her brother stepped backward. "Whoa, Bruce." Shaking his head, he lifted his hands slowly in the air. "Come on."

The killer took another step forward.

Chase ran toward his car as the killer aimed. "Don't do it," Chase shouted, and there was an explosion of sound.

The bullet struck, and Chase was spun around from the impact. Facing the shooter, he had his hand up, eyes wide with terror, as the killer aimed again.

Hannah sprinted, the fork gripped in her fist. Another shot fired as she struck, sinking the tines into the meat of his shoulder.

The killer howled, the gun falling from his grip. Hannah shoved her body into the fork and his shoulder, working the sharp points into his flesh.

The killer stumbled and fell onto the gravel. She grabbed the gun, planning to aim it at him. But the weight of it was terrifying. Without thinking, she threw it as hard as she could, watching as it flew across the road and into the tall grass.

The killer was still on his hands and knees. It would take him forever to find the gun, if he could find it at all. Hannah ran for Chase.

Blood soaked the side of his shirt and the front of his sweatpants. He'd been shot twice. His breathing was shallow, his face already a terrifying white.

"Chase! Chase!"

"Get my phone," Chase said. "In the car. Call 911."

She scrambled up and lunged into his car, finding the phone on the console. She tried to unlock it and couldn't. Remembered she could dial for an emergency. A sob escaped her lungs when she heard the ringing.

"911. What is your emergency?"

"My brother's been shot. Chase Visser. We're at a fishing cabin. On—" But the street address had vanished from her memory. "Crow. Crow something. Please hurry. He's bleeding."

"Okay. We've got police en route. What is your name?"

"Hannah," she said, breathless. "Hannah—" As she was about to give her last name, a hand wrenched her from the car. The phone flew from her grip and landed on the floor, out of reach, as she scrambled to grip the seat.

With one swift yank, the killer jerked her out of the car. She landed on the gravel road with a thud, the air rushing from her lungs. Gasping, she rolled over, fighting for her breath. She struggled to stand, but the killer planted a cowboy boot on her chest, holding her down.

Blood soaked the shoulder of his shirt as he gritted his teeth. "You're not going anywhere, Hannah Visser."

Chase shouted from the far side of the car, his words lost to the pounding of her heart. She twisted left and right, trying to free herself.

But the killer lowered his knees onto her arms, pinning her like a bug. Then he wrapped strong hands around her neck.

Reade. Bruce Reade. A doctor.

His hands tightened, and the air vanished.

A doctor had killed the Garzas, shot Chase . . . and now he would kill her.

Her eyes burned, her pulse throbbing in her temple. His face swam in her vision as his grip tightened. Her vision went black.

Chase's voice quieted as Hannah struggled to fight. She bucked her hips, but the killer was too strong, too heavy. He leaned down until his face was inches from her own. Sweat stained the front of his shirt, and blood began to soak through the side. His shoulder had to hurt. She had hurt him. The thought brought a surge of strength right as his grip faltered on one side.

Her throat opened, and she drew a breath, saw the pain in his face. He shifted to get a better grip, and her right arm was momentarily free.

His breathing was ragged, labored.

She dug her fingers into the gravel, searching for a rock. But it was all tiny stones.

He clenched his jaw and seemed to steel himself, clamping his hands on her neck again.

She grabbed a fistful of dirt and pebbles and threw it in his face. Open palmed, she swiped the dirt across his eyes, squeezing her own closed as dust and stones tumbled down onto her face.

The killer howled, lifting his hands to his face to clear the dirt.

Hannah drove her feet and shoulders into the ground and bucked as hard as she could. The killer reached out his right arm to catch himself. His hand hit the ground and his arm buckled, the injured shoulder unable to bear his weight.

Hannah rolled and scrambled to her feet. She glanced toward her brother. His silence was terrifying. He couldn't be dead. She needed him.

The killer stirred behind her. "You little bitch."

When Hannah peeked back, he was already struggling to his feet.

She thought of Chase's phone, the gun. She didn't have time to go for his phone, and she'd never find the gun in the grass. There was no time to make a plan.

She did the only thing she could.

She spun away and sprinted toward the woods.

CHAPTER 50

KYLIE

Sullivan's voice cut out midsentence. He'd been in the department in Hagen all night with Smith, researching Bruce Reade. He had been in the middle of telling Kylie about a call Doug Smith had with Reade's ex-wife when the line went silent. "Sullivan?" she called into the phone.

There was no answer.

Kylie pulled the phone from her ear and stared at the screen. The upper left corner now read *No Service*. "Damn it."

"Dead zone?" Gilbert asked.

"Another one." They'd been on the road for ninety minutes, and at least half of those had been spent in cell phone dead spots. She watched the upper left corner, willing the bars to return. Gilbert watched the road, keeping the Vissers in view ahead of them.

Every time they had a stretch of cell service, Kylie made phone calls. Back to the Hagen department to touch base with Doug Smith and Larry Sullivan, who were holed up at the department making calls and running reports, and to see if Marjorie had any better luck reaching the Molva deputies. She had yet to reach Marjorie.

Kylie sighed and set her phone on the console.

"What's the latest?" Gilbert asked.

"Sullivan's been in touch with Reade's ex-wife. I guess he was married in medical school. She had plenty to say about him." She tried to remember exactly what Sullivan had told her. Knowing they might lose their connection at any time, Kylie had urged him to talk fast, and he had. Maybe too fast. "Turns out that Reade was part of some ring of students who were accused of writing and selling fake prescriptions to pay for school."

"Did he serve time for it?" Gilbert asked.

"Was never even arrested," Kylie answered. "It didn't sound like any of them were."

"Why the hell not?"

"Three of them were expelled. Reade and another kid managed to get off with a warning. Probably the same reason as always—not enough evidence." That was the way it went in cases like this. The street kids who sold got arrested, but anyone higher in the food chain—doctors, distributors, the people who obtained the drugs or made them—often got off scot-free.

"Damn," Gilbert said. "And what's up with Baker?"

"She's coming, too. I tried to stop her."

"She found out she's got a kid, and that kid might be in danger," Gilbert said, meeting her gaze. "I'd be on my way, too."

Before she could respond, the Vissers slowed down and turned onto Route 23.

Kylie watched the Cherokee and wondered what the conversation was like in that car. "We still going to Molva?"

"Yep," Gilbert said. "We're about twenty miles out now."

That damn town. Kylie had never even been there—she'd been in a different town, meeting with the deputy sheriff about another missing girl, when Lily went back there almost four years earlier. Without ever seeing that town, Kylie was creeped out by it. She checked her phone again. Still no service. "Where the hell are the deputies in Molva?"

"You dial the inside line?"

"I called the number Sullivan gave me." She looked down at the scrap of paper on which she'd written the number. She didn't like that they weren't answering. Had Marjorie gotten in touch with them?

"No word on Reade's location?" Gilbert asked.

She shook her head, checked the phone again. Still no damn service. "No."

"His wife said he usually stays in town when he's working, Monday through Friday morning."

"According to the hospital, he's only on their schedule Mondays, Thursdays, and every third Tuesday," Kylie said. "So what does he do on those free Tuesdays and Wednesdays?"

"His wife seems to think he works at another clinic those days," Gilbert said.

She shook her head. "I don't know what that could mean. There's no other hospital with an emergency department within fifty miles."

"Closest is probably Sidney, Montana," Gilbert said. "He might go there."

"Maybe." Or maybe Reade ran another business on Tuesdays and Wednesdays, one he didn't want his wife to know about.

"Anything else from Sullivan?" Gilbert asked.

"Both Belt Construction and Chase Visser Interiors were on Lotari's distribution list."

"So it's possible that they were smuggling drugs along with the products, and she or Ben found out?" Gilbert said.

Again she noticed he didn't say Nadine's name out loud. "And then they told someone, and it got back to Lotari that they knew?"

"It's possible," Gilbert said.

"And Lotari sent his son-in-law to kill them? Seems extreme unless there was some pretty compelling proof."

"Something that could put him away," Gilbert agreed. "Maybe the lab will find evidence on Nadine's computer."

Maybe. But Kylie still couldn't figure out why it was Reade's mess to clean up and not Max Lotari's. Surely a guy in the drug business had people for that kind of thing. Or maybe there were others hunting Hannah as well. That thought was terrifying. She picked up her phone again. No damn service.

"There's service in Molva," Gilbert said. "Probably be back in the next five miles."

She fought the fear that they were too late. That Reade had escaped their grasp. That Hannah was . . . she thought of Lily. Lily was on her way to Molva. Why hadn't Kylie insisted Lily stay in Hagen? What good would it do to return to this town? This god-awful town . . .

"You okay?" Gilbert asked.

She nodded, resisting the urge to reach for her phone again. Her mother used to always remind her about a watched kettle. God, that saying drove her crazy.

"Whoa," Gilbert said suddenly. "What the hell's he doing?"

Up ahead, Charles Visser had doubled the distance between them.

Gilbert punched the gas, and they sped up. The speedometer read seventy, then seventy-five. Eighty.

She gripped the door. "The speed limit's fifty-five. Doesn't he know he's being followed by a cop?"

Visser shifted into the left lane to pass an old Dodge truck.

"Damn," Gilbert said, speeding up. "He's got to be going almost a hundred."

Kylie watched the road. "He was doing the speed limit, right?"

"He's been doing sixty, give or take, since we left Hagen." Gilbert glanced over. "Think I should pull him over?"

"Not unless we think he's going to hurt someone. For now, I think we follow."

Gilbert shifted into the left lane to pass the same Dodge truck and accelerated to catch up.

As Gilbert returned to their lane, Kylie's phone rang, and she jumped in her seat, snatching it up. The number was unfamiliar. "Detective Milliard."

"Detective." A man's voice came across a static-filled line. She gripped the phone tightly as though she might be able to keep the call from dropping by sheer will. "This is Deputy Tanner in Molva."

She felt a shock at the name. Scott Tanner. The same deputy who had called to tell Kylie that he'd found Lily Baker's car on the side of the road almost four years ago. Tanner had found the dog, Cal, sitting in the shade of the car and Lily gone. Despite the time that had passed, the rush of fear inside her now made it feel like it had been hours and not years. "What's going on, Deputy Tanner?"

"We're having an issue with connectivity in our department. No cell and no internet."

"Like someone is jamming a signal?" Kylie asked.

Gilbert glanced over and raised an eyebrow.

"We haven't had time to look into it. I'm calling because there's been a shooting at the cabin belonging to the Sutton family. I believe you know Priscilla Sutton. She's Priscilla Visser now."

A strangled noise came from her throat. Gilbert set his hand on her arm, his expression a question as she lowered the phone and put it on speaker. "Can you repeat that, Deputy?"

"There's been a shooting outside a fishing cabin that belongs to Priscilla Visser's family."

Gilbert's gaze tracked to the Vissers' car.

Had the Vissers just learned that Hannah had been shot? Was Visser rushing to try to save his daughter?

"We got lucky," Deputy Tanner went on. "Neighbor right off the highway called to complain about a car doing eighty down that road—some fancy foreign car, she said. We got a 911 call about ten minutes later, but I was already en route. Found the victim in the dirt, a through-and-through gunshot wound to the abdomen and another in the thigh. I called it in, and paramedics are on the scene. I called Charles Visser, too. He told me to call you."

That explained the way Dr. Visser was speeding. "Is she going to be okay?" Kylie asked.

"She?" Tanner repeated. "Victim's Chase Visser. He's alive now but in bad shape."

Chase Visser had been shot. By Bruce Reade? By Hannah? Or someone else? "You locate the shooter?"

"No, ma'am. Mr. Visser was the only one on the scene. No one else and only the one car at the cabin."

That was not good news. Where the hell was Bruce Reade? And Hannah? Kylie leaned into the phone. "Is he talking? Have you asked him what happened?"

"If the paramedics get him stable, we'll ask questions. But not before then."

Kylie thanked the deputy and ended the call.

"We're in Molva," Gilbert said.

A worn wooden sign announced the entrance to the town. **Population 370.** Up ahead, Visser took a left, his car spinning out before he straightened the wheel and kept going. Gilbert slowed and followed him into the turn. Visser made a series of rights and lefts, and Gilbert followed. A couple of miles down, Visser turned on a dirt road that made a long left curve before taking a sharp right. The street sign was riddled with bullet holes, making the name unreadable. Cabins dotted both sides of the road. They appeared to be closed for the season, windows shuttered, no signs of cars or people.

Molva.

"Here we go," Gilbert said as they came around a corner and saw the commotion. Two police cars and a Porsche Cayenne in the middle of it all.

Charles Visser was already out of his car, running across the gravel road. Priscilla emerged with a train of white gauzy nightgown. It might have been a strange dream, but not in Molva.

As far as Kylie was concerned, Molva was the place of nightmares.

CHAPTER 51

Lily

Iver slowed at the wooden sign that announced they had reached Molva. "Find an all-night coffee shop?"

Lily didn't want to go to a coffee shop. This wasn't a vacation. She dialed Kylie's cell phone again. It rang once, twice . . . she ended the call. "I just want to know where they are."

Iver turned toward town. "Has to be wherever Visser was going, right?"

Visser. Lily searched her contacts and found Charles Visser's cell number. She had all the doctors' cell numbers, to be used in case of an emergency only. This counted as an emergency. She dialed and held her breath as it rang.

Once. Twice.

"Hannah?" came the man's breathy response.

Lily's breath hitched in her throat.

"Hannah?" Visser called again.

"It's Lily Baker, Dr. Visser. I'm—" She glanced at Iver, who nodded. "I'm in Molva. I—"

"You're here? In Molva?"

"Yes." She couldn't think of how to explain it.

"Chase has been shot, Lily. One's a through and through, but the second bullet struck his femoral artery. Possibly the vein, too. I need your help to stop the bleeding. Can you come?" His voice pitched high, a fear like she'd never heard.

"Tell me where you are." She put the phone on speaker and held it up so Iver could hear the directions. Visser spoke quickly, his words breathless and tense. The doctor she'd only ever seen react with total calm in every emergency sounded broken, desperate. "You got that?"

"Got it," Iver said.

"We're on our way," Lily confirmed.

"I have to go, Lily," Dr. Visser said. "Please hurry."

The call ended, and Iver made several turns, then slowed to study the street signs. He turned left and followed the road until it became gravel. Visser had said to watch for the shot-up street sign for Crow Tower Road and make a sharp right. The road went on longer than she'd expected without a house or sign. They came around a bend, and right as Lily was certain they'd gone the wrong way, she saw a street sign tilted at an awkward angle, the metal peppered with buckshot holes. Then the first structure appeared—a small, square log cabin, the doors and windows shuttered.

"That has to be it," she said as Iver was turning.

He sped up, the tires spitting gravel against the truck's undercarriage. Around the next corner, the road was filled with activity. Iver parked behind two sheriff cars, their lights flashing, and Lily jumped from the car.

Kylie Milliard was speaking to a deputy as Lily moved past. The detective stepped in front of her. "You can't be here," Kylie said.

"Visser asked me to come. He needs my help to save his son."

Kylie glanced into the house, then at Lily.

"He's waiting for me," Lily said. A rush of heat coursed through her hands, the pressure of time urging her to run.

The detective stood aside.

Lily took hold of her arm. "Bruce Reade took the picture of Hannah from Visser's office on Sunday night, just hours after the murders."

A beat passed, and Kylie's eyes went wide. "How did he know she was the witness?"

"Right." Lily faced the cabin, imagining what she might find inside.

Kylie appeared to still be reeling from the realization as Lily looked back. "Hannah?" Lily asked. *My daughter.* But she couldn't get herself to say the words. "Is she okay?"

"We don't know. We're going to search for her now."

Both Visser children in danger. One seriously injured. One still missing. The fear Charles Visser had to feel in that moment. The fear she felt for a daughter she hadn't formally met. A daughter conceived in the most hateful way possible but still her flesh and blood. Lily grabbed Kylie's hand. "Please find her." And then Lily ran into the cabin as Kylie shouted at the deputies to let her through.

The cabin smelled of old cigar smoke and blood. The screen door slammed behind her, and Lily felt a wave of vertigo. She stumbled across a rug in the entry. It appeared Native American, a red-and-black diamond pattern at its center. The stepped edges of the design seemed to shift as she glanced away. She rubbed her face and moved past it. The room was freezing, and a cold breeze whistled through the space.

Priscilla Visser stood huddled against the wall, in a white nightgown covered in a coat. She looked frail and old. The refined air of her that had always intimidated Lily was gone now, replaced by pure terror. There were others there also—paramedics, a police officer.

"Lily," Visser called. Chase was laid across the dining room table, the chairs pulled away. One lay on its back some feet from the table as though it had been thrown. The space had been torn apart, the glass in the sliding door shattered.

The room was suffocating, too hot, though the air was cold. A painting of a Native American man at a fire seemed to leer at her, and Lily felt an overwhelming urge to leave. As she turned to the door, she spotted Iver through the screen. He watched her as though reading what she was feeling. He stepped closer, offering an out, and she hesitated, ready to run to him.

"Lily, please," Visser cried out. "A chopper's going to be here, but not for forty-five minutes. I've got to stop this bleeding, and I can't do it." He lifted a hand, and for only the second time since she'd known him, Dr. Visser's tremor shook his fingers. The desperation in his voice cut through her own fears.

With a deep breath, she took a last look at Iver and crossed to the makeshift gurney where Chase Visser lay bleeding to death.

CHAPTER 52

Kylie

Deputy Tanner had the dogs working the woods behind Visser's cabin while another of Molva's four deputies organized a volunteer search team and spread a description of Bruce Reade and his car through town. Reade was here. He'd been seen in town, where he had called himself Sam Jones and said he was Hannah's father. He had a massive head start, and there was no evidence that he didn't already have Hannah in his car. That he wasn't driving across the state at this moment.

Or taking her body to a dump site.

All they had was hope. Clinging to the possibility that Hannah was nearby, Kylie and Gilbert drove along the dirt roads around Visser's cabin, searching for signs of Hannah or Bruce Reade. With every passing minute, Kylie's hope faded, and the possibility that Hannah was with Bruce Reade grew more likely. Where would he take her? Not back to Hagen. He couldn't show up there now. Dahl was stationed at his Hagen place. And the Bismarck police were watching his home there.

Would he just kill her and hide the body? Would they ever find her? The thought made Kylie want to vomit. She pictured Hannah in the trunk of Reade's car. He was broad shouldered and strong where Hannah was petite. She was no match for him.

Gilbert hesitated at an intersection, and they scanned in each direction before he made a left. The roads were rutted and bumpy, this area of town clearly empty for much of the year. There was no indication as to which roads had been traveled most recently—no way to identify fresh tire tracks in the dry dirt, no noise coming from any direction.

Every second that passed felt like confirmation of Hannah Visser's death sentence.

"Left or right?" he asked at the next fork.

"Left," Kylie said, then second-guessed the choice. She stared right. Saving a life should never come down to a guess. How would she live with herself if she was wrong?

The car bounced down the gravel road, curving to the left, and she pried her eyes away from the disappearing road in the other direction. More boarded-up cabins. No cars, no people. They came around another turn, and she spotted smoke in the air through the trees.

"Carl," she shouted.

"I see it." He accelerated toward the rising cloud.

Gilbert drove to the edge of the woods, and they stared in. All Kylie saw was trees. "There," Gilbert said and pointed out a set of tire tracks.

Before she could tell him to wait, Gilbert pointed the nose of the patrol car down the embankment and drove between two trees. They bounced across the uneven ground, through a wooded patch, and into a clearing beside a creek.

Kylie searched for where the tracks continued.

"He must've crossed the creek," Gilbert said.

But as they approached, Kylie spotted a shadow in a cluster of dense trees. "What's that—"

Not a shadow at all. It was a black car—an Audi, the engine smoking.

"It's got to be his car." Gilbert drove over and halted behind the Audi. Without pausing for breath, he jumped out, leaving his door hanging open. Kylie was right behind him. They stood on either side of the Audi, peered in the windows. The car was empty, its bulk wedged between a tree and a boulder. The rear tires were sunk deep into the mud where the driver had clearly tried to free himself.

"Blood," Gilbert said, pointing through the window.

Kylie cupped her hands to the glass. There was blood on the driver's seat. "His?"

"I hope so," Gilbert said. He rushed to the edge of the woods and stared into the trees.

Kylie texted Deputy Tanner and dropped a pin for her location. A trick Amber had taught her. Reade's car is here. No sign of him or the girl.

"It's a good sign," Gilbert said, unholstering his gun. "Means she's still got him on the run."

Kylie felt the comforting weight of her vest settle over her shoulders as she returned her phone to her pocket. "Or she did."

"Hannah!" Gilbert shouted.

She and Gilbert froze, listening. There was a rustle, and her heart thrashed painfully against her chest. She glanced at Gilbert, who shook his head. She listened again, but there was only silence.

Gilbert aimed his weapon and strode deeper into the woods. From behind them, Kylie heard the wail of a siren in the distance. That would be Deputy Tanner. She exhaled her frustration at the noise. It was her fault. She hadn't thought to tell him to come on silent.

Kylie caught up to Gilbert, the sensation of someone watching prickly on her skin. Every step felt like a trap. She holstered her gun to text Tanner. Silence the siren.

But still it blared. Gun out, Kylie surveyed the woods.

"Kylie," Gilbert whispered, his tone sharp.

She looked up.

And then it came—a shriek and a grunt.

Gilbert began to run. "Hannah!"

"Help!" came the muffled response.

Gilbert and Kylie raced toward the sound emanating from a cluster of woods across the creek to their left. There was a crashing of branches and another scream as Kylie ran through the icy water, the cold air burning her lungs. Hannah stumbled into view, blood streaked across her face.

From behind, a hand swiped out at her, grabbing hold of her shirt. She was yanked backward, but her fingers caught hold of a tree.

Gilbert and Kylie sprinted the final distance to reach her. Hannah managed to gain another foot, but Bruce Reade stepped into view and lunged for the girl. He got hold of her hair, and Hannah's head snapped back. Kylie tried to aim her gun, but there was no shot. Hannah swung her hand and struck Reade in the shoulder. He dropped to the ground, cursing. Hannah ran to Kylie.

Still holding her gun, Kylie caught hold of the girl with one arm. "You're okay," Kylie whispered, blinking away the tears in her eyes. She thought of Lily. *I've got your girl.* "I've got you," she whispered.

Hannah leaned on her as though she was barely standing on her own.

Reade scrambled to his feet and bent forward as though to rush them, but he halted at the sight of Gilbert's gun, a wild-animal look in his eyes. His shirt was stained with blood, his right arm hanging limp at his side.

"On the ground," Gilbert shouted and approached Reade with a steady determination.

Reade glanced behind him before returning his attention to the officer.

"Down now," Gilbert repeated.

Some internal calculation told Reade that his chances were bad. He gripped his right wrist with his left hand and raised them both, a grimace of pain on his face. There was something satisfying in his pain.

"On your knees," Gilbert commanded, and Reade lowered himself awkwardly to the ground.

Kylie holstered her weapon and gripped Hannah's face in her hands to check her head and eyes. "Are you hurt? Did he hurt you?" The girl's neck was bruised, a thick band of finger marks on her skin. "We need to get you to a doctor."

Only then did Kylie notice that the sirens had gone silent.

Hannah pushed the hair out of her eyes. Dirt streaked her face and lined her fingernails. "My brother," she whispered.

"Your dad's there. He's with Chase."

Her eyes filled with tears. "Is he . . . ?"

"They're working to stop the bleeding," Kylie said. She had no idea if Chase Visser was still alive. "What hurts? Your neck. Is there anything else?"

Hannah stared down at herself as though taking stock of her limbs.

From behind them came the barking of dogs. "Detective!" Tanner's voice carried through the woods.

"We're here," she called out.

Tanner arrived, breathless, crossing the water as the two leashed hounds dragged him along. "You found them."

Hannah shifted closer to Kylie momentarily. When the dogs reached her feet, Hannah slowly eased herself down to one knee. They licked her face, and she began to pet the smaller one, her shoulders relaxing.

Tanner nodded to Bruce Reade. "You got him okay?"

"We do." Kylie knelt next to Hannah. "I want a doctor to look at Hannah."

"Our only active ambulance is at the cabin," Tanner said. "We're arranging air transport for the son."

"I need to see Chase," Hannah whispered.

"I'm going to have Deputy Tanner take you to the cabin," Kylie told her. "Chase and your parents are there, and we can get someone to check you over, make sure you're all right." Kylie thought about the fact that Lily Baker was there, too. How strange that mother and daughter would end up together for the first time this way.

Hannah seemed hesitant.

"My patrol car's up the hill here," Tanner said, hitching a thumb over his shoulder.

Hannah stared up at Kylie, who understood her fear. But Kylie knew Tanner would keep her safe. "Maybe Deputy Tanner will let one of the dogs sit up front with you on the ride."

Hannah turned to Tanner.

"Of course," Tanner said. "I'll bet Trixie would love that," he added, offering Hannah a leash.

Hannah pushed herself to her feet and took hold of the leash on the smaller hound. For a moment, she was a regular kid. Not a hunted witness to a brutal double murder and the product of rape. Just a fourteen-year-old who was happy to play with a friendly dog. Kylie fought off the rush of emotion she felt for all Hannah had lost. "We'll be five minutes behind you," she said.

Hannah took several steps forward. She didn't put weight on her left foot and guarded her right arm. Kylie stepped in beside the girl and wrapped her right arm around the girl's middle. "This hurt?"

Hannah shook her head, and Kylie helped her to the deputy's car, the leash still tight in her hand. "Please make sure someone checks your injuries, Hannah. Okay?"

Hannah's expression remained unreadable a moment, but then she nodded. They walked slowly, Kylie supporting the girl the entire way. At Tanner's car, Kylie helped Hannah into the passenger seat and watched as the girl lifted the hound into her lap, a shy smile on her face.

Kylie closed the car door gently and called over the top to Tanner. "Call a local doctor if you have to."

Tanner nodded.

Kylie turned and made her way back to the creek, where she'd left Gilbert and Reade. Gilbert should have had Reade handcuffed by now.

From the woods came a man's grunt and a curse. A shock of fear coursed through her. "Carl?"

Another grunt.

Unholstering her weapon, she broke into a run, gravity and fear dragging her down the hill toward Gilbert and Reade.

CHAPTER 53

Lily

Brilliant red blood saturated Chase Visser's shirt and jeans. His father's hands were coated in it. Lily could feel the blood, its thick, tacky texture. Arterial blood was a uniquely beautiful color, but there was a lot of it here. Too much. *Breathe. Focus.* She fought her own panic. *You're trained for this. A professional.*

Chase's jeans were unbuttoned and pushed down in haste, the fabric of his boxer briefs bunched upward. Exposed was the femoral crease, the natural fold between the pelvis and legs, where Dr. Visser fought to stanch the bleeding by applying pressure to the artery through the skin. Lily studied his face and wondered if he'd been a good father to her daughter. Then pushed the thought aside. *Not now.*

Chase had blood on his cheeks and neck, streaks of it like fingers. His hands, too, were coated in blood. Though his eyes were closed, the pain on his face made it clear he was alert. This kind of wound rarely rendered the patient unconscious. Not until they'd lost too much blood. His tortured expression was good news, as was the color in his cheeks. One paramedic was dressing the wound on Chase's abdomen, the one Visser had told her was a through and through. He had wadded gauze to create pressure and was taping strips across the skin to hold it in place until the wound could be surgically closed. A second paramedic stood against one wall, looking like he'd been dismissed. Ready, maybe eager to help, but Visser had asked her to come.

She stepped forward, drew a breath. *Treat it like any case,* she thought. *Start with ABC.* A—his airway was obviously open; he was breathing fine. B—breathing, check. Eyes squeezed closed, he sipped shallow breaths through clenched teeth.

Circulation. The problem was circulation. Lily stepped up to the table, drew a breath to steady herself. *Ready.*

"We're going to stop the bleeding on this leg wound, Chase," Visser said. "Just hang with me. You're doing great, son."

Chase nodded ever so slightly and took another swallow of air.

When Visser met Lily's gaze, his eyes were wide and glassy with fear. His characteristic calm had been burned away, and panic filled his face. He loved his son. He loved Hannah, too, she knew. Her daughter had known love. Again, Lily had to force the thought away, struggling to keep her own breaths slow and calm. *Panic won't help anyone.*

"Cut away the pants," he said briskly.

Priscilla Visser held out a pair of scissors in a trembling hand. Her face shone with sweat as she swayed on her feet.

"Give Lily the scissors," Visser commanded, working his fingers along the crease below Chase's pelvic bone. Without seeing the wound, it was impossible to say if it was still actively bleeding or if Visser had been successful in stopping the blood with pressure.

Priscilla was unresponsive, the words unable to penetrate her trance.

Touching her arm, Lily pried the scissors from the woman's hands. When their skin met, she thought about the strange bond they shared, their mutual daughter. *Not now. Focus on Chase.* Moving efficiently, Lily put her back to Priscilla and began to cut the pants upward from the cuffs. The scissors were dull, the denim fabric stiff. Motion was comforting but the process slow.

She called to one of the police officers standing aside, "Can you help me tear this?"

He came forward and took the bloodied fabric between two hands, ripping as Lily cut. The work moved quickly, and soon the wound was exposed. She estimated it was three inches below the femoral crease, approximately two inches toward the interior of his thigh from the midline.

The dull scissors made almost no progress through the thick waistband.

Blood leaked from the hole in short bursts, matching the beat of Chase's heart. The bullet had entered high in Chase's right thigh and traveled medial to lateral. From the inside of the thigh out. The exit wound was visible on the outside of the thigh. A good spot. Muscle and tissue aside, there was little of importance in that location. Nothing that might kill him. If they could stop the bleed, he'd be okay. Lily drew a breath.

Panic rose in her chest as she tried to saw through the remaining denim. It was too slow.

Iver, who had been standing near the door, approached the table. In his hand was his hunting knife, the one he always carried. "I can try this."

Lily held the fabric away from Chase's skin while Iver cut through it. He worked quickly, his movements confident, assured. She thought of his time in Afghanistan, of what he'd seen. The fabric fell free, and Iver stepped away. She felt a wave of relief and gratitude that he was there. Gratitude for him. She cut easily through the boxer briefs so the wound was fully visible.

Beside her, Visser leaned forward, applying his full body weight against the femoral artery. But blood continued to leak from the wound.

It wasn't working.

"I need to go in," he said.

Visser moved around her, lifting hands that were coated with his son's blood as they changed places. The paramedic adhered a final strip of tape to the second wound and shifted away from the table. Lily stood beside Visser, out of his way. Searched for a way to help.

Visser poked at the wound, then swiped a hand across the skin to clear the wet blood. "I can't see."

Using the pant leg of Chase's jeans, Lily wiped the skin around the wound to give Visser a better view. But the wound was a constant trickle of thick blood, coating everything.

Visser returned his finger to the wound.

She saw the tremor in his hand. "Tell me what I can do."

He just shook his head.

She held her breath.

A body's entire blood volume could fill the thigh cavity. Visser had told her this once, in a case where a bowhunter had accidentally discharged an arrow into his own thigh. His hunting partner had wrapped the leg to try to slow the blood loss, but the artery had emptied into his thigh. By the time he reached the hospital, his blood pressure was gone. He'd bled out into his own body. She rejected the thought now. There would be no bleeding out for Chase.

Dr. Visser pressed his index finger into the wound.

Chase writhed on the table. Lily felt his pain at her core as his mother cried out, touching her face to her son's head as she sobbed.

Chase cried out louder, and Priscilla began to wail. Her pained cries filled the air. Lily struggled to calm her breath, to focus. Visser cringed at the noise but said nothing.

"Take her out of here," Lily said to the paramedics.

One of them stepped forward and took hold of Priscilla's shoulders, and the woman melted into him without argument. He led her toward the kitchen.

Lily tried to push the sounds from her head.

"Chase, I need you to be still," Visser said. "Can you do that?"

Lily glanced up and caught Iver's attention. "Can you hold his feet?"

Applying pressure on Chase's shins, Iver pressed him down as Dr. Visser worked his finger into the wound.

Lily waited for Visser to direct her, staying focused on his hands, trying to anticipate his next need, the way she did in the ED. As Visser inserted his finger into the bullet hole, blood welled over the side and ran down Chase's leg. Lily swiped it again as Visser shifted his angle.

With his hand in a different position, Lily noticed a large red welt halfway up Chase's right thigh. A birthmark.

CHAPTER 54

Kylie

Breathing hard, Kylie came to a halt when she reached Gilbert and Bruce Reade. Reade was curled on one side, knees pulled to his chest and arms folded over his head. Above him stood Gilbert, his weapon aimed down.

"Carl, no!" Kylie shouted. "Don't do it." Her heart pounded in her ears. Gilbert didn't seem to hear her.

"Why them?" Gilbert shouted at Reade. "Why her?" His voice cracked on the words. He drew back a foot and kicked Reade in the spine.

"Carl!" she called again, lowering her voice as she moved closer. His face was tight with fury and pain. "Carl, he's going to jail. We're arresting him."

"I want to know why," Gilbert said, his voice cracking. He didn't take his eyes off Reade. "I *need* to know why."

"It was Visser. He made me," Reade grunted. "She found out."

A gasp caught in Kylie's throat. Found out? "Found out what?"

"Ask Visser," Reade said.

"No," Gilbert hissed, crouching down. "*You* tell me!"

"Please," Reade whispered.

Gilbert lowered the gun until it was inches from Reade's head.

Reade stared up at her. "Detective," he said. "Look at me." He spread his fingers, palms facing out. Dirt was smeared across the skin of his empty hands. "I'm not armed. I'm an unarmed man. Don't let him shoot me."

Gilbert looked up, eyes wet.

"You can't, Carl," she whispered. "I know you're angry. I'm angry, too. But this isn't who we are. It's not who *you* are."

Gilbert shook his head, tears tracking down his face. "He shot Nadine in cold blood. In front of her baby." He gritted his teeth and jammed the barrel against the back of Reade's head.

"I'm unarmed," Reade pleaded. "Don't shoot."

"Don't do it," Kylie said. Her voice cracked. "If you do that, you're no better than he is."

"Tell me. Tell me why," Gilbert said, dropping to one knee and swinging his fist into Reade's kidneys. "Tell me, or I swear to God I'll shoot you now."

Kylie waited for Gilbert to stand again, to get control of himself. "Carl," she whispered again, close enough to touch him. Gilbert glared at her when she reached out. "He's not armed."

He straightened his shoulders and pressed the gun to Reade's skull. "Neither. Was. Nadine."

Reade began to cry.

"Carl," she whispered and held her breath.

Pain was etched in the lines of Gilbert's brow and knotted the line of his jaw. Kylie could see the struggle in his grip on the gun. The barrel was buried in Reade's hair.

"Tell me why you killed Nadine," Gilbert said again.

"It was Visser. Visser told me I had to."

"Why?" Kylie said.

"Because she found out."

"Found out what?"

Reade said nothing.

Gilbert stood upright in an angry arch. The barrel lifted from Reade's head. The expression on Gilbert's face was pure rage. As he lowered his arm again, the gun aimed at Reade, Kylie let out a cry. Her noise seemed to awaken some bit of reason in Gilbert. He slowed a moment, drew a breath.

But then he lifted one work boot and pressed it into Reade's neck. "Answer the question, or I'll snap your damn head off, I swear to God."

Reade struggled to free his head as Gilbert applied weight. "Okay, okay. She found out about the drugs."

"What drugs?"

"The drugs we were moving. She was going to go to the police. If it got back to Lotari, he'd kill me."

Max Lotari. "Your father-in-law."

"Yes," he whispered, tears streaming down his face.

"You were using Chase's company to move the drugs," Kylie said. "Is that right?"

Reade said nothing, and Gilbert kicked him. "Answer the question."

"Yes," Reade answered, his voice cracking.

"Where do the drugs come from? Where do they go?"

Gilbert pressed his boot into Reade's injured shoulder.

Reade winced and kept talking. "Lotari has a source that delivers them to Chicago, and then Chase helped us get them into the Dakotas and Montana, Wyoming, and Idaho with shipments for his stores."

"So you killed the Garzas and tried to make it look like a murder-suicide?"

Reade nodded.

Kylie thought about what Lily had said, that Reade had taken the picture of Hannah from Visser's office Sunday night. "And how did you know Hannah witnessed the murders?"

"Chase texted. Said not to do it that night because his sister was babysitting." Reade took a shaky breath. "But I got the text too late. It was already done."

So he hadn't known Hannah was a witness until after the murders. But Chase must have known that his sister was in danger, after he'd sent that text. Had he been tracking her since she left Hagen? Or had he let Reade loose to deal with his sister? Willing to sacrifice her life for the money?

Gilbert stepped away from Reade, shifting his weapon to aim at the ground a few feet away. He wiped his face with one hand, his cheeks wet. "He deserves to die, Kylie."

Kylie drew the set of handcuffs from her holster and held them up. "He'll go to jail for the rest of his life."

"He doesn't deserve a life," Gilbert said again, the words edged in stone. He took another step away and waved at Reade.

Reade said nothing, and Kylie could see another wave of fury building in Gilbert. She pressed the handcuffs into his free hand. He scowled at the metal bracelets before holstering his gun and taking them from her. As though weighted by some tremendous burden, Gilbert dropped to one knee.

Reade lowered his hands slowly, glancing at Kylie, then over his shoulder at Gilbert. He shifted his back as though testing how much damage had been done by Gilbert's boots.

"Stay still, asshole," Gilbert snapped as he reached for Reade's right arm. Kylie wiped away the sweat with the sleeve of her shirt, felt the cold chill of the waning adrenaline. With a wave of relief, she realized it was almost over.

Hannah was alive. Reade was in custody, and if Chase Visser survived the gunshots, he was going to jail, too.

CHAPTER 55

Lily

Lily's heart drummed a sickening beat in her head as she averted her gaze from the strange red welt. People had birthmarks, she reminded herself. They weren't uncommon.

Instead, she shifted her focus to Dr. Visser, his head tilted back, eyes on the ceiling, as he felt his way into his son's leg. It was the same way Visser worked in the ED when he couldn't see the source of a problem. The same way he had reached into Nadine Garza's torso to try to stop her bleeding. Only now his expression was tense with fear. This was his son. They had to save him.

"The artery isn't transected. There's a nick, but it's not huge," Visser said with a beat of relief. His hand shifted under the skin of Chase's thigh. "Another in the vein. Two holes." His lips thinned into a line as he removed his hand.

Chase groaned.

He hesitated only a moment to speak to his son. "I can't hold them both without extending the wound. Hang on, Chase. This is going to be uncomfortable."

With a silent nod, Chase clenched his jaw. Iver adjusted his grip, increasing the pressure on Chase's legs. Visser slid both index fingers into the bullet's entrance wound and began to stretch them in opposite directions. Chase cried out. Sweat shone on his face. His skin was clammy as he lifted his hands to his face.

The wound hole opened, and Visser returned his fingers inside. "I'm going to need your fingers, Lily. I can't hold it steady." The tremor in his hand was visible now, growing more pronounced.

Lily's gaze found the painting on the wall—the Native American at the fire. She felt momentarily dizzy as a memory surged from the depths of her mind.

"Lily," Visser said, the urgency sharp in his tone.

Lily took a breath. "I can do it."

Exhaling loudly, Visser spread the wound opening. "Two fingers," he said, holding up his index and middle finger, stained red. "You'll have to push through the fat layer until you feel the pulse. There's one in the artery. The pulse there will feel stronger. Then a second one above and behind in the vein. You need to plug them both. Can you do that?"

Lily stared at Chase Visser's thigh, the blood pulsing. The strange red spot. Inside the shape were dozens of red dots, like the petechiae that resulted from strangulation.

"Lily?"

"Yes," she answered, switching her attention to the wound. With a glance at Iver, she pressed her index and middle finger into the opening and twisted them to move past the elastic layer of skin.

Chase gasped and groaned as Visser fingered the top of the skin and Lily pressed deeper into Chase's leg. "You'll feel the fat layer," Visser said. "I made a hole there. You'll have to work to get through it."

She felt the break in the tough, oily layer and pushed into it. It felt like gristle as she worked her fingers through.

Chase cried out.

"Keep going," Visser said to Lily, squeezing his son's shoulder.

Lily kept her attention on her task. An inch or so later, she felt the artery, like a thin rubber tube. "I'm on the artery."

"Work your finger down," Visser said. "Do you feel the hole?"

There was a pressure, like a tiny beat against her finger. The leak in the artery. She pressed her index finger against it. "I do. I've got it blocked."

"The second hole is in the vein right next to it. You should be able to feel it."

She shifted her hand, finding a second, softer pulse. She covered it with her middle finger. "I've got them." Visser wiped Chase's leg and everyone went quiet as they watched the wound. The skin of Chase's thigh remained dry, blood no longer leaking.

Visser exhaled, his entire body deflating. He scanned the room and found the officer who had helped cut through Chase's pants. "Officer, can you get some dish towels from the kitchen? The drawer beside the oven. And a bowl of warm water. Add a little dish soap. There should be a bowl on the table." The officer disappeared into the kitchen.

Lily drew a breath, unsteady on her feet. She tried to ground herself in Chase. Studied his face. His gaze shifted to hers, fear in his eyes. He looked away as though alarmed that she had seen him. He shifted, and the muscles in his leg moved.

"Don't move," Visser snapped. "You have to be still."

Visser studied Lily's hand, then her face. "Are you okay?"

The cabin was suddenly hot, and she unzipped her jacket with her free hand.

"Lily?" Iver said, and she met his gaze.

She reached her arm out to Iver. "Can you take the jacket off?"

"You can't," Visser said.

Lily shook her head. "Just this arm."

Iver pulled the jacket off, and she let it hang off one shoulder, returning her free hand to the table to steady herself. The Native American painting called to her, and she had to prevent her gaze from traveling to it. Sweat beaded on her lip, and she used the back of her free hand to blot it.

Chase glanced at her, scanning her face as though searching for something. But then he looked away.

The officer returned with a handful of dish towels and a bowl of water. Visser dipped a towel in the water and began to clean the area around the wound, washing away the coagulating blood.

Lily's gaze traveled the room. The rug on the floor, the leather couch, the darkened hallway . . . a wool blanket. Wool and leather. Lily felt like she was roasting from the inside. She shifted her position and took slow, even breaths.

"Can you bring her some water," Iver said to the officer, who nodded and walked toward the kitchen again.

"Thank you," she said.

Visser studied her face, but she shook her head. "I'm fine."

As Visser wiped the area around the wound, Lily touched the strange welt. "Is this a rash?" She knew it wasn't. She knew what it was.

"It's a hemangioma, a cluster of blood vessels. It's a birthmark." Visser rubbed the wet dish towel gently over the skin. "His red glove, he always called it."

Like a hand with the fingers pulled together.

Lily's knees buckled, and Visser caught hold of her. "Lily? Are you all right?"

She straightened her legs, moving her toes, and told herself to remain standing. She turned to Iver. His gaze seemed to read her. "What is it?"

She closed her eyes and saw the red patch of skin. The glove-like shape of the birthmark. Hovered over her. A man with blood running down his face. Stabbing her.

Raping her.

She opened her eyes to find Chase studying her. "Dad, she's going to let go. Is she still holding on?" Panic spiked in his voice.

Lily averted her gaze from his face.

"Lily?" Visser asked, a hand on her arm.

"I'm fine," she said. "I've got the bleed."

The officer pressed a glass of water into her free hand, and she drank from it. Her eyes found Chase Visser's, and she lowered the glass. How could she not have seen it? Without his smile, the dimple on his left cheek was gone. In the crease of skin, the scar was visible.

The scar she had caused.

Her hand trembled as she lowered the glass. "You," she whispered.

Chase started to shift on the table as though to sit up. "Dad, she's losing it."

"Don't move," Visser shouted, grabbing hold of his son. "Lily's doing great. She's keeping you alive."

"Lily?" Iver asked.

Lily gripped the edge of the table to prevent herself from falling. She imagined the tiny pads of her two fingers holding the life inside him.

She studied her own hand, considered its power.

Chase twitched beneath her. "Dad."

Visser shook his head. "Son, do not move."

But Chase lifted himself onto an elbow, working to sit upright. As he spoke, she noticed that one of his lower teeth was whiter than the others—a fake. "Dad, someone else has to do it."

"No," Visser said. "Lily's a nurse. She's saving your life."

Saving his life. The muscles in her arm began to tremble. She could see the missing tooth—the gap in her attacker's drunken grin.

Visser watched her.

Chase clenched his father's arm.

"Chase," Visser warned. "Lie back down."

Chase shook his head, a piece of hair falling across his eyes. The blood streaks on his face, the hair, the red welt on his thigh. "You," she breathed.

"Lily?" Both Iver and Dr. Visser called her name. Chase shook his head as though begging her to stop, not to say it.

And she could no longer hold it in. "You raped me. In this cabin. You. Raped. Me."

"What?" Dr. Visser gasped.

She studied her fingers in Chase Visser's flesh, the ones keeping him alive. How easy it would be to yank them out. How satisfying it would be to watch the blood pulse from his body.

To watch him die.

CHAPTER 56

KYLIE

A noise behind them made Kylie turn, a squirrel darting up a tree. She was jumpy, the adrenaline still coursing in her veins. Her attention distracted for a second. Maybe two.

From the corner of her eye, she saw Reade swing at Gilbert. The single handcuff connected with Gilbert's face in a sickening crunch. Gilbert fell. Reade popped to his feet. One fluid motion.

"Stop," Kylie shouted, reaching for her holstered weapon.

Rolling away, Gilbert caught one of Reade's feet in his arms. Held it, yanking and twisting. Standing, Reade had the advantage. He wrenched his foot back and kicked Gilbert's face. There was a massive crack, and Gilbert cried out. Rolled away, gripping his face as his hands filled with blood.

Kylie yanked the gun from her holster.

Reade stood upright, Gilbert's gun in his hand. Gilbert reached for it, but Reade stepped to the side. Aimed the gun at Gilbert's head.

"Pull the trigger and I'll shoot," Reade said.

Kylie froze. Gun aimed.

"Drop the gun, Detective."

"Shoot him," Gilbert said, wiping his face on his sleeve.

Reade took a step away.

"I mean it, Kylie. Shoot him."

Reade's hand shifted on the gun. The handcuff swung off one wrist, the barrel so close to Gilbert's head. Too close.

Kylie hesitated. If she put down her weapon, Reade would kill them both. Gilbert shifted on the ground. Reade glanced at him, and Kylie stepped closer. "You can't kill us both," she warned Reade. "Drop the gun."

"Not going to happen," Reade said.

Gilbert laid a hand flat on the ground, all five fingers showing. Then four and then only three. He was going to count down. He wanted her to shoot. No! It was too risky.

"Drop the gun," she shouted.

Two fingers.

One finger.

Reade tightened his grip on the gun as Kylie found his chest in her sights. Pulled the trigger.

The bullet struck Bruce Reade square in the rib cage.

Reade gasped in surprise, one hand reaching for his chest. He swung the gun in her direction, rage in his face.

Kylie shot again. And then once more.

Reade collapsed.

Her heart ramming against her chest, she lowered her weapon. Her fingers released, and the gun fell to the ground.

"Kylie," Gilbert whispered, pushing himself to his feet.

Reade lay on his back on the ground. Eyes open, he made a strangled sound, his lips moving.

A dozen horses pummeled her chest as she stumbled backward. Gilbert caught her shoulders as she bent over, trying to catch her breath. One thought circled her brain like a hornet. So close. Reade had been so close to shooting Gilbert.

"I can't believe you counted down," Kylie said, breathless. "What if he'd shot? What if he'd killed you?"

Gilbert pulled her hard to his chest, his arms solid around her. Blinking hard, she tried to inhale past the painful tightness in her lungs. "I'm okay," he said.

Reade wasn't breathing. She crossed to him, dropped to her knees, and pressed a hand on his carotid artery. He was dead. Damn it. "He could've testified against his father-in-law."

Gilbert took her hand and helped her to her feet. "You saved my life," he said. "I let him get hold of my service weapon, and . . . you. Saved. My. Life. There was no other way that could have ended better." His gaze held hers as he spoke. The intensity in his eyes, the firmness in his voice, reminded her that the good guys were still alive.

"I'm going to call Tanner and get someone over here to process this scene." He paused and scanned her face. "You okay?"

Gilbert had almost been killed, but he was okay. He was alive. Her throat too tight to speak, all she could do was nod.

CHAPTER 57

HANNAH

Hannah shifted the dog from her lap as the patrol car drove slowly down the gravel road. The place that had been terrifying and empty—where she'd learned that her brother was a criminal and watched him get shot—was now filled with cars. Her dad's car was in the street behind Chase's, as were a truck, a police car, and an ambulance. But there were no people in sight.

Staring at the cabin she'd so longed to find, she could think now only of the conversation between Reade and her brother. Chase had texted the killer that she was at the Garzas'. Her brother had known that Reade was going there to kill Ben and Nadine. Why would he let that happen? The older brother she'd looked up to, the one who had been teaching her to drive, who answered her calls and cheered her on and told her it would all work out. He was also the older brother who had told the killer how to find her.

She couldn't get the pieces to fit with who she knew her brother to be. Then she imagined the terror on his face when Reade had shot him. Whatever Chase had done, she prayed he wasn't dead.

As soon as the car stopped, she jumped out and ran up the walkway to the cabin, ankle throbbing. "Dad? Chase!"

Her mother stood at the end of the entryway hall, facing the living room. Dressed in her nightgown under a coat, she seemed to be leaning with her entire weight into the wall. Hannah caught herself, her mother's appearance filling her with fear. The light from the dining room cast her hair in a frizzy halo, her body too thin, out of the house in a nightgown. Everything about her was unfamiliar and wrong.

"Chase!" she cried out, her throat tight.

Her mother turned, her face splotchy and pale. In the strange dim light, she was a ghost of herself.

Where was her brother? "Chase?"

Her mother covered her mouth, shook her head, and drew Hannah to her chest. Beneath the gown, her mother was all bones that rattled as she cried. It seemed that Hannah was holding up her mother and not the other way around. Extracting herself, Hannah hobbled into the living room. "Chase!"

"Hannah, thank God," her father said. Tears filled her eyes as her father wrapped his arms around her. "I was so scared, Hannah. You scared me so much."

She felt the beat of his heart and the strength in his arms as he held her. "I'm okay, Dad."

Her father pulled her back and studied her face, lifted her chin and examined her neck. "Jesus, did Reade do that?"

"I got away," she whispered, tears blurring her vision.

"Thank God for that," he said, pressing a kiss to her head.

Chase was laid out on the dining room table. Covered in blood—his hand, his face—he reached out to her. She thought again about his words, about helping the killer track the Garzas' car. Prayed there was some way to explain what she'd heard, some other meaning. Hannah took his hand, and he squeezed, blinking hard.

"I'm glad you're okay," he said softly, holding tightly to her hand.

She studied his eyes, saw the fear there. For her? Or for him? She drew her hand away, stepped closer to her father.

Chase turned his head away and blinked hard. It seemed like he might cry. Only then did Hannah notice the others. Her father stood on one side of Chase, a woman on the other. A man held Chase's legs, and a police officer and two paramedics stood against the far wall. Hannah scanned their faces, trying to figure out why nothing was happening. Were they going to let Chase die? "We have to save him," she whispered. "Why aren't you saving him?"

"We are," her father said, motioning to the woman.

Her brother's nakedness was startling, and Hannah didn't want to see him that way. But then she noticed the woman's hand and her fingers—inside Chase's leg. Hannah gasped. "Why is she doing that?"

"She's saving his life," her father said. She flinched at his angry tone, the disgusted way her dad looked at Chase. Did her dad know what Chase had done? Had her brother confessed to knowing about the Garzas' murders? To telling the killer where to find her?

The woman with her hand in Chase's leg lowered her head. Tears streamed down her face.

Why was she crying? "What's happening?" Chase was going to be okay. He had to be okay. They could deal with what he'd done, but she didn't want to lose him. She didn't want to lose someone else. Hannah searched the faces around her for answers, for whatever they weren't saying.

But no one spoke.

The man who had been holding Chase's legs let them go and came to the crying woman. He gripped her shoulders. "I think you'd better find someone else to save this bastard," he said to Hannah's father.

"No," the woman said. "I can do it."

"Lily, you shouldn't have to save him." The way the man said *him* was thick with anger. Her father always said his job was to save everyone, no matter what kind of person they were. Wasn't that true for his own son?

Her mother gasped. "No. Please. Charles."

Hannah's father ignored her.

"Please," Chase said, lifting a hand toward Lily. "Please don't let me die."

The woman didn't look at him, her hand still inside his leg.

Chase tried to touch Lily's arm, but she met his gaze with cold, hard hate. "Don't. Touch. Me."

The woman's expression gave Hannah chills. Was this about the Garzas?

Chase yanked his hand away. "Okay. But please. Please save me. I need you."

"Iver's right, Lily," her father said. "You don't have to do this."

"Dad, you know me. It wasn't the way she's saying." Chase's voice cracked. "It wasn't . . . that."

"Then what the hell was it?" her father shouted.

"It was . . ." Chase shook his head. "We were drinking, and I didn't know she was—"

"Chase, be quiet! Don't say anything," her mother cried, rushing to the table. She smoothed her fingers through Chase's hair, across his face.

Hannah couldn't make sense of any of it. She stood at her brother's shoulders and watched the woman's hand in his leg. Why would she remove her hand? Why would she let Chase die? Doctors didn't make those decisions, her father always said. That was for the police and the courts.

When she looked up, Hannah saw the way her father stared at her mother. Mouth open, shock in his face. And fury.

"Please," Hannah cried out. "What is going on?"

Her father shifted to face her mother. Hannah had never seen him so angry. He lunged past Hannah and took hold of her mother's arm. Yanked her toward him. "You knew? Damn it, Priscilla. You knew about this!"

Her father looked ready to punch someone. Her mother cowered, and Hannah pushed herself between them. "Stop!" Hannah shouted, shoving against her father's chest.

He halted and stared down at her, releasing his hold on her mother's arm.

Taking Hannah under his arm, he moved her away from her mother. Gripping her brother, her mother started to cry. Hannah had never seen her mother cry. She glanced at her face, the strangeness of it. Her father brushed the hair off Hannah's forehead and rubbed his thumb along her jaw to draw her attention back to him. "Hannah."

He was scaring her. "Dad. What's going on?"

But her father's eyes went wide, and he shifted his gaze to her mother. "Chase's baby? Hannah?"

"Oh God," the man with Lily said. Iver, her father had called him. He pressed a hand over his mouth, his gaze on Hannah, then lowered his hand. "Oh, Lily. How didn't I see it?"

Lily let out a strangled cry, covering her face with her free hand. "I wanted to tell you last night, but she was missing . . . and she'd been right in Hagen all along."

Hannah studied them, trying to understand. *Why is he looking at me?* This wasn't about the Garzas. This was something else.

Lily gripped Iver's hand with her free hand, held it to her. He wrapped his arms around her, careful not to bump the hand that was keeping Chase alive.

The truth echoed in her head. *She was the baby. I was the baby.* Hannah watched Lily's hand in her brother's leg, the steady pressure she applied.

Terror ran through her like electricity. She felt ready to explode with it. "What are you guys talking about? What baby?"

But her father was shouting at her mother now. "How could you do this? How could you let him get away with—" Hannah waited for the word that never came.

Get away with what?

"And you put me in this position without my knowledge." Her father shook his head. "And Hannah. God, poor Hannah."

The emotions boiled in Hannah until they were too big to contain. "Why?" she screamed. "Why poor me?"

Chase was sobbing, tears leaking across his cheeks. "I was only a kid. It was a mistake."

"A mistake?" her father roared. "You call rape a mistake?"

Hannah stumbled, but her father's arm held her. *Rape.*

"It wasn't like that," Chase said, the words barely a whisper. "They had a party here, invited a bunch of people."

"They who? Who had a party?" her father asked.

"Ben, Mike, and Brian," Chase said.

"Of course. The Sutton boys," her father sneered with a hard glare at her mother.

"Who are they?" Lily asked.

"Cousins," her father answered. "Priscilla's brothers' boys, a bunch of illiterate animals."

Priscilla said nothing.

"It wasn't my idea," Chase said. "I was down for the night, staying here. All of a sudden, the place was full of people. I didn't even know any of them."

"Did your idiot cousins also make you rape a woman?"

"I was drunk," Chase said. "I thought—I thought it was consensual."

"Consensual?" Lily shouted. "I'd been a prisoner for at least a month by then. I was a prisoner in that cabin"—she aimed a hand toward the door—"not two miles from here for sixteen months." Every word was like a punch in Hannah's gut.

"I didn't know you were a prisoner," Chase said.

Her father made a sound of disbelief.

"I swear—"

Lily shook her head, wiping her face on her sleeve. Fresh tears replaced the old ones as Iver held her. She turned to him then, shook her head. "I didn't say anything that night because Hudson warned me. He said if I told anyone where he was holding me . . ." She paused to shake her head, Iver rubbing her shoulders.

"You don't have anything to explain," he said.

"Hudson told me he'd kill the others if I said anything."

"See!" Chase said. "I didn't know."

"Christ, Chase," her father shouted. "Do you hear yourself? You belong in prison."

"No!" her mother screamed.

Hannah gripped her father's hands. "Tell me what's going on. Dad, please." The pain in her stomach grew sharp. She pressed a fist against the ache. Prisoner. Lily was a prisoner? Whose prisoner? The room spun, and she held tightly to her father, trying to stay upright. She wished everyone would stop talking. Stop talking and explain.

"I didn't even remember being pregnant," Lily said. "I never knew I had a child." Her shoulders shook, and Iver pressed his lips to the back of her head.

Chase had raped this woman? And gotten her pregnant?

"For fourteen years I had no idea." Lily lifted her head and looked at Chase. And then she studied Hannah.

The experience was like a rush of ice-cold water and scalding heat at once. The stabbing pain in her stomach doubled her over.

Her father tried to take hold of her hands, but Hannah pulled away. "No." She scanned their faces—her brother and father, her mother, and Lily and Iver. They were all staring at her. The words swirled around her, pieces of a puzzle that she twisted in an effort to make them fit.

"You sick son of a bitch," Iver said. "You deserve to die right here. I'm tempted to pull Lily's hand out myself."

"No," Lily whispered.

"No," her mother howled at the same time. "You have to save him. Don't let him die. Please. Don't let my boy die."

Lily shook her head, the fight seemingly drained out of her. "No."

Forcing herself upright again, Hannah yanked on her father's arm. "Dad, he can't die."

"He's not going to die," Lily said. She glanced at Hannah's dad. "I'm still in the right place. I'm not moving."

Her dad put a hand on the woman's arm. There were tears in his eyes. Hannah wanted him to be relieved that Chase was going to live. And yet her father acted as though he'd been told Chase would die.

"I want him to live with what he did. I want him to face the truth." Lily turned to Chase, and her teeth were clenched as she spoke again. Tears ran in tracks down her face, falling steadily. "And I want to know how you ended up with her. Did Hudson blackmail you? Or did he make you pay for her? Did you buy *my* child?" Her hands trembled, and she hunched over, pressing her free palm on the table to still the hand that was inside Chase's leg.

Fourteen years. My child. Those words ricocheted inside Hannah's head. The breath was sucked straight from the depths of her lungs. Every molecule stolen as Lily watched her with that expression. Pain, sorrow, regret . . . love? "Fourteen years," Hannah whispered. She was fourteen. And without all the dots connecting, Hannah said, "I'm the baby."

"It doesn't matter," her mother cried out, sobbing. "It's over. The statute of limitations has passed. Whatever happened doesn't matter anymore." Her mother lowered her face to Chase's, pressed her lips to his forehead. "You'll be fine, darling boy. We're going to get through this."

"Hannah." Lily smiled at her softly. "I'm so sorry that you had to find out this way."

"Find out . . ." But she already knew. Chase and Lily. A baby. Fourteen years ago. Hannah. And then her father said the words: "She's your mother."

Hannah looked at her father, then her mother, who had covered up a crime and lied. Hannah's gaze slowly lowered to Chase's. Her brother had known Dr. Reade was going to kill the Garzas, had let that happen, and now she found out he'd also . . .

As though reading her thoughts, Chase looked away.

"And your brother . . . ," her dad said.

"Is my father," Hannah realized. She drew a steady breath around the pain in her stomach, the shock, the cold sweat, and the feverish heat. "I'm from the rape."

"You're a blessing," her father said. "No matter where you came from."

Hannah took a step toward him, and he opened his arms, pulling her in. She winced at the pain in her shoulder as he held her tight, but she pressed herself closer. He smelled like wood and his favorite charcoal aftershave lotion. She closed her eyes and wanted to stay there forever.

"I'm so sorry, Hannah," he whispered. "I had no idea. I should have known, but I didn't. I swear I didn't."

The front screen slammed closed, and Deputy Tanner entered the cabin, breathless and excited. "Chopper's coming in," he announced, unaware of all that had happened there. "They're going to try to land right on the street. They've got a transport nurse to take over. Should be ready to move him in five."

No one spoke.

Pressed to her father's chest, Hannah began to cry. "Please don't go away again," she whispered. "I need you, Dad." And then she caught herself.

He wasn't her dad anymore. But he was.

CHAPTER 58

Kylie

"Just need each of you to sign the last page," Deputy Tanner told Kylie, sliding the incident report across his desk. He picked up the cell phone jammer a deputy had discovered next to the department's printer and turned it over in his hand.

As the internet connectivity in the Molva Sheriff's Department ran exclusively off cellular data, the jammer had ensured that the APB Hagen PD had sent never reached the deputies in Molva. And that only landline calls were entering the building. They assumed it was planted by Bruce Reade. No one had seen him in the department. And with Reade dead, they might never be able to confirm whether it was his doing.

Beside Kylie, Carl Gilbert shifted the ice pack he held to his face into his left hand so he could sign his report, too.

His right eye was swollen closed, the skin around it a brilliant, angry purple. Blood stained his shirt and coat, and though he'd taken a couple of Tylenols, he had refused to see a doctor. At least not until they were done with the paperwork. From the moment Kylie had fired the shots that killed Reade, he'd been singularly focused on getting the report filed and getting out of Molva.

"Let us know if you need anything else," Gilbert said, standing. "And you'll let me know when I can come back down for my service weapon."

"Absolutely," Tanner said. "The deputy sheriff already called up to your sheriff. We're all on the same page about this one. Don't think it will take long to get through the judge. Guy got what he deserved."

"If only Chase Visser had," Gilbert said.

The realization that it was Chase Visser who had raped Lily Baker in captivity was still sinking in. Tanner had given them the story of what had happened at the cabin, which had been relayed to him by another Molva deputy. Lily with her hand in Chase Visser's leg, keeping him from bleeding out. The birthmark on his leg, the scar on his face that had emerged from her memories. Recognizing the cabin as the location of her rape.

According to the deputy, Lily recalled a party Derek Hudson had brought her to shortly after she was abducted. She'd been drugged and fed liquor and brought to the cabin where Chase's cousins were hosting a bunch of people. Hudson had warned Lily not to tell anyone at the party about the abduction, threatened to kill the other girls if she did.

Chase Visser was the man from her nightmares. He'd been right in front of her all along, her mind shielding her from the horror of that truth. Kylie hadn't gotten to speak to Lily yet, and she wondered if other memories had returned with that one. Had Chase known that Lily was the missing girl from Hagen? Had he lived free for all these years, knowing that he'd raped a girl who was being held prisoner?

What kind of a monster did that make him? Was it possible that he hadn't known? It was Priscilla Visser who had come to her son's rescue—sent him to boarding school, adopted his baby, and played Hannah off as her own. Gone to every end to make sure Chase never paid for his crimes. That came as no surprise to Kylie.

At least it seemed like Charles Visser hadn't been privy to his son's crimes.

There were a lot of questions Kylie wanted answered.

Kylie checked her text messages, but there was still no word from Lily Baker. Kylie didn't know that Lily would want to talk about what she remembered.

The desk phone rang, and Tanner answered. After a brief exchange, he returned the phone to its base. "That was Bismarck. Chase Visser is in recovery and stable. Surgery to repair the artery and vein was successful, and he'll be back up in no time." He said it with a dose of disdain. Priscilla Visser had gone in the helicopter with her son. Already, she had retained an attorney for Chase and was blocking all access to him. Not that it mattered. The local DA had already made it clear that he wasn't interested in pursuing a fifteen-year-old rape case. No doubt it helped that Priscilla Visser's family had always been big campaign donors in his township.

Lily had saved his life—the man who had raped her in captivity—and Chase Visser would walk away scot-free for that crime. But Kylie was determined to help make the case to put Chase away for conspiracy to commit murder and accessory to the illegal transportation of stolen prescription narcotics across state lines . . . and whatever else the Hagen DA and the FBI could throw at him. Reade was dead, but there were phone records, and the lab was already working to locate the cloud backup of Nadine's files. Kylie tried to feel some measure of satisfaction that Chase wasn't going to go free. The failure of the justice system to protect its victims was sometimes too gross to overlook.

She replayed Reade's death in her mind again. Wondered whether she would have shot if Gilbert hadn't been counting down. If there was a way they might have taken Reade alive. But there were certainly as many versions of that story, if not more, that ended with her or Gilbert taking a bullet.

She stood slowly, her bones aching. Every part of her was shaky. Some of it was the natural result of coming down from the adrenaline. Being up all night, the shooting. It was made worse by the fact that she hadn't eaten.

She would collapse soon. She just had to get home first. As she stood, her phone buzzed. A message from Lily.

We're at urgent care with Hannah and Charles. Be here a little longer, I think.

Too tired to speak, Kylie passed the phone to Gilbert. He read the message and nodded. "We'll go there now." She was grateful that they were going to a place where a doctor could examine his face. It seemed impossible that he didn't have a concussion or even a fracture.

Tanner shook their hands and told them he'd be in touch.

Kylie drove the three blocks to urgent care. Despite her exhaustion, she was in better shape than Gilbert. The building was a squat brick square that occupied the center of a block. As Kylie parked, she saw Iver's truck in the lot.

She waited for Gilbert to get out of the car, noticing that he seemed increasingly uncomfortable. The Tylenol was probably wearing off. Inside the small waiting room, Iver and Lily sat side by side. Iver held her hand as Lily stared at the floor.

Iver rose when he saw them. He saw Gilbert and cursed. "What the hell happened to you?"

"Bruce Reade kicked me in the face," Gilbert said.

"Reade?" Lily asked.

"He's dead," Gilbert told her. "Got hold of my weapon, and Kylie had to shoot him."

Kylie thought of all the moments that were eclipsed in that sentence. All the decisions they had each made. In the end, that summed it up. Reade had the gun. Kylie had to take the shot.

The sound of voices across the lobby came as a welcome distraction. Hannah Visser emerged from an exam room, wearing a boot on her left foot and a sling on her right arm. Dark circles shadowed her eyes. Fourteen, and she looked like a worn-out twenty.

Charles Visser thanked the doctor and turned toward them. He, too, appeared to have aged a decade since Kylie had watched him get into his car in Hagen eight or nine hours earlier. He held on to Hannah as she moved across the room, the others crossing to join her. "Where is Bruce Reade?" Visser asked Kylie and Gilbert.

She shook her head, not wanting to say it out loud in front of Hannah.

"He's dead?" the girl asked, and her father nodded at Kylie to answer.

"Yes," she said.

"Good," Visser said, his grip tighter on Hannah's shoulder. He shifted closer to Gilbert, still supporting Hannah, and he reached his free hand up to touch Gilbert's cheek. "Boot?"

"Yeah," Gilbert said.

"Sit down and let me see that," Visser directed.

They moved to a bank of chairs, all of them sitting. No one spoke as Visser probed at the bones around Gilbert's eye. Gilbert clenched his jaw and tried not to move, but it was obviously painful. "I don't think there's an orbital fracture, but you should have an x-ray."

A nurse crossed the lobby with a stack of papers and a white paper sack. "Here are her discharge instructions and the pain medication."

Hannah shook her head. "Not the medication." She glanced at her father, and something passed between them. Her eyes filled with tears, and Visser took her hand. "I don't want those," she whispered.

Visser nodded. "We'll manage without, thanks."

The nurse hesitated, then handed Visser the papers before retreating, the paper sack of pills still in her hand.

Tears streaming down her cheeks, Hannah covered her face.

"You're an incredible kid, Hannah," Kylie said, shifting to sit in the chair beside the girl. "We never would have caught Bruce Reade without you."

"And you saved Tiffany Garza, too," Lily said.

Hannah lifted her head, glancing between them. She said nothing as her gaze found her father's face. Kylie could feel her heartache, the longing. Lily studied Visser, and it seemed they were all waiting for him. But he didn't need any reminder. He lowered himself to one knee, then leaned forward until his forehead touched Hannah's. "That's my girl," he said.

And he wrapped his arms around her.

Iver reached an arm around Lily, and she looked up at him, tears in her eyes.

Kylie rose from her chair. "Let's get that x-ray, Gilbert."

Gilbert glanced up. "Probably a good idea."

She walked with him across the room, listening as the foursome started talking about heading home to Hagen. At the desk, Kylie and Gilbert rang the bell for the attendant. Standing beside him, Kylie nudged her shoulder to his. "Glad that's over," she whispered. "Thanks for the help."

Gilbert looked down at her. For a moment, he said nothing. Then he nudged her back and said, "You're welcome, Kylie Milliard."

CHAPTER 59

Lily

Four weeks later

Lily drove home from Dr. Visser's house, filled with thoughts of her daughter. She'd gone by to drop off groceries, replenishing supplies—brown sugar and vanilla—for their next baking session. Lily and Hannah saw each other most days now—even if it was a quick visit. Hannah also came to the house so she could cuddle with Cal. They baked a lot of cookies.

Having an activity seemed to make it easier for Hannah to express what she was thinking—the progress she was making with her therapist, how she'd started taking the pills, her unresolved issues with Priscilla and Chase. Occasionally she spoke of that night at the Garzas'. Today, Hannah had been struggling with the vividness of her memories of how Nadine and Ben had died. The way Hannah talked, it was like she was still in that closet. It broke Lily's heart, seeing the girl's pain.

And those conversations always returned Lily to her own terrors.

As though it were yesterday, Lily could recall the heady sensations of being high and drunk. Her young body had tingled in the night air, the skies brilliant overhead as she had floated through the dark. The smells of winter and pine, campfire and dust, as the drug pulsed pure joy through her veins. There had been both terror and also a strange lightness, getting out of that cabin, breathing night air.

From Hannah's birth date, Lily had calculated that the rape had occurred five or six weeks after she was kidnapped. Despite Hudson's warnings that he would kill the other girls, Lily had imagined their escape, dreamed of how she would return with the police and free the other three girls. That night she would never have imagined that her prison sentence was only beginning.

Kylie kept Lily up to date on the charges against Chase Visser. He would likely serve time as an accessory to the Garzas' murders and the illegal transportation of drugs, but there would be no jail time for her rape. Chase maintained that he had never known that Lily was a prisoner at the time of her assault. He had been sent to boarding school in Minnesota two months later, a plan devised by Priscilla once Hudson notified them that Lily was pregnant. Or that was Kylie's theory—and theories were all they had.

Kylie was pressing the FBI agents handling Chase's case to offer some reduced sentence if Chase and Priscilla provided some information about Hannah's origin. Unfortunately, the FBI wasn't interested in an old rape case, not when they might have a fish like Reade's father-in-law, Max Lotari, on the line.

Ironically, Lotari would also likely avoid charges, despite the fact that the FBI remained confident that Lotari ran a massive prescription drug ring, which had been under investigation for years. They still lacked the hard evidence to prove it.

Kylie and Lily agreed that Priscilla had known Lily was Hudson's prisoner, though she had sworn to Charles that she never met Lily nor heard her name. Priscilla claimed that she had thought it was Hudson's sister who had been pregnant and that the baby was given up willingly. But Priscilla was much too clever to take something like that at face value. Before adopting a child, Priscilla had undoubtedly done her homework, though all records of that would be long gone. Records of whatever money had changed hands were also long gone. Lily tried to focus on what she could control, and the cases against those people were far outside those lines.

In the end, Lily found it most palatable to allow herself the delusion that Hudson had been the intermediary, that he had kept her captivity a secret from Chase. Because Chase was two years older than she was and the two had never been together in school, it was easier to believe in the possibility that he hadn't known that the girl he'd raped was the same girl who had been abducted from his hometown.

But the delusion was often unmasked in the stark silence of night, leaving her with the bleak reality that her daughter's father was a monster.

As she parked on the curb at her house, she noticed the text message from Hannah.

Any chance for coffee after school tomorrow?

Lily smiled as she typed her response. Of course. Name the time/place. xx L

Her daughter. They had agreed that Hannah would call her Lily, the whole *mom* thing too strange for either of them. Seeing Hannah fighting the battle of her addiction made Lily wonder how life would have been different had she raised Hannah from birth. A child born of rape to a fifteen-year-old mother, Hannah would have had no chance at all. Lily was grateful to Charles Visser. In the end, it was his influence that had kept Hannah in a stable home. Priscilla's focus had been on keeping her marriage intact and preserving the reputation of her prized son. But Charles had successfully raised Hannah with the same tough love that had failed with Chase.

Lily looked up at the little house where she'd grown up, proud of what it had become. Iver had given it a fresh coat of paint during an unseasonably warm week in mid-October, and the maple he'd planted in the yard this past summer was growing steadily. The last of its red leaves were finally gone. Since his return from Fargo, Iver had installed a wooden swing on the front porch, and it swayed gently in the fall breeze.

Tonight she and Iver were taking dinner to his mother, Cathy, in the assisted-living center where she now lived. In the past month, she'd made huge strides with her physical therapy. While she had conceded to the need for a wheelchair, she was adamant about regaining her ability to talk clearly, and already her control of her facial muscles was impressive. It would be a long, hard road, but Cathy was a fighter. Like her son. Tomorrow Lily would go to work, back to the job she loved. She was always grateful for the respite those days brought, the intensity of the job a reprieve from the memories, the worries. And a chance to work for someone else, to make a difference.

Two days ago, Harrison Krueger had come in with his daughter, Stephanie, recovered after a tough battle with meningitis. In their arms were two massive baskets of homemade goodies—breads and cakes and cookies and tomato sauce and jam—to express their gratitude. Harrison had given Lily a fierce hug and whispered, "Thank you for saving my girl." *My girl.* How grateful she was to Kylie for saving Hannah from Reade.

Now, Lily got out of the car and made her way up the walkway. From inside, Cal barked to announce her arrival. The door opened before she could reach for it, and Iver stood in the entryway. He wore jeans and a flannel over a T-shirt, his presence calming her thoughts.

The sight of his stocking feet on her floor was a reminder of their home.

CHAPTER 60

Hannah

Two weeks later—Thanksgiving

Hannah adjusted the forks one more time, shifting each one a half inch closer to the plate. The table was meant to seat six people, but she'd managed to make nine place settings fit. Barely. Her father had suggested a second table, but the dining area in their little house was too small for that. It would mean another table in the entryway or the living room, and Hannah wanted them all together. The overlapped place mats made her think of her mother's grand table. That was the kind of table meant for nine people. But she didn't want her mother's table. She had not one good memory from that table.

Since Hannah had moved in, she and her father had settled into a comfortable routine. Her father had helped the hospital hire two new ED docs and was reducing his call to three shifts a month so that he didn't have to leave Hannah alone at night. During the first two overnight shifts he worked, he'd insisted she come to the hospital with him. She'd done homework, then slept in one of the sleeping rooms off the doctors' lounge. The next time, Hannah asked if it would be okay if Lily came and stayed in the guest room. Her father had been agreeable, and Lily had said she'd be happy to do it.

Her father must have known she was nervous that night. He'd given her a dozen outs, offered to call one of their neighbors or another mom.

But the night with Lily had been pretty great. Lily brought groceries, and they cooked a chicken stir-fry with rice and made Rice Krispies Treats. Then they'd curled up on the couch and watched a movie. Lily even helped Hannah brainstorm ideas for a paper she had to write in her social studies class. Since then they'd had three more overnights like that one. And now they saw each other most days.

Hannah hadn't been sure what to expect. The idea that Lily was her actual mother was still too weird. She would always think of Priscilla as her mother, though she never wanted to see her again. Nor did she have any interest in seeing her brother, who was actually her father. No. All that stuff was too impossible to think about.

For now, Hannah let herself imagine Priscilla and Chase were dead. Her counselor suggested thinking of them on a long trip was better, but dead was working for her. At least for now. Not that Priscilla had made any effort to see her. Or Chase, for that matter. As far as she knew, both of them had left town. Or maybe her brother was in prison. Hannah figured that if she and her dad were lucky, they'd stay gone.

There was a knock at the door, and Hannah checked her phone. People weren't due for dinner for another two hours. She felt a hitch in her throat, the way she always did now at the thought of something unexpected.

"It's Detective Milliard," her father called from the kitchen. "She had some news she wanted to share with us."

Hannah held on to the back of a chair as her father emerged from the kitchen, wiping his hands on a dish towel.

He watched her. "You okay?"

She wasn't, but she nodded.

He seemed to see right through her. "I think it's good news," he said, heading for the entryway. He opened the door, and the detective stepped into the foyer in a skirt and blouse.

"Wow, you look so nice, Detective," her father said, inviting her in.

"I figured I'd get dressed for dinner before I came in case we wanted to talk for longer." She shrugged. "Plus, you didn't want to see me in my sweats."

"You do look really nice," Hannah agreed, forcing her fingers to unclench from the dining chair.

"I know you guys are getting ready for dinner, but I wanted to talk to you before everyone arrived."

Her dad waved Hannah closer, and when she reached the foyer, he put his arm around her shoulders. "You said you have news."

The detective nodded, eyeing her dad. "You're sure?"

He squeezed his arm around Hannah's shoulder. "I want her to hear it from you," he said. "She deserves to know."

Hannah felt herself pull away. "Hear what?"

"The FBI arrested your br—" The detective stopped, smiled awkwardly. "Ugh."

Hannah shook her head. Her brother was her father and her father was her grandpa. How messed up was that? "It's okay."

"Chase," the detective said. "He's been arrested for drug trafficking."

"Drug trafficking?"

The detective nodded. "He and Bruce Reade were in business together, trafficking prescription medications across four states for Dr. Reade's father-in-law. Chase moved the drugs with building products and sold them through his showrooms." She paused a minute, then said, "He's going to federal prison, Hannah."

"But didn't he also help kill Ben and Nadine?" Hannah asked. Surely murder was worse than driving drugs around.

"He did," Kylie said slowly. "It's kind of confusing because a lot of this depends on what we can prove. Especially since Bruce Reade is . . . dead."

"You've got more evidence about the drugs," Hannah said.

"Exactly," Kylie agreed, looking relieved that Hannah understood.

Hannah studied her father's face, the sadness in his eyes. She reached out and took his hand. "Are you okay, Dad?"

"Chase made his own choices," he said. "Now he needs to deal with the consequences."

Hannah turned back to the detective. "How did the FBI find out about the drugs? If Dr. Reade is dead . . ."

"The arrests of several local dealers led them to Chase and Dr. Reade."

Hannah thought about Adam and wondered if he was one of them. But she said nothing. She'd never told her father about Adam, preferring to let him believe she'd gotten the prescription medications from her mother's supply. She was afraid of how he would treat her if she admitted to what she'd done for those drugs.

Hannah had heard her mother talk to Chase about money, about struggling with his business. But Dr. Reade? "Dr. Reade was a doctor," she wondered out loud. "Didn't he make enough money doing that?"

The detective shrugged, and her father let out a sigh. "For some folks, there's no such thing as enough money, Bean." She thought maybe he was also talking about her mother.

"Oh, and I thought you'd want to see this," the detective said, unlocking her phone and handing it to Hannah. She hesitated to look, worried it would be a picture of her brother in jail. Instead, it was a family—two parents and three little kids. Two twin boys and a baby girl. "Is that—"

"Tiffany Garza," the detective confirmed. "She's been adopted by her aunt and uncle."

Hannah handed the phone back. For a moment, she was in the Garzas' house again, in that closet. But she drew a slow breath like her counselor had taught her.

"She's safe," the detective said, pocketing her phone. "Thanks to you."

They stood there for a few more minutes before the detective excused herself. "I've got to go finish my stuffing and check in on Carl—he's making mashed potatoes. I'll see you all in a couple of hours."

Her father closed the door and crossed to Hannah, pulling her into his arms. He held her tight for a moment, and she smelled his sadness as though it were a cologne. She wished she could take it away, but her therapist told her that wasn't her burden to bear. They were both sad. It was okay to feel sad. Those were the words she kept running through her mind.

"You want to talk about it?" he asked, still holding her.

"I don't think so. Do you?"

"Maybe some time. But right now, I've got a turkey to baste." He stepped back and smiled at her. "You want to learn how to baste a turkey?"

She definitely did not want to learn how to baste a turkey. "Sure."

Three hours later, Hannah sat beside her father as he raised a glass of Martinelli's apple cider and toasted his gratitude. She held her own mismatched glass in the air and scanned the faces around the table. It was an eclectic group. Aside from her father, there was no one that Hannah had even known two months earlier. Weirdly, they all felt sort of like family now.

Across from Hannah was Lily Baker in a burgundy dress, her hair up and mascara on her lashes. She looked beautiful and happy. Twice when they'd gone to Fargo to shop, strangers had asked if they were sisters. The first time had caught them off guard—they didn't really resemble one another in an obvious way. When it happened last week, Lily had threaded her arm through Hannah's and said, "Yes. Sisters." They'd taken two steps down the street and dissolved into a fit of laughter.

Beside Lily was Iver Larson, who Hannah was slowly getting to know. He reminded her of her father—quiet, strong, kind. She watched as he helped his mother, Cathy, steady her glass. Each time Hannah saw her, Cathy seemed a little stronger. Her father said Cathy's improvements after her stroke showed that she was one very determined lady.

On Hannah's right sat little William with his green-and-yellow sippy cup of apple juice. On the other side of William was his mother, Amber, who had brought four different pies from the diner, including peanut butter, Hannah's favorite. Across from Amber were Kylie Milliard and Carl Gilbert. *The detective*, Hannah always wanted to call her even though Kylie kept saying it was okay to call her by her first name. The nine of them were practically shoulder to shoulder, and once again Hannah thought of her mother's enormous table. In her memory, there had never been many smiles around that table. Certainly never this many.

"To my smart and beautiful daughter, Hannah," her father said, and Hannah felt her face fill with heat.

"To Hannah," the table echoed.

"Thanks, Dad." She raised her glass a little higher to the group. "And happy Thanksgiving."

Then she took a sip of the sweet, bubbly cider and watched as this group of half strangers shared a meal with more love and joy than any family she'd ever known.

ACKNOWLEDGMENTS

My first thank-you is to you, the reader. You're the reason I get to sit in my basement and dream up stories. Thank you for reading this book, for following me back to the tiny town of Hagen, North Dakota, and for following Lily and Kylie in their adventure. While we're at it, thank you for every book you've ever read. It is the greatest gift you can give an author. A good review is the second-best gift.

Thank you also to the men and women who devote their lives to the pursuit of justice. As an author, I aim for a realistic portrayal of crimes and their investigation, but I certainly don't always get it right. Occasionally, I also bend (or break) the truth for the sake of the story. Any errors and poetic license are my responsibility entirely.

For research, I am, as always, indebted to the people at the San Francisco Police Department, who have been answering strange questions since I was writing my first book, *Savage Art*, in 1998. I'm sometimes amazed that you still answer my calls. Dr. Craig Nelson, associate chief medical examiner, North Carolina Office of the Chief Medical Examiner, has become absolutely invaluable in an accurate portrayal of death and death investigation—or as accurate as the story will allow. Thank you, Dr. Nelson.

The team at Jane Rotrosen Agency continues to blow me away. I am so lucky to call myself one of their authors. Thank you to all and especially to Meg Ruley, Rebecca Scherer, Michael Conway, Sabrina Prestia, and Hannah Rody-Wright. Thank you also to my fabulous editor, Jessica Tribble, and while Jessica went off to have her sweet baby girl, to Liz Pearsons, Gracie Doyle, and Laura Barrett for stepping in; to Sarah Shaw, who makes sure we're always having fun (we are!), and the incredible team at Thomas & Mercer; to Faith Black for helping strengthen the story; to Riam Griswold and Susan Stokes for the thorough edit; and to Shasti O'Leary Soudant for another fabulous cover design.

I am hugely grateful to those who support the process of writing a book and especially to fellow authors D. J. Palmer, Jay Shepherd, Jamie Mason, Christina Kovac, Angie Kim, James Hankins, J. T. Ellison, and Jaime, Jennifer, Lynne, Vanessa, and Wendy from the Rhode Island Writer Retreat that never was, and to the eagle-eyed proofreaders: Christy Delger, Dani Wanderer, and Whitney Pritham.

Above all, I'm grateful to my family for supporting this crazy dream from the early days. Chris, Claire, Jack, Mom, Dad, Nicole, Tom, and Steve. Because of you, I am the luckiest lady in the world.

If you enjoyed this book, please leave a review on Goodreads, BookBub, Amazon, and the like so that others might discover *Far Gone* as well.

Sincerely,
Danielle

FREE SHORT STORY

Join Danielle Girard's Readers Club and get "Too Close to Home," a Rookie Club short story, for free.

You will also receive regular news and access to exclusive giveaways. It's completely free, and you can opt out at any time.

Join here: www.daniellegirard.com/newsletter.

ABOUT THE AUTHOR

Photo © 2018 Mallory Regan, 40 Watt Photo

Danielle Girard is the *USA Today* and Amazon #1 bestselling author of *Chasing Darkness*, the Rookie Club series, and the Dr. Schwartzman Series—*Exhume*, *Excise*, *Expose*, and *Expire*, featuring San Francisco medical examiner Dr. Annabelle Schwartzman. Danielle's books have won the Barry Award and the RT Reviewers' Choice Award, and two of her titles have been optioned for movies. *White Out*, book one of her new Badlands Thriller series, is available now.

A graduate of Cornell University, Danielle received her MFA at Queens University in Charlotte, North Carolina. She, her husband, and their two children split their time between San Francisco and the Northern Rockies. Visit her at www.daniellegirard.com.